DEATH BLADE

The glass panel dropped, making a noise that was impossible to miss. Quickly realizing all surprise was now gone, Ramon heaved himself up through the narrow opening as swiftly as possible. Both Gallagher and Lorraine saw what was happening at the same time. Both brought their weapons up.

Ramon knew he was lost. He was trapped halfway through. His head, shoulders and arms were out, but his lower body hung helplessly in the saloon lounge. Even so, he was very quick. Bracing himself on one arm and a shoulder, he threw his knife at the source of what he thought would be the greatest danger.

His aim was true, but he was still too late. The shotgun round pulped his face even as the knife struck home and the round from the SC70/90 entered his throat, flinging him back through the hole and into the lounge below.

Also by Julian Jay Savarin

Trophy
Target Down!
Wolf Run
Windshear
Naja
The Quiraing List
Water Hole*

*Coming soon

Available from
HarperPaperbacks

VILLIGER

JULIAN JAY SAVARIN

HarperPaperbacks
A Division of HarperCollins*Publishers*

This is a work of fiction. The characters, incidents, and dialogues are products of the author's imagination and are not to be construed as real. Any resemblance to actual events or persons, living or dead, is entirely coincidental.

HarperPaperbacks *A Division of* HarperCollins*Publishers*
10 East 53rd Street, New York, N.Y. 10022

Cover photography by Herman Estevez

First HarperPaperbacks printing: August 1993

Printed in the United States of America

HarperPaperbacks and colophon are trademarks of HarperCollins*Publishers*

10 9 8 7 6 5 4 3 2 1

VILLIGER

PROLOGUE

The narrow strip of bush road disappeared into the distance. Roughly surfaced, it seemed to come from nowhere and to be going nowhere. But there were some strange things about it. Just under four meters wide, each side was remarkably clean, as if someone had passed along it with a huge vacuum cleaner. There was an absence of noise, giving the impression that every living thing in the vicinity had been removed. The road itself was clear save for the single carcass of a truck, a rusted and twisted skeleton. It sat on the road minus its wheels, the wrecked cab tilted forward in apparent genuflection.

There was no glass in the windows of the cab, or on the ground around it, and the single remaining door was a pattern of jagged holes. A bigger hole pierced the roof where something had gone through, making a peeling wound like a giant metallic flower.

On either side of the road and some forty meters from it, were a number of men. All but one were black. He was a tall, well-built white with cropped blond hair. Their leader.

The men, ten on each side of the road, had chosen their ambush position well. There were no indications that any other life existed within the immediate area. The men had now been there for five days and it was a tribute to their discipline that in all that time, only the calls of nature had caused them to move from their selected positions. Even then, only one would move at any given time. Each carried individual cold rations, and each ate and slept where he was. To anyone passing on the road, there was nothing to betray the presence of the waiting men.

They were heavily armed, with an assortment of assault rifles that had been manufactured in three countries. Four machine guns, four grenade launchers, and a selection of automatic pistols completed the arsenal. The quarry they awaited was a force twice their size, but they were quite confident that they would succeed in overwhelming their adversaries when the time came.

A good two miles down the road, the intended victims walked slowly toward the ambush. This group had a greater mix of white and black. They all wore the same combat fatigues, carried the same type of weapons, spoke the same language. There was an air of quiet confidence about them as if they had never lost a battle, and so they walked along the road, carefully scanning the undergrowth and the bush about them, heads and bodies turning this way and that, but not really seeing anything. They were committing the greatest of all errors in combat. They had become complacent.

When they came up to the truck they halted, milled about discussing its presence, smiling, laughing among themselves. Three of them were white officers. They too were relaxed, but one of them looked carefully about him, weapon at the ready.

The firing, when it opened up, was sudden and shocking in its ferocity. The men's reactions were commendably swift, but they were too late. Whole magazines from unseen assault rifles were emptied into unsuspecting bodies. Grenades blew limbs apart, and the heavy machine guns completed the murderous job. When it was all over, less than a minute had passed and not one of the forty men was still standing.

Five minutes passed. There was no movement whatsoever from the bush.

Another five minutes went by. Still no movement. Then at last, two men came forward cautiously, from either side of the road. One was the big white man. They were both heavily armed. The white man walked slowly among the dead, his rifle pointing at each corpse as if checking for signs of life. His companion followed, every now and then turning around, the snout of his rifle describing an alert arc as he did so. The white man continued his rounds poking here with his rifle, prodding there with his boot.

Then suddenly, he paused. One of the bodies interested him. Cautiously, he moved it with the toe of his boot. The body rolled over and flopped onto its back. It was a white man, youngish. He was one of the officers though for reasons of anonymity, he wore no badges of rank. The big white man's companion was now standing close to him.

"They won't be burning any more villages," the black one said.

The big white man said nothing, but kept looking at the body on the ground. He stared at the face now exposed to the hot African sun, the head bare, minus its bush hat which had fallen off during the attack. There were no wounds upon it.

The black one was speaking again. "Did you know him?"

The big man nodded slowly. "I knew him," he said quietly.

The white man now raised his rifle above his head, held it there for a few brief moments before lowering it again. Immediately, the bush on either side was suddenly filled with movement as the men rose out of their ambush positions, and came toward the other two already on the road. They inspected the bodies with guarded curiosity. It was a good day's work, and they looked pleased with themselves. But there was no look of celebration on their faces. Instead, their eyes were hard, determined, and as they looked at the bodies, there was no regret in them.

The white man looked about him, glancing at each one as his head turned slowly.

"Good," he said. "That will give them something to worry about."

1

London.

"As I live and breathe!"

Gallagher looked up. "Good God."

A tall, elegant blonde in smart business clothes was looking down at him, an amused smile upon soft lips. Lady Veronica Walmsley. "I'm so pleased you're happy to see me," she continued. "May I sit down?"

She was already doing so, even as he said: "Yes. Yes, of course." He was so surprised to see her that he was slow to marshal his thoughts.

She crossed one elegant leg over the other, continued to smile at him.

"How long has it been? Six years? Seven?"

"Nearer eight."

"Eight years," she repeated wonderingly. "You married that dark haired girl, didn't you? What was her name? Let's see . . . Cecile, Cecilia . . . no . . . Celia. That was her name wasn't it? Celia. Still happily married? I should be jealous, I suppose. You passed me over for her."

Gallagher smiled at her. "You know it wouldn't have worked."

"So this one has worked."

"No."

She had green eyes with gray flecks in them. They stared at him. "I'm sorry," she said.

"That was a long time ago." He didn't want to talk about it. "And what about you? What brings you to this neck of the woods? Married?"

She shook her head slowly. "No one can cope. You are a difficult man to replace."

"Oh come on, Veronica. You don't believe that anymore than I do."

She beamed at him. "Can't blame a girl for trying, can you?"

"Well? What brings you to this neck of the woods then?" Gallagher repeated.

"I'm with a promotional company. They have one of their offices up here, and I am sort of in charge. They think it's a good wheeze to have a Lady Somebody on the Board. And you? I've seen some of your photography around. Is that all you do? Or are you still working for that funny Department of yours?"

Gallagher felt a strange tingle. This usually happened when something to alarm him, as yet unseen, was on its way.

"What Department?"

"Now you come on, Gordon. Daddy once told me you worked for some funny people."

"Daddy told you?" Gallagher did not like the sound of this at all. What had Veronica Walmsley's father got to do with anything? What had he got to do with the Department?

"Daddy tends to mention you now and then. He always asks about you."

"Nice of him to be interested in my health. But I know nothing of any Department."

An eyebrow arched at him.

"That doesn't sound too convincing."

"Eight years is a long time. Why didn't you get in touch before?"

"You were married, for God's sake. Would your wife have approved?"

He made no reply. Whatever her insinuations, theirs had been a very casual affair. For all her remarks, she'd never had any intention of marrying him. His mind had therefore returned to the nagging question. Why had she sought him out? Or more to the point . . . who had sent her? He hoped it was not Fowler yet again.

"Tell Fowler to forget it."

"Tell who? Who is Fowler?"

She seemed genuinely confused.

"You mean you've never met him?"

The gray-flecked eyes stared at him. "I have no idea what you're talking about."

Gallagher was not sure whether to believe her. He decided to err on the side of caution, and assumed she was lying.

She continued to look at him, with the amused expression still upon her face. "Wondering whether I'm telling the truth?"

"I'm not thinking anything," he lied.

The Upper Street bistro in Islington was one of his favorite haunts when he had reason to be in the area. He had been commissioned to take photographs of an exhibition in the Trade Hall across the street, and had popped in for a cup of coffee. One of the waitresses came up to his table with a small order pad. She looked at Veronica, and waited.

"Just an orange juice, thanks," she said.

The waitress nodded, took the order and went away.

Veronica turned to Gallagher once more. "Look," she began. "Why don't you pop over to my place this evening? I'm having a little do. A small, intimate family thing. Daddy will be there."

Gallagher thought about what she had just said, liking it less with each passing moment. "Did you come here specifically to invite me?"

"Of course not. I was just passing, saw you get out of that amazing black car and come in here. At first, I couldn't believe it really was you. After all, eight years. But you don't seem to have changed at all."

"Is that good? Or bad?"

"Good," she said.

"I'm flattered."

"Then you will come."

The waitress had returned with the orange juice. They paused, waited as she put it on the table then moved off to serve other customers.

"I'd love to," Gallagher said, "but I've got to get today's photos ready by tomorrow. How about next week?"

"Can I reach you anywhere?"

"Nellads." He'd be dropping off the rolls of film to save time, instead of developing them himself.

"I know them," she said. "We once did a product launch with them. That's how I saw some of your photographs. I've also seen the book about the down and outs in London. What did you call it?"

"*Heart of the City*. I did another on drunks."

"Haven't seen that one."

He was not surprised. It was not the sort of book she'd go looking for.

Her eyes were studying him speculatively, as if trying to fathom what was going on in his mind. At last, she said: "You're not going to disappear for another eight years, are you?"

"I didn't disappear. You could have found me any time."

"Of course I could," she said skeptically. "And you could have found me."

What was she up to? Gallagher wondered. Precisely what did Lady Veronica Walmsley, heiress supposedly earning her living, really want? He watched as she slowly drank her orange juice, as her eyes absently studied the other customers, as she looked back at him and smiled once more. The smile was worrying.

Gallagher's gut instincts told him she had brought trouble with her, and he did not want any part of it. It was time to leave.

"I've got to start the job, so I'll be leaving you here, I'm afraid." He got out some money, then as she began to search in her purse, added: "I think I can afford orange juice."

"Thanks." The gray-flecked eyes were smiling at him much too intimately.

Nothing apparent seemed to justify the way he was feeling at the moment. Paranoia. It got to you sometimes. He stood up, placed the money on the table, picked up his camera case, and started to leave.

"How about that little restaurant we used to go to?" she now suggested.

He paused, surprised. "Is it still in business?"

"Thriving. I go there from time to time."

"Memories?" He didn't believe it for one moment. But let her play the game if that was what she wanted. It meant nothing to him, since he was not going to be involved.

She shrugged. "Who knows? How about next Wednesday?"

"Again, I'd love to, but I may have to go to Amsterdam on Wednesday. There's a job on."

"I'm not having much success with you, am I?"

"After eight years, what do you expect?"

"And now," she said, "you are angry with me."

"I'm not," Gallagher said.

She seemed to pause for thought then suddenly, brightened. "I know," she said. "Are you driving to Amsterdam?"

"Yes."

"Why don't I just come with you?"

"What?"

"I rather fancy a few days in Amsterdam."

"What about your job?"

"Oh I can arrange something."

I'll bet you can, Gallagher thought. Aloud, he said: "You wouldn't like it. I've got to take pictures of lots of canals and dykes."

"Oh I don't know," she said. "I think I could quite enjoy that."

Gallagher was not fooled. He knew Veronica was not one to go traipsing about the Dutch countryside. She could not have changed that much. "You really wouldn't like it," he told her.

She gave him a strange smile. "Alright, Gordon," she said. "I can take a hint. I'd better let you get on with your job. But call me." She handed him her card.

Gallagher took it and studied it briefly. A plain white card, embossed in gold. Superimposed upon a central design of whirling atoms was her name, telephone number, and office address. "FUTRON," it said. "We solve problems."

"What sort of problems?" Gallagher asked.

"All kinds."

Gallagher put the card away. "I'll call you."

He left her in the bistro, aware that her eyes followed him out. As he crossed the road to go to the exhibition center, he knew she was still watching him. Veronica Walmsley. It didn't make sense. She was still on his mind when he finished the job, and was on his way back home to his maisonette in Holland Park. Throughout the journey, he had kept a sharp eye on his mirrors. But no one appeared to have followed him. It didn't mean anything, of course. A group of shadowers who knew their job could wait at strategic points, record his passage, and collate the final results. But he didn't think that had happened.

The black car that Veronica had spoken about, a black Audi *quattro,* was his pride and joy. It was his one, real extravagance. He had an affinity with the car, and as a former fast jet pilot with the RAF, looked upon it as his earth-bound fighter. In moments of stress, he tended to talk to it, addressing it by name. He called it Lauren, after the girl he was to have married and who had been shot dead on the slopes of Courchevel. He would never forget Lauren. But a new love had entered his life. Unfortunately, Rhiannon Jameson had come close to death herself. As a result, she had taken a job in the States, and had not been in touch. It had been eight months of unbearable silence.

Gallagher had got on with his work and his life; but the pain of her leaving had not eased.

The car cruised toward Holland Park, its powerful engine rumbling deeply. The offbeat, five-cylinder sound of the power plant always gave him pleasure. It was a non-standard unit. Taken from the sports version of the *quattro,* the 20-valver had had its power raised to 325 bhp. Other aspects of the car had also been changed. There were no door handles, and access was gained by use of a remote about the size of a credit card. Gallagher had also had the car totally wired, so that the remote would sound should anyone try to place anything upon it or beneath it, or attempt a break-in. This security system had on more than one occasion foiled the Department's attempts to put a trace on him.

Gallagher parked the *quattro* in the quiet street off Holland Avenue, and got out. He paused, looked about him carefully. No one had apparently followed him. Taking the camera case with him, he walked unhurriedly to his door and let himself in. There were a few letters waiting on the mat, two of which were bills. In the firm belief that the bad news should be taken care of before moving to the good bits, he looked at these first. None of them were pressing, but decided to attend to them as quickly as possible. He hated outstanding bills. He put them to one side, and checked the rest of the mail. There were two assignments, one of which was for a very good fee. It was the one he'd been expecting: the Amsterdam job. The social invites could wait. The usual collection. But one was different. It was from his bank and by the window in the envelope, he could see it was a statement.

"I certainly didn't expect you," he said to the envelope as he opened it up.

He pulled out the single sheet of paper with its neatly set out columns, and checked his credit and debit. What he saw shook him. He refused to believe the figures.

They showed him a credit of well over £700,000!

He refused to believe it. The bank had made a mistake. Its computer had gone ape. He'd heard of such things happening and some poor sod, believing his luck was mysteriously in, would go on a spending spree, only to find the bank howling for its loot. That would not become his problem.

He glanced at his watch: 3.30 P.M. There was still time. He rang his manager to check.

The reply was an even greater shock. The Manager confirmed that someone had indeed deposited a sum of over £650,000 into his account.

"Are you sure, Michael?" Gallagher asked uncertainly. He'd known the Manager for some years and they were on quite friendly terms. "There's no mistake?"

"No mistake at all. Your already healthy credit has turned into something quite spectacular. I know of a lot of people who would be sounding a lot happier than you are at the moment . . . me for a start."

"Look . . . do you have some spare time this afternoon? I'd better come in for a chat."

"Can you make it in an hour? We're open late today."

"I can make it."

"Fine. See you then. And don't sound so gloomy. You're a rich man now." A chuckle ended the conversation.

Gallagher replaced the receiver slowly, sat

down, and began to think about his strange day. Lady Veronica Walmsley, who'd never needed to work for a living and could reasonably be expected never to suffer that need, had turned up out of the blue after eight years of no contact, *working*. She'd apparently been so pleased to see him, she had been prepared to take a few days off to accompany him to Amsterdam. Just like that. She'd also invited him to an "intimate" gathering where Daddy would be in attendance; the same Daddy who'd been making noises about the Department.

And now, someone had dumped over half a million quid into his account. If all of this didn't spell trouble, his paranoia was working overtime for nothing. Somehow, he didn't think his jangling alarm bells had got it wrong.

"Amsterdam," he said, "here I come . . . and without Lady Veronica."

But first, he had to see Michael Perowne at the bank.

Perowne greeted him with something very close to a grin, in the Piccadilly office.

"You should be celebrating," Perowne began, "not looking so glum."

"You don't know the things I do."

"And I'm very happy not to." Perowne knew nothing of Gallagher's previous work with the Department, though there were times when he had felt an undercurrent in Gallagher's life that had warned against too close a scrutiny. He opened a file. "The money came from the States. Boston, to be precise."

"What?"

"I see dawning comprehension. So you do know its source."

"Well no . . . What I mean is yes . . . but no. It can't be."

"It has to be one or the other."

"My God," Gallagher said quietly. He looked away, thinking: then turned to Perowne once more. "Are you sure?"

"Absolutely. No question. I thought you already knew all about it."

"This is as big a surprise to me as it is to you. Believe me."

Perowne was staring at him puzzledly. "But you do seem to know the source."

"If it's Boston . . . yes. But it doesn't make sense. I'll . . . I'll have to check. Look, can you put it into a separate account for me until I've sorted this out?"

"No problem." Perowne got a sheet of paper from his desk. "Sign this authorization and I'll do the rest. It will earn while it's in there, so you'll be even richer." He grinned.

Gallagher signed. "Thanks, Michael." He stood up. "I'll be in touch." They shook hands.

"A pleasure to do business with you, sir."

"Michael," Gallagher said warningly.

Perowne smiled.

Back in Holland Park, Gallagher rang Myron Tanner, Lauren's father, at his office in Boston. Gallagher had used the direct number, and got Tanner immediately.

"Gordon!" Tanner began, sounding genuinely pleased. "I did wonder whether you would call. I was not sure whether you had forgotten this number. It's been a long time."

"Yes," Gallagher admitted.

"There was no need for you to keep away just because Lauren's gone."

Gallagher shut his eyes briefly. Christ. Memories. What a day this was turning out to be. Lauren would still be alive if he . . . but Lauren was dead. There was nothing he could do about it now; nothing he could have done about it.

Memories slow you down, sir.

O'Keefe. O'Keefe was dead too. Killed on a mission that had gone sour. O'Keefe . . . Warrant Officer, mentor, teammate on many a successful mission until . . . More unwelcome memories.

Gallagher thrust O'Keefe out of his mind.

". . . are you there?" a voice was saying in his ear. Tanner at the other end of the transatlantic line.

"I'm still here. I got a surprise from the bank today."

"I know."

"I can't accept it."

"You can't return it."

"Why not?"

"The person who gave it to you is no longer with us."

"Not Lauren," Gallagher said. He'd feel like a ghoul, inheriting her money.

"Jake," Tanner said.

Jake Smallson, Lauren's maternal grandfather, had been shot dead by the same people who had killed Lauren. Gallagher had made them pay.

"He wanted you to have it," Tanner continued. "It was a wedding gift to both Lauren and yourself. Once all his affairs were sorted out, this had to be attended to. There was some opposition from the more distant family members, but I overruled them. I cannot stand naked greed in families."

"You can't ask me to accept," Gallagher pleaded. "I've already had my revenge. That was my payment."

"You're not hearing me correctly. No one is talking of payment. This is a gift from an old man who thought highly of you, and who loved his grand-daughter very much." A huskiness had come into Tanner's voice as he spoke, clearly remembering his own loss. "He made a specific change in his will . . . which I am determined will be honored. I happen to agree with his sentiments, Gordon."

It had been so different once. Tanner, New England patrician had not approved of his daughter's involvement with Gallagher. Then Lauren had been killed and the stern man had undergone a subtle change, extending sympathy to Gallagher when it had been least expected. Tanner had even called him son once or twice. Now Tanner, impeccable man of breeding, had fought off successfully a rear-guard action by distant relatives, to ensure Jake Small-son's bequest went where it was intended. Tanner would not be persuaded otherwise.

But I can't take it, Gallagher said in his mind.

As if he'd heard, Tanner said: "It seems as if we've got ourselves a Mexican stand-off. Leave it where it is. Get used to it."

"But . . ."

"And it's no use sending it back. I've instructed my bank not to accept a return. And Gordon . . ."

"I'm here."

"You must come and see us. Sara would like to see you once in a while."

Lauren's mother. Gallagher felt guilty. He'd

stayed away because he'd felt that with Lauren gone, there really was nothing for him within that family. Without Lauren, he was an interloper. Besides, there was Rhiannon now . . . if she ever came back. But the Tanners did not seem to want to let go.

The more he thought about it all, the more Amsterdam beckoned.

"I'll . . . I'll do that," he now said.

"Is that a promise?"

"Yes."

"That's enough for me. Don't give us a date. When you're ready, call me and I'll tell Sara. It would make her very happy, Gordon."

This was making him feel worse. He had to end the conversation gently; but Tanner, astute as ever, saved him.

"I'm sure you have many things to do," Tanner said, "so I'd better let you get on. Don't forget to give me a call. We'll always be glad to see you. Look after yourself, son."

"And you," Gallagher said quietly. "My love to Sara."

"I'll give it to her."

They hung up together.

Gallagher stared at the phone. What else, he wondered, did the day hold for him?

In a spartan office in a quiet London square, Adrian Fowler, Deputy Head of the Department, studied the transcript he had just received. He moved his glasses to the tip of his nose, pinched the bridge between thumb and forefinger, before moving them back.

"It would seem," he began, "that our Gordon's had a windfall."

"I thought we weren't supposed to be tapping his

phone anymore." Delphine Arundel, Colonel's lady but widowed by a bomb in County Armagh, Northern Ireland, was the Department's conscience. She had an uphill task, she also had a soft spot for Gallagher. She had brought the transcript.

"He's not always on tap."

"That's hardly an excuse, Mr. Fowler. He's no longer with the Department. Why do we keep interfering with his life?"

Fowler's eyes appeared to gleam behind the glasses. "I'd hardly call it interfering. His past seems to have a habit of catching up with him."

"Which conveniently for us, we tend to exploit."

"Why Mrs. Arundel," Fowler began mildly, "you're angry with me today."

"Why are we tapping him?"

"You don't really expect me to tell you, do you?" Fowler was smiling at her, but his eyes had lost their apparent gleam of amusement.

"Of course not, Mr. Fowler. Silly me."

She went out, closing the door hard behind her.

Fowler watched the closed door for some moments, the barest hint of a smile at the corners of his mouth, before returning to his scrutiny of the transcript.

Fowler was a tall, slim man in his fifties with neatly groomed hair just beginning to gray at the temples. If seen walking down the road in one of his perfectly cut suits, steely eyes probing at the world from behind his spectacles, he would easily be mistaken for a highly successful top executive. The observer would be correct in his surmise, but for all the wrong reasons. In the world that he inhabited professionally, Fowler was indeed a top executive and more often than not, was highly successful.

Though Deputy to Admiral Sir John Winterbourne, the Head of Department, consensus of opinion was that Fowler really ran the show while Winterbourne flapped about making noises. Winterbourne detested Fowler's wide-ranging grasp of all matters concerning the Department and seemingly, beyond the Department's sphere of influence. For his part, Fowler quietly despised Winterbourne, seeing the Admiral's appointment as Head as more of a political than practical decision. On occasion, Winterbourne's meddling had produced near-disasters, needing Fowler's expertise to salvage what was left.

Fowler's trump card was Gallagher, whom he had no compunction in using if such use helped produce the desired result. It mattered little that Gallagher was no longer on Department strength. Fowler was not averse to a little Machiavellian scheming in order to ensnare Gallagher into doing the Department's work.

Gallagher had resigned because of the soured mission on which O'Keefe had been lost. It didn't necessarily follow that a resignation meant no more Department work for Gallagher. Good operatives were not easy to come by. You could train an agent, but you could not give him or her the instincts that soared above the rest of the crowd; the instincts that told the instructors that here was a natural.

Gallagher was the Department's best. Why should a little matter like resignation get in the way of serious business?

But for once, Fowler was not doing the ensnaring. Gallagher was getting into something, and Fowler wanted to know what it was.

* * *

Gallagher had finished his packing. He double-checked, making sure cameras and necessary equipment for the assignment were all accounted for, together with the clothes needed for the two-week stay. It was a calendar shoot, the theme being scenes of the Dutch landscape, for an inland water transport company.

Satisfied, he took his luggage down to the car. It all went nicely into the boot of the *quattro*. He set the answering machine, locked up and went back out to the car. Before entering, he had a casual look around, searching for anything that seemed out of the ordinary in the immediate cityscape. His eyes hunted out the anomalies; anything that he instinctively felt to be wrong. He had long ago learned to trust his instincts.

But there were none. No out-of-place figure pretending to look occupied; no bicycle or motorbike that shouldn't be there; no car parked surreptitiously around a corner. Again, a current absence of all these did not positively mean they were not somewhere else but for the moment, the alarm bells were still. Whatever Veronica Walmsley had brought with her sudden appearance had for the time being, retreated.

He climbed into the *quattro* and snapped on his seatbelt. The car was clean, he knew. If anyone had tried to interfere with it, the remote would have bleeped, while the powerful alarm horns would have seared the area with their blast, accompanied by the lights flashing on full beam.

He started the engine, looked about him once more as it came to life. The sound should have alerted anyone carrying out a clandestine surveillance. Still nothing.

Gallagher eased the car out of the carport and into the road, wondering why an American firm would want pictures of the Dutch landscape for its calendar. There were enough Stateside lakes, bayous, rivers and inland waters of sufficient dramatic quality to suit the most jaded of tastes. Perhaps they suffered from overuse. Something special from Holland had been the brief.

Perhaps the head of the company had Dutch antecedents and wanted something from the old country to represent the company's image. Whatever the reason, they were paying Gallagher handsomely for his efforts.

Gallagher swung the *quattro* into Holland Avenue. He was heading for Sheerness in Kent, to catch the boat for Vlissingen near the Dutch/Belgian border, from where he would drive on to Amsterdam.

No one seemed to be following him, but he thought he saw a white Rover navigating the Shepherd's Bush roundabout behind him, going the other way.

Fowler was speaking into one of the three phones on his otherwise bare, polished desk.

"Heading toward the center of town," he was saying. He sighed. "No. Don't attempt to follow. He'd spot you within seconds. It doesn't matter if you were going in the opposite direction. His instincts are like targetting radars. I'd lay bets that he's spotted you already. We know he's on the move. That's enough for now. Come back to the square."

He put the receiver down, cutting transmission.

The door to his office opened and a big man, already well past his sixtieth year, entered. He looked like everyone's idea of a plodding policeman, complete with ruddy face; but George Haslam was no stolid plodder. In his younger days he'd been every bit as lethal as Gallagher now was, and during the Second World War, had operated with the *maquis* in France. It was said that various local Gestapo units vied with each other to capture him. They never succeeded.

Now, he was supposed to be a semiretired liaison officer for the Department, his specific area being the police.

"Hullo, George," Fowler began pleasantly. "Glad you could make it."

"Glad I could make what?"

"What's wrong with everyone today? First Arundel, now you."

"She says you're tapping Gallagher."

"Arundel talks too much."

"Perhaps it's because I listen to her."

"Are you implying I don't?"

"Why is Gallagher on tap?"

"I know that look, George," Fowler said. "Just this once, both you and Arundel are wrong. I have not initiated this. Gallagher's swanning his way into something and I'm merely keeping an eye out."

"Ha! Pull the other one."

"You know as well as I do," Fowler said, "that once you've been in this business, you never truly leave it. Resignation or retirement counts for little. You're only truly out of it when you're six feet under and even then, I wouldn't put any money on a bet like that. People have been haunted by dead spooks before, if you'll pardon the dreadful pun."

"Yes," Haslam said heavily. "It is dreadful."

Fowler gave a fleeting smile.

"Why did you call me in?" Haslam went on. "It's

been quiet for me recently and I like it that way. I'm a pensioner now. Or have you forgotten?"

Fowler made a noise of pure skepticism. "You may be of pensionable age, George . . . but a pensioner? No. You wouldn't know what to do with the time. I'm teaming you with Prinknash . . ."

Haslam sighed loudly. "Not Prinknash. Why do you always give me that deadhead?"

"You're our police liaison man, and Prinknash is a policeman attached to us. Besides, you're the only one who can put up with him. Your patience is infinite."

"Your barbs cut home."

"Come on, George. He's not so bad."

"He's worse. In any case, ever since he was shot up in France the last time Gallagher was involved, he's been a little twitchy. He still limps around because of that thigh wound."

"The Doc says he's physically alright. The limp is psychosomatic."

"Thanks for nothing. He was already halfway gone before he was shot. Now he's completely over . . . Good God, Adrian. Send him back to the boys in blue."

"Can't."

"Why not?"

"Prinknash is Winterbourne's idea of liaison. Now that he was wounded in action, so to speak, Winterbourne reads it as bravery . . . and bravery as you know, should be rewarded."

"Department personnel have had a lot worse happen to them."

"Ah yes, but they're not Winterbourne appointees."

Haslam made a noise of disgust.

"And besides," Fowler went on, "you visited him in hospital."

"I don't have to like the man. He was with me when he was hit. It was the least I could do. His wounds had done nothing to improve his brain."

"You clearly get on like a house on fire. Prinknash is coming in from a surveillance . . ."

"Gallagher?"

Fowler nodded.

"Don't tell me Gallagher didn't spot him?" Haslam said, disbelief plain in his voice.

"I'm almost certain he did. But that was not a problem. If I'd wanted a real job of surveillance, I'd have put you on."

"Gallagher would have spotted me too. He's a hard one to tag. So what are we supposed to do?"

"You wait for further instructions from me. Until then, keep an eye on Gallagher's home."

"What if he's not there?"

"We'll know soon enough. Oh by the way, seen this or anything like it before?" Fowler handed Haslam a white card.

Haslam looked at it, read the company name out loud: " 'FUTRON.' Who, or what are they?"

"Look at the representative's name."

"Peter J. Behrensen," Haslam murmured. His eyes narrowed as he studied the card.

"Yes, George," Fowler said. "The same Behrensen. Now tell me . . . what would a recruiter of mercenaries want with Gordon Gallagher?"

"Gallagher's no mercenary. He doesn't fight other people's wars."

"He fights ours but then, he's one of us. Your job, George. Find out what Behrensen's up to."

"But how do you know he's after Gallagher?"

"A young lady, whose father I happen to know, carries one of these cards. Prinknash was detailed to follow her. He saw her meet with Gallagher, but I ordered him off in case Gallagher spotted him."

"That still doesn't mean . . ."

"Eight years ago, she had a brief fling with our Gordon."

"Perhaps she wants to continue where they left off."

"That sort of thing only happens in soaps. People change. Gallagher's been radically changed by circumstances. He's a very different man under the surface."

"And this young lady . . . does her father know?"

"I very much doubt it. I'd be surprised; but in this job, we expect surprises. Don't we, George?"

2

Peter J. Behrensen was the kind of man who was disliked on sight. His detractors—who were legion—considered him a right bastard. His friends—who were very few—were of the same opinion. As in childhood, so in adulthood. Behrensen, a native of Dayton, Ohio, had left in his early teens, and had not been back since; for which Dayton was well pleased. Now, Behrensen was boss of a worldwide consultancy whose dealings were in the most lucrative of modern day markets: arms, and men. His education began on the streets of New York where he would sell weapons—flick knives, ice picks, filed-down scissor blades, knuckle dusters, etc.—to rival gangs. Every so often, he would sell better weapons to the side he decided he preferred at any given time. The fact that he survived such treachery bore testimony to his remarkable capability for survival. As he grew older, the wider world of arms dealing attracted him.

For many years, Behrensen disappeared without trace. When he resurfaced, he put it about that he had been with the US Special Forces. He also said he had been made a colonel. He supplied no proof of this but equally, no one came forward to deny it. His enemies maintained he had been in prison for all these years, as a result of a number of crimes he had committed. These ranged from protection rackets, to drug dealing, to murder. None of these accusations appeared to worry him.

Behrensen maintained a very low profile, perhaps with good reason. It was known that many law enforcement agencies throughout the world would have loved to get their hands on him, but for some reason, none seemed able to do so.

Behrensen's business interests covered the territories of many nations, among which were several tin-pot dictatorships. He still carried out his favorite trick of balancing the interests of one against the other, making sure whichever side won or lost, he was the eventual winner.

Behrensen was not a tall man. Large, with the build of an all-in wrestler, his head seemed to have been planted upon his shoulders with no room left for a neck. His eyes, protruding, appeared to have reached a limit whereby any further protrusion would have made stalks necessary. His forehead seemed to have been made for butting and his hair was cut so short, he could easily have passed muster as a bald-headed man. Behrensen had the pigeon-toed walk of the wrestler. His arm-swinging, head-jerking gait, gave him an aggressive approach which he always used to great effect. But there was one thing even more remarkable about Behrensen.

He was black.

No one who first heard the name Behrensen, imagined it. He used this to great effect, as many of his competitors had found to their cost, and he had shamelessly applied it as a potent weapon, when dealing with Third World countries.

While Fowler was wondering what Behrensen was up to, Behrensen was himself sitting in the state room of his luxurious motor yacht off the coast of Portugal, as it headed toward the Mediterranean at a speed of twenty-five knots. With him was a beautiful blonde woman. From their conversation, it became evident that her presence there was to do with business, rather than pleasure.

London.

Fowler picked up one of the phones on his desk. At the other end was Haslam.

"Yes, George?"

"Well he's not here. And I don't think he is going to be coming back for a while."

Fowler did not bother asking whether Haslam was sure. Haslam was not in the habit of making statements he did not believe in.

"Alright, George. What about Lady Veronica?"

"I've got another car on her. She is still at the office."

"Good, stick with her. I want to see where she goes to next."

"And then what?"

"Why George, you follow her."

"Wherever she goes?"

"Wherever she goes. Even if it's abroad."

"You expect her to go abroad?"

"Who knows, George. Who knows."

The gleaming white yacht, named *Stonefish,* seemed to skim across the surface of the still sea. When necessary, she could hit forty knots, a speed which in many cases was greater than several of the world's warships. It was an asset that greatly aided escape when the need arose. On one or two occasions, such a need had arisen.

In the state room, the blonde woman was saying: "So you are sure you can get them?"

Behrensen smiled. The woman felt suddenly cold. It was not a leer. Behrensen had little time for leering, or overt sexual games. He simply took, when he was ready. It was the smile. Many people had felt that chill before.

"F-16's are not the sort of thing you can pick up on the open market," he said. "But arrangements are being made, and I shall have the six ready for the time you have requested. And should you have a further requirement, I am certain I can arrange for another six."

"I thought it was difficult to get such aircraft even in your particular line of business."

The cold smile returned. "I can get them. There are many people with favors to return. Not only can I get them, I can also get the equipment and the armament, as a complete package."

The woman smiled at him. "Well, Mr. Behrensen, it seems as if our principals were right, after all, in recommending you. I look forward to our next meeting."

Behrensen reached forward to touch her hand. She flinched. Though as chilled by his presence as his smile, she was not truly afraid of him. Within her was the same revulsion she would have felt for a snake. She was wary of a snake, but would kill it rather than turn her back upon it. Behrensen knew what she was thinking. He withdrew his hand slowly, and the cold smile returned.

"And I," he said, "am looking forward to our next meeting. It has been a pleasure doing business with you. The helicopter will be arriving to take you to Faro, in time for you to catch your plane."

"Thank you, Mr. Behrensen." The blonde woman gave him one of her more devastating smiles; but it was totally devoid of emotion.

The accent in which she had spoken was South African.

The *Stonefish* was the kind of yacht even rich people dreamed about, but would have little chance of owning. To someone like Behrensen, ordinarily rich people were poor people and it always gave him a vivid pleasure to see the looks of envy the *Stonefish* brought its way whenever he took her into harbor. In many places, moorings were reserved for him. Not bad, he'd think at such moments, for a kid whose mother used to scrub other people's floors.

With a length of sixty meters and a displacement of exactly 400 tonnes, her triple screws driven by three 1500 hp engines, she could power herself through the water with arrogant ease. Her twin funnels had been designed so that they looked like flared wings, curving on either side of the superstructure. In place of the normal single outlet, slots had been incorporated, giving the funnels a ribbed look. She had a crew of twelve, each of whom was well schooled in the use of arms.

The owner's lounge, all bleached oak paneling and black lacquered furniture, was spacious and full of light. Behrensen sat in a gray suede armchair looking out at the blonde woman as she leaned against a high rail, looking out to sea. Her hair streamed in the wind of the ship's passage. She looked barely twenty-one.

I could have her, Behrensen thought, *and there's nothing she'd be able to do about it . . . despite her silly little pistol.*

But that would have spoiled the enjoyment. It was too easy. She had come aboard the *Stonefish* three days ago, and he had left her strictly alone. Business was business and this deal would be netting him enough of a profit to buy another *Stonefish* outright, with plenty of change to spare. He was not about to jeopardize that for any blonde piece of meat he could take any time he wanted.

As if she knew his thoughts, the woman turned, her eyes finding his through one of the spotless glass panels of the lounge. They were full of disdain.

Behrensen smiled at her.

She snapped her head around, turning away from him once more.

His smile did not die. There would be plenty of other occasions to teach her some manners. First things first. He picked up a white radio phone from its receptacle in the arm of his chair. A forefinger touched a single, numbered button.

"Yes, sir?" a voice answered immediately. The yacht's captain.

"Duquesne," Behrensen said, "how long before we meet up with the chopper?"

"Twenty-five minutes, Mr. Behrensen." Duquesne had a Southern drawl. "And we'll be off Cabo de Santa Maria five minutes before that."

"Thank you," Behrensen said and switched off.

He glanced again at the woman as he clicked the phone into its holder. She was still looking out to sea. He thought of the man who was captain of his ship.

Duquesne came from a reasonably monied Southern family and had grown up with motor yachts. Something had gone wrong with a promising legal career, forcing the young lawyer into a shadier profession that had eventually taken him around the world skippering boats of various kinds on sometimes hazardous undertakings. In his search for the right man for the job, Behrensen had found Duquesne in Singapore, about to be deported and with little money, having been double-crossed by a partner dealing in illegal immigration from Vietnam.

Duquesne came from the kind of family who believed that all association with blacks should be limited to the domestic necessity of requiring servants: but by the time Behrensen had found him, the real world had altered his own views radically. He was now as loyal to Behrensen as the black maid who'd looked after him as a child had been loyal to the Duquesne family. More so, perhaps, because Behrensen had not only given him a job that had brought some self-esteem back, it also paid ridiculously well.

Behrensen derived no particular satisfaction from the fact that a minor Southern aristo was now his employee. Duquesne was in his employ because the man was good at his job. Anyone who worked for him was required to display absolute professionalism, and loyalty. Failure on either of these two counts, merited instant dismissal.

In the case of the first requirement, there was also the accompanying penalty of a dearth of further employment by other organizations. Behrensen seemed able to block all doors within his particular world. The second requirement tended to attract a far more severe penalty for failure, and was fre-

quently terminal. One day someone would be in existence and the next, he would not be. Women in Behrensen's employ were not immune.

Behrensen glanced at his guest for a second
time. He would make her his project, but when he
was quite ready. It would give him great pleasure
indeed to spreadeagle her on the big circular bed in
the owner's suite.

He felt a stirring in his loins as he thought of it,
and prided himself on his control. Time enough to
taste the fruits of her body when the deal was complete.

Exactly twenty-five minutes later, the *Stonefish* lay
dead in the water, three miles off the hammer-
shaped peninsula that was the Cabo de Santa Maria.

The woman had collected her luggage—two ex-
pensive-looking travel cases of tan-colored leather—
and was waiting just outside the lounge. Extending
beyond the lounge whose stern section was beneath
the bridge of the ship, was a wide platform which
sometimes doubled as a sun deck. It had been cleared
of all furniture, and a full-sized covering of canvas
had been laid and secured in such a way, that not a
single wrinkle could be seen upon its smooth surface.

Behrensen was standing next to her. The May
sunshine was working itself up to a hot June and
beat upon the deck.

"You seem in such a hurry to leave," he said in
a calm voice, "if I didn't know better, I'd feel offended."

"I am in a hurry," she said without looking at
him, "to get to my next destination."

"I'm sure you are." Behrensen paused, listening.

"And you won't have much longer to wait. I believe I can hear your chariot on its way."

Even as he spoke, a faint sound had made itself heard. Soon, a speck had appeared, coming from landward. Before long, the speck had grown into a fast-traveling MD 500 helicopter equipped with floats where skids should be. It thrummed up to the *Stonefish,* swinging in to land with a flourish. It touched the deck with barely a jolt.

"Dan Murchison's one of the best," Behrensen informed her. "Treats the deck like his living room. You'll have a very safe flight to Faro."

The helicopter's blades were now slowly rotating as it waited. One of the ship's crewmen had come to take the woman's luggage and was moving toward the aircraft. Another was holding a door open.

She began walking, head slightly down, following the man with her luggage.

Behrensen remained where he was, and called after her: "I expect to hear from your people soon."

She paused briefly to glance back at him. "You will."

The crewman ahead of her put the luggage inside the helicopter, then moved back for her to get in. She took her seat next to the pilot and secured her straps. She stared out at Behrensen who raised a hand in farewell.

She looked back expressionlessly at him. "Let's go," she said to Murchison.

He did so without comment, raising the helicopter smoothly off the deck.

Behrensen was slowly lowering his hand as the aircraft tipped over on its side and headed back toward Faro.

Almost immediately, the *Stonefish*'s powerful

triple engines came to life and very quickly the white ship, gleaming in the sunshine, was surging its way across the gulf of Cadiz.

The helicopter landed at Faro airport and within half-an-hour, the woman was aboard a Boeing 737 on the first leg of her journey northward.

London, 2100 hours.

Haslam entered Fowler's office. "I've got a home to go to," he began. "So have you. Why are we here? It's clear Gallagher's gone away for some time and as for Lady Walmsley, she's having what appears to be a party. We know where she'll be for the next few hours. I've got a car parked not far from her place. So if the world's not about to end in the next five minutes, I'm off to bed."

"I'll have a doze in my room," Fowler said. "I want to be on this for a little longer."

"I don't know how you can call that cubicle a room," Haslam said, peering into it. "More like a broom cupboard."

Fowler gave one of his illusory smiles. "I've heard there are people these days who will happily pay a small fortune for broom cupboards, or their equivalent."

"The ones with air where their brains should be, you mean. Yes. I've heard of those."

Fowler had two sheets of paper on his desk. He toyed with them absently. "Behrensen," he said. "Behrensen. He's the key."

"To what?"

"Everything, and perhaps nothing."

"That's what I like. Clear-cut choices."

"It's too late in the day for sarcasm, George."

"And too late for someone my age. I should be in bed."

"So you keep saying." Haslam's sarcasm was having little effect on Fowler. "You've never actually seen Behrensen, have you?"

Haslam shook his head. "Not even a photograph. But I've heard of him in some of the most sensitive places."

"No description."

"No."

"Doesn't that strike you as odd?" Fowler queried. "Here's a man known in the trade from Aleppo to Zanzibar and yet . . . no one seems prepared to put a face to him. An epidemic of amnesia seems to strike both those of the high life, and those of the low. Even his competitors appear reluctant to shop him. Why?"

"He's got long arms, and a very good memory. There must also be quite a few state officials whose careers would descend very rapidly to earth if he got annoyed with them."

"That's still not enough, George. He's got more weight behind him. Government weight."

"Whose?"

"Take your pick from the alphabet. Here's a man who's been in every trouble spot in the world. You'd think someone somewhere would have put him on a dossier by now."

"He is on the dossiers . . ."

"Except his description." Fowler held up a sheet, and studied it. "Listen to the number of places where evidence of his handiwork has been found . . . Angola, Ecuador, Namibia, Nicaragua, Venezuela, Eritrea, Labuan, Afghanistan . . . it goes on and on . . . over a hundred countries, including some in

Europe. I'm certain we've only touched the surface. In some cases, he was involved with both sides in a given conflict."

"Sounds like some governments I know," Haslam murmured.

"That's not the point, George. Behrensen's not a government. Which means if he goes out of control, a Department like this has to do the cleaning up afterwards. Normally, I'd leave him alone; but this time Gallagher's involved, and a daughter of a peer of the Realm. I can smell something getting ready to hit the fan."

"Or someone's running an operation under our noses."

"Using *Gallagher?*" Fowler was skepticism itself. "Gallagher works for us under extreme duress. There's not another group on this planet who could succeed in coercing him. The first people he would suspect would be our very selves. He'd come fuming in here, and we'd be in the know. No, George. No one's running him."

"Who said anything about duress?"

Fowler stared at Haslam. "There's no one in the business Gallagher would do that kind of favor for. His closest friends are all dead."

"Not all. How about von Talheim?"

"Freddy von Talheim? The chap who was wounded getting out of Czechoslovakia with that woman he later married?"

Haslam nodded. "Gallagher helped him to get out and last year, he helped Gallagher out with that spot of bother that finished up in Norway."

"Yes, yes. I remember. But Talheim's out of the game. Been out for some time and runs a restaurant in that town near Munich."

"Ingolstadt," Haslam said.

"That's it."

"As you've reminded me more than once," Haslam went on, "no one leaves completely."

Fowler shook his head. "Not von Talheim. If something connected to Behrensen were touching him, I'm sure we would have got wind of it from our German counterparts."

"Then who?"

Fowler stared at the sheet of paper, as if expecting it to yield pertinent information. "We've got to wait," he said. "Something will turn up."

"Oh Micawber," Haslam began drily, "wisdom is thy name."

"Leave Dickens out of this, George, and make sure we don't lose the lovely Lady Veronica."

"Prinknash is on it. Can I go home now?"

Fowler looked at him with the tiniest of smiles. "I thought you were going to do that ages ago."

Haslam shook his head slowly. "Good night, Adrian."

" 'Night, George."

Gallagher had caught the 21.30 ferry from Sheerness and was on his way to Vlissingen. Arrival was 0700 local time the next day, so he had booked himself a cabin for the crossing, paying the substantial price for one he wouldn't have to share. What the hell, he thought. It would go on his expenses. The clients were being very generous, and Nellads had not indicated any limits to be observed.

He had checked all the way to Sheerness for shadows, but no one had seemed to display the slightest interest in him. Careful scrutiny of the passenger and vehicle decks had likewise given him no cause for alarm. Yet he didn't think he was being paranoid. Something was running. His instincts told him so. He intended to take very close heed of them.

The crossing proved to be without incident and as he drove the *quattro* off the ramp the next morning and onto Dutch soil, his fellow passengers continued to be more interested in their own plans rather than his. He hoped it would remain like that all the way to Amsterdam.

He took the Breda motorway, the A58, and obeyed the speed limit, though most of the other motorists didn't. No one seemed to be following. Through Breda, and on to Utrecht, heading north. The road was almost deserted, making it easy to spot a shadow: but there was no shadow to spot.

Surely, his instincts could not have been so wrong?

Although they did not specify any particular area of Holland, the clients had insisted on some shots of Amsterdam to choose from. Thereafter, Gallagher could go wherever he liked, choose whatever he thought would go with the Amsterdam selection. It had seemed perfectly logical to begin with the capital city.

He still kept his eye on the mirrors. With only 206 kilometers to Amsterdam, the car would use only about a fifth of its fuel capacity at motorway cruise. There was thus no need to stop for petrol. But partly because he felt ready for breakfast and because he wanted to check for a tail, he pulled in at a restaurant on the A2 just outside Utrecht.

He took a window seat that gave him a good view of where he'd parked. It would enable him to see if anyone of interest put in an appearance. Three-quarters of a leisurely hour later, nothing had happened in the car park to cause worry. He went out to the *quattro* and resumed his journey.

Amsterdam. Gallagher loved the city. He had fallen in love with it during his student days when it had seemed a place full of gorgeous young women on bicycles. Many things had changed since then; but the bicycles and their riders were still there each time he came.

He had a friend who felt very differently and who would talk about dog feces and July mosquitoes. This negative bias had been brought about by the friend's very first trip to Amsterdam. He had come by car and on the first night of his stay, the car had been broken into and his very expensive car stereo stolen. Gallagher, three years later, had still not managed to change that jaundiced view. The car had been parked barely yards from the hotel he'd been staying at.

Gallagher parked the *quattro* in front of his hotel, near the Leidseplein. A hopeful radio thief would not have much luck. Touching any part of the car in an attempt to force entry would start the secondary alarm system. If the thief believed he'd still be quick enough to continue, the primary alarm, loud enough to bring the police if only to stop the noise, would add voice to the chorus. Should the thief stubbornly persist and actually break the glass, he would still be unable to open the door when he put his hand through. Forced entry automatically prevented the internal handles from being used. The doorman was approaching.

Gallagher unloaded the car, secured it with the remote just as the doorman came up to him.

"We can park it for you, sir," the doorman said in perfect English.

"It's alright, thanks," Gallagher told him. "I'll be going out again soon. Can I leave it here for the moment?"

"Certainly, sir." The doorman turned to a porter briefly. "The porter will help you with your bags, sir."

"Thank you," Gallagher said. He carried the camera case, while the porter followed with the luggage.

As he went inside, Gallagher glanced about him. Nothing. It didn't make sense. His instincts were still warning him.

He was given a very pleasant room overlooking the Singelgracht and as he peered down at the canal from the fourth floor, his eyes searched across it for anyone or anything that might have followed him here. But again, he saw nothing to disturb the pattern.

He changed his clothes for black jeans, a white shirt and a black, full-length leather jacket. Might as well start the job. He picked up the camera case and went out to the *quattro*.

He spent the next hour and a half cruising around the city, looking for shots that had not already appeared in just about everything that could be printed. Eventually, his travels took him to the district of Noord on the other side of Amsterdam's biggest waterway, the river IJ. After ninety minutes dodging cyclists, trams, and tourists, it was a calm haven. Few cyclists were about, the street was tram-free, and no tourists apparently ventured this way. There were no parking restrictions that he could see, and none of those fiendish spiked things that made

London wheel clamps look positively benign. It was perfect for his needs, and the beauty of it all was that the bustling center of the city was a mere 300 or so yards away across the water.

He had found himself driving along the wide cobbled surface of the Meeuwenlaan. Across the busy waterway, was the rear of the central railway station. He parked the car, and climbed out to have a good look at the location. It would give him the shots he needed. He had stopped virtually at the end of the road. Beyond it, were the slipways that led down to the water, from where two flatdeck ferries plied to and fro about every fifteen minutes.

He went back to the car to set up his camera, and returned to position it on its tripod. As he watched, the two ferries, with their aircraft carrier-like islands, were passing each other just beyond the slipways. For moments, they appeared stationary.

Gallagher triggered off some shots. The long rear of the railway station, with passenger and working boats moored at the water's edge, formed a good backdrop. A lone motorcyclist was waiting for the incoming ferry. As it drew closer, it seemed to dwarf him, its raised ramp giving it the look of a landing craft. Heads and shoulders lined its lip, strengthening the impression of anxious marines waiting for the off. A single-decker bus seemed to be the only motor vehicle carried.

Gallagher triggered off some more shots as the ferry reached the slipway, and stopped. Yellow signs with red and black lettering, were mounted on either side of the river ship.

VERBODEN, the sign said, VOOR (BROM) FI-ETSERS. That was the red message. ALLEEN VO-ETGANGERS, the black one added.

That was easy enough. The tunnel-like shelters on the otherwise open deck were strictly for pedestrians.

The ramp dropped, and a horde of cyclists surged off. While this was going on, the longest ship Gallagher had ever seen on an inland waterway coasted into view, moving across his vision, heading for the petroleum docks to his right. The ship was beautifully in position and filled the viewfinder. He took some rapid shots of the entire scene.

Pleased with himself he straightened, and looked about him for more possibilities.

And stiffened.

A car was slowly approaching from the far end of the lane. It braked suddenly, as if aware he was looking at it. The car, a silver-gray Volkswagen Golf with Dutch plates, remained uncertainly where it was for some moments, before pulling into the side where it again stopped.

Gallagher began to slowly pick up the tripod. He had seen the car before, on two previous occasions. It had been behind him as he'd gone down the Nassaukade toward the Western Docks. He had not given it much importance, despite having noted its presence. At least four other silver-gray versions of the same model had trailed him at one time or another. Two of those had been driven by blonde women.

The second time had been on the Noordzije in Slotermeer district. Again, he had registered it, but it had passed him without the slightest of pauses. A blonde woman had again been driving, but she had given him not even the most surreptitious of looks and had turned off soon after. Throughout his wanderings about the city, the Golf had not put in another appearance.

Until now.

The way it was parked, it was difficult to tell whether a blonde woman was in the driving seat; but he was not going to give her the benefit of the doubt. The only way back seemed to be up the lane. He looked at the ferry. The motorcyclist was aboard, and the flat deck was virtually empty. No other car seemed to have been waiting to cross. A few cyclists had pushed their bikes on, but that was it. Gallagher had no idea whether this was a regular car ferry. No cars had accompanied the incoming bus.

He decided to chance it. Unhurriedly, he collapsed the tripod and leaving the camera still attached, walked back to the car. He placed camera and tripod on the back seat, then climbed in. He chose his moment well. Just when it looked as if the ferry was about to raise its ramp, he started the *quattro* and drove aboard. There were more cyclists, but no other car. From the high island, the captain and one other crew member stared down at him strangely, but made no move to make him disembark. Other passengers gave him weird looks too. No one asked for a ticket.

Silly tourist, they were probably thinking, Gallagher told himself. Given the circumstances, it was not the time to stand on dignity. He turned around to look through the back window, and saw he had made the right decision. The Golf was tearing down the lane.

But it was too late. The ramp was coming up and soon, the silver-gray car was blotted out by the massive barrier. The ferry began to move off.

There was a sudden shout from the passengers.

Gallagher propped himself out of the car to look. The Golf had nearly overcooked it, leaving its braking almost too late. It had stopped at the very edge. The people on the ferry were talking animatedly to each other about the incident. Feeling scrutiny, Gallagher looked up at the island. The crew were now looking down at him even more strangely.

A man came up to him. "You shouldn't be here," the man said pleasantly in English.

Gallagher looked out at the river. They were in midstream.

The man smiled, and nodded. "Of course, they cannot put you off now."

"No," Gallagher said. "I suppose not."

"The ferry you should use is over there." He pointed. "Distelweg. But because you are English and do not know, that is why they have done nothing."

"Thank you," Gallagher said. He glanced back to shore. The Golf was still there, its driver probably in shock.

"My pleasure," the man said, and went back to his friends.

Gallagher watched him for some moments, but came to the conclusion that he was just a chatty soul wanting to help. However, by the way he was smiling with his friends, it was clear he had found humor in what he saw as yet another tourist who had made a fool of himself.

Gallagher got back into the car. It was the same all over the world. The man had quite probably been a tourist himself and had conveniently forgotten his own gaffes abroad. Or perhaps he hadn't, and now took some pleasure from Gallagher's apparent mistake.

Gallagher put the man out of his mind. Of greater import was the blonde in the Golf. Who was she, why was she following him, and whom did she work for? He felt certain none of the answers would please him.

He cast his mind back to the only reasonably clear view he'd had of her. That had been in Slotermeer, when she had overtaken him. A glimpse of a very attractive face, perhaps even beautiful, with a healthy tan.

Dutch? She was driving a Dutch registered car; but that meant nothing. It could have been hired. She could be working in Holland . . . There were all sorts of possibilities.

He thought of her tan. Even with the recent good weather, it was still too soon for her to have acquired such a hue, unless she was the sort of person with enough money to follow the sun; or she had lived or had worked for a long time in a hot climate.

Gallagher felt frustration. This was getting him nowhere. There was a whole range of locations from Acapulco to Zanzibar where she would have more than enough sunshine for such a tan. He'd just have to wait and see what the next development would be. At least things had changed. He was now fully on the alert. From the moment the Golf had put in its latest appearance, his senses had moved into top gear. Knowledge of skills, suppressed in memory, was being called up for potential use. Instincts were tuning themselves, quivering like antennae, probing at the environment about him, seeking out the danger. The familiar metamorphosis had begun and by the time the ferry scraped its way to a halt behind the station, a subtly different Gallagher drove off it. Beneath the controlled exterior, the lethality that the Department had used so well was now in place.

He returned to the hotel and left the car in its car park. He fitted the camera with a zoom lens, slung it around his neck, and went walking. If the Golf turned up again, he intended to get some shots of both the car and its driver.

At the time that Gallagher started out to hunt down his persistent shadower, an airliner was approaching the runway at Schiphol with Lady Veronica Walmsley aboard. As soon as she had cleared customs, she went to a taxi and gave the driver her destination.

It was the same hotel as Gallagher's.

3

"**Amsterdam, is it?**" Fowler said into the phone. "Got your toothbrush?"

In the Department Rover, Haslam sighed into the radiophone. "Why can't we get them to tag her over there?"

"Sorry, George. Don't want to excite our EEC partners unduly. There may be nothing in it, you see."

Haslam made a skeptical noise. Fowler never chased anything that had "nothing" in it.

Fowler said: "Did you say something?"

"No."

"Got enough money?"

"Yes."

"You're not being very cooperative, George."

"I wonder why. How do you expect us to find her? It does not necessarily mean she'll stay in Amsterdam."

"That's easy. Watch Gallagher. If she's going there to meet him . . ."

"And what makes you think he's out there?"

"That's another easy one. I called the ad agency

he works for, or rather, who contract him. At first, they would not give me the name of his hotel; but I invoked national security. Always works. Got the boss of the company, who knows Gallagher's got a Security Service background." Fowler gave Haslam the name of the hotel.

"Gallagher's not going to hang around once he knows we're following him."

"I'd be very disappointed in him if he did. Which is why you should find young Lady Veronica quickly. My guess is she'll go to the hotel."

"And if she doesn't?"

"Don't make an already difficult life more difficult, George. I'm sure you'll think of something."

Haslam took the phone away from his ear and stared at it as if he wanted to strangle it. Then he brought it back up.

"I'm too old," he said into it after a while.

"Nonsense. Stay where you are. A car will be coming to you with more cash and passports for Prinknash and yourself. Hire a car when you get over . . ."

"A hired car will never keep up with Gallagher once he gets going."

"Neither will a Department car, so it hardly matters. Got your credit cards with you?"

"Yes," Haslam answered heavily.

"Don't use them. Wrong name."

Haslam closed his eyes. In anticipation of a quick trip abroad, Haslam had packed a small case, and had advised Prinknash to do the same. Both cases were in the boot of the Rover. Now, Fowler wanted a change of identity and while they awaited the other car, Veronica Walmsley's plane would be leaving.

Haslam said, "Right."

"Good," Fowler said. "Keep me posted."

When Fowler ended the conversation, Haslam had the uneasy feeling that Fowler was amused by something.

That had been two hours ago. As he now signed for the Mercedes 190E from the car hire firm at Schiphol, he thought wryly of Fowler's little twist of humor. He and Prinknash were traveling as father and son. They even had driving licences to back up the passports.

Haslam decided to drive for the time being.

As they headed into the city, Prinknash's eyes ranged like hungry animals over the female cyclists.

"My God, Mr. Haslam," he exclaimed. "No one told me Dutch girls looked like that."

"Keep your eyes on the job they're supposed to be doing," Haslam said. "And don't call me Mr. Haslam. I'm supposed to be your father." Haslam sounded as if he would choke on the word.

"Uh . . . yes, Mr. . . . ."

Haslam gave him a baleful glance.

"Er, yes . . . Father."

"Not a difficult word to remember, is it?"

"No."

They drove on in silence, but every time they passed a young woman in shorts astride a bicycle, Prinknash's eyes did a sort of manic dance.

Their hotel was not far from the one Fowler had said Gallagher was booked into. Haslam parked the Mercedes between two other cars, nose-on to the canal.

Prinknash said as he got out: "One false move and this motor goes for a swim." He looked about him. "Bridges, canals, women. Not a bad little town.

They speak English too." To Prinknash, that was a definite plus.

Haslam shook his head slowly. Prinknash was a terminal philistine whose remarks frequently defied comment.

"Let's book in," he said, "then see if we can find that young lady. Who knows? We might even see Gallagher."

"Then what?"

"We follow them, son," Haslam replied, putting heavy irony on the last word. "We follow them and see what they're up to."

"And after that?"

"Let's take one little step at a time, shall we?"

They went to the hotel and booked in as John Peyton and his son James. They were given adjoining rooms, each of which looked out upon the same canal as Gallagher's. The Singelgracht, outermost of the inner group of partially encircling canals, was also the longest at six kilometers. Their hotel was thus sufficiently distant from Gallagher's to enable them to carry out their surveillance without running into him before they were ready to. Haslam hoped.

He knocked on Prinknash's door and entered. Prinknash was still at the window. He turned as Haslam entered.

"Bit like Venice, isn't it? This whole place is on the water."

Haslam said: "Ever been to Venice?"

"No, Mr. . . . er Father."

"It's nothing like Venice. You wouldn't say London is like New York, would you, just because they've each got streets?"

"I've never been to New York."

Haslam paused, patience thin. "Two things to remember: while we're on this trip, never wait for someone to enter the room while your back is turned, and get it into your head you're supposed to be my son . . . God help me."

"I can't keep saying Father. It's not easy."

"Then don't say it. Call me "sir" if you feel the need, the way the Americans sometimes do with their own fathers. Got it?"

Prinknash nodded.

"Fine," Haslam said. "Let's go. And keep your eyes off the women. You can do that on your own time."

Prinknash brightened.

"Not while you're here," Haslam told him. "You're on Department time for the duration."

There was still a good two hours of daylight left when Gallagher decided to stop at a canal-side café. He had seen no sign of the blonde in the Golf, and was certain no one else followed him. He had carried out a series of backtracks that would have betrayed any shadow, no matter how good. None had fallen into the laid traps. He therefore made the decision to become more accessible. Flush her out. Give her time to catch up.

He took a seat at an outside table at the corner café. Directly ahead of him, was the curving hump of a canal bridge. He could clearly see the cobbled street across the canal, in both directions as it ran up to two other bridges. On his own side, he also had an unrestricted road view to the same bridges. If she came, he would see.

He was halfway through his second cup of coffee when the Golf appeared on the opposite side of the canal, coming slowly from the right toward the café bridge. Gallagher watched interestedly.

She found a parking place, got out of the car with studied calm and shut it, taking her time. She wore a white blouse, a plain blue skirt that cleared her knees, and low-heeled shoes. As she crossed the bridge, Gallagher saw she was a very tall woman, with long golden legs and a superbly shaped body. A classic, he thought. What some men would call a dangerous woman. Irresistible, but get involved with her at your peril. What did she want with him?

She approached with the kind of purposeful walk of someone who was unsure of an outcome, but was determined not to be put off.

She stopped at his table, and looked down at him. Very beautiful too, with startling translucent eyes tinged with blue. In the tanned face, they were riveting.

"A dangerous person," she said, opening the gambit.

"Funny. I was just thinking that about you."

"You nearly put me into the river." The accent was familiar.

"You should drive more carefully," Gallagher said. She must be nearly six feet tall, he thought. A mere inch or so less than his own six one. "Take a seat," he continued. "After all that hard work, you need a drink. Coffee? Or something stronger, if they've got it?"

Unaccountably, she smiled, the planes of her face shifting in a manner that enhanced her beauty. It was a smile to look upon for long wondrous moments.

She sat down with feline grace, her eyes fixed

upon him. "Aren't you worried about who I might be?"

He looked about him. "I don't think you're going to shoot me in the street."

"He did tell me to watch out for your strange sense of humor."

"He?"

At that moment, a young waitress arrived. The blonde woman ordered a coffee in perfect Dutch, confirming Gallagher's suspicions. This was no foreigner with just a grasp of the language, nor was she Dutch. The waitress returned inside.

"He?" Gallagher repeated.

"My name is Lorraine Mowbray," she said, as if in reply.

A name so close to Lauren's made him twitch inside. Lorraine Mowbray's eyes seem to be studying him intently.

"And yes, Mr. Gallagher," she continued, "I am South African."

"You're quite something," Gallagher said. "You know my name, and you know what I'm thinking."

She gave a strange smile. "I saw it in your eyes. A South African accent is a very hard one to shake. It's like a mark of Cain. These days, some of us try to disguise it when we're abroad. I don't."

"Good for you."

The eyes were still studying him. "You're difficult to place in a neat box. That's not the response I would have expected."

The waitress came with the coffee. Lorraine Mowbray thanked her in Dutch.

"I always try not to do what's expected of me," Gallagher said.

She nodded, as if confirming his remark. "It's obviously good for survival."

"It helps."

She took a swallow of her coffee. She seemed to be waiting for something to happen; but Gallagher felt no icicles between his shoulder blades. Whatever she wanted, it was not a canal-side assassination. But why would the South Africans send her to him?

"He said you were good at that," she now said, eyes speculative; then she glanced at where she'd left the Golf. "Survival."

"He?" Gallagher said for the third time, and followed her glance.

Someone was standing by her car. The person gave him a little salute; informal, American style.

"You look as if you just went into shock," she said calmly. "You look as if you've seen a ghost, in fact."

"I think I just have," Gallagher said, giving her a rapid glance.

When he looked at the Golf again, there was no one standing by it. His eyes searched rapidly up and down both sides of the canal. Had he been dreaming?

"I think I must have," he repeated, mind defying what his eyes had seen.

The man by the car was supposed to be dead, killed by the same people who had killed both Lauren Tanner and Jake Smallson, and who would have killed Gallagher too, had not Lauren's falling body thrown him out of the line of fire.

The man he had seen was Piet Villiger.

Veronica Walmsley went to the hotel receptionist. "Has Mr. Gallagher not returned?"

"I'm sorry, Lady Walmsley. Not yet, I am afraid."

"Do you have any indication of when he might be back?"

The receptionist shook her head. "I'm sorry," she said again. "But unless our guests leave instructions, there's nothing we can know about their whereabouts."

"I see. Thank you."

Wanting to help, the receptionist said: "Was Mr. Gallagher expecting you, Lady Walmsley? I can leave a message in his box, if you would like."

"Er . . . no," Veronica Walmsley said. "I want to surprise him." She smiled.

Misunderstanding, the receptionist smiled too. Clearly, this was a special, private occasion.

"Very well, Lady Walmsley."

Veronica gave a little nod. "Thank you," she said once more, and walked away.

"I've got questions," Gallagher said, "and you've got a lot of answers I want."

Lorraine Mowbray sipped at her coffee, and looked at him with her translucent eyes. "He'll give you all the answers you could want."

"He?"

"The man you saw."

"I thought you said it was a ghost."

"I said you *looked* as if you'd seen one. He's very much alive and he wants to see you."

"Am I supposed to go running off to meet this person on your say-so?"

"He did say I'd have a job convincing you."

"You keep saying 'he.' Does 'he' have a name?"

"Piet Villiger."

"Oh yes. Of course."

"You don't believe me?"

Gallagher just stared at her.

She sighed. "He said you'd be difficult, but I didn't think he meant impossible."

"Put yourself in my shoes," Gallagher began. "A strange woman follows me all round Amsterdam, comes to my table when I stop for a quiet cup of coffee, then shows me a man who looks like someone who's dead and finally, tells me Piet Villiger—the dead man—wants to see me. How am I doing so far? Would you, in my place, leap into the sunset to meet this dead man, on the say-so of the strange woman? You have five seconds to claim the prize."

"He warned me about your sense of humor too," she said. She was not smiling. She then nodded to herself, coming to a decision. "Fine," she continued. "He said that if things got bad, and believe me, I can't say I approve of his even wanting to get in touch with you . . . considering your attitude . . ."

"Ah. Daylight. Can I go now?"

"He said," she went on firmly, "there was one other chance to convince you . . . and that only the two of you would recognize these words. He said to you: 'If things were different I'd ask you for a drink, up Table Mountain.' And you said: 'If things were different, I'd accept.' Do you recognize them?"

Gallagher felt himself go very still. "Where were those words spoken?"

She answered without hesitation. "Australia."

"My God," Gallagher said softly. "He really is alive. But I don't understand. Everyone said he was dead. Even the . . . ."

"Department? Oh yes. I know what you used to

do before this." She glanced at the camera. "Before you became a fancy photographer."

"That's not how I would describe what I do."

"We never see ourselves as others see us."

"Are you looking for a fight? You don't know me. What gives you the right to be cross with me? Or is it because you're so accustomed to having people jump to attention when you speak? You're not in South Africa now. It helps to be civil over here."

The translucent eyes seemed to blaze. "I don't think I'm going to like you, Mr. Gallagher."

"Guess what. I'm not going to lose any sleep over it."

Her lips tightened. "Don't jump to conclusions about me."

"You seemed quite happy to do it to me. Fancy photographer. Remember? But let's put that aside, for now. Who was the poor sod who died instead of Villiger?"

"He'll answer all your questions. I've done my job."

"Our pride's all injured now, is it?"

"Mr. Gallagher, you're . . ."

"I know your problem. You're still angry because of what happened by the ferry."

"I could have injured myself."

"If you follow people around, you can't expect to be treated like some kind of princess. As I've said . . . over here, the human beings bite back."

"You're wrong about me," she said tightly. She put a plain postcard on the table. There was writing upon it. "He'll meet you there. Tomorrow, at ten in the morning. If you're as good as he seems to think you are, I'm sure you won't leave this card lying around where everyone can have a good look at it."

She stood up. "Goodbye, Mr. Gallagher. You can pay for the coffee." She walked purposefully back to the Golf.

Looking at her, Gallagher thought her angry stride was very seductive. She did not turn once to look back at him; but her continuing anger was evident in the way she crunched the gears as she set off.

A tiny smile on his lips, Gallagher studied the card. There was no message; merely a location. He had no idea whether the writing was Villiger's. He had never seen Villiger write. The first and only time they'd met, there had been more pressing matters to worry about: like staying alive.

He tore the card into tiny pieces and put them in a jacket pocket. He was still not certain whether he'd turn up at the indicated location.

Unless someone had somehow managed to record their conversation that day in Australia, there was no way in which Lorraine Mowbray could have known what to say, unless Villiger had told her himself. And as the chances of their words being recorded at that particular time were virtually zero, he had to assume that Villiger was indeed alive.

Even so, it would not do to take chances.

The two men sitting in the parked taxi looked on as Gallagher continued to drink his coffee. One was black. He was in the passenger seat. The taxi was some distance away, on the opposite bank of the canal.

"He's a cool one," the black man said. His accent spoke of Africa. "Drinking his coffee as if nothing has happened."

"He's supposed to be good," the other said. His accent was of Africa too; South Africa. His mouth turned down at the graffiti message, painted in white, on the other side of the canal.

MANDELA FREE, it demanded.

"Bloody kaffir," he said.

His black companion followed his gaze, but said nothing. A short while later, the black one saw Gallagher stand up.

"He's leaving. Do we follow?"

The other did not speak. Instead, he continued to look in Gallagher's direction.

"Let's see what he does," he eventually said.

It did not take Gallagher long to establish he was being followed. On leaving the café, he had deliberately driven aimlessly for ten minutes, sometimes covering the same ground twice. The taxi had stood out like a sore thumb.

They were not very good at their job, he thought disparagingly. He wondered who they were this time. Colleagues of Lorraine Mowbray? Someone from FUTRON, Veronica Walmsley's lot? Or could it even be the Department was nosing in as well?

The taxi's passenger was in the back. The driver apparently Dutch. Gallagher had once caused them to slip up so that they had been forced to stop by the side of the *quattro,* at a set of traffic lights. He had not looked at them; but delaying his start from the lights, had forced them to yield to the pressure of traffic from behind and to draw ahead. He'd been able to get a brief look then, though the black passenger had been indistinct. The taxi driver had a baseball cap pulled low on his head.

The taxi disappeared soon after.

* * *

The men parked the taxi, and walked away from it.

"This is no use to us now," the black one said. They had hijacked it, after first booking it for a long ride out of town.

The taxi driver was now dead, lying in some woods off a deserted lane on the outskirts of the city. The black man had not approved of the killing; but his companion had a fondness for it.

As they walked on, the black man said: "You didn't have to kill him."

The other paused, looked at him with dead eyes. "We. We did the job. Remember that. *We.* You were there too. If the Dutch just happen to find out who was responsible, they won't make the fine distinction about who actually committed the deed. Think hard about that when you feel your nerve slipping away. Now come on. We need another taxi." The man with the dead eyes smiled. "This time, no killing. We're only going back to the hotel."

They did not take a taxi immediately but walked several streets before doing so.

Gallagher returned to his own hotel deep in thought. If Piet Villiger were truly alive, what did he want? Gallagher could not think of any reason why Villiger would go to such trouble to seek him out unless it was for a very serious matter. Experience had shown that serious matters concerning someone in Villiger's line of work could only mean bad news, making involvement potentially very dodgy indeed.

But he had himself once sought Villiger out, needing help . . . and had been told Villiger was dead. "Help" had nonetheless been forthcoming; but there had been a price. Villiger's unknown colleagues had forced Gallagher into taking part in an operation on the borders of Angola, as the price of a safe ticket out of Africa for himself and Sigga von Kregelmann. But that was history.

Now a supposedly very much alive Villiger was in Amsterdam, needing to see him. There was a connection between all that had occurred since that meeting with Veronica Walmsley in London; and Gallagher was sure he didn't want to find it. What he really wanted was a quiet life.

As usual, it was being denied him. The knock on the door of his hotel room made sure of that.

He stared at it for some moments. The knock came for a second time. He went up to the door, opened it, shielding himself behind it as he did so.

Veronica Walmsley breezed in. "See?" she began. "I couldn't keep away." She paused in midstride. "Gordon?"

He pushed the door shut. She gave a startled little jump and gasped, then relaxed when she saw him.

"My God. You gave me a fright. What were you doing behind the door? You look as if you expected someone else, and not very friendly either."

"What are you doing here, Veronica?"

"That's not much of a welcome."

"You haven't answered me. What are you doing here, and how did you find me? Amsterdam may not be as sprawling as London, but it's still a fair size. Finding me on your own would not be easy."

"What a suspicious mind you have, Gordon. You weren't like that eight years ago."

"More's the pity," he said.

She looked about the room. "Nice. Photography pays you well."

"Fine," Gallagher said drily. "You can answer

me later. Help yourself to a drink from the bar. I'm having a shower. When I come out, I want answers."

"I haven't the sort of answers you seem to want."

"Oh yes, you do."

"I only came . . ."

"On the spur of the moment."

"Yes. I did. I thought it would be nice to enjoy Holland together. I was always impetuous. You can't have forgotten that about me, surely?"

"No. I haven't forgotten . . . but I also remember that your idea of fun is one party after another, not traveling around the countryside . . . unless it's to more parties. I'm here to work."

"People change. You're different. I'm different too."

"But still impetuous."

She nodded. "Still impetuous."

He looked at her silently.

"What are you thinking?" she asked.

"I was thinking you're a very attractive woman . . ."

She smiled. "You've already found out just how attractive."

"That was some time ago."

"That part of me hasn't changed." She was still smiling.

"I was wondering," he said, "who sent you, and why."

She stopped smiling. "No one sent me, Gordon."

"As I said . . . answers after the shower."

He left her, and entered the large bathroom.

She walked about the room, classed by the hotel as a King, idly touching items of furniture here and there. She seemed unsure of what to do. The muted sound of the shower came to her from behind the bathroom door as she walked to a window, and looked out. At 6:30, the day was still a long way from turning into night and she could see Gallagher's car clearly. She could not know he had left it there deliberately, so that he would have an unrestricted view of it when looking out of that very window.

She watched uninterestedly as a slim man came bouncing along the canal. The peculiarity of his walk, however, changed her lack of interest into curiosity. He seemed to be limping as well.

The limping, bouncing man went up to the *quattro,* and peered in; then he began a slow walk around it. He paused, made another circuit, and paused again.

Veronica ran to the bathroom door and pounded upon it. The shower was still on. She slapped at the door with an open palm. The shower stopped.

"What is it?" came from within.

"I think someone's after your car."

A few seconds later, the door opened and a hastily dried Gallagher, wrapped in a huge white towel, appeared.

"Wouldn't do him much good," he said, but he went to the window. "Well, well," he continued, eyes upon the man.

"You don't seem worried," she remarked, staring first at him, then at the man in the street below.

"He's not trying to steal it."

She looked at him once more. "How do you know?"

"I know." He moved away from the window and began walking back to the bathroom. "I see you haven't given yourself a drink. I hope you've done better with the answers."

"I've got no answers," she insisted. "I don't know what you're talking about. I came over on . . ."

"Impulse. Yes. So you've said."

"It's true, Gordon."

"Of course it is."

He entered the bathroom, and shut the door behind him.

When he later came out, she was gone. He checked all his personal belongings. Nothing had been touched. It didn't make him feel any better about her. He still thought her reasons for being in Amsterdam highly suspect.

He went over to the window. The *quattro* sat low on its fat wheels in black splendor. Prinknash, whom he had recognized, was nowhere to be seen. It didn't matter.

Gallagher smiled, but there was no humor in it. So the Department was snooping around too.

"So many interested people," he said to himself. But it was the kind of interest he could well do without.

Prinknash had not attempted to put a tracer on the car, for the remote had remained silent. Gallagher assumed Prinknash would have a partner, who would not be far away. Haslam? He wondered. But he found it difficult to believe Haslam would have allowed Prinknash to have shown his hand so clumsily. Perhaps Prinknash was working on his own initiative.

Again, Gallagher found that difficult to believe. Fowler would never have sent Prinknash out, even to buy a loaf of bread, if he could help it. That meant someone senior to Prinknash. Haslam seemed the most likely, but Haslam would never have allowed . . .

Gallagher stopped. He was going over old ground. Forget the Department and Fowler and the rest of them; forget Lorraine Mowbray; forget the taxi that had tried to tail him; forget Veronica Walmsley forget Villiger . . .

To hell with the lot of them, he thought. He was going down to the hotel's brasserie for a light snack and coffee, and then back up for an early night. He would even think about whether he would meet Villiger the next morning on the Ijsselmeer causeway.

In any case, he had decided to leave the hotel and continue the rest of the assignment away from Amsterdam. There were now too many sniffers around, and he wanted no part of them.

He went down to the brasserie and had been there for about fifteen minutes, when Veronica Walmsley joined him. So much for a quiet evening.

"I thought you decided to dump me," he said to her.

"You were so unwelcoming," she said, "I thought it best to leave you alone."

"And here you are."

She frowned at him. "This is not like you, Gordon. Not the Gordon I remember."

"I've learned a few things along the way."

"Why don't we call a truce?"

"I'd be very happy to . . . provided you tell me why you're really here. Ah. Here comes the waitress. Would you like something to eat?"

She ordered coffee and pastries. "I'll put on some weight, but who cares?"

"You're one of those lucky women who looks good with or without weight on."

She smiled, pleased. "You're being nice to me. Should I worry?"

"It's my other technique."

"You still believe I've got answers."

"I'm quite sure you have. Someone's asked you to keep an eye on me. I want to know who's responsible. It's as simple as that."

"Why should anyone send me after you? I can do that by myself."

"While it would be a lovely massage for my ego, Veronica, I can't believe you pined so much for me over the past eight years . . ."

"Alright," she said. "It was daddy."

"What? Your father? Don't be ridiculous. He barely knows me . . . well, he hasn't seen me for eight years, so why would he want you to check up on me?"

"He doesn't want to check up on you. He wants to see you."

Gallagher said drily: "Everybody wants to see me. Must be my aftershave. Why does he want to see me?"

"I don't know."

"That's a help."

"I'm telling you the truth. I really don't know."

Gallagher paused in the act of slicing a chunk of delicious pastry. "Your father, if I remember rightly, was a diplomat. Foreign Office for a while . . . let me see . . . Africa was his patch, then it was on to the Ministry of Defense. Correct me if I'm wrong." He completed the cut, popped the slice into his mouth.

"You've got a good memory."

"I may have a good memory, but my vision's shot. All I'm seeing is fog. Clear some of it for me.

How did you really know I was going to the trade hall?"

"I phoned your agency to ask for you about a job. They told me you were on assignment."

Gallagher nodded. That would have been simple enough for her to do, but Nellads never gave information about the location.

"They wouldn't have told you where," he said.

"Ah well." She had a slightly sheepish look upon her face. "I told them we were old friends, and it would be nice to see you for a cup of coffee."

"And they fell for that?"

"The girl I spoke to did. I can be very persuasive when I want to be."

"I don't doubt it." He would have to talk to the agency about that. "How about over here? How did you find my hotel?"

She seemed reluctant to tell him.

"You're doing so well," Gallagher said. "Don't spoil it now."

She continued to hesitate. At last, she said: "Daddy found out . . . through some connections he still has."

The alarm bells went into their routine. Whom did Lord Walmsley know who could do that? Just about everybody, Gallagher answered himself sourly. At least one of those would have a line to the Department. It wouldn't be Fowler. Fowler would not let light get away from those outwardly innocuous offices in the sleepy London square, if there was some way to prevent it.

Gallagher thought he knew the culprit.

"Does your father know someone called Winterbourne?"

She stared at him. "How did you know?"

Bingo.

"Put it down to my shady past," he said.

"Then you will see him when you get back to England?"

"It depends."

"On what? Daddy seemed to think it was very important. I'm certain he wouldn't have asked me to find you if he didn't."

If Veronica's father had a line to Winterbourne, Winterbourne could have got Fowler to . . .

Again, Gallagher stopped his train of thought. Winterbourne knew as well as Fowler, just how a summons from the Department would be treated. Winterbourne had therefore left it up to the noble lord to carry out his own entrapment. But what was in it for the Department? The presence of Prinknash, and almost certainly Haslam, was not something that encouraged good cheer.

He was glad he had decided to leave in the morning.

"Look," Veronica was saying, "now that all the mystery's been cleared up, why don't we go out and enjoy ourselves?"

"Why not indeed?" Gallagher said.

In the morning he'd be gone, and she wouldn't know where.

4

"Will I do?" she queried of him later in the hotel foyer. Attired in a simple body-hugging black dress whose skirt seemed to be minimal, and showing copious lengths of bare leg and thigh, she looked exceedingly good.

"You most certainly will," he said, "though I'm not sure what."

She smiled. "You can find out later . . . perhaps. Well? What delights of Amsterdam are you planning to show me tonight?"

"That depends on what you'd like to see."

"No concerts, no operas, and no trips on the canals. I want to get into the real spirit of the city."

"Oh well, it's the café tour then. Give you a taste of the *gezelligheid.*"

"The gezzy*what?*"

"You'll find out. We'll leave the car. Much more fun walking, or going by tram." He glanced at her shoes. The heels were sensible enough for what he had in mind. "Do you mind walking?"

"I can keep up with you any day."

"In that case, let's go tell Amsterdam we're in town."

"Ah *shit!*"

A scuffing sound told Haslam the dogs of Amsterdam had struck again. Prinknash was furiously rubbing the sole of his shoe against edge of a canal wall."

"Bloody hell, Mr. Haslam. How many of these animals do they have in this place? That's the fourth time I've stepped in the bloody muck."

"You must have the knack," Haslam said with a straight face. "My shoes are clean."

Prinknash, who felt like kicking any dog that came within shoe range, made no comment. Instead, he watched as Gallagher entered yet another café with Veronica Walmsley.

"They must be sloshing about with coffee by now," he said to Haslam. "We've been on them for nearly two hours. What's he up to? His version of a pub crawl? That's café number three or four."

"Four," Haslam said. "He's showing her around."

"Another of those dark places that looks as if it's afraid to pay the electricity bill," Prinknash remarked unenthusiastically, thinking of the nicotine-stained wooden interior. "We're not going in, are we? It's not as if he's trying to lose us."

Haslam sighed. "Prinknash, you manage to confound me time after time. After so nicely taking the bait Gallagher left outside his hotel . . ."

"You sent me . . ."

"I sent you to check out the hotel, not to admire his car. I thought that even you would have worked that one out." Haslam paused and cursed Winterbourne in his mind. "Gallagher left the car there deliberately. He will have positioned it so as to give him a clear view from his hotel room. Of course he's not trying to lose us. He wants us where he can keep tabs. All the initiative is with him now. He can lose us anytime he likes. That's why we'll go into every café he decides to visit, in case he chooses one to make his break."

Haslam sighed and wished a plague of piles upon Winterbourne. It did not improve his demeanor to know that Winterbourne was quite probably having a nice time of it in his club at that very moment.

Haslam's feet ached from all the walking. It was worth going into the brown café, if only to sit down. Prinknash could moan all he liked. Tough shit.

Haslam smiled at his little private joke, and felt slightly better. Perhaps Prinknash would slip on the next lot and fall into the stuff.

The thought cheered him up some more.

"Here come your friends," Veronica said.

Gallagher glanced to where Haslam and Prinknash had found themselves a dark corner within which to skulk. "They're not my friends."

"You waved to them a couple of cafés ago."

"Just letting them feel wanted."

"Aren't you going to tell me who they are?"

"Assuming you don't already know . . ."

"You've said that before. I really don't know these people, Gordon. I only recognize one because he was looking at your car."

"So they're not your minders?"

"Minders?" She stared at him. "Why would I need minders?"

"Good question."

"It's you they're following. You're the one who waved to them."

"Acknowledging their presence doesn't mean I know them. But let's not allow them to spoil the evening. Are you enjoying the café tour?"

"Mmm," she said. She looked about her. "These especially. Is the wood really stained by smoke?"

"Oh yes. No fake chemical stuff. Genuine natural, killer tobacco."

"I feel as if I've gone back in time."

"You have. These places are as they were decades before we were born." A couple of tough-looking old men were playing chess in the dim lighting. "Those two have been playing for years. I've seen them in here before."

"When were you last in here?"

"Three years ago. Well . . . nearly four."

One of the men glanced up from his game, saw Gallagher looking. He smiled, raised a small glass of clear liquid, and silently toasted Gallagher and Veronica. Gallagher raised his coffee cup in return. The man went back to his game.

"That's *gezelligheid,*" Gallagher said to her. "At least, my interpretation of it. There's no adequate translation. It's a form of letting you do your own thing in privacy, but without isolation. You'll be included in the proceedings if you wish to be and if not, while your privacy is respected, you won't be frozen out. As I've said . . . a clumsy interpretation. Each person will give you a different explanation while meaning the same thing. Compare this with London where you can be crammed up against someone on the tube but be a million miles away from real contact."

"Would you like to be in contact with some of the people you meet on the tube?"

He smiled. *"Touché.* But that says a lot about London." He glanced about the dimly lit establishment. Haslam and Prinknash were still on station. But now, someone else had entered. "Ready for another café, Lady Veronica?"

She was looking at him in surprise. "We've only just got here."

He stood up. "I've got lots more to show you."

"Promises, promises." Despite her reluctance, she too had got to her feet.

Gallagher nodded in the direction of the chess players who briefly nodded back at him, before returning to the serious business of destroying each other's moves. He paused to allow Veronica to walk past, then followed her out.

The newcomer, the black man Gallagher had seen in the taxi, did not look in their direction. It did not dissipate his feeling of unease. He paused outside the café, looked up and down the brightly lit canal. Nothing.

With Veronica at his side, he walked a short distance, stopped to look around. Haslam and Prinknash were just coming out. The black man was nowhere to be seen.

"What's wrong?" Veronica was asking, perplexed.

He continued walking. "We're going back to the hotel," he said, instead of answering her.

"Why? I'm enjoying . . ."

"We'll grab a taxi and head back."

Taxi. Even the taxis had to be watched. He glanced at Veronica. She would slow him down. He would prefer it if they made it back to the hotel without incident.

Suddenly, the bright lights had taken on the guise of a cheerful screen that hid an unseen menace.

Sensing his unease, Veronica had glanced around.

"Gordon!" she said in a tense voice. "Those men are following us!"

He looked. Haslam and Prinknash, walking quickly. But behind them, something else. A taxi, moving slowly.

Suddenly, the taxi picked up speed. It swerved past Haslam and Prinknash, and came hurtling directly for Gallagher and Veronica. Gallagher assessed their chances. On one side, the canal. On the other, tall houses with no spaces in between to rush into. Get wet or get squashed. Seconds within which to decide. Haslam and Prinknash running. Haslam reaching for something.

Then Gallagher saw it: a tiny space between two of the houses. How had he missed it before? No time to analyze. *Move!*

He grabbed a seemingly mesmerized Veronica about the waist and hauled her unceremoniously toward the impossibly small space between the buildings. The roaring of the taxi's engine filled the night, its main beams coming on now, blazing at him. It seemed to be almost upon them.

Then he was shoving Veronica through the crack and was pressing his body against hers, pushing her through.

The taxi swept past, the wind of its passage buffeting him. He felt the heat of its engine as it went by, its bonnet missing him by inches.

There was the sudden squeal of brakes and the crunching of gears. It was coming back! It would not be able to turn. The cobbled one-way street was too narrow. Whoever was driving would be risking a quick dip in the canal.

Gallagher looked about him. This was no narrow passageway, but an indentation between the houses. Their exit was blocked by the solid rising wall of the joint. It would have to be back out into the street, and he'd better be bloody quick about it. The taxi would soon be reversing, when the driver found the right gear, with the intention of blocking the only exit. It was time to go.

Even as he was considering the options, Gallagher was already moving. Then he froze.

Two shots had barked suddenly into the night, followed almost immediately by the sharp report of shattering glass. Another crunch of gears and the taxi was accelerating away. It sounded eager to put the greatest possible distance between itself and that particular field of battle. Soon, its noises had died away.

Gallagher eased himself out of the narrow space. Veronica stood rigidly behind him. Haslam was running heavily toward him, Prinknash limpingly bringing up the rear.

Haslam stopped, peered past Gallagher. "Bit of a trap you picked for yourselves."

"It was either that, or a swim. I didn't fancy a lungful of canal. Doesn't go well with coffee. I didn't realize her Majesty's serva. .s could shoot up Dutch streets, but thanks for the help."

Haslam seemed to be smiling. "Always happy to serve. I think we should get away from here before the good citizens decide to look, or a passing police-man takes an interest."

The three of them began walking quickly but without seeming haste. Veronica, still in an apparent state of shock, kept up with them shakily.

Gallagher said: "So you were minding her, after all."

Haslam shook his head. "Wrong."

"Tailing me, then."

Haslam said nothing for a while. "Not their taxi," he remarked eventually. "Made a mess of the gear change. Lucky for you. Gave me time to scare them off."

"Lucky for me indeed," Gallagher said. He glanced at the limping Prinknash. "Is he hurt?"

Haslam seemed to pause for thought before replying. "An old war wound." He sounded as if he wanted to laugh. "Got it chasing you, as a matter of fact."

Gallagher glanced at Prinknash for a second time. "And here you are again."

Prinknash grunted. It could have meant anything.

"I suppose it's no use asking what your plans are," Haslam began. "It would save me a lot of hassle."

"I don't mind telling you. I'm here on a job. Photography. I'm likely to go anywhere in pursuit of a good photo."

Haslam sighed. "Thanks for nothing. Might as well walk you to your hotel."

"Might as well," Gallagher said genially. "You know I'm here, and I know you're here."

"So who were those jokers?"

"God knows."

"Oh come on."

"The truth. I haven't a clue. Was one of them the man who came into the café as we left?"

Haslam nodded. "Yes. As soon as you were out the door he turned, waited for a little while, then hurried out."

"Naturally, you were interested."

"Of course . . . and . . . lucky for you . . ."

". . . lucky for me . . ." Gallagher said at the same time, drily.

Haslam seemed to be smiling. He turned to Veronica Walmsley. "Are you alright now, Lady Veronica?"

She'd been hanging on to Gallagher. "Yes. Yes," she said quietly. "I'm . . . I'm fine." There was, however, an edge to her voice.

"Be at your hotel soon."

"Yes." She did not look at Haslam.

They made it back to the hotel without further incident. Haslam glanced at the *quattro*.

"Like leaving the jam jar open and waiting for the bees to come."

"One did," Gallagher said.

Neither of them looked at Prinknash.

"Expecting more?" Haslam asked.

"Only time will tell."

Haslam nodded slowly, apparently admitting defeat. He glanced up at the hotel. "Nice. Must cost a bomb. Department funds make going downmarket a necessity."

"You're not going to plead poverty to me, Haslam. Are you?"

This time, Haslam was smiling. "No. I'm not. Come on, Prinknash. Time to let these youngsters have their beauty sleep." To Gallagher, he added:

"Next time you decide to leap into a dark passage, make sure you've got an escape route."

"I usually do."

"Once is all it takes."

Gallagher nodded. He knew that well enough.

"Will you be in town tomorrow?" Haslam now asked.

"Of course."

Haslam didn't look as if he believed it. "Of course," he said drily. Then he turned and walked away, accompanied by the limping Prinknash.

As he stood back for Veronica to enter the hotel, Gallagher noted a familiar shape. It was the silver Golf, parked out of the direct blaze of the hotel lights. He did not turn to look at it but instead, followed Veronica inside.

They were by themselves in the lift. Veronica was trembling.

"Can I spend the night in your room?" she asked. "I . . . I don't think I could sleep in mine tonight." As if thinking he would hesitate, she went on: "I'll sleep anywhere . . ."

"Of course you can stay," he said. It still did not mean he trusted her.

The two men had dumped the taxi at the earliest opportunity. They had not killed the driver of this the second of their hijacked vehicles. He had been knocked out, never having seen his assailant. They had left him in a deserted cul-de-sac and had poured over him a whole bottle of Jenever, bought specially for that purpose. Anyone entering the cul-de-sac would smell him long before he was seen, make the wrong assumption, and leave; unless it happened to be a police officer, who would check the supposed drunk.

"We should have killed that taxi driver," one of the men was saying as they walked away from the tram that had taken them to the Europaplein.

"You like killing," the black one said, "too damn much, man. And if you hadn't tried to run down the man and the woman, we wouldn't have been shot at by those other two we didn't even know about. They probably didn't know about us either. But now . . ." He let his words die, shaking his head.

"Are you quite finished?" his companion demanded sharply.

"No. Think about this . . . they could have killed us if they had wanted to."

The other was dismissive. "They were lousy shots."

"Believe that if you want, but I'm telling you . . ."

The man who liked killing stopped suddenly, rounded on his black companion. "Now *you* listen, man. Because we're not at home doesn't mean you can talk to me just as you like. I'm leading this mission, and don't you forget it."

The black man was unmoved. "Why don't you shout it for all of Amsterdam to hear?"

The other looked about him quickly, as if expecting to see a crowd of people listening intently. But there was no one close enough to hear what was being said.

"When we get back . . ." he began warningly.

"If we get back," the black one amended.

They continued walking in silence. A short while later, they boarded a bus that took them northwest to its terminal on Bertelmanplass. From there, they boarded another tram which returned them to the city center and the Central Railway Station. They arrived just before midnight.

It was the black man who broke their silence as they went to where they had left their car, a small, two-year-old BMW saloon.

"I was told this was to be a low-key surveillance job," he began. "I'm beginning to feel we're starting a war."

The man with the dead eyes said: "We're already in a war. It was started a long time ago."

The black one unlocked the car. He had taken the precaution of removing any tempting articles from view, including the radio cassette player. An easily slotted unit, it was in his hotel room. As a result, the car had been left untouched by opportunist thieves.

The man was called Zamba, not his real name, and had been living quietly in Rotterdam for over two years. That had been his "posting." He did not like being saddled with the man who had introduced himself as de Vries, and whom he considered a raving psychopath. But he had to live with the unpleasantness. He had been told to expect de Vries—no more real a name than his own—and to give him every help. De Vries seemed to think that meant no opposition to any crazy scheme.

They entered the car. Zamba started the BMW and drove slowly back to their small hotel near Erasmus Park. Left to him, he'd change the surveillance team. He was sure the man they had been following would recognize him from now on, if he hadn't already done so. He may not have seen de Vries, but it was not safe to consider that a certainty.

But here was de Vries, who seemed to want to

solve everything by killing. Why had they sent such a man? This was not South Africa. Two hijacked taxis in the same city on the same day, was clumsy in the extreme, especially as one of the drivers had been murdered. It was alright for de Vries. His stay in Holland was temporary.

Neither man spoke to the other throughout the drive.

Gallagher sat in the darkness and looked out at the car park. He could see the *quattro* clearly. On a small table close by was the remote, its audio warning switched to mute. The tiny red alarm beacon would still blink, should anyone attempt to interfere with the car. Within the vehicle itself, six other tiny red lights—one each on the dashboard, the rear parcel shelf, and on each door and quaterlight capping—would blink intermittently at the first stage of the alarm sequence. It should be enough to warn anyone off. Persistence would bring a nasty aural suprise in its wake. He wondered if anyone would try tonight.

Gallagher turned his head to look at the shape on the bed. Veronica Walmsley had coped with the shock of almost being deliberately run-over, by removing her shoes and falling promptly asleep, fully clothed. He had pulled the quilt over her. Now she lay there, curled fetuslike, protecting herself from a terror she could not understand. Whatever she was involved in, he thought, it had certainly not prepared her for this. People reacted in all sorts of ways to combat stress.

But she was not in combat.

He turned his scrutiny away from her. The remote was blinking. His eyes switched to the *quattro*. Someone was standing next to it. Lorraine Mowbray.

He waited. The Golf was not in view.

She seemed to be standing uncertainly. He knew why. She must have touched the car and had set the warning lights off. She was now clearly wondering what to do next. She remained where she was. Soon, the light on the remote went out. Those in the car, save for the single activation light, would have gone out too.

Gallagher waited, smiling.

After a casual glance around, she began to walk slowly until she reached the rear of the car, where she again stopped. She stooped, apparently to pick something up. Now she was reaching forward.

"Dear, oh dear," Gallagher said, and waited for all hell to break loose.

But something made her stop. Gallagher knew exactly what. The remote was again blinking. If she waited until the lights stopped for a second time then decided to try again, the alarm system would be fully triggered.

She decided against it. Clearly frustrated by her failure, she walked angrily away.

Gallagher smiled in the dark once more as the remote returned to standby. Might as well get some sleep.

He undressed, picked up the remote and placed it on his bedside table. This time, he switched it back to audio. He climbed into bed, keeping well away from Veronica. The bed was big enough to leave plenty of space between them.

Sometime during the night, she moved over to his side and pressed her still-clothed body against his. An arm held on to him tightly. She was still asleep.

They spent the rest of the night like that.

* * *

In the morning, hair tousled and face slightly plump from sleep, she climbed slowly out of bed. She stood up, absently smoothing down her dress.

He'd been awake for some time. He lay there, looking up at her. The remote had been quiet all night.

"You . . . you didn't do anything," she said.

"Is that a question? Or an accusation?"

Her body moved slightly. It could have been a shrug.

"I never take advantage," Gallagher said. "Not my style. You wanted some comfort. That's what you got."

"I . . . I was making a heavy play before . . ." She paused. "Thank you. Some men would have . . ."

"I'm not some men."

She smiled at him, a little hesitantly. "The same Gordon, after all, despite everything and eight years."

He shook his head. "No. I've changed more than you can imagine. You look good in the morning," he added.

"Still, you mean. I know I look a mess."

"Not still. You look good. Period."

"I remember the first time you said that to me." She glanced down at her dress. "I had rather less on." As if she were indeed naked, she put her arms about herself. She was clearly remembering the incident with the strange taxi for she was looking anxious now. "Who were those men who tried to kill us last night?"

"I was hoping you'd tell me."

Her eyes widened as she stared at him. "Tell

you? Do you think I'd know people who'd want to kill
me? Perhaps it was you they were after."

"For what reason?"

"How should I know? You're the one who had
the funny job. What about those two last night? The
big man with his funny limping friend?"

"I'm certainly not with them."

"Good thing they were there, though."

He looked at her for some moments. She was
still hugging herself.

"Veronica," he began, "all this started after you
came up to my table in London. You've triggered off
something that's seriously disturbing my peaceful
existence. When that happens, I prefer to take myself well away from the source of my troubles. I'll tell
you what today's plan is. You go right back to London, and I get on with my job. Nothing could be
simpler. Whatever it is you're involved in, I don't
want to know."

"I'm not involved in anything."

"You may think it, but that doesn't mean you're
not."

She kept staring at him. Gone was the self-assurance of that day in London. The uncertainty and
fear in her eyes were so strong, he felt himself prepared to believe she was indeed innocent of whatever
was going on beneath the surface.

She brought her arms down to her sides. "All I
know is that Daddy asked me to get in touch with
you. That really is all. He didn't tell me why."

Gallagher threw the quilt back and got out of
bed. "Breakfast," he said.

Her eyes followed his naked body as he went to
the bathroom.

"What?" she asked weakly.

But sounds of the shower were coming to her. When that eventually stopped, she heard him brushing his teeth. Then he came out and began to dress.

"Breakfast," he repeated when he had finished. "Down there? Or up here?"

"I don't think I want to go down."

"I'll order it brought up." He picked up the phone.

She said: "I'll . . . I'll freshen up a bit." She smiled sheepishly.

He watched as she entered the bathroom and shut the door behind her. Then he ordered a large breakfast for two to be sent up. When he'd put the phone down, he went over to the window. The *quattro* had no one near it. He looked at the remote.

"Just stay quiet," he said to it.

London.

Fowler read the message twice over. It had come from Haslam, via the Consulate, and had been in one of his peculiar codes. "Shot at two dogs chasing hares. Missed."

Fowler smiled thinly. Haslam never missed unless he wanted to. So Gallagher and Veronica Walmsley had been in deep enough trouble to warrant Haslam's use of a firearm. Even as a warning, it was serious.

Fowler stared at the message. Who was after Gallagher? And why?

He lifted his spectacles to briefly rub the bridge of his nose, then glanced at his watch. 0800. Haslam should be up by now. It was 0900 over there. The message had been sent during the night. That meant Haslam must have disturbed the Consulate staff.

Not the best way to win a popularity contest, Fowler thought.

Haslam would not have wanted to use the Consulate. He preferred autonomy in the field, even at his age. Fowler therefore reasoned that Haslam had wanted to warn him of the escalation of the situation.

"You'll just have to keep following him, George," Fowler said to the slip of paper. "And try not to alarm the Dutch by shooting at more people on their streets."

It was pointless speculating on how Haslam had got hold of a gun. Both he and Prinknash had flown to Amsterdam unarmed. But Haslam's long experience in the field had left him with all sorts of contacts, and he knew just where to get hold of weaponry when he needed to. Fowler gave another of his thin smiles. So did he, for that matter.

He squeezed the bridge of his nose a second time.

Veronica Walmsley, FUTRON, Gallagher, and Behrensen. Where was the connection? He stared at the printout.

He was sure he was not going to like the answer.

The aroma of fresh coffee hung pleasantly in the room. Veronica had brightened considerably and was almost her old self.

"Are you really serious about putting me on the plane?" she asked Gallagher as she gave their cups a refill. She had eaten breakfast with a gusto that led him to believe she was still reacting to the previous night's incident, despite the return of some of her self-assurance.

"You can count on it," he told her. "Better for you if you're safely back in London."

She gave that some thought. "I don't understand why I should be in danger. I haven't done anything to anyone."

Gallagher smiled without humor. "Oh the number of people who must have thought that as the bomb or bullet or whatever got them."

She drank her coffee silently. The gray-flecked green eyes studied him.

Gallagher said: "Who are FUTRON? Really?"

"I've told you. We're a promotional company."

"I know what you've told me. It still does not answer the question. What do you promote?"

"Everything. People, merchandise . . . you name it."

"And you're on the Board."

"Yes."

"How come?"

"Gordon . . . from anyone else, I'd consider that insulting. It assumes I haven't got the capabilities."

"How long have you been with them?"

"Three years . . ."

"Three years and you're on the Board?"

"Why not? I know people who have done it in one. And I do have a Double First, if you remember. Rather more than cotton wool between these little ears."

Gallagher knew all about her degree. "I'm not doubting your intelligence, Veronica. I never have. But I do also remember your distinct reluctance to seek any form of employment."

"People were afraid of me. All my interviewers were men who seemed to take fright. Perhaps they thought I'd be having their jobs one day. Even today, some men don't like women to be too clever."

"But FUTRON changed all that."

She nodded. "Oh I know they like having the title as a sort of publicity stunt, but they do treat me as if I've got brains." She smiled at him. "Alright. So the way I look has a little to do with it. But the brains came first in priority."

"Who's boss of the company?"

She gave an amused smile. "Silas John Becker, Jr."

"Have you met him?"

She shook her head."

"In *three* years? But you're a Board member."

"He's a busy man, Gordon. He has business interests all over the world. There's a company in Singapore that hasn't seen him for six years, so I've been told."

"So you asked about it."

"Well yes. You know me. I sometimes become curious."

"Not 'sometimes,' " Gallagher remarked drily. "Whom did you ask?"

"J.D. That's what we all call him. J.D. Quinlan. He's our American member. He has direct access to Becker. I did hear Becker's voice once. J.D. was on the phone to him and called me in. He had the phone on the speaker so I could hear."

"What was the conversation about?"

"Me. Becker was saying how pleased he was to have me on the UK Board."

"And that's it?"

Veronica nodded. "I'm afraid so."

"What about Quinlan? What kind of a man is he?"

Her shoulders moved slightly. "American. Umm . . . neat suits, neat haircut, soft spoken, glasses . . ."

"I know someone just like that. Put him next to a crocodile and I'd worry about the crocodile."

"Oh J.D.'s not like that at all. He's the most mild-mannered man I know."

"And the man I know is so mild-mannered, he makes a stagnant pool seem animated; and most certainly, I'd not give much for the crocodile's chances."

"It's that funny world of yours. You think everybody's someone else."

"They usually are," Gallagher said.

She got up from the table, shook out her golden hair, then stood on tiptoe and stretched, arms reaching upward. The minimal skirt of her tight dress reached up her bare thighs to her bottom. She froze in that position, and looked down beneath an arm at him.

"I can see it in your eyes," she said. She settled back, brought her arms back down. "You used to like me doing that. There's still time before you take me to the airport."

She could forget about that for a start. He could not deny that seeing her stretch, bare legs tautening, had set his pulses racing; but if they began anything, it would be goodbye to making it to the plane in time. His day's schedule would be ruined too.

She saw the refusal in his eyes, looked disappointed, and misunderstood.

"I'm feeling a bit . . . silly for offering myself like that."

"Don't be," he said. "I'm not refusing you. I just want you safely out of Amsterdam. If we start anything, we'll miss your plane."

She seemed prepared to accept the explanation. "I'm not having much luck with you, am I? Is there . . . someone?"

"There is . . ."

"Ah. Now I understand."

"No you don't. I haven't seen her, nor heard from her for eight months."

"You have been counting. Where is she?"

"The States."

"She's American?"

"No. She went there to work."

"Did she need to?"

"Not for reasons of work."

"You're getting more and more reluctant to talk about her, Gordon. She must have gone deep."

He stood up. "You'd better get your things sorted out and packed."

Veronica went up to him, standing very close. "It was very foolish of her to leave you like that."

"She had good reason," Gallagher said flatly. "Being with me nearly got her killed. You saw what happened last night. I'm trying to prevent their success next time round . . ."

The gray-flecked eyes danced with apprehension. "You expect them to try again?"

Gallagher sighed. "Get packed, Veronica, and go home. Please. Be ready to move in ten minutes. That's all I'm giving you. Now off you go."

She didn't move. Instead, her eyes searched his face for long moments. Then she put her arms about his neck, pressed her body against his, and kissed him fully on the mouth. She released him and stepped back, smoothing her dress as she did so.

"That's for you to get on with until you get back. A sort of down payment." She was breathing slightly faster than normal.

She went to pick up her shoes where they had been dumped by the bed and barefoot, walked to the door. She gave him a last look over her shoulder and with a hesitant smile, let herself slowly out.

She pulled the door shut quietly after her.

Gallagher stood looking at the closed door for some moments, before beginning to pack his own gear. When he had finished, he went over to the window. It was going to be a bright, hot day.

No one was by the *quattro*.

5

The Mercedes was parked some distance from Gallagher's hotel, but both Haslam and Prinknash had a clear view of the *quattro* from their seats.

Prinknash watched as Gallagher loaded the boot. "He's leaving! But he said he wouldn't be."

Haslam sighed. "And of course, you believed him."

They saw Veronica Walmsley approaching the car, a porter close behind with her bags.

"She's going with him," Prinknash said.

"Looks like it." Haslam sounded puzzled. It was not what he had expected.

They continued to watch as she tipped the porter then entered the car. Gallagher took his place behind the wheel. Soon, the black car was moving.

The Mercedes followed at a discreet distance. Prinknash glanced at a road sign after they'd been traveling for about ten minutes.

"He's going to the airport!"

Haslam said nothing. Now he understood. They followed the *quattro* to Schiphol, maintaining their distance. They parked, and watched as Gallagher

took Veronica Walmsley's luggage out and accompanied her to the Departure lounge. Fifteen minutes
later, they saw him return to the car and climb in.

"Right," Haslam said to Prinknash. "Out. I'll do
the driving."

"But I . . ."

"Out!" Haslam repeated sharply. "And be quick
about it." He had already left his seat.

Not understanding, Prinknash swopped seats
hurriedly.

"And now," Haslam said as he settled in, "he's
going to try and lead us a merry dance, before setting
off for where he's really going." He eased the Mercedes out of the car park.

"But why didn't he try before?" Prinknash
asked.

"What was the point? He was only going to the
airport to see the lady off. She was a weight he didn't
want to carry. I know how Gallagher works. And I
understand," Haslam added softly. He saw much of
himself as a younger man, in Gallagher.

"I could have kept up with him."

"I doubt it, even if you knew this city and this
car was one you were familiar with. Gallagher
knows his way around, and so do I. We do not have
his acceleration and speed, but I doubt if he knows
the shortcuts I do. We'll match our cunning with his
power."

Gallagher watched the Mercedes in his mirrors. He
had seen it come onto his tail soon after leaving the
hotel, and had made no attempt to elude it. He had
not even mentioned its presence to Veronica. At the
airport, he had noted the swopping of seats and had
smiled. Haslam clearly knew what was to come, and

was banking on his own knowledge of Amsterdam's traffic system to keep up.

For a good half hour, Gallagher led the Mercedes on a meandering tour of the city, waiting for the opportunity he had already set up in his mind. When it came, he almost missed it.

A tram, which had right of way, was crossing the junction of Overtoom and Constantijn Huygenstraat. Gallagher gave the accelerator a sharp stab with his boot. The *quattro* leapt forward, well clear of the tram, but leaving the Mercedes hopelessly trapped.

The tram shrilled its warning bell angrily at him. The driver, Gallagher decided, having noted the UK license plates, would assume here was yet another British driver who had forgotten which side of the road to drive on.

Gallagher was heading south, but his eventual route was southeast of the city where he would take the Muiderstraatweg which would lead on to the A1 motorway for Apeldoorn. He was not going there, but this was the route to his rendezvous with Villiger.

Several side streets later, the *quattro* headed out on the Hartveldseweg. The same road became the Muiderstraatweg. He was on the correct route. There was no sign, either of the Golf, or the Mercedes.

No sign, either, of the people who had tried to run him down during the night.

Haslam pulled up near a canal north of the city, sighed, and switched off the engine. After the incident with the tram, his attempts to pick up Gallagher again had proved totally fruitless.

"Don't say anything," he warned Prinknash, "if you know what's good for you."

Prinknash knew better than to speak, but the suggestion of a smirk hovered about his lips. He made sure Haslam did not see it.

Just outside Naarden, the A6 motorway joined the A1. Gallagher turned on to it and thirty-four kilometers later, he came to the exit sign that said LELYSTAD, DRONTEN, HARDERWIJK. The yellow national route signs were also on it. N302, N309. The one he wanted was 302.

He left the motorway, and took the road that bypassed Lelystad. He was heading for the twenty-eight-kilometer causeway that separated two of Holland's largest, manmade inland bodies of water: the smaller Markermeer, and the outer IJsselmeer.

He followed the signs for the N302 and eventually came to the approach to the causeway. There was an air of newness about it, and the two-lane road surface looked spotlessly clean.

Gallagher stopped the car at parallel white lines that crossed his side of the road. Over to the right, a low-mounted traffic signal was showing alternately blinking red lights. He glanced in his mirrors. There were no other cars behind.

Up ahead, he could see traffic coming to a halt and over to the left some thirty meters away, was a white, three-storeyed building that reminded him of an air traffic control tower.

He looked in his mirrors again. No car approaching from behind.

Twin barrier poles, painted with red and white warning bars, had now come down across the full width of the road and beyond that, a whole chunk of

its surface was rising upward like a vast drawbridge.
Gallagher heard the sound of a marine engine. He
looked to his left and saw the masts of a ship almost
as tall as the tower, going past. He could not see the
hull. Then the masts were briefly hidden by the
raised portion of the road.

He glanced at his mirrors once more. Two cars
approaching, but none he recognized. No Mercedes,
no Golf, and no taxi.

The ship had passed, and the chunk of road was
on its way back down. Soon, it was part of the surface
again and the barriers were being raised. The lights
had stopped their blinking.

Gallagher drove slowly forward, then picked up
speed. Almost immediately, the road curved sharply
to the right and 200 meters later, it went left. This
gave him an opportunity to check his mirrors and
the short line of cars that had joined him. Still nothing to cause worry. The road had straightened now,
and seemed to stretch interminably into the distance. Beneath the bright, cloudless sky, it appeared
to fade into the water.

About halfway along, Gallagher saw the place
that had been designated for the rendezvous. It was
a lay-by, on the right side of the road. He pulled into
it. A dark blue, Dutch-registered Range Rover was
parked there, but no one was in it. Gallagher
brought the *quattro* to a halt some distance from the
Range Rover. He kept the engine running and
looked carefully about him. Villiger had chosen his
meeting place well. There was a clear view of the
road for a considerable distance, in both directions.

Traffic was light and every so often a car would
rush past going one way, or a lorry would thunder in
the other direction. Gallagher looked at each care-

fully as he began to wonder why he had decided to come. Curiosity, perhaps? To check that Villiger really was alive? Curiosity was always a bad reason.

From where he sat, with the vast tracts of water on either side, he felt as if he were in the middle of the Channel; but neither Dover nor Calais was at either end. Beyond the low metal barrier on the right side of the lay-by, was a wide path that apparently paralleled the entire length of the causeway. Gallagher soon noted its main purpose. In the distance up ahead, he could see a cyclist approaching. As the cyclist drew closer, he thought the shape familiar.

Before long, there was no denying the big frame. It really was Villiger.

Gallagher turned off the engine and climbed out. He walked the few feet to the barrier, and waited. He glanced quickly about him. Still clear. He kept well away from the Range Rover.

Villiger rode the bicycle up to the point near the barrier where Gallagher was waiting and stopped, placing one foot on the ground. He looked across at Gallagher.

Gallagher saw the same close-cropped blonde hair that had been bleached by years of strong sunshine; the same small eyes set deep in the heavy face; the same tall solid frame with its deep tan; the same aura of physical power. But there was something else he had not expected. It was in the eyes. Far within them, a haunted look was trying to keep itself hidden.

Then Villiger was smiling. He held a hand out across the barrier. "Man, it's good to see you."

Gallagher shook the hand warmly. "You too, Piet."

"Thought I was dead, hey?" The unmistakeable Afrikaner accent too.

"You gave a good impression of it."

Villiger got off the bike, lifted it, and crossed over to Gallagher's side. He sat on the barrier and began to dismantle the cycle. It was one of those fold-away jobs.

"Still a careful man," Villiger said as he worked. "That's good. I saw you arrive, of course." He patted a pouch on the bicycle. "Binoculars. When you didn't get out, I knew you'd be ready to move if anything looked wrong to you."

"I thought the Range Rover might be yours. Wasn't sure, though."

Villiger had finished. The cycle had become two wheels clipped together within a seeming tangle of frame, handlebars, and cables.

He stood up, and carried it over to the Range Rover. "Remind you of our little adventure in Australia, did it?"

"A little." Gallagher would never forget. They had been the survivors of a hijack, fleeing for their lives across the fearsome Australian Outback, with the hijackers in hot pursuit, determined to ensure none survived in the end. With Villiger's invaluable help, Gallagher had brought the remnants to safety. A bond that was not quite friendship had subsequently grown between them. Villiger was a South African intelligence man. Afrikaner.

Villiger loaded the folded bike into the back of the Range Rover. "Saw you kept well away from it," he said with a brief twitch of his features. It could have been a smile.

"People can do wonders with booby traps these days."

Villiger shut the hatch. They walked back to a spot midway between the two vehicles.

"You don't think that I . . ." Villiger began.

"Not your style," Gallagher said. "You might have tried a pot shot at me from long distance, if you'd wanted to. But that was not likely. You're really a close-in man . . ."

"Well thank you."

Gallagher grinned at him. "Anytime. It's just that it did cross my mind," he went on, "that someone could have got me out here under false pretenses, using the possibility that you were still alive."

"You saw me in Amsterdam . . ."

"I saw someone who *looked* like you."

"Ever the careful man."

"Is there another way?"

Villiger turned to look out at the IJsselmeer. "No. There isn't."

Gallagher kept his own eyes on the road.

"This is an amazing thing," Villiger was saying. "Do you know from its southern shore to the dyke up north, complete with a motorway running along it, this patch of water is wider than the English Channel? Thirty miles from point to point and all inland. I'm talking about the Dover to Calais run, of course."

"Weird," Gallagher said. "I was thinking about the Channel myself as I drove up. But you didn't call me out here to talk about water, Piet."

"No. I didn't." Villiger gave a brief chuckle. "You seem to have upset my lovely messenger. She does not like you at all."

"You've got to give her a little more training. I saw her trying to put a trace on the car last night."

Villiger's chuckle sounded again. "I told her you

would know. The alarm lights began to flash. She's
very cross with you. You nearly drowned her, she
said."

"She nearly drowned herself," Gallagher cor-
rected. "She should have been more careful."

"Not her line of work, really. But I've got to use
her."

"Whatever it is she's doing, she's certainly stirring things up. I came to Holland for a nice quiet
photo assignment. Instead, I find myself being followed all over the place by a beautiful blonde which
under normal circumstances, I'd have found flatter-
ing. But I find I'm also being followed by two other
sets of people, one pair of which tried to smear me all
over a car last night."

Villiger turned around sharply. *"What?"*

"All true," Gallagher said. "Someone was out
for a little dodgem practice."

Villiger's eyes narrowed, almost disappearing
into his face. "Can you describe them?"

"One was black. I'd recognize him if I saw him
again. The other . . ." Gallagher shook his head.
"White . . . might be Dutch . . . might be any national-
ity."

Villiger looked thoughtful. "And the other people?"

"You'll laugh at this. My old Department."

Villiger's face went still. "No," he said. "They
couldn't know," he added after a while. "They must
be following you out of habit."

"They never do anything out of habit. I ought to
know."

Villiger was again looking out over the water.
"Of course." He seemed to be thinking deeply.

"I really thought you were dead," Gallagher

said into the ensuing silence between them. Two cars went past, followed by a convoy of two lorries. Nothing to cause anxiety.

Villiger made no comment, seemingly still deep in thought.

At last, he said: "Mistaken identity. The people who came for me got the wrong man. He bore a superficial resemblance. I was out in the bush at the time. An interrogation job. When we realized what it was all about, it seemed a good idea to continue to remain dead. It had its uses."

Gallagher did not ask what uses, nor about the interrogation. He didn't think he'd like to hear.

"Do you remember that young officer you worked with on those missile sites on the border?"

Gallagher remembered. He'd been chasing Lauren's killers and had stumbled upon a plot to nuke Pretoria. He'd been virtually shanghaied into leading the commando officer and his men to the hidden site.

"Beukes," Gallagher now answered. "I didn't like him much. A diehard; but he was a good man in a firefight. When it was all over, I detected a little bit of serious questioning of what he stood for."

"He's dead."

"How?"

"Whatever serious questioning he was doing didn't go far enough. He was out on a search and destroy mission and walked into an ambush. They all got it. Forty of them."

"Shit. How much more blood are your people going to lose, Piet," Gallagher went on, "before some common sense penetrates?"

Villiger looked at him. The haunted look in the

eyes flickered briefly. "That's what I want to talk to you about."

"I don't think I'm going to like this."

"I need your help."

"I know I'm not going to like it."

"Hear me out."

Gallagher looked about him. "Much as I'm enjoying the view, I didn't come here just to admire it. I'm listening."

"We'd like you to command a force of F-16's . . ."

Gallagher started laughing. It took him some time to stop, while Villiger looked on expressionlessly. The laughter faded slowly.

"Even assuming you could find anyone to give you just one F-16 . . . although given Iran and Nicaragua, anything's possible these days . . . Even if you could lay your hands on some, and even if I were current on fast jets, never mind that little electric hotrod, what makes you think I'd even consider flying for your lot? You and I have a mutual respect pact going, Piet. It doesn't extend to your country as it stands at present."

"You helped Beukes . . ."

"I didn't do it for him. I told him so at the time."

Villiger was silent once more, his back again to Gallagher. Gallagher continued his scrutiny of the passing traffic. A couple of cyclists went along the path, heading north. Gallagher wondered whether they were just out for a spin or whether they made the return journey each day. Good way to keep fit. He wondered what happened during the winter.

"We've been working on this for three years," Villiger was saying, "checking out various fast jet pilots, seeing who would be suitable. This year, when we became sure of the aircraft, we made our approaches. We've got fourteen."

Gallagher turned to look at him. "Are you telling me you've got fourteen fully qualified pilots to agree?"

"Yes."

"Better than a cricket team, I suppose. And what are they going to fly? Mirages turned into Cheetahs?"

"F-16's. We've got a supplier who has secured six, with full spares support, and who is able to acquire at least six more, should we want them."

Gallagher was staring at Villiger who had now turned to face him. "You're bloody serious. Who the hell would give you those aircraft?"

"There are seventeen air arms using the F-16 at the present time," Villiger said, "the US Air Force and Navy included. In all, I'd say about 2,200 are currently in service, give or take the odd dozen or so. Twelve is a very small number among all that."

"And out of whose inventory would they come?"

"People can get hold of plastic explosives, poison gas, surface to air missiles . . . it's a supermarket out there. There are plenty of customers, and plenty of people willing to sell . . ."

"Aircraft are a little more difficult."

"Not always. Our . . . representative has good connections."

"The answer is still no, Piet. Glad as I am to see you alive, you must have known what my reaction would be."

Villiger said: "I heard about Lauren. I'm sorry."

Gallagher did not want the memory, but he could not help seeing again in his mind, her falling body on the slopes of Courchevel, the sniper's bullet already having taken her life away. She had survived the pursuit in the Outback, only to die where she had thought herself safe.

"Her falling body saved me," he now said in a voice that seemed to be addressed to himself rather than to Villiger.

"She was right for you."

"I thought so at the time. And how's this for irony?" Gallagher went on. "Do you remember her grandfather?"

"The old man? Jake? Yes . . . I remember. They got him too."

Gallagher nodded. "He's left me a ridiculous sum of money in his Will. God knows what I'm going to do with it."

"Spend it, like any sensible person."

"I don't want it . . . and you've very nicely changed the subject."

"Not for long. You haven't heard all that I have to say. You are quite mistaken about the aircraft. They're not destined for the place you think they are. They're going to the ALA."

"And who are they, when they're home?"

"The Azania Liberation Army."

"Never heard of them."

"All to the good. We're not looking for publicity."

"*We?* You belong to this . . . Army?" Gallagher's expression showed his disbelief.

Villiger nodded. "It's a multiracial group of people who believe in a non-factional counter to what's going on in our country. We're motivated in a way that makes us quite potent in the field. Many of us are ex-professional soldiers. Guys who have been in the bush and seen the reality of what the future holds. We're hoping to prevent a civil war that will make the Lebanon look like a minor aberration."

Gallagher was shaking his head slowly. "You, Piet, are not trying to tell me you've turned rebel, after years of serving the establishment."

"I didn't 'turn rebel' as you put it. I've had years to watch my country head down the path to suicide. Don't get me wrong, man. I'm not looking for a black government that wants to get its own back for what was done to its people; and I'm not one of those who wants to become a refugee. I love South Africa. It's the only country I want. I'm not prepared to stand by and watch people . . . white or black . . . destroy it from within. I believe that until something hard and positive is done, we'll lurch down the same old road until one day, we all wake up to find ourselves bathed in each other's blood. When that happens, the country I love will become just another Third World state, with most of its people dead. That's the nightmare I see."

"And you think that a few F-16's will bring about the changes you want? Piet, you disappoint me. Or you think me a fool. You've been a top Intelligence man for years. You can't expect me to believe you've suddenly changed sides . . ."

"I haven't changed sides. I'm still serving my country. I've merely altered the methods in which to do so. The aircraft are not to be used to attack South Africa, but to prevent incursions into neighboring states. We're not affiliated to any of the other movements as yet. They don't really know of us, although they must be wondering who's been taking out the S&D teams so effectively."

"Others too, I suspect," Gallagher said drily. His

eyes continued their frequent scrutiny of the traffic. No one, it seemed, had managed to follow him.

"Our security is good."

"I wouldn't count on it. How do you explain the men in the taxi, *and* the Department?"

"They're not following me. I'm not even in Europe, as far as anyone outside the immediate circle of Lorraine and yourself knows. I'm meant to be in the bush conducting a special search with just two other men . . ."

Gallagher stared at him. "You're still in your old job?"

"Of course. How else could I get to spend weeks in the bush out of contact? That's been my job for the past two years."

"And no one's rumbled you?"

"Not yet."

"Christ. You like living dangerously. You're in shit street if they ever find out. God knows what they'll do to you."

Villiger gave a tired smile. "We are always more vicious with our own kind. They won't find out."

"And the men with you?"

"Members of the ALA . . . er . . . when they're in the bush. They're black. We've got white ex-soldiers too. It's a bigger movement than you'd think."

"Christ," Gallagher said again.

"There are many people in reasonably high places," Villiger went on, "who see the future of South Africa in the same nightmarish glare that I see it, and would like a different solution. They'd never admit it if you asked them to their faces. They make all the usual noises in public of course, using the communism red herring which even they realize is going stale. These people have helped in getting the aircraft.

"The condition is that there'll be no offensive operations across the borders. We wait for incursions, then take them out, whether in the air or on the ground. We bleed them, make it counterproductive to continue. If these incursions are not halted, it will only be a matter of time before the MiG-29's and the tanks start appearing in our particular theater; especially now that the Afghan honeymoon is over."

"No way," Gallagher said. "They won't get involved. Too soon after Afghanistan."

"Don't bank on it. The MiG-29 is meant to be an export fighter."

"You're crazy, Piet. It won't work."

"We've got pilots of all sorts of nationalities: Yanks, Brits, a couple of Arabian gentlemen, even an Israeli . . ."

"Even if I wanted to join your crazy air force, I'm not qualified to fly the Falcon, let alone lead guys who've got more experience than I on the type."

"You're saying no?"

Gallagher sighed. "I'm saying it's a mad scheme. Shifting twelve . . . even *six* F-16's into the African bush is not going to go unnoticed. The bloody sky's riddled with spy satellites . . ."

"Getting the aircraft there is our problem. If we can't do it, you've got nothing to worry about and can forget you ever heard of the idea. If on the other hand . . ." Villiger paused. "You're still saying no."

"I'm saying," Gallagher began patiently, "that even six months out of the cockpit is six months too long. I've been out of it for years. I've had exactly three flights in the F-16. Each time, it was the two-seater 16B. Once in the rear seat, twice in the front. That's the full extent of my time on type. These people you've talked about were operational pilots with recent experience . . ."

"I want someone to lead them. I know enough about you, Gordon, to convince me. I know something of your flying skills." Villiger's eyes seemed to be pleading. "Look. Don't think about an answer now. One other thing I'd like you to do for me, especially if you decide not to come with us." The deepset eyes were fixed upon Gallagher with a strange intensity. "I want you to look after Lorraine for me while she's over here. She's . . . she's a bit of an innocent abroad."

"I like your sense of humor. She hates my guts."

Villiger smiled. "Not really." They began walking back to the Range Rover, then paused by the driver's door. "Change will come down there, you know," he continued. "The status quo is no longer sustainable, no matter what some people may think. The ALA, and the economic imperative will see to that. When all the opposition sorts itself out and combines, then change will be unstoppable. It's only a matter of time. The sooner the better, because the longer it takes, the nastier it will be." He climbed into the vehicle.

Gallagher said: "Have you heard of something called FUTRON?"

"No. It sounds like a fruit cocktail in a science fiction movie."

"What about a man called Quinlan?"

Villiger suddenly went very still. His eyes seemed to lose all life. "J.D. Quinlan?"

It was Gallagher's turn to be surprised. *Villiger knew Quinlan.*

"Yes," Gallagher replied.

"Describe him."

"I can only relay someone else's description of him. I don't know the man personally. Neat suits, neat haircut, glasses, mild-mannered . . ."

"That's the bastard."

"I don't understand." Gallagher was already sensing an unpleasant twitch in his stomach.

"If there's such a thing as a war broker," Villiger began grimly "then Quinlan is it. The dirtier the war, the better. Think of all the little cesspit conflicts on the face of this globe . . . El Salvador, Nicaragua, Honduras, Chad . . . he's been in there at some stage. The Middle East and even, I've heard, Afghanistan."

"Africa too?"

Villiger nodded. "So how come you've heard of him?"

Gallagher gave the question some thought before replying. "I've got a friend who works for him."

Villiger's eyes were hard. "I'm not very pleased to hear that, man."

"It's not what you think. This is a woman I last saw eight years ago. She works for FUTRON, a promotional company . . ."

"Hah!" Villiger exclaimed with harsh skepticism. " 'Promotional company.' They certainly promote. Wars. And how did this woman suddenly come to make contact?" While he'd been talking, Villiger's eyes had darted from time to time in a swift survey of the traffic. He seemed to be straining at a leash.

Gallagher said: "I was at this café in London when she appeared at my table. Said she'd seen me get out of my car . . ."

"And you believed her?"

"Of course I didn't believe her. We talked briefly and she invited me to a small party at her place. Gave me a card. That's how I know about FUTRON. I told her I couldn't make it. Had a photo job to do in Amsterdam. Suddenly, all sorts of people are following me . . . your blonde, the Department, and those homicidal maniacs in the taxi. And she turns up in Amsterdam as well, in *my* hotel . . ."

Villiger's grin was without humor. "It's the effect you have on women."

"Even my ego questioned it," Gallagher said drily. "If what you say about Quinlan is true . . ."

"It's true."

"Then I don't think she realizes what she's got herself into. Those people would have killed her last night as well."

"Sounds pure Quinlan. Where is she now?"

"I put her on the plane back to London."

Villiger gave a brief nod, as if in approval. "Clearing the decks. That was a good move. How long has she been working for FUTRON?"

"Three years, she said."

Again, Villiger nodded. This time, he appeared to be confirming something to himself. His face had grown as hard as his eyes.

"Are you going to tell me what this is all about?" Gallagher demanded. "Why has everybody taken a sudden interest in my movements? And don't tell me it's routine Department activity."

Villiger looked up and down the causeway before replying. "In a few minutes, Lorraine Mowbray will be arriving. I've arranged it with her to put in an appearance about then. This was to give us time to discuss matters, while at the same time watching out for anyone who might have followed you." His big hands gripped the steering wheel. "Forget what I said to you about just looking after her. I want you to stick to her like glue, and don't take any nonsense from her."

"You're not telling me you suspect her of working for Quinlan."

"You're right. I'm not telling you that. You may not want to join my crazy air force, but I'd appreciate it if you did this as a favor to me." Villiger started the engine. "I may be wrong. I *want* to be wrong . . . but if I'm not, a lot of people could be in danger. Three years." He said the words bitterly.

"What the hell are you saying, Piet?"

"I'm saying," Villiger began grimly, "that I think I'm being set up . . . or the ALA is. I'm not sure, but I'm bloody well going to find out, man. Keep your eye on Lorraine." So saying, he sent the Range Rover hurtling onto the causeway, heading north.

"But . . ." Gallagher had begun, but the Range Rover was already well on its way. "Shit," he said. *"Fuck it,"* he added for good measure. "Why the devil does everybody seem to think they can interfere with my life?" he shouted at the IJsselmeer.

A pair of passing cyclists, young girls in skimpy shorts, giggled at him. His eyes followed their firm bottoms without real interest. His mind was churning, trying to sort out all that had occurred since Veronica Walmsley had chosen to drift back into his life after eight years of silence. Veronica and Quinlan, Villiger and Lorraine Mowbray; and beyond them, unseen manipulators.

"I ought to get into the car," he told himself, "and get out of here before she comes . . . if I'm smart. This is none of my business."

But Villiger had asked.

The sound of a car slowing down made him look. The silver Golf was approaching, coming from the direction of Lelystad.

"But I'm not being very smart," he muttered as the Golf swung into the lay-by and stopped close to the *quattro*.

He walked up just as Lorraine Mowbray climbed out.

The translucent eyes stared at him. "Well?" She was not even smiling.

"That's a good way to start."

A smile was even further from coming. "Don't bandy words with me, Mr. Gallagher."

His eyes held hers unflinchingly. "You must give me the name of your charm school. I'd like to enroll."

Her expression was cold. "You turned him down, didn't you."

"I told him what I thought. I said it was a crazy idea. I know a little more about air fighting than he does. It is a crazy idea."

Her lips tightened. "I knew it. I told him he was making a mistake coming to you. I knew I was right."

"And how long did it take you to come to that illuminating decision?" Despite his own reservations about Villiger's plans for a mini air force, Gallagher discovered that her words rankled.

"Right after I met you." She began to move back toward her car. "Clearly, valuable time has been wasted. We'll leave you to get on with your life." Her hand was on the door.

"There's nothing I'd like better!" Gallagher said

to her sharply. "But I don't have a bloody choice now."

The vehemence of his words startled her and her hand came unconsciously away from the door. "What . . . what do you mean?"

"I mean, Miss Mowbray . . . that Piet has asked me to keep an eye on you. Stick like glue, to quote him, and don't take any nonsense."

She stared at him, head turned slightly, a tiny frown between her eyebrows. "He said that?"

"Words from the man himself."

Her reaction was unexpected. He had thought she would have shown a furious defiance. Instead, she had become very quiet, turning away from him to stare unseeingly at the water.

"Something very serious must have happened," she said at last. She did not turn around.

"It did. I told him about Quinlan." He watched her like a hawk, waiting for her reaction to the name.

There was no reaction.

"Who's Quinlan?" she asked. She turned around to look at him. "I don't know any Quinlan."

"Piet certainly does. He took off from here as if rocket-assisted."

"Did he say anything else?"

"Only what I've just told you." Gallagher had decided to leave out the part about a suspected set-up.

"So what are you going to do?" The eyes were challenging.

"What I'm not going to enjoy doing . . . watch you, guard you, wet-nurse you. I may not agree with his air force idea, but I can at least do that. He would have done the same for me under similar circumstances. I hope."

That did not amuse her either. "Don't strain yourself, Mr. Gallagher."

"It's no strain, but I can see it's going to be a pain in the neck."

Her lips tightened even more and she opened the door of the car to reach inside for something. It was a radio. Gallagher reached in swiftly and took both the radio from her, and the keys from the ignition.

She rounded on him furiously. "Just what do you think you're doing? Give me those keys and that radio!"

"You do like giving orders, don't you? Why the radio?"

"None of your business!"

"I'd dearly love it not to be . . . but I'm stuck with you for the time being. Hopefully, Piet will meet up with me somewhere very soon and haul you away. In the meantime . . . why the radio?" Gallagher's hazel eyes had become very hard and within them, was something that appeared to frighten her.

"I've got to get in touch with Hennie," she answered with reluctance.

"Who, or what is Hennie?"

"Hennie Marais. He's my backup."

"No contact," Gallagher told her. "The radio stays with me."

"You can't . . ." she began, anger coming to her eyes.

"I don't know what this is all about," he interrupted firmly, "but Villiger asked me to watch you . . . and until he returns to take you off my hands, that's exactly what I'm going to do. I'm not looking forward to it, but there it is. No radio."

The translucent eyes blazed at him, but his own eyes sent her a deadlier message. The anger that had come into the pale eyes began to show signs of fading. The lips remained compressed, as if she dared not trust herself to speak.

"Does this Hennie Marais know about Villiger being in Holland?" Gallagher asked her.

After a long pause, she chose to answer. "No. Piet thought it best that only I knew. Now you do as well," she continued, making it sound like an accusation. "As far as Hennie knows, I've come here to make the contact with you myself."

"That's a small mercy, I suppose. Does he know my name?"

"No. Piet wanted as little as possible to go beyond himself and I at this stage."

"Thank God for his caution." Gallagher scanned the traffic. He felt no unease, for the time being. "Is your car hired?"

"Yes."

"Get rid of it. Is it one of those you can leave at any depot?"

"Yes," she said again.

"Fine. Check your brochure, see where the nearest place is from here . . . except Amsterdam. You'll hand in the Golf, then come with me."

"So now you're giving the orders?"

"Get one thing straight, Miss Mowbray," Gallagher began with heavy patience, "you haven't a choice. Come to terms with that and we'll pass our enforced time together with a reasonable lack of stress. I'm doing this for Piet . . . but I'm not going to get into any trouble for you. Make life easy for both of us and just do as I say. Please?"

"I don't know what he saw in you," she said scathingly.

"Beauty," he said, "is in the eye of the beholder. Now are you going to check out that hire depot?"

She stood her ground for a few defiant seconds before crossly reaching into the Golf for the hire company's publicity blurb. She studied it before reluctantly passing it on to him. There was a small map of Holland with the brochure, with the vehicle handing-in points marked by small red stars.

"We're in luck," he said to her. "There's a depot over on the other side, at Hoorn." From where they were, Hoorn was about thirty-six kilometers away. Hardly any distance.

Gallagher returned the brochure to her.

"Can I have my keys now, please?" Her eyes showed him no warmth.

"Of course." He did so, but held on to the radio.

"What's to stop me getting into the car and driving away?"

"Nothing," he said calmly. "But you'd have to answer to Villiger. I don't know how well you know him, but from my own experience, I'd advise against making him angry. Now you can follow me to Hoorn, or stand here and admire the view." He turned from her, went to the *quattro,* and climbed in.

As he clipped on his seat belt and started the engine, he glanced at her. Her eyes blazed back at him. He ignored her, and began easing the car toward the road.

She remained stubbornly where she was for some moments, then entered the Golf, slamming the door in her fury.

Gallagher heard the engine start, then smiled to himself as she followed him into the sparse traffic. There were some vehicles ahead, but none whatsoever behind them. He selected Rodrigo's *Fantasia para un gentilhombre* on the CD player, and glanced into his mirrors at the Golf following meekly in his wake.

He smiled once more. It was fitting, he thought. In the warmth of the bright sun and with the causeway stretching its way across the water, he could temporarily forget the people who had come to place their disruptions into his life.

The Adagio had come on. He glanced again in his mirrors. Lorraine Mowbray, in her silver Golf, was still on station.

6

Gallagher pulled up behind a short line of vehicles at the other end of the causeway. The road had been opened up to allow another small ship, this time coming from the north, to pass through. At the side of the road, teenaged youths with heavy tans were offering to clean insect-spattered windscreens.

One came up to the *quattro,* bucket and chamois leather in hand. The windscreen was dirty. Gallagher nodded, then regretted the decision almost immediately as the leather went to work, initially smearing the screen. Suppose the youth were in fact an assassin?

Paranoia. Shut up, Gallagher.

He looked in his mirrors. The Golf was getting the same treatment. For some reason, the whole affair made him feel uneasy. He could no longer see Lorraine Mowbray. Just as he was about to climb out, her screen was wiped clean, and there she was. His own screen was clean too. He smiled his thanks, and paid the boy. The traffic had begun to move.

He started off, Lorraine Mowbray faithfully keeping station.

They followed the N302 into Hoorn where she returned the Golf to the rental company, then joined Gallagher in the *quattro*. Her only luggage was a medium-sized handbag.

Her expression was frosty as she snapped on her seat belt. Then she leaned against the door and passed a hand through her hair. She did not look at him.

"Great," he said drily, and set off, heading for the intersection with the A7 motorway that would take them to the Afsluitdijk, the northern shore of the IJsselmeer. Gallagher wanted some pictures. No one was going to interfere with the work he had come to do.

Twenty-five kilometers after joining the motorway, he said: "There's a petrol station coming up. I need to fill the tank. There's a restaurant too. I fancy a bite to eat. How about you?"

She had not spoken throughout the journey so far, and he had filled the silence with Rodrigo on the CD.

"Alright," she now said without much enthusiasm. "And can you change the music?"

"To hear is to obey." He switched to Bruce Hornsby—one of his favorites—then after a moment's hesitation, selected Bob Seger instead. *Mainstreet* came on.

She looked pointedly out of the window.

"Don't you like it?" he asked.

"It will do."

"I can see we're going to have a wonderful time."

She said nothing.

* * *

The BMW was cruising from Hoorn, going toward the causeway.

Zamba, now in the passenger seat, said: "We can't be sure they're going to be around here." He did not like the way de Vries drove. The car was his, after all, and did not belong to de Vries.

"Our information—reliable information, I might add—gives this area as their meeting place."

"They could be anywhere."

"Our informant specified the dyke . . . the causeway to Lelystad."

"What if we are already too late?"

"Man, you worry me sometimes," de Vries said impatiently, narrowly missing a towed caravan going the other way. "I'm not sure you should remain here for much longer. You should be sent back home. I think you are beginning to forget your place, hey? Being in Europe is not so good for you."

Zamba said nothing, but the latent hate in his eyes could not be hidden.

De Vries was quite aware of it. "You know what I am thinking? I'm thinking," he carried on, not really wanting a reply from his companion, "you dislike me so much, you would kill me if you could." He laughed, as if this were an immense joke.

De Vries had a way of laughing that was all his own. The mouth was opened wide, but no sound came out of it. A strange ripple seemed to course through his body as he moved about in his seat, hands gripping the steering wheel. His entire frame was involved.

Zamba watched him warily, as one would a crazed dog and unconsciously moved himself away, within the restrictions of his seat belt and the closed door of the car.

Abruptly, de Vries stopped his bizarre laughter. It was as if a switch within him had suddenly been flicked to a new position.

"Perhaps you really have been here too long," de Vries was saying. "Perhaps a little riot duty in Soweto, eh? Get the blood going again. It's been too quiet for you over here."

The silent laughter began once more.

When they had gone all the way to Lelystad without a sighting, de Vries' mood turned ugly.

"We're going back across," he said tightly.

"But why?" Zamba asked. "If they were not there . . ."

"We are going back!" de Vries snarled. "And you be careful, man. I might start thinking you don't want to find them."

Zamba stared at him. "And you are crazy, man. Why should I not want to find them?"

"That's what I'd like to know. I'd better not find out you have been talking to the wrong sort of people. They can fill your head with nonsense. Give you wrong ideas." De Vries stopped the car just before the approach to the causeway. "The wrong kind of thinking can find you looking after the drunks in Kaffirtown in no time at all. You drive." He climbed out of the car.

After a moment's hesitation, Zamba climbed out of the right-hand seat to take his place behind the wheel.

De Vries was dressed in faded blue jeans, a white T-shirt, and a pale blue lightweight blouson which was zipped halfway up his chest. On his feet were blue and white trainers. He climbed into the passenger seat and reclined the back fully. He shut the car door and lay down.

"I feel like a nap," he said. "Wake me when we get to the other side." He folded his arms across his chest, and closed his eyes.

Zamba stared at him silently and still saying nothing, started the BMW on its return trip.

Mainstreet came to an end just as Gallagher pulled off the motorway and headed for the petrol pumps.

"I liked that," Lorraine Mowbray said as the car stopped.

He turned off the engine. "Would you like to hear the rest?"

She shook her head. "It's just this song."

He re-selected it. "Enjoy," he said, then got out to unlock the petrol cap.

While he filled the tank, he could see her moving her head slightly to the music. Once, she turned to look up at him through the window. The pale eyes studied him keenly, but there was a curious lack of expression in them. She turned away to concentrate on the music as he replaced the pump nozzle and secured the cap. The windows were raised so the music, though loud inside the car, barely escaped into the outside world.

Gallagher went to pay, taking care to look casually about him as he did so. No lurking vehicle. No one who seemed remotely interested. He returned to the car and drove it to the restaurant car park. He positioned it where he could keep an eye on it while inside. They were able to get a table at a window which afforded a clear view of the *quattro*. No one would be able to approach it unseen.

They gave their orders and while waiting, Lorraine Mowbray said: "You're a strange man." The translucent eyes seemed to have a depth that went on forever.

"That's one way of looking at it."

She did not expand upon her theme. "Where are you taking me?"

"First, I'm . . . we're going to the Afsluitdijk where I want to take some photos . . ."

"And then?"

"I'm hoping that by the time I've finished, Villiger will have made contact and I'll be able to pass you on to him."

"How?"

"How what?"

"How will he make contact? He doesn't know where we are."

"That's easy. You must have a way of getting in touch with him. You make the contact when I'm finished with the day's work and tell him where we are, or we arrange to meet. Simplicity itself."

"And then you'll return to London?"

"Oh no. I've got some more traveling to do for a few days yet. I think I'll go up to Groningen. See what I can find there. Then it's back to London."

She tightened her lips briefly, and nodded to herself. Their orders came and they ate in silence.

Gallagher wondered where the men from the taxi were, and what they were up to.

"We're coming to the end of the causeway," Zamba said. He had to repeat himself before de Vries acknowledged.

De Vries remained in his reclining position. "You drove well. You didn't even wake me. Look, man . . . perhaps I've been a little hasty. I was just annoyed we missed them . . ."

"If they came here at all," Zamba said, glancing briefly down at de Vries.

"Just what I was thinking. And it's alright. I won't ask them to send you back home."

Zamba said nothing to that, but looked pleased. You never knew with de Vries.

Then Zamba said: "We have left the causeway."

De Vries raised himself just long enough to peer out. Some minutes later, he had another look. They were entering a shallow left-hand bend.

"Over there," he said. "On the right. That parking place."

"You want to stop?"

"Yes. I feel better now. I'll drive."

Zamba was reluctant, but decided not to have another argument. Besides, de Vries had stopped being nasty.

The bend had developed into a long straight and the lay-by was a short distance from where it began. Zamba pulled into it, and stopped the car. A low bank led down from the side of the road to a narrow man-made stream. De Vries got out and stared at the stream briefly, before moving around to the other side of the car. He left the seat in its reclined position.

De Vries was already in the left-hand driving seat before Zamba had completed the swap. He watched as the other man got in and began to raise the back of the seat.

"You might like traveling like this . . ." Zamba began to say.

The bullet from the small silenced automatic that de Vries had swiftly pulled out of his blouson took Zamba squarely in the heart. He died so quickly, he barely had time to register shock as he fell back onto the still reclined seat. His eyes had opened wide, as if trying to pop out of their sockets. He had uttered no sound.

De Vries put the gun away, and glanced up and down the road. He had chosen the moment well. There was a lull in the traffic and nothing was coming from either direction. He started the BMW, and drove back onto the road. To anyone in a passing car, Zamba was invisible; and to the occupants of a higher vehicle, whether behind or going past, he would appear to be sleeping . . . if they bothered to look.

De Vries smiled to himself and drove a little faster.

"That's it," Haslam said in disgust after their third circuit of Amsterdam. "I've done more tours of this city today than a coachload of bloody tourists. If I'd wanted a tour, I'd have come on holiday." He glanced at a quiet Prinknash. "I wouldn't have taken you with me either."

"No, Mr. Haslam . . ."

"And don't call me Haslam!"

"But last night . . ."

"That was last night." Haslam stared balefully at the Ringvaart, the narrow canal that encircled the district of Watergraafsmeer like a ring road. "Gallagher's gone for good," he continued, "and we won't know where. Not what I would call a successful trip."

"His car's not exactly inconspicuous," Prinknash said. "Why don't we get the Dutch police . . ."

Haslam gave one of his heavy sighs. "Sometimes . . . If we wanted the Dutch police to know we were shadowing him, we would have let them know before

we left London. We don't know what he's involved in
. . . quite probably, he doesn't either . . . and if we
cover the operation with bloody coppers . . ." He said
this with added emphasis for Prinknash's benefit.
". . . if we do that, then we might as well shout it from
the rooftops. And the people involved in whatever
this is will simply go to ground. They'll still get on
with their plans, but we'll have lost this very tiny
lead we've got." Haslam made a noise that betrayed
his own sense of frustration. "Assuming we've still
got even that."

"What about Lady Walmsley?" Prinknash suggested.

"What about her?"

"She could be a lead."

Haslam stared at the canal through the windscreen of the Mercedes, mind elsewhere. "They'll be
keeping an eye on her in London."

Prinknash had a bright idea. "Perhaps Gallagher will come back to Amsterdam."

Haslam interrupted his blank scrutiny of the
canal long enough to favor Prinknash with a glance
of pity. "Got that on good authority, have you?"

"Well . . ." Prinknash began lamely, ". . . in that
car of his he can cover long distances and with it not
getting dark till late, he can do all his photography
for the day and come back here for the night. I mean,
it's a great hotel. Must be a nice place to make your
base if you're on his sort of expense account . . ." His
voice faded. Haslam was staring at him again.

"Did you work that out all by yourself? What
possible reason could Gallagher have for returning,
especially as he knows *we're* here?" Haslam shook
his head in exasperation. "Sometimes."

"It was just a thought," Prinknash said, managing to sound both defiant and defensive.

"Put it back to sleep. Let's get out of here."

Gallagher and Lorraine Mowbray had finished their meal and were on their way out of the restaurant when he paused by the small newspaper kiosk near the entrance. A headline and a photograph had caught his eye. He wondered how come he'd missed it when they had first entered. The relevant edition was prominently displayed. It must have arrived while they were eating, he decided.

His knowledge of Dutch was rudimentary, but there was no mistaking the headline. Murder was not a difficult word to understand. But what made the victim more than of passing interest was the other photograph. It was of a taxi, with a shattered rear window.

Gallagher bought the paper and studied the lead story as they walked back to the car.

"I didn't realize you could read Dutch so well," Lorraine Mowbray said. There was no suggestion of sarcasm in her voice, but Gallagher got the impression she was having a quiet laugh.

"I can get the gist of what it says," he told her. He continued to study the article.

"What's so important about that story?" she asked.

Until he heard from Villiger, he felt he should tell her as little as possible. "It interests me."

She thought about that for some moments, then tried again. "May I have a look? I'll read it aloud for you. You may be missing the important bits."

They had reached the car, and the pale eyes were upon him. Her offer seemed genuine enough.

She did not appear to be trying to show off her linguistic skills in an attempt to get one back on him.

Gallagher switched off the alarm system before leaning on the car and laying the paper flat upon its warm roof. She came close, and also leaned against the *quattro* to have a closer look at the article. As if she had suddenly become aware of their proximity to each other, the faintest of flushes rose from the base of her neck to her cheek, before fading rapidly. It was an unusual display, but it looked good on her and gave her outwardly cold aloofness a certain degree of warmth. He preferred her that way, despite his having to play the jailer. He hoped Villiger would find nothing incriminating about her. Until then, she was still to be watched.

"Mystery surrounds the strange death of Amsterdam taxi driver Jan Leender," she began to read, *"near a path in the Speulderbos . . ."*

"Where's that?"

She read on silently, then: "Er . . . that's a wood northwest of Apeldoorn."

"Okay. Go on."

"It is not known why Mr. Leender went to the Speulderbos," she continued, *"nor how he got there. There were no radio messages from him. It is possible he was killed before he could send any. Death was instantaneous, and was caused by a small caliber bullet to the heart at close range. His taxi was found unattended in the city. It is being examined for traces of blood but as yet, none have been found. Mr. Leender leaves a wife and two small children.*

"Another taxi driver, Mr. Cornelis Heukel, was also attacked and his taxi stolen. Luckily, he was not seriously injured, but his attackers poured alcohol over him and for some hours, he was ignored as he lay

*unconscious. He was thought to be drunk. Mr. Heu-
kel's taxi has been found, with its rear window shattered, and a bullet hole in one of the other windows.
Mr. Heukel can give no reason for this. Are we perhaps witnessing the beginnings of a kind of gang
warfare between the taxi drivers of Amsterdam? The
idea seems preposterous on the face of it. However, the
police feel there is more to it . . ."*

"I've heard enough, thanks," Gallagher said.
"Well . . . it doesn't concern us."

She folded the newspaper. "Then why were you
so interested?"

"I thought I would be. I was wrong."

The pale eyes were disbelieving. "You expect me
to swallow that?" She had moved a little away from
him.

He went around to the driver's side. Her eyes
continued to follow him.

"Are you getting in?" he asked, looking across at
her. "I've got work to do. You can chuck the paper
away, if you like. Or keep it. I don't mind."

There was a bin close by. She went over to it and
almost flung the newspaper into it. She returned to
the car and got in, then silently secured her belt.

Gallagher entered and shut the door as he
looked at her. She was staring firmly ahead. He
clipped on his belt slowly. She still did not look at
him.

"Great," he said, and started the car.

It was less than ten kilometers from the motorway service station to Den Oever, where the Afsluits-
dijk started. They had been traveling in silence for
a few minutes when Gallagher decided to try again.

"Do you realize," he began, "that what we're
traveling over was open sea before the Second World

War? And up ahead, Wieringen was an island? The whole thing fascinates me. Good stuff for the kind of photos I'm after. The clients I'm doing this for should be pleased."

"I'm sure you'll be very happy together." She did not sound the slightest bit interested in land reclamation.

Gallagher said: "Look. I'm just trying to ease the atmosphere in here. I've got to do my job. I'm not pleased you're along for the ride, and neither are you. But we haven't a choice. So let's accept that and grin through it until we make contact with Piet. Alright?"

"Why won't you tell me what so interests you about those taxi drivers?"

"There's nothing to tell. I don't know them."

"That doesn't answer the question."

Gallagher gave her words some thought. "Tell you what," he began. "I'll have a word with Piet Villiger, then he can tell you all about it."

"But if it concerns him . . ."

"Then he's the one to be told."

"But . . ."

"Look. I'm sorry to keep interrupting you, but there's nothing that I can say to you at this stage."

She didn't like that one bit, and her expression spoke louder than words.

"You're an impossible man," she said after a while.

"A careful one."

Her eyes were disbelieving, as if he had just insulted her. "You've got to be careful of *me?*"

"Of everyone. I learned a long time ago it was a good way of ensuring survival."

"And Piet?"

"We . . . have an understanding."

She fell silent again, and seemed thoughtful.

Then she was saying: "I hope this little trip of yours doesn't last till nightfall. All my things are back at my hotel. I've got just my personal documents with me, and my money. I don't intend to buy new clothes just because you want to do your job."

"Don't worry. We'll get in touch with Villiger in plenty of time. I'm certain he'll find a way to get you back to Amsterdam."

She made no comment, then after another short pause, said: "Can we have some music? I'd like that song again, if it's no trouble."

He glanced at her for a hint of sarcasm, but she was looking out of her window.

Mainstreet, a ballad of unrequited love for a body-swaying dancer, came flooding into the car from eight speakers.

Gallagher wondered why she liked the song so much. Did she somehow identify with the haunting and haunted young dancer? He glanced at her once more. Her eyes were closed, head moving gently to the rhythm of the music. She had totally immersed herself within it.

The *quattro* sped on its way toward the Afsluitdijk.

Haslam was again on the Consulate telephone to Fowler.

"You don't sound very happy, George," Fowler said mildly.

"I'm not." Haslam had no intention of mincing his words. "The merchandise is missing."

"Oh dear. Suggestions?"

"We stay one more night, then come home."

"Are you sure?"

"Yes. Incidentally, a packet should be arriving
. . ."

"It's arrived. We're covering."

Haslam grunted. It could have been approval.
At least, the Department would have Veronica
Walmsley under constant surveillance.

"Traffic's getting hotter," he went on to the distant Fowler.

"Perhaps you should return tonight."

"No . . . no . . . we'll be fine."

"How hot?"

"There have been accidents." Haslam had read
about the taxi drivers. His Dutch was fluent.
"Local."

"Nothing to do with you, I hope." Fowler
managed to convey alarm, while remaining as calm
as ever.

Haslam said: "I don't think you really expect a
comment from me."

"Sorry, George. Just expressing anxiety. Any
idea who was responsible?"

"There are unknown players in the game. Perhaps those we met the other night."

Fowler gave that some thought. "Serious."
There was another pause. "Very well. I'll leave it up
to you. You decide what's best."

"I'm too old for all this," Haslam said in a voice
that was at once world-weary and pleading.

"Of course you're not," Fowler said, and ended
the conversation.

Haslam stared at the phone before slowly re-
placing it. "What do you know about it?" he said to
the silent instrument.

He had been given a private room from which to

make the call to Fowler. He walked thoughtfully out of it, closing the door softly behind him. One of the Consulate staff approached, smiling.

"Everything alright?" the newcomer began brightly.

"No. It's not." Haslam scowled at him and went on his way.

A young woman going the other way stopped by her colleague. They both looked at Haslam's departing figure.

"What's up with him?" she asked. "He went by with a face like thunder."

The man shrugged. "Who knows with these people? Ours is not to reason why."

"Well he can do the dying," she said. "That's what he's paid for."

The man stared at her. "God, you're cold-blooded."

"It's true, though. Isn't it?"

The man had no answer.

De Vries was on the A2 motorway, going south. He had just passed Utrecht. He glanced down at Zamba's reclined body, and smiled. Hardly any blood. No one had stopped him. It was going to be alright. He had wanted to put as much distance as possible between the actual scene of the shooting and the disposal of the corpse, before returning to Amsterdam.

Sixteen kilometers later, he came to the Deil motorway intersection and went left on the A15, in the direction of Arnhem. He glanced in his mirror and felt a sudden frisson of uncertainty. Two motor-cycle policemen were coming up fast.

He held the steering wheel with one hand, while

the right reached into his blouson for the small automatic. He held it there, in readiness. He made sure his speed was just inside the limit.

Killing the policemen was not what he wanted, though this was only for reasons of convenience. If they stopped him to look inside, then it would be unfortunate for them. They would die very quickly indeed. One shot each to the face. He would ensure that the range was such, he could not possibly miss. Besides, he was an exceptionally skilled marksman. Those who had trained him had said so.

The motorcycle policemen would live for another day. They swept past, with hardly a glance at the BMW.

De Vries removed his hand from the gun. "Kiss your girlfriends for me," he murmured at the fast-receding patrolmen. "They won't know how lucky you were today." He glanced at the body. "Not like you, eh, Zamba man? No more kissing for you."

He smiled again, as he continued on his way.

Gallagher listened to the soft whirr of the camera as it loaded the new roll of film he had just inserted. The whirring stopped. The Nikon was ready.

From the center of the walkway that spanned its four lanes, he looked up and down the Afsluitdijk. Traffic, as usual, was sparse. It never ceased to surprise him how free-flowing the Dutch motorway traffic tended to be. Nothing like the nightmare back home.

He glanced up and down along the road once more. No sign of any suspicious-looking vehicle. He wondered where Villiger had got to. He turned to look out over the IJsselmeer. Behind him, was the raised bank of the dyke that kept out the Waddenzee, beyond which was the crescent barrier of the Wadden Islands. Beyond those were the open waters of the North Sea. He had used a 1000 mm lens to give him unusual shots of Texel, the largest, some 24 kilometers away. The day was bright and clear, and the surface of the water was like an ever moving mirror. He had used black and white film with a strong yellow filter. The results he was sure, would satisfy his clients.

He had changed to a color film and a zoom lens for the shots he wanted of the IJsselmeer. He raised the camera to look through the viewfinder at Lorraine Mowbray. She was standing with her back to him, down below at the end of a small, narrow, T-shaped pier. It was bordered by pristine white guardrails and at the edge of the T, six white-topped posts had been driven into the bed of the inland sea, three to each arm. Lorraine Mowbray stood close to one, her arms folded, her bag hanging from her right shoulder. A gentle breeze fanned her hair over to the right and was just strong enough to bare part of her neck.

Gallagher decided he'd start the roll with a few shots of her. She had been very accommodating, all things considered, and had neither got in his way, nor had she once complained as he had trekked from one side of the dyke to the other, looking for the shot he thought would work.

She turned just as he triggered the first series of five. Her eyes zeroed upon him in the same instant and he saw the alarm in them. He had zoomed to 210 mm and could see her expression clearly.

Then she was rushing off the pier toward him.

What the hell, he thought as he stopped. He glanced quickly about him. Had she seen something?

Ample parking facilities had been provided on either side of the dyke and the general area had been turned into an observation point, complete with a tower next to the walkway. Two short flights of concrete steps led down to the car park where he'd left the *quattro*. His eyes found the white flagpole from which flew the Dutch national tricolor. It stood directly before the nose of the car. He had chosen to park there deliberately so that from any position, he could find the *quattro* swiftly. There was no one next to it.

He turned to look for Lorraine Mowbray. She was now hurrying up the steps. Breathing hard, she rushed up to him, translucent eyes wide with a strange fear, the skin at their outer corners showing palely.

"How could you be so stupid!" she said to him, only just managing to keep her voice low. A few other cars were parked on either side of the road and their occupants were sauntering about. "Did you just take my picture?"

"Why the big drama? I was merely . . ."

"So stupid!" she repeated, interrupting him. "I don't want my picture taken."

Gallagher glanced about him. There were quite a few cameras being used. "Any one of these people could have included you in a shot."

She shook her head. "I made sure. I moved out of the way each time."

"What about the ones I just took? Someone else could have been focusing on you while your back was turned."

Again, she shook her head. "You were the only one. You were quicker than they normally are."

He knew what was giving her so much anxiety.

"Do you think I'm going to hand photos of you around? I do my own developing and printing. No one's going to see them."

She was not convinced.

"I was setting up a new roll of film," he went on, "and I thought you looked good in the shot . . ."

"No," she said. "No pictures."

"Anyone following you in Amsterdam could have taken a picture of you," he said reasonably. "What's the difference? At least you know I have no hostile motive . . ."

"No," she said again.

"Fine," Gallagher said with weary resignation. Before she could make further comment, he opened up the camera and removed the offending roll of film. "Here," he continued, handing her the cassette with its exposed shots now fogged. "Be my guest." He turned away and squatted on his heels to get another roll from his equipment case.

She stood uncertainly, staring at the ruined length of film. "Can't you use the rest? I . . . I don't want to spoil all of it."

"It's only a roll of film," Gallagher said as he reloaded the Nikon. "I've got plenty more." He squeezed the body shut and the camera whirred to the first frame. He stood up. "I'll soon be finished, then we'll be on our way."

He moved past her and went down the steps to road level, conscious that she was staring after him, the exposed film still in her hand. Another flight of steps led down the tight-packed slope of the dyke to the loose grouping of broken rocks at the water's edge. White swans lined the rocks, hunting for food in the shallows. Close by, a more enterprising pair were coasting to and fro in regal splendor, hoping to con a teenaged couple into feeding them.

Gallagher thought the swans might be a good subject. While he waited for the boy and the girl to leave, he looked about him every so often, checking each new face he saw. At last, the teenagers left without succumbing to them, and the birds now looked upon Gallagher as a possible soft touch. They came closer, filling the viewfinder nicely.

He'd triggered off a lengthy sequence when he heard footsteps behind him. He stopped to look around. Lorraine Mowbray. She was still holding on to the ruined film.

"You can chuck that away," he said. "It's no good now. And if you're worried that someone might come along and somehow manage to get a print out of it. Forget it. There's a bin by the car."

The eyes were seemingly fixed upon him. "Did you really think it was a good picture?"

He found that a strange question, given her earlier attitude. He nodded. "Yes."

"I'm sorry."

"What for?"

"That I ruined it. I'll pay for the film."

Gallagher shook his head slowly. "You do take some understanding. Do you know that?"

"You're not so easy yourself."

Gallagher looked at the swans who were still hopeful, then again at her. "I can afford the film. Time to leave. I'm finished here."

"I'd like to get back to Amsterdam," she said as they started back up the steps.

"We'll have to make contact with Villiger first."

She glanced at her watch. "There's a number I can call, in one hour."

He stared at her. "Why didn't you tell me about this before?"

She did not reply.

"Great," he said.

They made it to the car in silence. The rubbish bin was next to the flagpole and with seeming reluctance, she lifted the lid briefly to drop the spoiled film into it. Then she climbed into the *quattro,* which Gallagher had already unlocked.

He glanced about him before entering. There were now more parked cars than when they had first arrived, many with non-Dutch plates. He saw nothing to cause him alarm.

"Let's find you a telephone," he said to her as he got behind the wheel.

De Vries had come to the end of the motorway at Bemmel, near Nijmegen. He skirted Bemmel, drove through the small towns of Gendt and Doornenburg on the Waal canal. He was heading eastward, in the direction of Pannerden. Out of Doornenburg, the road he had taken abruptly ended. He had come to the Pannerdens canal. A small, open ferry laden with cars was approaching. Other cars were waiting to be taken across.

De Vries quickly took Zamba's sunglasses which were in the glove compartment of the BMW and put them on the corpse. No one bothered to look into the car, nor give it more than a cursory glance. De Vries sat calmly at the wheel as the ferry beached and the cars drove off. He remained calm when it was his turn to board. Again, no one paid him undue attention.

As the ferry set off, a youth came up to the car to collect the fare. De Vries paid for himself and the corpse. The young man glanced at Zamba's reclined body.

"Your friend finds our sun too hot," he said to de Vries jokingly in Dutch.

De Vries smiled knowingly and made a drinking sign with his hand. "Too much *genever* last night."

"Ah," the other said in understanding. "That explains it. He looks like death. Not many foreigners can handle our little drink."

"You're right there."

The youth nodded and with a friendly wave, moved to another car.

De Vries glanced down at the body. "Man," he said. "You should not drink so much." He smiled again. "You look like death."

The crossing was completed without further incident and he drove out of Pannerden along a road that skirted several small lakes. He decided he had come far enough when he saw one that looked a good kilometer long. He stopped the car and studied the water.

The road was on a high dyke, and was totally deserted. To his left, a steep track went down to the water, but between the base of the dyke and the lake itself, was an expanse of flat sandy ground. Here, the track widened, but was bordered by acres of tough, stunted grass. Within the lake itself, were small low-lying islands, some with tree stumps that had grown tufts of foliage. A mild breeze teased at them, giving the impression of hair being blown sideways.

"I've found you a resting place, Zamba," de Vries remarked softly as he took the BMW down the track.

He drove slowly along the edge of the water until he came to a spot where he thought it looked deep enough. There were plenty of underwater nooks and crannies to trap the body. He stopped the car broadside on, with the passenger side toward the lake. He climbed out, and looked about him. He was completely alone.

Working quickly, he opened the passenger door, released the seat belt and hauled the body unceremoniously out and rolled it into the water. The ground was low here and Zamba went in with hardly a splash. His body floated briefly and as the clothes became waterlogged, it began to sink.

De Vries watched with the calm of a surgeon studying his handiwork. The body sank lower until, a good meter beneath the surface, it began to move rapidly downward at an angle. De Vries saw why. The lake was not totally enclosed but was in fact a spill off from a tributary. Perhaps of the Rhine, he thought. Whatever it was, it seemed to be helping him. The body was caught in a fast moving undertow and was swept beneath an overhang. It did not reappear.

"Couldn't be better," he murmured.

Satisfied, he got into the BMW and drove slowly back to the road. Throughout, no one had turned up to observe him. Pleased with himself, he eventually joined the A12 motorway at Zevenaar. His route back to Amsterdam would take him via Apeldoorn. Once in the city, there were a couple of finishing touches he'd be adding to the sudden disappearance of his erstwhile colleague.

"And if they ask back home why I did it," de Vries said to himself, "I'll tell them you had spent too long in Europe, Zamba, man. You mixed with the wrong people and they gave you a lot of biased propaganda. Your head began to turn. You were getting ideas above your station." He grinned without humor. "They'll understand. We've lost people that way before."

De Vries began to hum tunelessly.

7

Gallagher had continued along the Afsluitdijk until about halfway, where an exit curved over the road to join the opposite carriageway. He had taken it to head back toward Amsterdam. There was a petrol station on the dyke where he felt sure there would have been a telephone, but he had not wanted to linger there. Instead, he had continued toward Den Oever and had found another petrol station about two kilometers along from that exit.

He was now sitting in the *quattro,* watching as Lorraine Mowbray made her call to Villiger. He hoped Villiger would find some way of picking her up. He did not intend to go all the way back to Amsterdam just because she needed to get the rest of her gear.

She was looking at him and beckoning urgently.

Gallagher got out of the car and joined her at the telephone. She thrust the receiver at him.

"He wants to speak to you." Her expression gave nothing away.

Then the phone was suddenly in his hand and

she was moving out of earshot. Something had clearly displeased her.

He put the phone to his ear. "Gallagher."

"Ah, Gordon," Villiger's voice began. "I need your help. I can't stay long to discuss it. It's got to be a yes."

"I don't like the sound of this."

"Man, I wouldn't ask if I had a choice. This is not what we discussed earlier. It's to do with your friend's bosses. Something very serious is going wrong. I want you to stay with Lorraine . . ."

"What. Piet, for God's sake . . ."

"Don't use my name!"

"I'm sorry. Silly mistake. But I wasn't expecting this. I can't take her in tow . . ."

"You must. I'll be in touch later, if I can . . ."

"If you can?" Gallagher was decidedly unhappy. "Don't do this to me."

"Stay with Lorraine," Villiger repeated firmly. "Have you got a gun?"

"A gun? What the hell would I want with a gun? That's it. I'm out of here. Send someone to pick her up."

"You can't just leave her there."

"And why not?" Gallagher found he was beginning to shout.

"She's in danger."

"But I thought . . ." Gallagher stopped to stare furiously at the phone. The line had gone dead.

Villiger had hung up.

Gallagher slammed the receiver back down. *"Sod it!"* he snarled at the machine.

He went back to the car, his expression, while not hostile, showing little friendliness. Lorraine

Mowbray was standing next to the partially opened passenger door, looking uncertain.

"Get in," he said roughly. "I'm taking you, against my better judgment, back to Amsterdam to collect your things. Then we're leaving Holland, though God knows where we'll be headed. I'll have to think on the move. Bang goes my bloody assignment, damn it! I've got my clients to think of, you know."

She entered wordlessly and he sent the *quattro* rocketing away, almost before she'd finished clipping on her seat belt.

She stared at him, but remained silent.

The *quattro* roared down the motorway toward Amsterdam.

They had traveled for nearly thirty minutes in silence before she decided to speak.

"He talked a lot about you," she said. "Mainly about how he respected you. You're one of the few people he seems to trust. He took a great risk coming to Europe since officially, he's supposed to be in the bush. If you had asked him to do you a favor, he would have done it."

Gallagher said nothing. She may be in some danger as Villiger had indicated; but it did not necessarily mean Villiger trusted her. Gallagher wanted to say he would not have asked Villiger to lead a squadron of dubiously acquired fast jets on clandestine missions in Africa. Some "favor."

"I'm doing one for him right now," he told her. "I'm looking after you."

"With as much bad grace as you can muster."

"You're hardly all sweetness and light," he retorted.

That brought another fifteen minutes of silence from her and it was not until they were approaching the Amsterdam Noord exit that she said: "He told me about Lauren. I'm sorry."

Taken by surprise, Gallagher took a quick look at her. She was staring out of her window. She was certainly a difficult woman to read. Why had she chosen to speak of Lauren at that particular moment?

He said: "Thank you." What else could he say to something like that? But part of him resented her mentioning it. Since Rhiannon's departure to the States, unwanted memories had found it easier to invade his mind; but though he missed Rhiannon as badly now as when she had first gone, he could live with it. Visions of Lauren were altogether a different matter. How do you lay such a ghost?

Lorraine Mowbray was looking at him. "You didn't like my mention of her name."

"Is it that obvious?"

"You don't look pleased. I'm sorry."

"You've nothing to be sorry about. You were not responsible for what happened."

There was a pause before she said: "I'm glad Piet told me. It helps me to understand you."

Gallagher again felt he had been caught on the hop. There was simply no telling which tack she would choose to take. "Why do you feel you need to understand me?"

"It's always better to try and understand others."

"Was that a not so subtle dig at me?"

She shook her head slowly. "Everyone's guilty of not trying hard enough at one time or another. I

know I am . . . and so are you. Turn here," she added.
   They were now back in the city.

De Vries' route after Apeldoorn had taken him past
Amersfoort where he turned off the motorway at
Bunschoten. Using the back roads, he had found
himself on a deserted bank of a small river that
emptied itself into the Eemeer, south of Flevoland.
There, he had taken Zamba's conveniently remov-
able radio and had thrown it into the water. As he
now headed back to the city, there was just one more
touch to add when he dumped the car.
   For that, he would have to wait until it was quite
dark.

Gallagher stopped the *quattro* a short distance from
the small hotel. From his position, he had an unrestricted view of the entrance. He toyed with the idea
of waiting for her in the car, then decided against it.
He locked the *quattro* after he'd followed her out,
using the remote; then he accompanied her to the
hotel.
   "What's the matter?" she asked. "Don't you
trust me?"
   "I don't trust someone not to be waiting to give
you a rough welcome in your room."
   She looked at him as if she didn't believe it, but
made no objection.
   "As we're going to cross borders," he continued,
"what passport do you carry?"
   "British," she replied, without looking around.
   "What else?" he said drily.
   "I've got relatives in England," she said, a little
defensively.
   "How convenient."

She still did not look around, but the sudden stiffening of her body told him what she thought of his comment.

In the event, no one was waiting in her room, and nothing had been disturbed. Whatever the suspected danger, it had clearly not yet reached that far. Gallagher wondered whether Villiger had conned him into remaining involved, no matter how tenuously. It was not a thought that gave him pleasure.

Commendably, she traveled lightly, and had soon packed her two expensive travel bags of rich leather. He thought they were a giveaway in such an unpretentious hotel, but said nothing. She was obviously not very good at undercover work.

Gallagher gave a mental sigh and again wished Villiger had not lumbered him.

"Right," he now said to her. "Are we ready?" He picked up the bags.

"I can manage," she began, reaching for them.

He moved away. "This is not the time to start playing the I-can-carry-my-bags game. Let's get out of here. I'll go to the car while you settle your bill."

He walked out of the room without waiting for her response to his words. Sod it, he thought. Now I'm babysitting.

It was coming up to 2010 hours when Prinknash stamped on the brakes of the Mercedes, nearly causing another car to slam into the back. A furious pounding of horns greeted his sudden action as the following motorist swerved past. It was about forty-five minutes to sunset.

"Mr. Haslam!" Prinknash shouted.

Haslam, who had been severely jolted by the

abrupt halt, was in a foul mood. "Prinknash . . ." he began ominously, then stopped when he saw the target of the younger man's pointing finger.

"I told you he'd be back," Prinknash said, trying hard not to sound smug. He failed.

More horns had taken up the chorus.

"I'd pull into the side if I were you," Haslam advised. "Unless you want the fastest course in Dutch swear words." He stared at the *quattro* thoughtfully as Prinknash moved the Mercedes safely to the side of the road.

A passing car gave an outraged blare for good measure.

"Shut your face!" Prinknash snarled at the driver who neither heard, nor cared.

Haslam was thoughtful as he said: "Gallagher would not have returned unless he had a very good reason. Much as I have to admit you appear to have been correct, I do not believe it was for the reasons you gave. Something forced him back." The Mercedes was neatly parked, ten cars behind the black Audi. "Let's wait here for a while."

Barely a minute had passed before Prinknash again spoke. "Look, Mr. Haslam," Prinknash had whispered.

"He can't hear you," Haslam said. He had given up expecting Prinknash to stop calling him by his real name.

They watched as Gallagher approached the *quattro* with the two bags.

"They can't be his," Prinknash observed. "What's he doing out here, anyway? It's not the kind of hotel he would use, a bloke like that."

"How do you know?" Haslam challenged.

"Well . . . look at his car . . . and that hotel he used . . . well, it's not like him . . ."

"Prinknash," Haslam began wearily, "stop talking such bullshit. You know nothing about Gallagher. He's stayed in more fleapits than you've had hot dinners. When it comes to predicting his actions, the best advice I can give you is don't. Gallagher never does what's expected. That's why he's so good."

But Prinknash was off on his own, wrapped in his theories. "Well, well. The lucky, jammy sod. He gets rid of one woman and just look at what he's been hiding. She's bloody tasty. My God." He watched admiringly as Lorraine Mowbray went to the Audi and got in. "Some people have all the luck. What's a woman like that doing in such a hole, anyway?"

"Just what I was thinking," Haslam said, getting quickly out of the car.

Prinknash was staring at him, peering across to look up. "Mr. Haslam . . ."

"Just stay where you are." And Haslam was hurrying toward the *quattro*.

Gallagher had just started the engine when Haslam appeared at his side of the car. He pressed the switch to lower the window halfway.

Haslam said: "You're getting rusty. I could have been someone with a gun."

"I spotted you as soon as I came back into the street," Gallagher said calmly. "The Mercedes was not there when we first arrived. I waited to hear what you've got to say."

Haslam gave a rueful twitch of the lips. "I might have known. Prinknash will be disappointed. He thought we had caught you out. So why are you back?" He leaned on the car to peer in. "Care to introduce me to the lovely young lady?"

"No."

"Well that was to the point."

"You know me."

"I know you may need our help."

"I doubt it."

"I thought you wanted to hear what I've got to say."

"I'm listening."

"No," Haslam said. "We ought to talk out of the car." He peered in again at Lorraine Mowbray. "Don't mind, do you, Miss? We won't be long." To Gallagher, he added: "Well?"

Gallagher thought about it for a few seconds, then he raised the window and turned off the engine.

He climbed out, taking the key with him. "A few minutes, Haslam. That's all. Okay. This is as far as we go."

Haslam had moved a few feet away.

Gallagher reached into the car, put the key into the ignition to turn it one notch. Then he removed the key.

"The player can be switched on," he said to her. "Put a cassette in. We won't be long."

As he joined Haslam, he saw her face looking back at him through the rear window, then she turned away and he saw her moving, searching for a cassette. Presently, the muted sounds of music came to him.

"She's not listening," Gallagher said to Haslam. "What's so interesting that you've got to tell me about it?"

"Have you ever heard of a man called Behrensen?"

"No. Next question."

"You should have. You're playing around in his pool."

"I don't see how you've reached that conclusion. How can I be playing in someone's pool, as you've put it . . . someone I don't even know?"

"If you were still with us, you'd know all about Behrensen."

"But I'm not still with you. Thank God."

"You're going to need us if you remain in this little game."

"I'm not in any game, Haslam. I'm minding my own business, as usual."

"Oh really," Haslam remarked, sounding unconvinced. "And the young lady? Is she, as Prinknash's lustful mind would have it, going on a romantic sojourn with you? Or could my own nasty suspicious mind be more on the right track?"

"Such as?"

"She's very much involved in what I'm talking about."

"With this . . . Behrensen?"

Haslam nodded.

"You're out of your mind," Gallagher said.

"Am I? Try asking her."

"About the state of your mind?"

Haslam smiled thinly. "Ever the wit, Gordon. Ask her about Behrensen. After all, you took one of his employees to the airport earlier today."

Gallagher could not hide his surprise. "Veronica? Nonsense."

"FUTRON."

"What?"

"She works for FUTRON."

"So?"

"FUTRON and Behrensen are one and the same."

"I thought that was a man called Becker."

Haslam gave a short laugh. "One of his many aliases."

Gallagher paused, then decided to throw in another name to see what would come up. "What about J. D. Quinlan?"

The effect was interesting. Haslam was staring at him. "You know of Quinlan?"

Ironic, Gallagher thought. Quinlan's name had had a similar effect on Villiger.

"Well, well," Gallagher said. "And you didn't even know he was with Behrensen or Becker or whoever."

"Oh we know who he is, and what he is. Are you still maintaining you know nothing about it?"

"Not 'maintaining.' I know nothing . . . which is exactly how I'd like it to remain."

Haslam looked even more unconvinced. He tried reason. "Look, Gordon. I'm not a schemer like Fowler. I'm telling you this for your own good. Get out of it. You don't want to tangle with either Quinlan, or Behrensen. At least, not without the kind of backup we could give you."

"Ah. Now it comes. First the warning, then the pitch. Help us, Gordon, and we'll give you all the muscle you need. No thanks, Haslam. Tell Fowler it didn't work. And for your information, I'm not involved. In fact, I'm doing all I can not to be. Pass that on to Fowler as well."

"It may surprise you to know that we were not sent here to reel you in . . ."

"It does surprise . . ."

"I can be as cynical with the best of them," Haslam said. "I can beat you at cynicism . . ."

"Oh yes?"

"I'm older for a start. I've seen more than you have." Haslam gave a loud sigh. "Still, if you won't take my first piece of advice, perhaps you'll take this one . . . get a gun. You'll need it."

Gallagher stared at him. "That's the second person to mention guns to me today."

"Do I know this paragon of commonsense? I don't suppose you'd care to tell me."

Gallagher looked at him silently.

"I didn't think so," Haslam remarked drily. "I'll give you something for free. Behrensen and Quinlan are major sharks in the world of clandestine armament sales. They seem able to supply highly sensitive equipment; from electronics to . . . you name it. Even aircraft, I've been told. Sometimes, the equipment supplied may not even be on the standard military inventory, except perhaps on those used by specialist forces. Yet, they seem able to get clients, and to supply them."

"Somebody somewhere likes them."

"That's obvious enough. For people engaged in an ostensibly illegal trade, they do seem to enjoy an amazing degree of freedom, while making a pile out of their activities."

Gallagher said: "War is hell, war is money. A lot of people worked that one out a long time ago. Whole economies run on it."

"Come on, Gordon," Haslam said. "You're not going to bleed all over me, are you?"

"Just letting you know I've got no cobwebs over my eyes."

"We'd like to know why Behrensen and Quinlan

felt the need to contact you," Haslam said. "After all," he went on with some irony, "who knows better than the Department how capable you really are? You wouldn't be thinking of going into the business as a sort of . . . er . . . private enterprise, would you?"

Gallagher gave a smile that possessed little humor. "Do you mean it would let the side down? Don't worry, Haslam. You can be assured that neither Behrensen/Becker, nor Quinlan, have asked me to do anything for them."

"But someone else may have." Haslam glanced meaningfully at the *quattro*. Lorraine Mowbray seemed engrossed in the music.

"You're floundering," Gallagher said. He took a quick look at his watch.

"Anxious to go somewhere?" Haslam's tone was needling.

Gallagher did not rise to it. He glanced up at the darkening sky. Already, the city lights were coming on.

"I've got some more shots to take before the light's gone completely."

Haslam did his own glancing around. "Got cameras that see in the dark, have we?"

"You know how it is. Modern technology can do anything these days." Gallagher began moving toward the car. "I wouldn't try to follow."

Haslam remained where he stood. "I won't," was his dry comment. He looked briefly at the waiting Mercedes. "Not in that anyway."

Gallagher had reached the driver's door. He paused to look at Haslam. "Thanks for the other night."

"All part of the service. I suppose it's no good telling you to watch your step."

"I always watch my step," Gallagher said, and climbed in.

He started the engine and as the *quattro* moved away, he saw in the mirrors that Haslam was still standing where he had left him.

On the stereo, *Mainstreet* was playing. Lorraine Mowbray said nothing to him as the car headed out of Amsterdam.

The song came to an end and she stopped the music, but chose not to speak.

Their silence lasted for a good half hour before she said: "Have you decided where we're going?"

"Yes," he answered. "Belgium. There's a little place in Bruges where we'll stay for a day or so till we hear from Piet."

It had become properly dark during the past few minutes and the motorway traffic was sparse enough to leave long distances between vehicles. They were making good time. Gallagher kept a constant watch in his mirrors. Haslam had said he would not follow; but that did not mean no one else would.

"And after?"

"After what?"

"After we've been to Belgium."

The red glow from the digital display of the instrument panel shifted upon his face as he glanced at her. "You're asking *me*? I'm hoping Piet will come up with some answers."

She retreated into another of her silences as the *quattro* roared deeply into the night toward Rotterdam. Gallagher had decided to take that particular route to Antwerp, from where he'd make for Bruges. He saw nothing in the mirrors to excite his interest. He hoped it would remain so.

After a while, Lorraine Mowbray began to fidget in her seat. Gallagher left her to it, taking pleasure in the powerful tremor of the car as its fat wheels sped over the dark surface of the road. When he needed to think, when pressures were put upon him, the open road and the subdued thunder of the car served to relax him. Tonight, however, a disturbed spirit was with him. Total relaxation would not be his.

"What's up?" he was eventually forced to ask.

She took some time before replying. "I wish I could have made contact with Hennie. He'll be wondering what's happened to me."

"No contact," Gallagher said. "That's the rule as long as you're with me. What you do afterwards will be your own affair. Besides, I'm sure Villiger will have made arrangements. Your Hennie will know you're safe."

"My Hennie?"

"The way you talk about him makes me think he's more than just another member of the team."

She seemed to give that more thought. He sensed she was looking at him, so he glanced at her. In the gloom of the car, the pale eyes had an eerie glow.

"I've known him for years," she said. "That's all. He's had a rough time back home for his beliefs. He's colored, although you wouldn't think so at first. Bloody shit!" she said with sudden anger.

"What?" Gallagher queried, startled by her vehemence. "Your good friend Hennie Marais?"

"No, no. The bloody shit situation back home. The bloody system that perverts people, turning them from decent human beings into . . ." She paused, as if choosing what she wanted to say with great care. "What kind of system takes pleasure in categorizing people like laboratory animals . . ." She paused a second time, her emotions apparently getting the better of her.

Gallagher once again found himself intrigued by yet another of her transformations.

"Hennie can't go back," she said, more quietly now. "Piet and I can. They don't know about us as yet."

Don't be too sure about that, Gallagher thought grimly, keeping his opinions to himself. Villiger could tell her.

"All he wanted was a quiet life. Now . . ."

"If he wants a quiet life," Gallagher began, "he's on the wrong planet."

She was staring at him once more. "Is that all you can say? Don't you have any feelings about *any*thing?" Then she seemed to remember Lauren. "I'm . . . I'm sorry. I shouldn't have said that. It . . . it was uncalled for . . ."

"Don't lose sleep over it."

He had spoken more harshly than he'd intended and the result was another sudden end to all conversation.

The *quattro* sped into the night, carrying their strained silence toward Antwerp.

In Amsterdam, Haslam was again on the consulate phone to Fowler.

"You must be getting quite popular by now, George," Fowler was saying.

"They're not exactly brimming over with joy. I think they'd prefer it if they never saw me again."

Haslam could imagine the fleeting smile as

Fowler said in his calm voice: "Don't take it too hard. They think we're the glamor boys."

The sound Haslam made could have been one of disgust. "They're welcome to swap places."

"Why do you think he returned to Amsterdam?" The conversation had gone back to Gallagher.

Haslam said: "I can make an educated guess . . ."

"Your educated guesses are usually better than most people's certainties, George. So give."

"I think he's been asked to join."

"By whom? This new young woman?"

"Possibly."

"But would he? Doesn't sound like him. He prefers to be left alone, as we know only too well. She'd have to be very convincing. He wouldn't do it for the money . . . especially not now he's become rather wealthy."

"Perhaps she wasn't the one," Haslam remarked thoughtfully.

"Then why is she with him?"

"Contact. No other reason that I can think of at the moment."

"And now you have no idea where they could be."

"Shouldn't be too difficult to find out. His car's hardly inconspicuous."

"No, George. We don't want outsiders in on this. Never know who might have links. It's got to be the hard way. You'll have to find them all by yourselves."

Haslam sighed. "Remind me to get you a birthday present."

"I never celebrate birthdays."

"Lucky for you," Haslam said with feeling.

"George, George," Fowler said soothingly.

"As I'm struck with this, I need a decent car. I want accounts clearance for whatever I want to hire, or I'm going to sit in this city until you send one of our cars out."

"Hire anything you want. If it suffers a few unfortunate shunts, we'll cover that too."

Haslam thought about it. "I ought to be worried. You're not even complaining."

"This is too important, George. Find him, and talk some sense into him."

"I've already tried."

"You'll just have to try again." Fowler hung up.

Haslam stared at the phone. "I should be drawing my pension, for God's sake!" He put down the receiver just as the duty officer entered the small room.

"All going well?" the man queried brightly.

"Of course it isn't," Haslam told him roughly. "Haven't you been in long enough to know that by now? It's a one percent game."

"One percent?"

"Yes. Ninety-nine percent of the time it's a right cock-up." Haslam went irritably out of the room.

The younger man stared briefly at the phone, then at the departing shape. He looked around the room then left, shutting the door quietly behind him. He was not paid to wonder what was going on.

It was none of his business.

De Vries had decided it was well enough into the night to carry out the final part of the deception about Zamba's death. He had parked the BMW in the Warmoestraat where inside various establishments, pleasure was up for sale and for grabs. Music from the small darkened bars competed with each other. It was perfect for his requirements.

He climbed out of the car. No one bothered to look at him. Those passing by were too busy with their own plans for the evening. He leaned against the car and placed a small, spring-loaded punch gently against a quarterlight. The punch looked like a toy pistol.

De Vries waited until a car had gone slowly past then while the sound of its exhaust was still loud, fired the punch against the glass. The quarterlight crystallized with a barely discernible noise. De Vries struck at it with a denim-clothed elbow. The crystals fell into the BMW, leaving a gaping hole.

He put the punch into a pocket and walked unhurriedly away. Anyone noticing the shattered glass would assume yet another vehicle had been broken into for its radio. It happened all the time.

De Vries wiped the punch carefully and quickly when he came upon a litter bin in a dark side street. He dropped the punch into it, and strolled calmly away.

By the time the forces of law and order managed to work out what had happened, he'd be back in South Africa, his real job completed.

He smiled at the thought.

Haslam said: "Let's go back to that little hotel where we saw Gallagher."

Prinknash was surprised. "But Mr. Haslam, he's not going to return . . ."

"Humor me. Let's go." Haslam's tone brooked no further argument. "If you can't find your way back, I'll direct you."

Prinknash complied silently.

When they'd got there, Haslam said: "Pull in just here." And when Prinknash had obeyed, went on: "Now we wait."

"For what?"

"For something to turn up. And turn off the lights, for pity's sake." Haslam sighed. "You don't have to broadcast our presence."

Prinknash, who was seriously wondering whether Haslam had finally lost his marbles, said nothing as he switched off.

They waited for nearly an hour, watching people and traffic go by. Prinknash, increasingly coming to the conclusion that they were wasting their time, began to look sulky. Haslam gave him expressionless glances from time to time, but said nothing. Another fifteen minutes passed.

Then a dark-colored Golf GTI pulled up before the hotel with a soft squeal. A young man in a pale suit and open-necked shirt climbed out. He locked the car with some care, and entered the hotel. Soon, he was back out. He reentered the car, but made no move to drive off.

"It would appear," Haslam began softly, "that he's waiting for something, or someone. Let's see if it's anybody we might know."

Ten minutes.

The man in the pale suit was out of the Golf again. He entered the hotel once more, this time without bothering to lock the car. When he came out for the second time, he was clearly anxious. He climbed back into the Golf. Minutes later, the engine started.

"Follow him," Haslam ordered.

Still not convinced this had anything to do with Gallagher, Prinknash obeyed silently.

They tracked the Golf to another small hotel. The journey took fifteen minutes through reasonably traffic-free streets. Prinknash had stayed well back so as not to alert their quarry. They waited inconspicuously as the target car was parked and the man entered the hotel. They settled down to wait.

After about five minutes, Haslam said: "Grab a taxi and go back to our hotel. It's not far. Pick up our things and check us out, then come back here. If I'm gone, go to the Consulate. I'll be in touch. Remember the name of this hotel so that you can tell the taxi driver. And don't attempt to speak Dutch to him. Everyone speaks English." He climbed out, in preparation for getting behind the wheel.

"But . . ."

"Don't argue, Prinknash," Haslam interrupted mildly. "Just do it."

A moment's hesitation, and Prinknash got reluctantly out of the Mercedes. A taxi came soon after. Within twenty minutes he was back, openly relieved to find Haslam still on station. He dumped their bags on the back seat while Haslam went back to the passenger side. Prinknash got in.

Less than five minutes after his return the man, carrying a small bag, dashed out of the building and almost entered the Golf at a run. It set off with a churning squeal of rubber.

"After him!" Haslam barked. "And whatever you do, don't lose him!" He glanced at the fuel gauge. "At least we've got plenty of petrol. I just wish we had more power in this thing. We'll change it tomorrow."

"Where are we going?" Prinknash asked.

"Wherever he goes."

"And where do we sleep tonight?"

"In the car if necessary. Just you make sure you don't lose him." Haslam added wistfully: "I should be drawing my pension. Instead . . ."

Prinknash would not leave it. "But Mr. Haslam . . . what if we're chasing him for nothing?"

"Let me worry about that, shall we? Concentrate on keeping that Volkswagen in your sights."

Prinknash finally gave in and did as he was told. Before long, it became clear what the Golf was doing.

It was leaving Amsterdam.

The *quattro* was approaching the motorway bypass that ringed Antwerp. Throughout the journey so far, no shadowers had been detected. Gallagher had made a continuous, careful scrutiny of his mirrors. Taking the roundabout route via Rotterdam had enabled him to check whether they were being followed; but unless there had been some clever switching of cars, nothing of an alarming nature had occurred. He hoped it would continue to remain so.

He had stopped only once, to make a call to the hotel in Belgium to warn of their impending arrival, and to top-up the tank. He had also paid a visit to the lavatory. Unknown to him and during his brief absence, Lorraine Mowbray had rushed to a telephone to make a call.

As they now took the Antwerp ring road, a totally unaware Gallagher said: "We're on the home stretch now."

Instead of continuing on the motorway to Bruges, he joined the N49 which would take them on a more direct route to Knokke-Heist on the Belgian coast. From there he intended to go through to Zeebrugge before heading back to Bruges. The convoluted routing was deliberate. It was unlikely that another motorist would be making exactly the same journey. There were several other, shorter routes. It would give him the opportunity to smoke out a tail, if one were indeed in place. Traffic was so sparse at that time of night, the road both ahead and behind was devoid of any other vehicle. A possible tail would be a virtual beacon in the darkness.

"You seem to know your way around," Lorraine Mowbray remarked a while later. The long night drive seemed to have mellowed her. She had become almost friendly.

"Zeebrugge and Ostend are two very busy ferry ports for the UK. I've been up and down different routes to them for more times than I care to remember."

The timer on the instrument panel said 00.30.

"Will the hotel still be open?" she asked after she had leaned over to check.

"It's a small place, but someone will be waiting to let us in. Don't let its size fool you. It's very comfortable indeed. More like a small mansion. I know the owners. You'll be alright there until Piet lets me know what he's up to."

No one followed them to Zeebrugge and nothing of interest showed in the mirrors as they doubled back to Bruges. It was just after one o'clock in the morning when the *quattro* rumbled into the enclosure of the hotel courtyard. An electronically operated steel gate whirred softly down to seal it from the outside world.

After they had booked in, they went straight to their rooms. Neither was particularly hungry and so were not bothered by the fact that the kitchen had long since been shut down. In each room, was the usual minibar and small fridge, filled with a selec-

tion of alcoholic and nonalcoholic drinks. Gallagher
went to the fridge and took out a well-chilled bottle
of orange juice. As he opened it, a soft knock
sounded.

He shut the fridge and still carrying the bottle,
went to open the door. Lorraine Mowbray stood
there, an already opened bottle of Coke in her hand.

"Care for a nightcap?" she greeted. The pale
eyes were enigmatic.

He stood aside for her to enter. "Satisfied with
your room?" he asked as he shut the door.

She nodded. "Yes, thanks. You were right. This
is a nice place."

He went over to the minibar. "Glasses? Or will
you drink out of the bottle?"

"It's late. Save the glasses." She put the bottle
to her mouth to take a drink.

"In that case," Gallagher said, "please take a
seat."

She chose to sit on the edge of the wide bed.
Gallagher sat down next to her. They clinked their
bottles.

"You are in a good mood," he observed.

"I felt a bit mean for being so difficult," she said.
"So I've come to make peace."

"I'll drink to that." They clinked bottles again,
and drank. "If it's a nice day tomorrow . . . or rather,
later today . . ." Gallagher went on, "I'd like to go to
Ostend. There's a fine old pier out there that would
make a good subject for a photo session . . ."

"So you're still working."

"Until we hear from Piet, we'll have time on our
hands. I'd like to make good use of it . . . if you don't
mind putting up with . . ."

"I don't mind," she said quickly. "Really," she

added, noting his skepticism. "I've always heard about Bruges," she went on. "Can we have a look around later?"

"Okay with me. We can do that after Ostend. When do you have to make contact?"

"At four, but from a public phone."

"That won't be a problem. Lots of phones all over the place."

They finished their drinks.

She got to her feet. "Bedtime for me. See you for breakfast?"

He stood up and followed her to the door. "I'll come and collect you. You're perfectly safe here, but lock your door all the same . . . as a matter of routine."

"Do you? Always?"

"Always."

She smiled at him. "Goodnight."

"Goodnight, Lorraine." It was a nice smile, he thought.

Her room was next to his. He watched as she went to her door and was safely inside. He waited to hear the lock click home, before closing his own and locking it. He went over to a window which looked directly onto the courtyard. Floodlights were on, bathing the area within the high walls. A definite plus, he felt. There were two other cars there: one with UK license plates, the other from Luxemburg. They had been there when he'd arrived. Unless someone scaled the wall, there was no way that anyone on the search was going to find out where the car was bedded for the night. Satisfied, he began to get ready for bed.

Within five minutes, he was drifting into sleep.

* * *

In her room, Lorraine Mowbray lay on her bed and stared at the telephone on the small cabinet next to it. She reached out to place a thoughtful hand upon the instrument, leaving it there for long seconds. Then she withdrew the hand, moving it to the bedside lamp.

After another pause, she switched it off and settled down beneath the quilt. She'd make the call before going down to breakfast.

8

Gallagher rapped twice on the door. Inside the room, Lorraine Mowbray replaced the phone quietly.

Gallagher listened as the footsteps approached and the door was opened. Sunlight streamed through the windows.

"Hello," she greeted him cheerfully. "It looks like we're in for a fine day. You'll be able to get your photos."

"Sleep well?" He studied her appreciatively. In tight jeans and a loose white shirt, she looked good.

"Umm. Very well. The beds here are lovely. Now I'm hungry. Lead me to breakfast. I can smell some great coffee."

"Your wish is my command."

She gave him a sideways glance. "A good mood as well. Does that now mean we're really going to make a nice day of it?"

"It does indeed."

"That sounds promising." Another sideways glance. "Like what you see, do you?" It seemed to please her.

Thickly carpeted stairs took them to the ground floor where they made for the cozy breakfast room. The eight tables were laid, but only four were currently occupied. They were shown to a table next to a french window, which pleased Gallagher.

From his position, he had an unobstructed view of the courtyard, and of the parked cars. The roller door had been raised, and a couple of newcomers had joined the throng: a black Mercedes 190E with German plates, and a Belgian-registered Renault.

He glanced at his fellow diners. Two middle-aged couples, and a family group needing a pair of tables to accommodate them. Nothing to worry about there. He wondered briefly about other guests who were still to come down, but decided he'd just have to wait and see what transpired, and act accordingly.

Breakfast was enjoyable, and without incident. Gallagher made a thorough check of their rooms afterward, but there was nothing to worry about. The cleaners were at work in other rooms and the sounds of their machines filled the small corridor. They worked with the doors open.

Gallagher knew them by sight, but when it was time to go down to the car, he made certain he took everything with him and instructed Lorraine Mowbray to do the same. While he thought it unlikely that anyone interested in their whereabouts would have found the hotel so soon, there was no point in being complacent. He checked the rooms again, just to make sure.

At ten o'clock, the *quattro* moved slowly with the traffic along the one-way system of the Smedenstraat. Just ahead was the Smeden Poort, a small fortlike building that straddled the road. Because of its narrow arch, the road was just big enough for cars to pass singly. As a result, there were traffic lights on either side. The lights were against Gallagher.

He came to a stop, fourth in the line of waiting vehicles, checked his mirrors and saw a dark blue Golf sliding in, eight cars behind. He gave it no more attention than the others.

The lights changed. He followed the cars through the arch, the *quattro*'s exhaust echoing briefly within the little fort. A third set of lights were just ahead and Gallagher pulled over to the left, in preparation for a sharp turn that was almost doubling back on itself. He made a second check of the mirrors. The Golf had not come through in time to beat the change in the lights.

He got the green, but had to wait for oncoming traffic to pass. Just as he found a gap and accelerated around the tight turn, the lights again turned red, effectively baulking the Golf that had just come through the arch.

No, Gallagher thought. *It's coincidence. I'm being paranoid.*

Even so.

Gallagher continued to accelerate until the road fed into a wide thoroughfare that led to the motorway for Ostend. It was a long stretch with three sets of lights and each time, he was fortunate to get the green just before it turned red. At one stage, he thought he saw the blue Golf at one of the lights; but after he had joined the motorway for the twenty-one-kilometer journey to Ostend, constant scrutiny of the mirrors showed no sign of it.

From time to time, Lorraine Mowbray had turned to look at him, but she had made no comment. As he now cruised along the Visserskaai toward the pier, he decided the Golf had been just another car going about its business. He also decided to remain alert; just in case.

"This is a good sign," he said. The bright, warm day had brought out a lot of people and cars. The seaside restaurants were full of diners having late breakfasts, and cars were having difficulty finding somewhere to park.

"What is?" she asked.

"The weather. Most of the time, whenever I've come across the channel, it's chucking it down. Water, water everywhere. But today, we've got the luck. You must have brought some of that African sun with you." He checked the mirrors.

"I've been watching you do that ever since we left Bruges," she said. "You've been studying those mirrors more frequently than I would have thought was necessary for normal driving. You don't think we've been followed all the way from Amsterdam, do you?"

"I take nothing for granted. First rule."

"You just said the weather was a good sign."

"It is. But that doesn't mean I think nothing can go wrong."

He turned right, off the Visserskaai, and onto the short cobbled lane that led to the harbor breakwater. His luck continued to be in. There was enough space among the parked cars for one more. He slotted the *quattro* neatly into place and turned off the engine. He climbed out, and began to get his camera gear from the back. Everything else was left in the boot. Lorraine Mowbray had also climbed out and was stretching contentedly in the warmth of the sun.

Gallagher paused to watch her appreciatively. She glanced at him just then, looking sideways at him from beneath a raised arm. The pale eyes were again enigmatic, but the lips smiled slightly. She lowered her arms and shut the door on her side of the car.

He had got all the equipment he needed. He shut his door and armed the remote. The tiny red lights came on within the black Audi.

"If anybody fancies his chances," he said to her, "the car will make enough noise to warn us, even at the end of the pier. Besides, the remote will shriek, as well as wink away with its warning light."

"You don't take chances, do you?"

"Not if I can help it."

"Have you never made a mistake?"

Gallagher looked at her thoughtfully, remembering O'Keefe who had died on a mission when Gallagher's jammed gun had failed to give covering fire in time. He remembered Lauren, too vividly for comfort.

"More than once," he replied. "Come on. Let's go."

The port of Ostend with its ferries, yacht basins and shrimp boats, bustled about them as they made their way toward the west pier. With its solid white-painted railings it curved, a great wooden road, toward the mouth of the harbor.

"Look," she said. "Someone else thinks this is a good place to take pictures."

He followed her gaze. Halfway along, was a group of people; three women in designer clothes, and three men with equipment he recognized all too easily.

"I wonder what sort of expenses they're charging," he said drily. "One will be the photographer

. . . the one doing all the work, although he may well have a poor assistant lurking about somewhere. One will be calling himself the creative manager. Another is probably a boyfriend who fancies himself as an agent, and there's bound to be a makeup lady somewhere . . ."

"There is. Look."

On the other side of the pier, a woman was coming up some steps that led down to the water. She went to one of the models who, as Gallagher and Lorraine drew nearer, appeared to be less than happy.

"They're going to have trouble with that one," Gallagher said.

"How do you know?"

"I've been there."

Even as he spoke, he gave each person a swift inspection. He felt no unease. A bona fide gathering then. No worries.

He relaxed imperceptibly as they moved past the group and carried on.

It was a longish walk and from time to time, Gallagher stopped to take a few shots of the harbor and the east pier. Toward its end, the west pier expanded tadpolelike to about three times its normal width. In the middle of this was a large, flat-roofed cabin in white, an island in a sea of wood. On a landward outer wall, were two blackboards, each with a chalked menu printed upon it.

Over to the left, was a parked Range Rover.

Gallagher paused. It was a different color from the one Villiger had used in Holland, and it was a Belgian registration.

I'm bloody jumpy, he thought. He stared at the Range Rover for a few seconds as if mesmerized. It was the first one he had seen since the meeting with Villiger.

"It's not his," Lorraine Mowbray said behind him.

"I know," Gallagher said.

They walked slowly around the café. There was a substantial number of people about, many having decided to dress as if for the beach. Around the building, several tables with parasols had been set out, a good number of which were occupied. Gallagher saw one that overlooked the shore.

"That one's free," he said to her. "Have a coffee, if you'd like, while I see if there's anything promising on the other side."

"Trying to get rid of me?"

"Something like that."

She smiled at him. "In that case, I'll wait here."

"I knew you'd understand."

"Be careful," she said. "We'll start liking each other."

"Can't have that," he said as he left.

He felt the pale eyes upon him as he moved away, but did not turn around. Directly in front of the café was the white tower of one of the harbor lights, standing at nearly forty feet. Beyond it, at the curved railing of the pier's end, were a few hopeful anglers. Then Gallagher saw a great plume of spray, fast approaching. The Jetfoil from Dover.

He got some good shots of it and the light tower, and felt that one or two might please the clients. He returned to the table, having decided he'd taken enough for his purposes.

"I'm still here," she said as he sat down.

"So I see."

A waitress came to take his order. He decided on

a coffee and a pancake. As the waitress went off, he heard a growing and familiar sound that made him look up.

A pair of Belgian Air Force F-16's were screaming in from the sea. He watched as they continued inland, holding a tight formation.

"The Beauvechain boys," he murmured, eyes following the receding dots.

"How do you know?" she asked, repeating a previous query.

"I know." He looked at her. The pale eyes seemed to be studying him intently.

"Why don't you admit it?" The eyes were challenging now.

"Admit what?"

"That you'd like to be up there with them. That's one of the reasons why Piet . . ."

"Oh no you don't," Gallagher interrupted. "It's not going to work." He glanced quickly around to make certain no one could eavesdrop.

"I could see it in your eyes. There was a longing . . ."

"There may well be, but it's not strong enough for what you want."

"We'd pay . . ." She stopped when she saw the look that had come into his eyes.

Further conversation was temporarily halted as the waitress returned with his order.

"If I did become involved in something like this," Gallagher said as the waitress left, "it wouldn't be for the money. Besides, I've got more than enough for my needs. I make a good living. If you're looking for a mercenary, you've come to the wrong person. *He* knows that. He wouldn't have offered me money." He began to eat his pancake.

"Have I offended you?" she asked.

He wasn't sure whether she was being sincere, so he did not reply immediately. Instead, he studied her closely. She had tilted her head slightly so that the sun caught the hair about her forehead, in a way that made it seem like a mass of fine golden threads. Though the perceptible hairline began high, wispy blonde strands began on the forehead itself, growing close to the skin and backward into the main body of hair. These strands were so delicate, that under normal lighting conditions they were virtually invisible. But now, the way the sun had caught them gave the impression that her brow was being lit from within.

"No," he said at last. "I cannot be offended by a remark I did not take seriously."

"What's wrong with my forehead?" she asked suddenly.

"What do you mean?"

"You're staring at it."

"It looks as if it's full of light."

"Is that a compliment?"

"I should say so."

She had begun to smile at him, then the quality of the smile changed into one of open pleasure. Pleasantly gratified by this, Gallagher basked in it until he realized she was looking past him. He turned to look, and saw a man with wavy blonde hair, dressed in a pale suit and open-necked shirt, approaching.

Looking at him, Gallagher was startled to find that had he not already been told by Lorraine Mowbray, he would never have imagined the newcomer to be colored. He felt an instant twinge of sympathy for the man who had been humiliatingly branded by his own society. It was obscene; an offense against common decency.

But Gallagher felt his sympathy evaporating. A growing anger was taking its place. What did Lorraine Mowbray think she was playing at? By the time the man had reached their table, Gallagher was furious. His eyes, when he'd turned back to her, left her in no doubt.

"Gordon," she began hesitantly, "this . . . this is . . ."

"Hennie Marais," Gallagher interrupted coldly, "and owner or driver of a dark blue Volkswagen Golf."

He stood up, seeing the surprise in her eyes, but feeling little satisfaction. He felt no better at seeing the same surprise mirrored in Marais' own eyes. Ignoring Marais, he took her by the arm, holding her so firmly, she began to rise involuntarily.

"You don't have to grab so tightly," she said in a tone of censure.

"There are a lot of things I don't have to do," he said tightly, "but if I told you, your ears would blister. Come on. We're going to have a little talk." To Marais, looking bemused and sheepish at the same time, he went on: "Excuse us for a few minutes, won't you? I'd like a few private words with your not-so-clever little friend."

"Don't patronize me!" she told him sharply.

People were beginning to look.

"Are we going to do this in a civilized manner?" he asked. "Or is it your intention to bare your secrets to the world on a Belgian pier?"

She pulled her arm away from him, turned to Marais and said, reluctantly: "We won't be long, Hennie. Wait here." She drew herself to her full height, raised her chin at Gallagher, sighting at him along her nose. "Let's get it over with."

Gallagher turned away from her and began moving between the tables. He came out of the tables and continued along the pier deck, heading for the light tower. She followed, barely in control of her own anger.

The anglers behind the tower had given up for the day or had changed to another fishing spot. Gallagher and Lorraine Mowbray had the place all to themselves.

She launched into the attack immediately. "That was very rude of you. Hennie . . ."

Gallagher's suddenly cold eyes stopped her. "Think what you like of me," he began, "but never take me for a fool. I was suspicious at first of the sudden change in your attitude. Care for a nightcap?" he mimicked. "She's learning, I thought. She wouldn't be planning anything as stupid as deliberately getting in contact after having been told not to. Do you think I don't know when you made that call? You had one opportunity when I went to the gents on the motorway, and several more at the hotel. I could have had your line disconnected, but I preferred to rely on your own sense of discretion. Instead, I've paid for that stupid mistake.

"What the hell did you think you were playing at? Don't bloody interrupt! I don't want an excuse, because you have no justification whatsoever for what you've done. If I spotted him so long before you let me in on your little secret, what do you think happened when he left Amsterdam? Was he still in Amsterdam? Well? *Was he?*"

"Yes," she answered grudgingly, after one of her silences. Her face was flushed with anger and embarrassment.

"More than likely," Gallagher went on, "he was

followed. God knows who by. But I can think of at least two different sets of people, one of which may well be the homicidal maniacs who are so determined to do whatever job they've come to do, they'll quite happily kill innocent taxi drivers, if convenience demands it. Has it occurred to you that they may well be after Piet Villiger?"

Her eyes widened.

"Oh God," Gallagher said in disgust. "You do need a bloody babysitter."

The eyes looked hurt. "Do you have to be so rude?"

"I'll be as rude as I like if it means I might stop you from getting your silly head shot off. More importantly, while I'm not prepared to join Piet's guerilla air force, I'm not going to let your headstrong incompetence get him assassinated . . ."

"But I've told you . . . no one knows he's here except me, and you, of course . . ."

"Don't put your shirt on it."

"I've told no one. Hennie doesn't know . . ."

"If what I've seen of him today is the best he can do, they'll probably take him out as soon as they're ready. Quite likely, he's only still alive because they think he can lead them to the really big fish. You've managed to leave a trail so clear, you might as well have lighted it. Before you make that call to Piet at four, you've got to sort your friend Hennie out. It's either that, or I leave you here to your own devices and you can explain it all to Piet."

The pale eyes narrowed at him. "You would do that, wouldn't you?"

"That you can bet your shirt on."

"Are you always so nasty?"

"Oh this is really great. You're calling *me*

nasty?" After what you've just done? Let me tell you something, Miss Lorraine Mowbray . . . your friend Hennie Marais whom in your infinite wisdom you decided to contact, has in all probability towed all sorts of people, whom you'd definitely not like to meet, in his wake. If you want to attend to them by yourself, that's fine with me. The ferry's just over there. I can be on my way to London this afternoon. It just takes a phone call and my credit card to check out of the hotel. I've left nothing in my room. So if you want me around when you call Piet, make your Mr. Marais useful."

"What do you mean?"

"I mean you send him away. In so doing, he'll probably take whoever's following with him. They'll think he was just meeting you on his way to another rendezvous. I hope that's what they'll think."

"But he'll be on his own. We've always worked together . . ."

"I'm not babysitting for the two of you . . ."

"Stop saying that! We're not babies."

"Then stop acting as if you were. I'm going back to the car. I've had it with these arguments. This is not some sort of school game. People get killed . . ."

"I know people get killed," she snapped at him, eyes blazing. "Have you forgotten where I come from?"

"Then start behaving as if you understand its realities. As I've just said, I'm going back to the car. I'll wait there for ten minutes. No more. If you're not by the car by then, you're on your own."

Gallagher turned away from her and went back to the table. Marais was still there.

"Nice to have met you, Hennie," he said to the still bemused Marais, as he picked up his equipment.

"Your lady friend will be along in a moment for a little chat."

He left Marais to his own devices and headed back toward the car. He paused halfway along, to check every item. They were clean. Marais was either a truly trustworthy chum, or very clever.

Gallagher was not prepared to take chances to find out which.

Gallagher was listening to Frescobaldi's *Toccata Ottava,* when he saw her hurrying toward him. He did not stop the music until she had reached the side of the car. Marais was nowhere to be seen.

She opened the door and entered. She stared expressionlessly through the windscreen, and maintained a stubborn silence.

After some seconds of this, Gallagher said: "Let's begin with the ground rules. I gave you a chance to do things your own way. The fact that you are here means you have willingly chosen to try it differently."

"So what are your ground rules?"

"Not mine . . . *the* ground rules. And they are simple. You do as I say."

"That's all?"

"Yes, Miss Mowbray. That is all. You can open the door and go back to your friend, if you don't agree. I'm not forcing you."

For reply, she snapped on her seat belt.

"And don't take it out on the car, please."

She glared at him. "What's so special about this car? It's not alive, is it?"

Gallagher gave her a fleeting smile as he started the engine. "Love me, love my car."

That brought a silence that would last most of the return journey to Bruges.

Marais had watched Lorraine Mowbray walk away from him, his expression neutral. A fairly handsome man, he was three inches under six feet tall; but the slimness of his body gave the impression of greater height. The slim form belied a tough core that had been shaped by the harsh social realities of his native land.

He remained at the table, slowly drinking his coffee as he thought of her instructions, and of his next move. She had clearly not wanted to go with Gallagher, but had seemed to have no choice.

What, he wondered, did Gallagher have on her?

He knew from experience that it was usually an uphill task to get her to do anything she did not want to; but she had evidently met her match in Gallagher. There had not been much time to study him closely.

A man worth watching, and very carefully indeed.

Marais stared out across the gray sea. He would be meeting Gallagher again. Of that, he was quite certain.

The *quattro* was heading off the motorway, when Lorraine Mowbray decided to speak.

"I hated leaving him like that," she said, looking at Gallagher accusingly.

"It is sometimes necessary to make a tactical decision that may go against the emotional responses . . ."

"Tactical decisions, emotional responses . . . What are you talking about?"

"A war. You're in it, and you don't seem able to come to terms with that." He shook his head slowly. "Villiger must have been out of his mind to bring you over here, and to give you so much responsibility. You're a walking menace."

"Did you get me to stay with you just so you could throw insults at me?" The eyes were blazing at him once more.

"I didn't get you to do anything. I gave you choices. You took one. So please, let's try to get through this until we have made contact with Piet. Okay?"

"You're not making it easy, you know."

"I'm not here to make it easy for you. I'm trying to keep you from getting your head blown away . . . mine too, for that matter. Forget what you may or may not feel about me, and just concentrate on that. Concentrate too, on the fact that any mistake you make might cost Piet his life."

He had glanced at her as he'd said this and had caught a stricken expression upon her face. He felt a certain degree of satisfaction. She might appear unconcerned about her own safety but clearly, the thought of causing Villiger's death had gone deep. If this served to give her a more professional attitude, it was a small victory. It was about time she woke up.

"I'm not . . . I'm not as incompetent as you seem to think," she said. She had moderated her tone, and appeared to be declaring a truce. "I've asked you before, not to prejudge me. There are things about me you don't know . . ."

Gallagher thought he might as well do a little fence-mending himself. "And I'm not about to ask you to tell me. Perhaps I was a little harsh just then. I know Piet would not have brought you unless he thought he could rely on you. Even so, I've got to be honest and say I've got the feeling he would have preferred it differently. You are new to this particular kind of game, and I'm trying to steer you away from the mine fields."

After a while, she said: "You're right. He would have preferred me not to have come. But he felt I was the one person in the Movement who could get around sufficiently openly, and whom he felt he could trust with the knowledge of his presence in Europe."

"He doesn't trust the people in the Movement?"

"Oh it's not as bad as it sounds. In a way, you two think alike. I suppose that's really why among other things, he came to see you. He believes in telling as few people as possible about matters like this. Less chance of its getting into the wrong ears."

"Sounds like a good insurance policy to me. Which means, if someone's really after Piet, you are the stalking horse. And that makes you very important to whoever it may be. Now do you understand?"

For once, she took no offense. "I do understand. And I'm tougher than you may think."

"I don't doubt you're tough. It must take guts to carry on a normal life back home. But in this game, you need more than guts. You need cunning . . ."

"And ruthlessness."

He knew she was looking at him. "That too," he admitted.

"Piet says you're the most ruthless man he knows, under certain circumstances."

"Such flattery." He glanced at her, and saw a tiny smile at the corner of her lips. "Friends now, are we?"

"Let's make a truce."

"Fine by me."

"Hennie agreed to go back to Amsterdam and wait to hear from me," she said into the brief silence that had followed.

"That's good news. It will help split any shadowers. They must follow him, if only because they can't afford not to."

"He had some good news of his own."

"Oh?"

"The first batch of six F-16's are on their way."

"My God. You really are going to do it."

"Of course we are. Piet is serious about this. We all are."

"You can say that again. Where did all the money come from?"

"Even if I did know," she said, "I couldn't tell you. It's up to Piet."

"I'll say this for him," Gallagher began. "Whoever's bankrolling this, has weight. Falcons don't come from supermarket shelves."

She made no comment, saying instead: "Hennie will be meeting me in Greece."

"*Greece?* Why Greece?"

"The container ship with the planes is heading that way, and I've got to meet . . . someone else there. On one of the islands. Hennie will accompany me."

"Bodyguard?"

"If you like."

"Is he dangerous . . . this someone else?"

"He's the one who got the planes. He's been much quicker than we dared hope."

Gallagher remembered what Haslam had said about Behrensen and Quinlan, then thought of Lorraine Mowbray and Marais going out to meet with one, or possibly both of them. Lambs to the slaughter.

"I can't believe Piet agreed to this. Marais will be worse than useless to you."

"You don't know him," she said, springing to Marais' defense.

"Perhaps not. But I do know of one, or perhaps two of the people you might be meeting. Big sharks in an already shark-infested sea. A person who knows about these things said so. Marais is so outclassed, it's almost funny."

"Are you offering to go in his place?"

"No."

"I didn't think you were." The familiar edge had returned to her voice.

"Truce," Gallagher said. "Remember?"

She said nothing.

Haslam and Prinknash had spent the night in Gent, thirty-five or so kilometers from Bruges. They had followed the Golf there and when their quarry had stopped for the night, had done likewise. They had slept in the Mercedes, while the driver of the Golf had booked into a hotel. In the morning, they had refreshed themselves with travel tissues, and swapped the Mercedes for a BMW 535SE. It was far more powerful than the previous car and was good for 140 mph, at the very least.

"There you go, Prinknash," Haslam had said. "Now you might be able to keep sight of Gallagher."

Looking at the gleaming BMW, Prinknash had said sniffily, "Give me the Jag any day." Prinknash was an irredeemable xenophobe.

They had followed the Golf to Ostend and parked on the Albert I Promenade, from where they had witnessed the meeting between Gallagher, Lorraine Mowbray, and Marais. Or rather Haslam had, through his binoculars.

"Shouldn't we have gone after Gallagher, Mr. Haslam?" Prinknash now said. "He could be anywhere by now."

Haslam had again raised the binoculars to his eyes. The man in the pale suit was still at the same table.

"Clever sod, our Gordon," Haslam said as he lowered the glasses. "It's clear he didn't want to be followed by our man in the Golf, a man the young lady clearly knows . . . if the little act I saw was anything to go by." Haslam was almost talking to himself. "Gallagher hauls her away, gives her a ticking off, then leaves. But he doesn't drive off. Young lady goes to our boy in the lightweight suit, talks to him, and they seem to reach agreement. Then back she goes to Gallagher. What do you think he was up to, Prinknash?"

Prinknash looked blank.

"Call yourself a copper," Haslam said wearily. "He's forcing us to decide between targets. He has assumed the man in the Golf was followed and while he has no idea who may be following, he has still taken action. He was followed by the Golf, which was followed by us and having neutralized the one, he's presented the other—us—with a problem."

"So we've lost Gallagher again," Prinknash said.

"Perhaps," Haslam murmured, raising the glasses once more. "Then again, perhaps not. Our man's moving. Let's see where he goes."

"Back to Amsterdam, with our luck," Prinknash said gloomily.

* * *

1300 hours, 250 miles west of Crete.

The *Stonefish* had worked up to her max of forty-six knots, slicing a great wake through the calm Mediterranean waters. At that speed and in the current sea state, her stability was such that the three glasses of champagne on the burr-maple table spilled none of their contents. Next to the glasses was a large ice bowl, which contained a magnum of rare vintage champagne. There was still plenty left in it. It was, however, the second magnum to sit in the bed of ice within the past hour.

The champagne was in the large bedroom of the owner's suite and the vast bed was occupied by Behrensen, and two young women who were entertaining him with great vigor. One was a lithe black girl from Los Angeles called Lona Mason. The other, white, with a full head of raven hair, came from the southeast of England. Her name was Tessa James. Both girls were just eighteen.

They had met in England, and had backpacked to the south of France. Walking along the Nice seafront in shorts and T-shirt, they had caught Behrensen's eye on one of his rare visits ashore. He had invited them to the yacht and flattered, they had accepted. He had subsequently discovered they were on their way to Greece and had offered them passage. They had been delighted by their good fortune. He put a luxurious stateroom with its spacious twin beds at their disposal. He gave them champagne breakfasts and with the exception of two specific no-go areas, virtually gave them the run of the ship.

For an entire day and night he made no advances, treating them instead with great courtesy. They experienced meals that were the stuff of dreams and no restrictions were put upon their drinking. Designer drugs were there for the taking.

It had not taken them long to get into the spirit of things and when on the second day he had begun his advances, they put up no resistance. If anything, they were more than willing to succumb.

As the *Stonefish* sliced the water with her 46-knot prow, Behrensen thumped his body at the glistening, sinewy shape of Lona Mason. He was roaring at her.

"Forty-six knots!" he was saying. "Forty-six knots, baby! Ever had it in you at forty-six knots?" He punctuated every other word with a thrust.

Lona Mason was whimpering, but not in pain or fear. She was enjoying herself and made noises that were like little screams. Next to them, Tessa James lay spread-eagled. Her body, still with a few vestiges of puppy fat, gave her legs and thighs a softer, fuller look that contrasted sharply with Lona Mason's streetwise sinuosity. Behrensen had his hands upon her generous breasts, holding on to them tightly. She squirmed beneath his touch.

Behrensen was working feverishly at Lona Mason who had now begun to scream. His roaring continued until suddenly, he strained at her in complete silence. He held thus for long moments as her slim legs clamped themselves to him. Then her body relaxed and the legs fell limply back to the bed.

With barely a pause, Behrensen left her and seemed to launch himself at Tessa James. Her soft body yielded to him. This contrast with Lona Mason served to drive him to new heights of sexual arousal. He seemed to want to devour her with his body and pumped himself at her with an almost demented urgency.

She began to make squealing noises and he held on tightly, arms locked beneath her now, squashing her breasts against his broad chest. His eyes seemed to pop even more than was normal, and huge beads of sweat covered his brow. His neck muscles stood out like great hawsers as he strained at her. He seemed to have left his surroundings and to have entered his own special world. It was almost as if Tessa James were herself not there.

Watching languidly from a side of the bed, Lona Mason said softly: "Jesus." But she could not resist her own feelings of renewed arousal.

She reached forward to touch Behrensen. He brushed her aside with a remarkably quick swipe of an arm that was again soon locked beneath Tessa James's heaving body—upon whose glistening face a strange mixture of ecstasy and loathing had appeared.

About them, the hurtling ship throbbed beyond perceptible awareness.

Then Behrensen was again roaring, but speaking no words this time. His body strained and trembled, and Tessa James gave a prolonged gasp that shuddered her entire body before it arched and slowly relaxed into stillness.

Behrensen rolled off her. After a few moments, he picked up one of the two bedside phones.

"Mister Duquesne," he said into it. "Give us ten knots."

He replaced the phone as the *Stonefish* suddenly went from its headlong rush to a sedate cruise. The glasses on the table barely registered the abrupt change of momentum.

"More champagne, ladies?" Behrensen said.

Tessa James was gently rubbing an inner thigh.

Lona Mason looked at the glasses, smiled at him, and nodded.

"You don't approve, Mr. Duquesne?"

Behrensen was on the bridge. The *Stonefish* was still cruising at a leisurely ten knots and Lona Mason and Tessa James, in skimpy bikinis, were standing by the port bow rail.

"You pay me enough not to have an opinion one way or the other, sir," Duquesne replied.

"And if I did not pay you enough?"

"I'd still have no opinion."

Behrensen's smile was wolfish. "Spoken like a man who's seen all the cesspits of humanity." He looked at the young women. "A man needs distractions from time to time. They're energetic, and they don't suffer from puritanical constraints. They would not have accepted my invitation otherwise." His eyes lingered upon their bodies a while longer, particularly upon Tessa James's.

"An interesting combination of character," he continued. "The black girl has street cred. She's wiser beyond her years. Tough, no nonsense. She knows the world will take what it can from her, so she's out to get what she can from it. Her illusions left her a long time ago. The other girl's as different as it's possible to be. She's got a soft body . . ." He paused, remembering. "Soft," he repeated quietly, "with an innocent fire. I like that . . . but she still expects the world to play fair. Pity. But no matter, Mr. Duquesne. This business we're engaged in will net us a very substantial sum. Why, your share will buy you a real boat instead of that toy you keep in the Spanish islands."

Behrensen's description of Duquesne's own

motor yacht as a toy could not have been further from the truth. Many people of reasonable wealth would not have been able to afford it. It earned its keep doing weekly charters. Duquesne was never directly involved.

"I'm happy with it," Duquesne said. "It fulfills my needs."

Behrensen shrugged. "As long as you're happy."

A crewman entered with a message which he handed to Behrensen who smiled rapaciously, before passing it on to Duquesne.

"She'll be back soon," Behrensen said with quiet satisfaction, "now that they know the cargo is heading for the rendezvous. And this time . . ."

Behrensen allowed his words to die, but his mind was racing ahead, contemplating the plans he had in mind for his blonde customer. She'd been cold toward him that last time, but after the business was complete . . .

Thinking about her gave him a powerful arousal that needed immediate attention. He walked quickly off the bridge without another word to Duquesne, and made his way down to the main deck, heading for the bows and the young women.

It would be a further seven hours before they'd be able to leave his suite for their stateroom.

2

Bruges, 1600 hours.

Lorraine Mowbray made her call to Villiger from outside the medieval city. Gallagher had suggested doing so, and she had not objected. He sat in the car keeping watch as she spoke into the phone. They were in Lichtervelde, a village just off the Bruges-Roeslare motorway. No one had followed them.

She had been in conversation with Villiger for about five minutes when, as on the previous occasion, she began to beckon urgently.

He got out of the car and after a quick look around, went to the phone. She handed it to him wordlessly.

"Wait in the car," he said. "And keep your eyes open."

"Yes, sir," she said, those same eyes giving nothing away.

He waited until she had entered the *quattro* before saying into the phone: "Gallagher."

"What was that all about?" came Villiger's voice.

"She doesn't like taking orders from me."

Villiger gave one of his short bursts of laughter. "I've told you before, man. She really likes you."

"You could have fooled me."

"Be patient. It's difficult for her. I'll meet you tomorrow," Villiger went on.

"Thank God for that."

"Come, come, Gordon. She can't be such bad company. There are a lot of men who would give a lot to be with her."

"Until they feel her fangs," Gallagher retorted. "So when and where do we meet?"

"How well do you know the Ardennes?"

"That's a lot of ground. I know all sorts of places."

"Give me a few."

"Spa, Malmedy, Marche . . ."

"What about routes into Germany?"

"There's one I use when I want to beat the Aachen traffic if I'm going south. I go via Trier. The motorways are usually practically empty. After Verviers, that is. It's not all motorway, but even so . . ."

"Let's use the Trier route . . . the section just before the border." Villiger gave detailed instructions.

Gallagher knew just where he meant.

"It's a bit of a drive from Bruges," Villiger continued, "but it's best for keeping this thing secure. I'll see you there at 11.00. You'll have time for breakfast, and still make it in that car of yours."

From Bruges to the rendezvous Villiger had decided upon was roughly 230 kilometers—140 miles or so—mostly by motorway. A seven o'clock breakfast would leave plenty of time.

Gallagher said: "What do I do about . . ."

"You bring her, of course. And Gordon, there's no need to worry. I trust her with my life."

You may well have to, Gallagher thought, but said nothing.

"But you told me the other day . . ." he began.

"I never said I didn't trust her," Villiger interrupted.

"No. You didn't. Will she be remaining with you, so that I can go back to my normal life?"

"Well . . ."

"Don't tell me . . ." Gallagher began.

"Alright. I won't."

"For God's sake . . ."

"Just a while longer."

"Now why did I think I'd hear you say that?"

"Gordon, Gordon. Your old sarcasm is rearing its head again."

"Oh I am surprised. You wouldn't still be trying to con me into your crazy scheme, would you?"

"As if I would."

"Of course you bloody well would."

"You should be more trusting, Gordon."

"Ha bloody ha."

"It won't be for much longer," Villiger told him soothingly, and hung up.

Gallagher stared at the dead phone. "Sod you, Villiger," he said quietly, and placed it back on the hook. He returned to the car. "Well," he said to Lorraine Mowbray as he entered. "We've got time for you to play tourist in Bruges."

A long way from Gallagher and Lorraine Mowbray, de Vries was also in conversation on the telephone.

"I've followed the quarry," he was saying, "but those two who interfered the other night are still in the game. They've changed cars for something faster. They mean business."

"If they get too close, you'll have to stop them. The job has to be done. Any identification of the target?"

"Not yet."

A swear word came down the line. "We need a result soon. He must be identified and terminated. We cannot stress that too strongly. You're supposed to be good . . ."

"I am good. You've got my record to prove it."

"You know the old saying . . . you're only as good as your latest success. I've paraphrased a bit, but you get my meaning. And don't forget to take out the quarry as well when the time comes, will you?"

The line went dead.

De Vries slammed the phone down. "I know my job!" he snarled at it.

The car had been left in the hotel courtyard, and they had walked for some time through the cobbled backstreets of the city. She had gaped, childlike, at the ancient buildings; been surprised by the unexpected quietude of the narrow lanes; had lingered on the many small bridges to stare into the canals, and had even forced him to go on a carriage ride with her.

"Good grief," he'd said. "This is so touristy."

"Don't be such a snob," she'd countered. "I am a tourist. You said so yourself."

All the while, he had kept a careful watch for shadowers. The idyllic surroundings, he knew, could so easily be shattered by sudden violence from an unseen quarter.

But nothing had served to disturb the peaceful afternoon.

"This is so normal," she now said, "it makes what is happening back home seem unreal."

They were standing near the Jan van Eyck statue, looking out along the canal. Gallagher sensed there was something important she wanted to say to him. He waited, wondering what it could possibly be. When she finally spoke, it was about a subject he would never have imagined.

"What do you see when you look at me?" she asked.

The question took him by surprise, and he had to consider his reply carefully.

"I see a fantastically attractive woman," he began. She smiled at that, but made no comment, so he continued. "I see someone who would have preferred to lead her life normally, instead of putting it deliberately in danger. I see someone brave, but uncertain. I see a woman who tries to be tough, but isn't in the true sense of the word . . ."

"As I've told you before, I can look after myself. I can shoot quite well too."

"I don't doubt it. But my words still stand. You're a good actress . . ."

"Very astute, but you don't know how good."

Gallagher watched her, waiting. The pale eyes surveyed him almost humorlessly; but it was a strange humor. There was no joy in it.

"You had parents who loved you," she said. "They were able to give you what any parent in such circumstances would . . . the right school, the right university. That went a long way toward helping you become a commissioned pilot with the RAF, which in turn led to your job with that Department . . ."

"Which with hindsight, I could well have done without."

"You know what I'm getting at. You were given the chances to stretch whatever talents you've got. That's all anyone needs to ask for."

Gallagher was looking hard at her. "You don't look like someone who was denied any chances."

Her smile was enigmatic. "You see a beautiful blonde with nice eyes and to some, a sexy body. Oh don't worry. I'm not coy about it. I know what I look like. But there's something you miss. Yes, I'm a good actress: a chameleon under some conditions. You still don't know what I'm talking about, do you?"

Gallagher shook his head slowly. "Suppose you put me out of my misery."

"My father," she said, "was colored. Ah!" she went on. "The shock hits. To the outside world, I'm a fantastic blonde, to use your own description. To some bureaucratic shit in his cesspool back home, I am a colored."

Gallagher was so stunned by her revelation, he could only stare at her. In a brief moment of embarrassment, he found himself searching for evidence of "color." It served to vividly illustrate to him how quickly the virus could grow. He had always considered himself above such banality. His father had schooled him long and hard about his own worth as a person. As a result, it had never been difficult for him to put his mind to anything he wanted to do. Being aware of something did not necessarily mean one had to be inhibited by it. It was his credo.

"Up to the age of sixteen," Lorraine Mowbray was saying, continuing her apparent need to confess her secret to him, "I believed I was white. After I found out, I still found it hard to accept. I met a white boy and went out with him for two months." She paused, reliving the humiliation that had come with discovery. "We met in a store. There were people of all races about, so it never occurred to him that I was not . . ." She paused once more. Her lips twitched slightly, the memory still searing at her.

Gallagher said: "Look. You don't have to . . ."

"No! I want to tell you. I've begun, so let me finish."

Gallagher kept his peace.

"When he found out," she went on, "do you know what he said? 'How could you do this to me? I've shown you off to all my friends.' " She gave a soft, dry laugh. "How could I do it to *him*. He was the one doing it to *me*, the gutless little bastard." She took a slow breath, her voice remaining quiet as she spoke. "I think that was when I really decided to do something about what was going on. Any system that humiliates like that has to be fought. That's how I met Hennie a couple of years later. He was a student activist. And no, not a boyfriend."

"I didn't say anything."

"You didn't say it, but you must have thought it."

"I've only seen the man once. Whatever you say, he has the look of someone who thinks of you as rather more than just a good friend. You're not going to tell me you don't realize it. In any case, it's nothing to do with me."

She decided to ignore his remarks about Marais, preferring instead to return to that first discovery of the real world. "I've always thought I've been hard on that boy all these years. After all, he was the product of his environment. It's his parents I really despise." She gave a slight shrug. "Still . . ."

Her words had died suddenly. She folded her arms about her, a hand holding on to each elbow as she stared at the water. Gallagher was not sure of what to say. It struck him that she seemed peculiarly alone. Almost unconsciously, he put an arm about her shoulders. She stiffened, but did not pull away.

"Why are you doing that?" she asked. The pale eyes were staring at him.

"I felt you needed a hug. People who need hugs should get them."

The barest hint of a smile came and went. "You're not so tough."

"Soft as butter inside. That's me. I know a little place that gives you chunks of raw steak and a hot slab of stone to cook them on. Fancy trying it?"

She had relaxed in the embrace of his arm, and now leaned a little against him. "Alright," she said.

London.

Sir John Winterbourne entered Fowler's office without warning. Fowler looked calmly up from his desk, and waited.

"Well?" Winterbourne began.

"Well what, Sir John?"

Winterbourne, his petulant cherub's face beginning to swell with outrage at what he perceived as Fowler's lack of respect, said tightly: "It has come to my notice that funds were approved for Haslam to hire a *BMW*!" Winterbourne's emphasis made it sound as if Haslam had just bought the car. "Why was I not informed of this before you chose to approve it?"

Fowler felt like sighing wearily, but restrained himself. "I did try to reach you, Sir John," he began civilly, "but you were on the way to your club . . ."

"Good God man! I've got a telephone in my car!"

"With respect, it is not necessary to burden you

with every request for contingency funds. We get so many of those, you'd have no time for other, far more important matters . . ."

"Don't try the silver tongue trick on me, Fowler. I'm the one who has to prize a decent budget from the finance department. I'm the one who has to justify it to the Minister."

"You do so admirably, Sir John . . ."

"And the blatant flattery won't work, either."

You're getting cleverer than you look, Fowler thought uncharitably.

"Did you say something?" Winterbourne demanded suspiciously.

"No, Sir John. But I was about to say that I authorized the hire of a car that Haslam felt would keep up, in some measure, with Gallagher's. There was hardly time to send one of our special Jaguars."

"Why didn't Haslam and Prinknash go over in one in the first place?"

"Because, Sir John," Fowler began with a patience he did not feel, "they were following someone else at the time. Someone who traveled by airplane."

Winterbourne paused, aware that yet again, he had been maneuvered into another stalemate. It frustrated him, and angered him further.

"Why are we following Gallagher?" he demanded.

"I believe he is being approached for mercenary service . . ."

"Just up his street," Winterbourne said nastily. He couldn't get Fowler and saw no reason why he shouldn't use the absent Gallagher as a more convenient target.

But Fowler was not going to give him the petty victory. "Not his style at all, Sir John," Fowler said mildly. "Gallagher will not work for anyone he does not want to, and no amount of money will induce him. Besides, he hardly needs it."

"I repeat . . . why are we following him?"

"We believe he will be coerced."

"We?"

"If you prefer, *I* believe it, Sir John."

"So this operation is sanctioned only by you? Fowler . . ."

"Nothing is being kept from you. Prinknash is with Haslam, after all. There's also the question of Behrensen."

Winterbourne looked unhappy. "I sense an unease about this, Fowler. Behrensen's an American. Let the Americans take care of their own . . ."

"Gallagher's British. Lady Veronica Walmsley is British. Behrensen, or someone connected with him, has involved them. That makes it our problem."

"Why do I get the feeling you are telling me rather less than you know?"

"You'll have a full report, Sir John."

"That may well be the case, but when, Fowler? *When?*" Winterbourne strutted out, slamming the door behind him.

Fowler stared for some moments above the rim of his glasses, at the closed door.

"At the proper time, Sir John," he said, in his mildest voice.

It was 19.30 in Bruges when Gallagher asked for the bill. At about the same time some streets away, a man walked along one of the many cobbled back lanes of the city. The man's steps took him past the rear of the small hotel where Gallagher and Lorraine Mowbray were staying. The roller door to the courtyard was up. It was not normally lowered till midnight.

The man stopped when he saw the *quattro*. A young woman was in the courtyard, looking at it.

"Nice car," the man said in English, having noted the number plates. "Yours?"

"It is a nice car," came the reply, also in English; but she was not speaking her native tongue. "And it isn't mine," she added wistfully. "I could not afford it. It belongs to one of our guests."

"Very nice," the man repeated appreciatively. He smiled at her. "'Bye."

"Goodbye."

The man walked on, came to the end of the lane, and turned a corner. As he disappeared another man, this time older, came into the lane. He too walked up to the roller door and without pausing, glanced into the courtyard. He saw the *quattro,* and the young woman.

He gave her a courteous nod, and continued on his way.

Gallagher would have been surprised by the identity of the two men. One was Hennie Marais, the other, Haslam.

Haslam sauntered on, heading for where the BMW was waiting with Prinknash at the wheel. A short distance away was the blue Golf. No one was in it.

Haslam rapped on the window. Prinknash jumped.

"Always watch your back," Haslam said as he got in. "Someone could have walked up and put a few rounds into you."

Prinknash looked sheepish. "I was keeping an eye on his car."

"That wouldn't have been of much use, would it, if you couldn't see anymore."

Prinknash took the admonishment with surprisingly good grace. Perhaps it was because he knew Haslam was talking hard sense.

"Did you stay with him?" Prinknash now asked.

"I stayed with him. He checked his back very often. He's had practice. Expected, of course, given where he comes from. It must be second nature to check over your shoulder in that country, these days. But he was not good enough." Haslam sounded pleased with himself. "I know rather more about surveillance techniques than he does about evasion. And by the way," he added offhandedly, "he led me nicely to where Gallagher's staying."

"You've found him!" Prinknash looked excited.

"As I knew I would." There was no smugness in Haslam's voice. He had read the situation correctly, and it had developed in the way he had expected. "Now that we know where Gallagher's bivouacked, so to speak, we can dispense with our friend in the Golf . . . though not completely. I'd still like to know where he fits into the scheme of things."

"Are we sleeping in the car again tonight?"

Haslam stared at his younger companion. "What are you, Prinknash. A copper, or a girl guide? And I apologize to all guides." Haslam gave his familiar sigh. "There's a little hotel close by. We'll use it."

"But how will we know if he decides to leave . . ."

"Traffic in that lane is one-way only, and anyone coming out of it has to turn left to pass right in front of the hotel I've chosen. I've preempted you, Prinknash. We're already booked in, and my room overlooks the street. We'll keep watch on Gallagher's hotel until after midnight. There's a small courtyard with a gate that can be lowered, which I suspect they close at night. We'll wait until they've done so, before packing it in for the night ourselves. I'll be up early enough in case he decides to leave at the crack of dawn. That answer your questions, Prinknash?"

Prinknash nodded, but said nothing.

"Good," Haslam said. "Now you'll be able to get your beauty sleep."

"I enjoyed it in there," Lorraine Mowbray said to Gallagher as they left the brasserie. "Thank you for taking me. You should have let me pay."

"My treat," he told her. "You can pay for the next one."

"I'll hold you to that."

"Then we've got a deal."

She linked her arm in his, doing so unselfconsciously as they crossed the cobbled bridge near the now-empty fish market. Every so often, her hip brushed against his as they walked. A seductive warmth came from her body with each touch.

"Do you think differently about me now?" she asked.

"In what way?"

"Now that you know my background." She did not look at him as she spoke.

"Why should I think differently? I see the same blonde who interrupted my coffee in Amsterdam, and who nearly drove into the water. And as for that little deadhead you met when you were sixteen, you're better off without him. He didn't know a good deal when he had one."

She squeezed his arm briefly. "That was a nice thing to say. Thank you."

"No need to thank me for telling the truth. Besides, you're talking to someone whose mother was a half-Scottish Jamaican, and whose father was a full-blooded Irishman."

"Well," she said, smiling at him, "I like what they produced."

"Careful," he began. "That's dangerous talk. I might begin to believe . . ." His words died suddenly.

"What . . ." she started to say.

"Keep walking!" he commanded. "No, no. Don't stiffen. Relax. Good, good. That's it."

They had passed through an arch and were entering a small square which was fairly crowded.

"Isn't this where we took that carriage ride?" she asked.

"How can I forget?" he replied drily. His eyes were swiftly tracking the various groups of people, hunting out a target, though apparently not settling upon any.

They continued walking, cutting diagonally across the square.

"Are you going to tell me?" she asked. Her arm was still linked in his.

"Tell you what?"

"Did you see something? Or someone?"

After a while, he said: "I thought I saw someone. Can't be sure."

"Who?"

"I'm probably wrong. Jumpy."

"Who?" she repeated.

"If I did see anyone, it was someone who should not be here."

"I don't understand."

"Neither do I."

He had seen Hennie Marais. But Marais was supposed to have gone back to Amsterdam. What, he wondered, was the depth of the game she was playing? What had that story about a colored father and teenage rejection been all about? Had she been playing for the reaction she had received from him? And if so, why? Was she hoping that making him feel sympathetic toward her would make it easier to persuade him to join Villiger?

It didn't make sense.

He glanced at her, remembering how she had been in the brasserie, laughing and joking as she had tried to cook the meat on the hot slab. He found it hard to believe that had all been an act; but he also knew that survival in this kind of game depended more than anything else upon one particular rule.

Never take anything at face value, sir. O'Keefe.

And for most of the time, his former mentor had been shown by subsequent events to have been correct. O'Keefe had drummed it into him and on at least two occasions, that rule had saved his life.

He glanced at Lorraine Mowbray once more. There was nothing visible that betrayed her alleged ancestry. Nothing about Hennie Marais, either; and there was nothing about their respective tans that made them seem different from Villiger, or any number of white South Africans he had seen either in the flesh, or on the box. If she had spoken the truth, it only served to demonstrate the terminal insanity of the philosophy that had bred the system she lived under.

"I can almost hear you thinking," she said.

"Can you? And what am I thinking?"

"I'm not telepathic. I can simply hear the grinding of rusty cogs." She smiled guilelessly at him.

If it worried her that he might have spotted Marais, Gallagher mused, the possibility had apparently not disturbed her.

He would not, he decided, tell her about Marais. At least, not just yet. He would go along with her little game until the time was right to jolt her with his knowledge of Marais' presence in Bruges.

"Grinding of cogs," he said cheerfully. "That's one way of putting it. And what would Madam like to do now?"

"Madam would like to go back to the hotel for a longish nightcap."

"Would she indeed."

"It would round off a perfect day." She was now holding on to his arm as she looked up at him.

The pale eyes were bold.

21.30 hours, aboard the *Stonefish.*

"Woooeee!" Lona Mason exclaimed as she flopped onto her bed in their stateroom. "My Gawd. I thought we'd never get out of there tonight."

Tessa James was more subdued. Barefoot and barelegged, she sat on her own bed, absently rubbing at the inside of her upper thigh. She was dressed in a loose T-shirt, and a very brief pair of shorts. She wore nothing else underneath. There were slight discolorations on her arms, legs, and thighs where Behrensen had handled her roughly.

Lona, a burgundy-colored robe wrapped loosely about her own bare body, raised herself on an elbow to stare at the other girl. Her eyes studied the marks on her companion's limbs.

"You turn that guy on. You know that?"

Tessa James said nothing.

"Hey c'mon, Tessa. Don't go all prudish on me. We knew what we were doing when we came aboard this floating palace. You didn't really think we'd get a ride to the islands for free, did you? Sure, we're not paying money, and we're living better than half those guys on their yachts at St. Tropez . . . but there's always something to pay. You've heard about lunch? Well there's no such thing as a free ride either . . . especially when it's a millionaire giving it."

Lona stood up, securing the robe about her. She stalked about the stateroom, a slim feline on the prowl.

"Look at this stuff," she went on. "I've got to admit it gives a kick to know a brother owns it all." She stopped by Tessa James's bed. "Hey, girl. You'll put this all behind you when we get to the islands." She looked about her once more. "I don't mind telling you I'd be happy to stay on for the trip back."

"No!" Tessa's voice was shrill in its suddenness. Then the voice was as suddenly quiet as she continued: "I didn't expect this. Not quite like this. Kevin . . ."

"Kevin? You're not talking about the boyfriend you left back home? If you really cared for the guy you wouldn't have gone away without him. *C'mon,* Tessa. What about that French boy in Nice? He got so many tunes out of you, I thought you were auditioning for an opera. Don't tell me about Kevin . . ."

"As soon as we get to Crete, I'm getting off this boat. It's not fun, Lona. You can stay if you like. He frightens me."

"Every man with power is a little frightening.

That's why women find them attractive . . . even when they're ugly."

"I'm not staying," Tessa insisted.

Lona went back to her bed and again sat down. "What if he doesn't want you to go?"

Tessa's eyes were wide. "He can't stop me. That would be kidnapping. It wouldn't do his reputation any good, would it? I mean . . . *kidnapping*. I agree we came on board of our own free will but now, I'm changing my mind. This is not what I had really expected, and I'm leaving before it gets worse. He can't stop me," she added, as if to reassure herself.

When Lona had made no comment, Tessa continued: "Just think about this . . . why are there no more guests on board? All we've seen are the crew. We haven't stopped anywhere for more people. Didn't he tell us he was meeting up with another yacht and a whole group for some big party? Where are they?"

"We're not in the islands yet . . ."

"I'm not staying." Tessa was still rubbing at her thigh. "He's left bruises all over me. Say what you like, Lona. I think we've made a big mistake with this one. If you've got any brains, you'll come ashore with me."

"Oh Tessa, Tessa. He's a brother. He's cool."

"I don't care. He frightens me."

Later that night, both came awake in the darkness of their stateroom. The ship was lying dead in the water. Both heard a noise which they soon recognized as that of an approaching helicopter.

Lona was the first to speak. "You awake?"

"Yes," came the reply.

She turned on her bedside lamp. "Looks like

those guests you were talking about are coming aboard. You see? Nothing to worry about."

Tessa was getting out of bed. She went over to a chair to pick up the robe she had flung on it after a pre-bed shower. It was blue, with the *Stonefish*'s monogram discreetly embroidered upon the left breast in white. She put on the robe, and went to the door. She turned the handle. It did not move. She tried again, with the same result.

"Lona, it's locked!" she said in a high voice, squeaky with fear.

The sound of the helicopter had risen in volume.

Lona got quickly out of bed and naked, hurried over to the door. "What do you mean it's locked? Here. Let me at that thing." She tried to open it. "Shit. You're right."

Tessa's eyes were wide with her mounting fear. "Of course I'm right. Now what do we do? We're miles from land . . ."

"Shhh! Keep your voice down. Let me think."

The helicopter was close now and its sounds, despite the proofing of the stateroom, came loudly. Lona, street gaining ascendance, rushed back to turn off the light. The stateroom was again plunged into darkness. She groped her way to one side of the room. Thick curtains covered the solid glass panes of the windows. She found one, and cautiously drew its curtain aside a fraction of the way.

Subdued lights were glowing out of her line of sight, but the contrast was so great, she had to blink to adjust her vision. Tessa had crept up behind her. She put out a warning hand to prevent her from speaking.

Lona could see nothing more, but she heard the helicopter come to the hover. Then an alteration of its sound told her it was landing. She could hear no voices, but realized this was because the helicopter would have drowned all else with its noise. She continued to peer. Then she froze, not daring even to draw the curtain back. Someone was coming. One of the crewmen.

The man walked right past, even glancing at her window; but he gave no indication of having seen her. As he disappeared from view, she felt her heart thumping. The man had been carrying something.

She had seen enough war movies to recognize an assault rifle.

She closed the curtain just as cautiously, then groped her way back to her bed. Tessa stumbled after her.

"Put on the light," Tessa said. "I can't see what I'm doing."

"No lights."

"No li . . . Lona! What did you see?" Tessa's voice had a slight tremor to it. "What's wrong?"

"Keep it down! Sometimes," Lona went on ruefully, "having a dark face really pays off. That guy looked right at me."

Tessa tripped over something. "Oh shit!" she said.

"Keep it down, Tessa!" Lona hissed. "Haven't you got to your bed yet?"

"Okay. I'm there. What's wrong?"

"I dunno, but I owe you an apology. I'm getting off this boat with you. We're in the wrong place, and at the wrong time."

"What made you change your mind?"

"Men with guns."

"Guns! Are you sure?"

"This is one time I wish I was wrong. Go back to sleep . . ."

"How can I . . ."

"Go back to sleep," Lona repeated firmly, "and in the morning, act like you know nothing. You've had a nice long sleep because you were so worn out. You know nothing, you heard nothing. Got it?"

"Y . . . yes."

"Just remember that and pray we get to an island soon."

The helicopter was lifting away as the passenger it had brought came toward Behrensen. A neat man with glasses. Quinlan.

Behrensen held out a hand. "Good to see you, J.D."

"Glad to be here, Mr. Behrensen, and looking forward to the successful conclusion of our operation."

Behrensen grinned into the Mediterranean night. "Worth waiting for, J.D. Worth waiting for."

Gallagher looked at his watch. "You'll never believe the time."

Lorraine Mowbray gave him a sideways look. "Time flies when you're having fun. Or are you trying to get rid of me?"

It was eleven o'clock. Gallagher said: "You're welcome to stay all night."

"Is that a proposition?"

"You would be quite safe."

"I don't know whether that's a compliment, or a backhanded insult. I'll take it as a compliment."

They had spent the evening sitting together, watching the video channel on the TV. They had laughed at some of the material, quietly enjoyed others. At times, he had put an arm about her, and she had seemed content to lean against him. Once, they had switched to the news and had caught an item on South Africa. It had been depressing enough to silence her for a good half hour.

"We've got to change," she had said at the end of her silence. "We've got to."

Gallagher had listened neutrally, not sure whether to believe her apparent sincerity. He was still playing the waiting game.

She stood up slowly, with obvious reluctance. "I suppose I'd better leave. I don't think we'd make it chastely through the night. What do you think?"

"Probably not." He got to his feet.

"What do you mean 'probably'?" She was standing quite close, eyes challenging.

"I don't think I'll answer that." They walked to the door. "I'll see you home."

"Thank you, kind sir," she said. "It's such a long way."

They went to her door. She handed him the key and he opened it with a flourish, handed the key back to her.

She stood for a moment looking at him then without warning, put her arms about his neck. She kissed him fully on the lips for long seconds, body pressed against his. When she at last stood away from him, the pale eyes looked hot, and her breath came quickly.

"That's for . . ." she began. "That's for . . . When this is all over I'd like . . ." She stopped, walked into the room and shut the door.

He turned away to return to his own room. The door opened once more. He turned to look. She stood there, staring at him as if unsure of what to do next.

"Goodnight," she said softly.

"Goodnight."

She closed the door slowly.

Gallagher went back to his room and prepared for bed. As he climbed in, he heard the whirring of the courtyard door as it was lowered for the night.

Haslam walked slowly past the lowering door. He caught a glimpse of the *quattro* just before it was hidden from outside view. Haslam walked all the way to where the Golf was parked. It had not moved. He gave a tiny smile of satisfaction. It would be interesting to see what the morning brought.

He turned, and retraced his steps back to his hotel. He had spotted the driver of the Golf just once during the course of the evening. The man had done a quick circuit of the block that included Gallagher's hotel, and that had been it.

Haslam was certain he had not seen the last of the driver of the Golf.

He reached his hotel and entered thankfully. It would be good to sleep in a bed tonight. Sleeping in cars was not his idea of fun.

But he'd never say that to Prinknash.

10

In the morning, as they went down to breakfast, Lorraine Mowbray said: "Sleep well?"

Gallagher stole a quick glance at her. Her expression was giving nothing away. "No," he said.

"Oh good."

She'd sounded too smug and the warmth of her presence was too distracting, but he made himself pretend this had little effect upon him.

They had a quick breakfast and again taking everything from their rooms, went out to the car.

Haslam and Prinknash were already on station when the black snout of the *quattro* eased its way out of the courtyard, and turned into the cobbled lane.

Haslam knew that Gallagher would be forced by the one-way traffic system to turn left at the end of the lane. In preparation, he had ordered Prinknash to position the BMW just beyond the hump of the narrow canal bridge that was a few meters from where Gallagher would be making the turn. This would take the car in a direction away from the bridge.

They were close enough to hear the deep note of the approaching car, but out of sight. They heard it slow down, then the exhaust rumble grew in volume as the Audi gently accelerated away.

Prinknash, who had kept the BMW's engine running, was about to slot into gear when Haslam's hand rested briefly on his arm.

"Wait for it," Haslam said. "He's got to follow the one-way system. Plenty of time to catch up with him." Haslam waited a few moments longer before saying to the increasingly impatient Prinknash: "Now you can go and *don't* screech off after him, for God's sake. He'd spot you in seconds. We're going to do this nice and easy. We're stalking . . . not hunting. No Hollywood-style chases. If we're careful, we might keep up with him and find out where he's going to so early in the day. You will keep up with him, won't you, Prinknash?"

"'Course I will, Mr. Haslam."

Haslam looked most unconvinced, preferring not to expect too much from Prinknash.

They had been following Gallagher out of Bruges, keeping a discreet distance for about fifteen minutes, when Haslam glanced in the passenger mirror. He had adjusted it so that he could check their tail, without seriously impairing Prinknash's use of it.

The mirror showed a dark blue Golf keeping station two cars behind.

"We've got company," Haslam said mildly.

Prinknash glanced upward at the interior mirror. "The Golf. He's sussed us."

"I doubt it. I think he's following Gallagher and using the other cars and ourselves as a shield. Let's see what happens when we reach the motorway. It looks as if that's where Gallagher's headed."

"Ostend again?"

"I think not. Look. He's taken the Brussels route. Keep on him."

Several other cars were also going toward Brussels and the BMW was not exposed as it followed the *quattro*. Once on the motorway, the black Audi streaked off in a massive burst of acceleration.

"Shit!" Prinknash said. "Look at the bastard go."

Haslam gave him a hard stare. "Forget the colorful language. Department funds are paying for this fancy machine so let's see you make proper use of it. You won't like my mood if you let him get away. But do remember we're stalking. My mood will suffer an equally drastic change if you allow him to spot us."

Prinknash sent the BMW rushing forward, chasing after the hurtling *quattro* and finding various marks of Mercedes giving him a tough contest.

"Isn't there a local speed limit?" he asked.

"There is," Haslam confirmed.

"Look at these people."

"When in Rome," Haslam told him, adding with another glance at the mirror: "Now we know. Our Golf is with us."

After the initial thrust of acceleration, Gallagher had eased back to a more sedate speed that was close to the 130 kph limit. There was no particular hurry toward the rendezvous with Villiger. The time margin was quite healthy. The sudden acceleration had been a device to flush out any tails.

He had seen a blue Golf. He was sure of it, but

had said nothing to Lorraine Mowbray. Besides there were many other VW Golf GTI's on the road. At least two of those were blue. He had also seen a BMW that appeared content to cruise. That did not necessarily mean a possible danger, though it would do no harm to keep an eye on it. His interest was drawn to those particular cars because even though several other vehicles separated them, they appeared to be keeping station. Whenever they chose to overtake, they seemed to do so in unison.

Gallagher decided to keep an eye on them from time to time. He could well be wrong; but gut instincts told him he wasn't. He always listened to his instincts. He only got into trouble when he didn't.

The dislocated convoy continued toward Brussels, Gallagher at times thinking he'd been mistaken when both the BMW and the Golf would disappear from sight. But on each occasion when he had begun to persuade himself they had gone their separate ways, their tiny images would reappear in the mirrors, in the far distance behind him. Now, as the Brussels ring road took him on its curving way past the airport and toward the Liège intersection, the cars were still with him. Every so often, they would be screened by the traffic, only to eventually emerge like divers coming up for air, to take up station in the mirrors.

He had still said nothing to Lorraine Mowbray. For most of the journey, she had so far been content to work her way through the music CDs, sometimes making light conversation. Apart from her remarks just before breakfast, she had made no further comment about what had occurred the previous night. Her manner was very relaxed, as if she at last felt completely at ease with him.

Traffic had been building up since Gent, and as Gallagher took the *quattro* off the ring road and onto the tight left-hand curve of the junction, it began to thin out considerably. Not many going on to Liège, it seemed.

Judging his moment, Gallagher accelerated onto the Liège motorway. He checked the mirrors. The BMW and the Golf were nowhere to be seen. Had they been heading for Brussels, after all? The gut reaction told him otherwise. He believed it.

Prinknash said: "Doesn't look as if he's going to Brussels."

"It would seem not." Haslam looked into the mirror as the BMW swept along the curve of the Liège junction. "This is a popular route," he continued softly. "Our Golf is still with us."

"Do you think he's sussed us yet?" Prinknash joined the motorway with barely a pause in speed. Another BMW, coming up from behind, seemed to want to argue but at the last moment changed its mind and swerved out of the way with a blare of indignant horns. "Piss off!" he snarled at the offended motorist.

"Oh very good," Haslam said. "A little longer at this and you'll make Genghis Khan seem like a model of social etiquette."

"He should have seen me coming." Prinknash was unrepentant. "Well, Mr. Haslam? Do you think the bloke in the Golf knows by now?"

Haslam glanced in his mirror. The blue Volkswagen had not yet appeared. Probably baulked by traffic.

"Hard to tell," Haslam replied thoughtfully. "I'm inclined to think not. He's more likely to be expecting to be trailed, and will be keeping an eye on his mirrors. I still believe he's looking upon us as a convenient screen from Gallagher. Talking of which, you'd better get some speed on. I can barely see Gallagher's car." He took another glance at the mirror. "And there we are."

"The Golf?"

"Right on station, three cars behind." Haslam looked at his watch. The time was precisely 0802.

0902 local time, a hundred miles west of Crete.

The *Stonefish* was barely making headway, its engines apparently shut down. In their stateroom, Lona Mason and Tessa James were ready to face the new day. Both were dressed in bikinis. There should be no change in their pattern of behavior, Lona had warned. Behrensen would expect them at breakfast in bikinis and dressing differently would make him wonder. Tessa had been reluctant, feeling an overwhelming need to cover her body; but she had taken Lona's advice.

"All I want now," she said, "is to get off this bloody boat. I wish he'd hurry on to Crete. I wish he hadn't stopped out here, miles from the nearest land."

"Don't crack up on me, Tessa. We're going to get off, but we've got to be cool about it. Now let's go to breakfast like the good little girls he expects us to be. Okay?"

Tessa nodded, and followed Lona Mason out.

But matters did not work out as planned. Behrensen would not be joining them. Instead of the owner's private dining room to which they had regularly gone since coming aboard, they were shown into the guest's dining room by Behrensen's sleek

Filipino chef. A table for two was set, complete with two bottles of champagne, a pitcher full of freshly squeezed orange juice, and croissants so recently baked, the heat was still rising off them. The aroma of fresh coffee mingled with that of the croissants.

Lona said, with genuine surprise: "Why this room, Ramon? Where's Mr. Behrensen?"

Ramon was apologetic. "Mr. Behrensen sends his regrets, ladies. He's got some visitors . . ."

"Hey, that's great," Lona interrupted enthusiastically. "We're gonna have some partying. When did they arrive?"

Ramon's dark eyes were fathomless. "Last night." He had a strong Californian accent. "Didn't you hear?"

"No," Lona replied quickly, before Tessa could say anything to the contrary and warn Ramon about what they had seen. "We were so bushed, only a war could have woken us."

Ramon appeared satisfied with that. "They came in by chopper . . ."

"So when do we see them?" Taking Lona's lead, Tessa forced gaiety into her voice. "It would be great to have a party."

Ramon was again apologetic. "I'm afraid, ladies, the visitors are not here for partying. These are business people. Mr. Behrensen has some urgent affairs to attend to. That's why you're in here today. He's having breakfast with the gentlemen. But as you can see, he's instructed me to give you the best. Just press the buzzer when you want more. If you'd like a couple of sunnyside eggs, or waffles, just call me. In the meantime, enjoy." He left them with a friendly smile.

"I don't like it," Tessa said as they took their places at the table.

"What's to like?" Lona told her. "Don't let all this go to waste. Unless you marry a millionaire, you're not going to get more breakfasts like this. So eat up, kid, and drink your Buck's Fizz." Lona poured champagne into Tessa's glass and topped it up with orange juice.

In his stateroom, Behrensen watched them on the video screen that was normally hidden by clever paneling. He had recorded every conversation the two young women had had within the various enclosed parts of the ship since they had boarded. Every action too. He had recorded them in the shower, undressing for bed, or simply walking around. The lavatory was not exempt. Even their conversation of the previous night had not escaped his notice and though Lona had kept the stateroom dark when she had gone to the window, she had still made it on tape. Behrensen had recorded her in infrared.

It was his way of keeping total security aboard the *Stonefish*. There was a secondary reason which, in the past, had served him well. Many an unfortunate in a position of some power or influence, had been recorded committing an indiscretion or two. Behrensen had found such evidence a potent card to play when he needed a favor.

He switched off the screen and watched as it slid back into its hiding place. He pressed another button on the slim remote he held. A second screen came from the paneling. He turned it on, and ran a tape. A blonde with perfect curves was taking a shower. Lorraine Mowbray.

Behrensen's eyes stared at the image. Every so often, he would lick his lips slowly.

"Now there," he said hoarsely, "is a real woman. I tell you, J.D., I'm going to have her."

Quinlan, who had been watching the show impassively, said: "Once business is complete, you'll be able to do what you like with her."

Behrensen turned dead eyes upon Quinlan. "You wouldn't be trying to tell me how to handle this, would you, J.D.?"

Quinlan knew when to back off. "Not at all, Mr. Behrensen."

"Keep remembering it."

Quinlan remained silent as Behrensen returned his attention to Lorraine Mowbray in her shower.

After a while, he said; "What about the two women?"

Behrensen did not turn from the screen. "What about them?"

"Will you be putting them ashore first?"

Behrensen switched off the video. The screen slid back. The panels shut themselves over it.

He turned to Quinlan. "Don't be ridiculous."

Lona Mason dabbed at her lips delicately with a monogrammed napkin. She gave the bottles of champagne a brief glance. One was empty.

"I'm full," she announced. "How about you, Tessa? You haven't eaten much, and I drank most of that champagne. Be happy, kid. We'll be off this tub soon."

"I hope you're right."

Lona stood up. "I'm right. Now let's go out on deck as usual, and all we've got to remember is to do exactly as we've always done. A little stroll, before going to the sunbeds at the stern." She gave a cheese-cake smile. "Give the crew their daily thrill."

"Lona, I don't think we should." Tessa said worriedly. "Perhaps we shouldn't parade on deck . . ."

"Look, kid," Lona interrupted firmly. "We don't know what we're playing with here. We thought we were going to have some fun, but it's turned kind of sour on us. Now that you've got me agreeing we should make ourselves scarce, I want nothing to foul us up . . . even if it means giving those bozos their floor show. Okay?"

Tessa got to her feet slowly. "Okay." But her heart wasn't really in it.

They went through the motions of their daily routine, eventually ending up on the luxurious reclining deck chairs that Lona had called sunbeds. With sunglasses on, they soaked up the pleasant warmth of the Mediterranean morning, seemingly without a care in the world. They knew various members of the crew would be taking turns to have a good look at them. By now, they had got used to it. They also knew the crewmen would keep both their thoughts and hands to themselves. No crewman in his right mind would risk offending Behrensen.

The ubiquitous Ramon appeared with more chilled champagne and a fresh pitcher of orange juice.

"It's going to be a fine day, ladies," he said to them.

Lona glanced at the still surface of the sea. "Why are we drifting, Ramon? I thought we were going to Crete."

"We are, but it's such a nice morning, Mr. Behrensen decided to hang around out here for a while. He has an important meeting, and it's better to have a quiet ship, if the sea state allows. As you can see, it's like a lake this morning. Enjoy, ladies. I've got to get back to my kitchen. Got a lot of food to prepare."

"Oh," Lona said interestedly. "More guests?"

Ramon nodded. "They'll be coming in from Crete."

"So we'll be there soon?" This from Tessa.

Again, Ramon nodded. "Yes, ladies. Now I really must get back." He smiled at them, and left.

"There you go," Lona said, when he was well out of earshot. "We'll soon be out of this, Tessa."

"Do you think Behrensen gets all his money from drugs? That's why they've got all those guns you saw . . ."

"Tessa," Lona interrupted, "questions like these can get you shot. Me too. I wouldn't like it one bit, and neither would you. So let's just stick to our little plan. No see, no hear, and no goddam talk. Okay, kid?"

Tessa's eyes, full of fright, stared at her.

"Hi!"

They looked in the direction of the call. Behrensen was standing outside his stateroom, and was carrying what looked like a video camera. From where he stood, he was about 20 meters away.

"I'd like to make a video of you. A record of your trip to take with you." Behrensen smiled at them.

"For us?" Lona asked, sounding pleasantly surprised.

"Sure. You can prove to your friends you really were on the *Stonefish.*"

"Okaayy!" Lona stood up, looking enthusiastic. "What do you want us to do?" She reached for Tessa. "Up, Tessa. Let's strut for the man."

Behrensen followed them about the ship, even up to the bridge, camera whirring softly. None of the crew members got into shot, and there was no sign of the guests that had arrived by helicopter during the night.

They were moving back toward the deck chairs, when Behrensen said: "I'd like some film of you on the chairs, then of the two of you by the guardrail, backs to the ensign. Yeah. Good, good. Now against the rail. Closer together. That's it. Perfect. Hold it for a moment."

Behrensen was again near his stateroom and he paused to take a telephone from its socket on the superstructure.

"Mr. Duquesne?" he said quietly. "In thirty seconds, I want forty knots. Go to it." He replaced the phone. "Okay," he called to the young women. "Stay like that while I get this shot."

Lona was smiling at Tessa when her eyes were attracted by something in the region of the other's ample left breast.

"Hey," she said. "You've got an allergy, or something. There's a red spot on your breast."

"What?" Tessa looked down quickly. The spot seemed to be moving infinitesimally. "It's moving! It's . . . it's not a spot. I think it's a light of some kind . . ."

She never finished. The red spot suddenly blossomed into a crater of blood just as the *Stonefish,* with a sudden bellow of its powerful engines, seemed to leap forward. Tessa was flung right over the guardrail by the force of the impact, and the unexpected surge of the ship.

Eyes wide in horror, Lona was in the act of turning to see Tessa's body flung into the boiling wake, her mouth opened to scream. She did not see the two red spots settling upon her own back. Then a double blow of immense power struck her between the shoulders, and she was aware of being suddenly airborne. There was a strange numbness brought about by the shock of the blows, and pain seemed to have been left far behind in an immeasurable distance.

Then she was falling swiftly and the water hit her full in the face, flooding into a still-open mouth that had not even had the time to give voice to the intended scream. By the time the water had closed over her, she was dead.

Behrensen stopped filming. "Pity," he said to himself.

Two men came from either side of the ship to join him. They carried silenced rifles with laser sights.

"Good work," he said to them. He tapped the video camera briefly. "Got it all in." He glanced at the weapons. "You can put those away now."

The men, both white, nodded silently and went off to store the weapons. If they had any opinions about Behrensen's filming of the killings, they kept them to themselves. Their faces were totally impassive.

Behrensen again pulled out the phone. "Ten knots, Mr. Duquesne, if you please . . . and give us a nice slow circle." He snapped the phone back into its mounting.

The *Stonefish* seemed to come to a halt as the headlong rush was abruptly cut to an apparent crawl. Despite the residual momentum, the *Stonefish*'s change of speed was remarkable. Duquesne now took her into the slow circle demanded by Behrensen, the diameter of which was about a mile. At its center, was the spot where the two bodies had gone in.

Behrensen continued to film, zooming in on the patch of water. A dark fin-shaped image appeared in the lens.

"Ah," he murmured.

Soon, another fin had appeared; and another and yet another, until half a dozen were in the vicinity, cruising and cutting sharply into each other's own circles. Then one darted forward. Fractions of a second later, there was a sudden frenzy. The others joined in. The patch of water had become red. In their madness, they began to turn upon each other. The churning sea appeared to bleed for a long five minutes; then it was over. The calmness returned. Behrensen had filmed it all.

"You want to watch that, Mr. Behrensen. It's one thing having films of clients as insurance; it's another to leave yourself open to the same risks. Your own private films . . ."

Behrensen had finished. Now, he turned to look at Quinlan who had quietly joined him.

"Bet they never thought they'd have a breakfast like this today," Behrensen remarked calmly. His eyes, however, were cold. "You wouldn't be thinking of setting yourself up as a blackmailer, would you, J.D.?"

"Even if I needed the money," Quinlan said, deadpan, "I don't think there's anyone around who could pay me enough." Quinlan was many things, but being suicidal was not one of them.

"That's why I like you," Behrensen said. "You're smart."

"We've also been to many wars together, and we've pulled each other's tails out of the fire. A man does not forget these things. But I've always worried about your er . . . private movies, Colonel . . . guys falling out of choppers over some boondocks somewhere . . . getting into the wrong hands . . ."

"You let me worry about that, J.D. Those tapes are safe."

"But Colonel . . ."

"You don't have to call me that. A field commission . . ."

"Ratified by Capitol Hill. You're a long way from First Lieutenant."

Behrensen gave a wry smile. "An officer, but no gentleman. West Point never saw my ass."

"After all this time it matters to you?"

"With my background, J. D., I wouldn't have got past the cookhouse. But look at me now, eh?" Behrensen glanced upward. The ship's bridge was above their heads. "Up there is a guy who's never worn a uniform except the one he had at school, and the one I've bought him. But he looks every inch a naval officer when he's in it." He gave another of his wry smiles. "A descendant of a big slave-owning family, all the right schools, plenty of money, a car every birthday from the age of sixteen. Then something goes wrong and he washes up in southeast Asia, where I found him. No officer, but still a gentleman."

Behrensen reached for the phone a third time as the *Stonefish* continued to describe its slow circle.

"Mr. Duquesne, back on course now, thank you. Yes, maintain current speed." Behrensen's voice was almost sly as he went on: "I don't suppose you approve of what just happened either." Behrensen waited as Duquesne made reply. "Thought you'd say that." He hung up, and turned again to Quinlan. "I get the same answer every time. 'It's not for me to have an opinion one way or the other,' " Behrensen quoted. "That's the kind of man he is, J.D. A moralist."

As the *Stonefish* changed course, the sun flashed upon Quinlan's glasses. For a moment, it seemed as if the sockets of his eyes were on fire.

"A *moralist?*" he said disbelievingly.

"Oh yes. The best kind too. One that has sunk so low, his loyalty is assured. You see, J.D., people like Duquesne are sometimes far more ruthless than we are, when they play in our kind of pool. I have no illusions . . . had none when I was a kid and you, well even with your Ivy League background, you're a cobra when you get going. Duquesne found out the hard way what we already knew. He feels betrayed by his own kind so he has no respect for them. We got there long before he did."

"You trust him?"

"As I do you, J.D., but for different reasons. I'll always remember what a training officer once said to a group of us. 'I want no moralists here. In a tight spot, a moralist can get you killed while he's thinking about what to do. Morals have no place in this game.' " I took his advice. When I started my business, he came to work for me."

"Does he still?"

"No."

"What happened?"

"I shot him. The bastard tried to double-cross me. He forgot one thing . . . morality and immorality are two sides of the same coin. If you look closely, you'll see one creeping up to the other. It's a policy of mine to keep my eye on both, because they are both as dangerous."

"And you?"

"I, J.D., am the most dangerous of all. I am amoral." Behrensen placed the video camera on a nearby table that was fixed to the deck, and went to the side of the ship. He gripped the polished wooden capping of the rail with both hands and stared out to sea. "I'm going to enjoy the next forty-eight hours."

Quinlan came to stand next to him. "What shall we do about Veronica Walmsley?"

Behrensen thought about it for some moments. "She's served her purpose, although she did not do as well as I'd hoped. But it's not a problem. I have more than one string to my bow. When this is all over, sack her."

The ship turned a few degrees into a new course and again, the sun caught Quinlan's glasses. His sockets seemed to catch fire for a second time.

"Just sack her?"

Behrensen looked at him. "As I've just said . . . you can be a cobra sometimes. No killing there, J.D. That would be stupid. She's no danger. Those two girls were. They were dead when they first came aboard. No one saw them. I made sure of that. And everyone's going to think that another pair of traveling young women got into a situation they couldn't handle. Happens all the time, and I doubt if the sharks will have left much evidence.

"Veronica Walmsley is a different proposition. Questions will be asked and besides, I'm certain she's being watched. No, J.D. This one you don't get. Just sack her when you get back. Pay her off well, and make suitable apologies. Say we're rationalizing our staffing situation. That's common currency these days, so it will have the ring of truth." Behrensen inhaled deeply. "There are times when I think life is truly wonderful. Don't you?"

"It has its moments," was what Quinlan said.

The A3 motorway, just after the Herstal intersection, 0842 local.

Gallagher turned off the motorway and took the filter road that led to the service station at Barchon. He did not need fuel as yet, but the car had used enough to make the stop appear genuine. As he stopped by the pumps and climbed out, he took a swift glance around. The large parking area was barely occupied. This pleased him and while the tank was being filled, he waited to see who would turn up.

By the time the tank was again full, he knew.

"I was afraid of this," Haslam said as Prinknash stopped the BMW a long way from the petrol pumps. Haslam had directed him to choose a parking slot that was behind a low barrier of young trees. "I'll bet anything he was not really short of petrol. This was a flushing out operation, and it worked."

"He can't have seen us come in," Prinknash insisted. "We were behind that bloody great articulated lorry."

"You don't learn much, do you, Prinknash? Did you expect him to stand in the middle of the place to wave us in? Of course he's seen us. Probably did so a long time ago. His pulling us in here behind him just confirms it. It's what I would have done in his place. And look at that car parked over there . . . next to that red Volvo."

"The blue Golf. Think he's worked it out about us?"

"It's an even bet. He may be too occupied with Gallagher's car to pay us much attention. On the other hand ... Ah. Look. See that white Citroen with the Belgian plates? It's been on this route since well before Brussels. If our man's noticed it, he could easily think it's involved, though the driver may just be someone traveling on business. Perhaps that's what he'll think we are for the moment. Business travelers."

"Gallagher's leaving," Prinknash said urgently.

"We may as well follow."

Prinknash started the BMW. "Think he'll try to lose us now?"

"That's an absolute certainty. It's only a question of timing. Be on your guard." Haslam watched the Golf. It had begun to move. "He seems only to be worrying about Gallagher. Let's see where he decides to position himself this time."

Gallagher watched as the cars sorted themselves out in his mirrors. The Golf had again chosen to stay behind the BMW, leaving four cars to fill the space. The BMW was itself six cars behind the *quattro*. At the Chaineux intersection, he took the A27 south toward Malmedy and Francorchamps.

Traffic had become very light now, and it was some time before the BMW put in an appearance. The Golf, a speck in the distance when view of the road allowed, had taken the same route.

Gallagher had said nothing to Lorraine Mowbray. Even at the filling station, she had been occupied with the CDs and had not looked around to see the Golf in their wake. He wondered whether that was because she already knew.

They were going down a steep sweeping curve when she stopped the music and suddenly said: "And lo we sprang, fully formed, out of the loins of the sky."

"What was that all about?" Gallagher began. "Has this hill given you a rush of inspiration?"

"I was just thinking about the situation back home. You'd think we so-called Coloreds were created by some form of magic, and not by black and white people sleeping together over the centuries . . . mainly white men screwing black women. Yet there are those who look on them as animals. What does that make all those generations of whites who have gone to bed with them?" Her voice had become tense and full of anger. "If I had a time machine I'd go back to 1487 and shoot Bartolomé Dias. Save a lot of people a lot of grief, man. I tell you."

It was the first time Gallagher had heard her use that particular style of speech: a measure of her agitation.

"Someone else would only have come along to discover the Cape," he said. "What would you do? Sit in 1487 to shoot every seafarer who came by? Besides, shooting Dias would possibly eliminate your very existence which in turn would mean you wouldn't be around to go back in time . . ."

"The last thing I need right now is a lecture on the paradoxes of time travel."

Gallagher gave her a quick look, noting again her flawless beauty and wondering about the warped ideology that made life a horror for so many in the country she clearly loved.

"Sorry," he said.

"No. It's my fault. I'm just passing my frustrations on. My anger too. But there is hope, you know. People of my generation, of all races, are beginning to realize that the older ones have let us down. We are the ones who will be living with the future, and we are the ones who can decide what that future will be." She looked at him, and smiled. "I shouldn't be so angry."

"You have every right to be."

"Yes, but not with you."

Gallagher took a quick look in the mirrors. Nothing. But that did not mean the BMW and the Golf had given up. It was merely that a right-hand bend past Verviers had temporarily hidden them from view. But he had a little surprise planned for them.

He meekly allowed them to trail him all the way to Baronheid where the motorway came to a temporary end. The section to Malmédy was currently incomplete but beyond Malmédy, it continued to the German border.

He turned right when he came to the end of the section and onto the N640. The road here was a 2-kilometer straight, narrow, with several undulations in its surface. There was no room for overtaking. There was also no other vehicle ahead of him in his lane. He drove fast along it.

By the time the BMW came off the motorway, the *quattro* was far into the distance and receding rapidly.

"That's it!" Haslam told Prinknash sharply. "This is where he's going to try to lose us. Get moving. I have a nasty feeling he knows his way around here. Once he gets away, we might as well give up."

He looked into his mirror. "The Golf's not here yet, but I suspect he won't be far behind. There's no other route off the motorway at this point."

"I think he's turning right, Mr. Haslam. Gallagher, I mean."

Haslam stared ahead. The Audi's indicator was blinking. "Why is he letting us know?"

"He wants us to follow."

"I've worked that one out, Prinknash. It still doesn't tell me why."

"Shall I follow?"

"Of course. What else can we do?" Haslam again checked the mirror. The Golf was coming up fast. "The blue wonder's on its way. Things should get interesting."

Gallagher had stopped at the T-junction with the N92. To the left was the small motor racing circuit town of Francorchamps and to the right, eight kilometers away, was the larger town of Spa. The junction was itself on the apex of a rising bend, with the right turn sharper than the left. Gallagher went right, accelerating hard.

After the turn, the road was straight for about a kilometer before curving gently right through the village of Malchamps into another straight. In his mirrors he saw the BMW, baulked by an oncoming lorry, impatiently waiting to follow.

Lorraine Mowbray said: "Are we being followed?"

She was either a very good actress, or she really didn't know; which brought all sorts of different questions in its wake.

"I prefer not to take chances," was what he replied.

The road bordered a marsh and some woods. Gallagher briefly considered the idea of coaxing the BMW into the marsh, but discarded it as unworkable. He'd have to rely on the *quattro*'s power and speed to give him sufficient distance within which to carry out his intended deception.

The road began to curve gently left three kilometers later and on the curve, was a side turning to the left. A temporary lack of traffic from either direction enabled him to go into the turn without indicating. He thought he caught a glimpse of the BMW storming up, but wasn't sure.

Again, the road was a long straight, but narrower. He made good time and when after another three kilometers he turned left, there was still no sign of the BMW, let alone the Golf. He hoped they were both on their way to Spa. They could have fun trying to find him there.

A further left at Le Rosier took him across country on a tiny twisting lane that was roughly parallel to the route he'd taken on the N62. This went on for nearly five kilometers before he was again going left, heading for Francorchamps. His route had described a loose square and when he had reached the little town, he felt certain his 20-kilometer ruse had shaken off both his pursuers.

At Francorchamps, he turned right to continue his journey along the N640 which on race days, was part of the circuit. Two kilometers before Stavelot, he went left. He would be rejoining the motorway less than five kilometers later.

Lorraine Mowbray had been silently watching him. She now turned briefly to peer through the rear window.

"You really do know how to handle your car, don't you?" she said.

"I hope I didn't frighten you on those narrow roads."

"I'd have screamed if you had."

He smiled. "No you wouldn't. You'd never admit it . . . not to me, anyway."

"Oh I don't know."

He glanced at her. The translucent eyes seemed amused.

She took another peek at the back window. "Think we've lost them? Whoever they are?"

"I know we have."

Prinknash pulled into a Spa side street and stopped the BMW

Haslam was ominously silent. He looked in his mirror and saw the blue Golf turning into the same street to park sheepishly some distance behind them.

"That will teach you to play follow-my-leader," Haslam said to the image harshly.

"What now, Mr. Haslam?" Prinknash began uncertainly. "I mean, what do we do? God knows where he's got to now."

"You've got the whole of Belgium within which to look, Prinknash."

"Me, Mr. Haslam?"

" *'Me,* Mr. Haslam?' " Haslam mimicked. "Yes. *You.* You lost him."

"But that lorry . . ."

Haslam sighed. "When are you going to learn? To keep up with Gallagher you've got to practically read his thoughts. Think of all the normal things you would do, then chuck them out. You can be sure he won't be doing any of them. When you've cleared the decks, think of all the outrageous and unexpected things you might contemplate doing. One of them *might* be the one. The trouble with that theory of course, is the lack of guarantee. He might have come up with something so simple, we're blinded by it. Come on, Prinknash. Get those rusty cogs working."

"Perhaps he's gone back to Brussels," Prinknash offered tentatively. Then warming to his theme, added: "Perhaps he was going there all along."

Haslam was thoughtful. "Good try. You've got the drift . . . but I don't favor Brussels, even if he did come back this way. This is a route to Liège and from there to Brussels, but I don't think he'd have come all the way out here just to give us the slip. My guess is it's somewhere around this area. Keep working at it."

11

The day had become bright and warm when
Gallagher pulled off the motorway and onto the slip
road, a short stretch of tarmac about three hundred
meters in length. It ran alongside the motorway,
with its own hard shoulder which was used for parking.

Gallagher brought the car to a slow halt and
switched off the engine. The 20-valver ticked quietly
to itself as its turbo whirred inaudibly to a stop. The
West German border was a bare two kilometers
away. The time was 1059.

There were two other vehicles on the hard
shoulder: a vast truck with what looked like four
smokestacks, and the Range Rover he had last seen
on the IJsselmeer causeway. The truck, pointing the
wrong way, seemed to be some kind of roadworks
vehicle. The relative newness of the section of motorway appeared to confirm that. In the space between
the truck and where Gallagher had parked, was Villiger's Range Rover. As on the IJsselmeer, there was
no one in it.

"Stay here," Gallagher said to Lorraine Mowbray, and climbed out.

She leaned across to look up at him. "Why isn't he waiting?"

"He's here. He's checking us out. More to the point, he's out there somewhere making certain no one's tagged along."

Gallagher left the door slightly ajar and walked the short distance to the low barrier at the edge of the slip road. He looked slowly about him. Traffic on the motorway appeared to be so infrequent, not a single vehicle had passed in either direction since their arrival. Beyond the high banks on each side of the road, were thick woods. He wondered if Villiger waited under cover up there.

After about five minutes, Gallagher heard a rumbling sound that grew in volume. It came from the direction of the border. Soon, a big white Mercedes, traveling fast, hove into view. It hurtled past, the type of road surface making its tires roar like a low-flying jet fighter. The sound faded quickly as the car vanished out of sight as the road inclined downward. The quiet descended once more.

Gallagher walked back to the car, unconsciously listening for new tire sounds that would betray traffic coming from the opposite direction. He hoped the BMW and the Golf would continue to waste time in Spa.

He leaned on the warm roof of the *quattro* and looked in. "He must be here somewhere," he said. "When we last spoke, something had given him cause for alarm. He's clearly not taking any chances."

"What if . . . what if whatever it is has already

gone wrong? Because the Rover's here doesn't necessarily mean he brought it."

"He's here," Gallagher repeated. "Piet does not get caught out easily. We'll wait."

"It's because you're anxious to get rid of me."

He stared at her.

"It is true, isn't it?" she went on. "You're hoping he'll take me off your hands. I'm a nuisance in your life. Oh I know you were nice to me yesterday, but you can't deny you're hoping to be let off the hook . . ."

"Well . . ." Gallagher began, but a familiar voice interrupted him.

"You were one minute early!"

Gallagher straightened, and turned to look. Villiger was climbing down from the truck. Lorraine Mowbray looked very pleased to see him, and got out of the car. She walked quickly over, almost eagerly, to meet him. Gallagher remained where he was.

Villiger smiled at her, gave her shoulder a quick clasp and together, they approached the Audi. Something nagged at Gallagher, but it didn't crystallize into anything he could identify. He let it be. Perhaps it would surface later.

Villiger stopped and extended a hand. "And here we are again." He held his other hand against his thigh. There was a weapon in it, pointing downward.

Gallagher had never seen anything like it. His attention was drawn to the pistol-like gun even as he shook Villiger's hand.

"What the hell's that?"

Villiger glanced down. "A new kind of toy, not yet on the market. As far as I know, there are only two outside the factory where they're made. I've got one, and the man who hopes to sell them to us has the other."

"It looks like a cross between an automatic and a submachinegun. Were you expecting company?"

"It is, and I wasn't . . . but it doesn't do to take chances, as you know."

Gallagher nodded.

"Here." Villiger handed him the gun. "Get the feel of it."

Gallagher took the weapon, noting the strange cylindrical shape that looked like an enclosed sighting system.

"Lighter than I expected," he said. "What's that thing on top?"

"A close-quarter dream. It's a helical magazine. A hundred rounds in a single load."

"You're joking."

"It comes in a 50-round capacity too, for the truly frugal. Fires well, 9mm. Makes your average 15- or 16-round auto look deprived. Good piece of kit to have with you."

A faint rumble made Gallagher hand back the weapon. "Car coming. Better put it away."

A truck thundered past, heading for Germany. Villiger held the gun straight down against his side. There was little chance of the trucker seeing it from his vantage point on the far carriageway, but Gallagher was still uneasy.

Villiger gave a thin smile. "It's alright." He turned to Lorraine Mowbray. "Wait here by the car. I'd like to have a word with Gordon."

She nodded, gave Gallagher an unfathomable look, before going around to sit in the car with the door open and her feet on the ground.

"Let's go to the truck," Villiger said and Gallagher accompanied him, wondering why she had not been included. "You two getting on?" Villiger continued.

"We're doing okay."

Villiger gave a sideways glance. "Only okay?"

After a moment's hesitation, Gallagher said: "I like her, but she can be a bit of a pain at times. Green though. Very green at this kind of business. Not like you, Piet, using her. She's a danger to herself and you, if you're not careful."

"I'm careful. And as I said to you before, I trust her with my life. I don't make such decisions lightly. Has she told you about herself?"

"About her mixed parentage? Yes. I'd never have believed it."

They had reached the truck. "Here," Villiger said. "Let's go this way."

They moved around the vehicle so that they were hidden from the road. On the ground, between two of its massive six rear wheels, was a spread raincoat. It looked as if someone had recently lain upon it. Villiger had set up a firing position.

"I had a good field of fire," Villiger said, looking down at the coat. "If anyone had followed, I'd have taken them out before they knew what hit them." He sat on the raincoat. "So . . . you'd never have believed it. Because she's so blonde? Sit down, for God's sake. Do I need a crick in my neck while I'm talking to you?"

There was an edge in Villiger's voice that added an extra dimension to the brutal sound of the Afrikaner accent.

Gallagher sat down on the space Villiger had left for him, arms about drawn up knees. A confusion of smells came from the truck: fuel oil, hot rubber and grease mixed with tar. The concoction was almost overpowering. From where he sat, he could see between the wheels. The *quattro* was in full view, as was the approach road. As usual, Villiger had chosen well. It was a spot Gallagher would have himself chosen.

"The way she looks," he now said in reply to Villiger's question, "makes your whole system even more of an aberration. But you don't need me to tell you that."

"She's suffered more than you can imagine."

"It doesn't show. At least, not unless you are aware of her history."

"She's a good actress. Good at her job too."

Gallagher said: "You don't have to sell her to me, Piet."

Villiger had kept the weapon ready and now, he peered briefly along his line of fire. He made no comment.

"I hope you don't intend to use that out here," Gallagher said.

"If I have to, I will. You're sure no one followed?"

"Two cars tried. They're still sorting themselves out."

"Where did you lose them?"

"Spa."

"Not far enough, but I suppose it will have to do." The edge was back in Villiger's voice. Something was really worrying him.

Gallagher pointed at the gun. "What is it called?"

"No official name as yet, but I've given it one that I believe suits it. I call it the Taipan, after that monster of a snake in tropical Queensland." Villiger's deep-set eyes seemed to twinkle briefly. "Appropriate, don't you think . . . keeping our Australian connections? After all, if we hadn't met over there, we wouldn't be here talking about how you're going to do a little extra favor for me."

Gallagher shut his eyes briefly, gave a loud sigh. "I bloody knew it. You've no intention of letting me off the hook, have you? I'm not going to fly your airplanes, Piet. I haven't changed my mind. Okay. Look. I'll help you keep those people off your back. I've got the distinct feeling it's you they're after. I could be wrong, but I never doubt my instincts. I've had too many harsh lessons when I've ignored them in the past . . . but no flying of fighters."

"Good. I'm glad we agree."

Gallagher stared at him. "I think I've just been suckered."

Villiger's smile was brief. "It's a job you shouldn't have difficulty in carrying out. I want you to accompany Lorraine to Greece. Crete, to be more precise. Fly with her to Chania. A helicopter will pick her up, and your job's finished. Here," Villiger reached into a pocket of the raincoat and put an envelope next to Gallagher. "Return tickets, and expenses. I hope your passport's in order. But of course it is. You wouldn't be here otherwise."

Gallagher looked at the envelope, looked at Villiger, peered through the gap between the wheels to look at Lorraine Mowbray's feet showing beneath the bottom of the *quattro*'s opened door, before turning to Villiger once more.

"You had this all set up," he accused.

"No. I really did hope to persuade you to fly for us. This is a totally new arrangement. I believe it's

Lorraine who's in danger. I want you to deliver her safely to Crete. I hope you'll do it."

Gallagher remembered what it had been like for them in the Australian Outback, fleeing for their lives from a murderous band of hijackers. He remembered how Villiger had saved his life. Already feeling guilty about refusing to fly for Villiger, he decided to do that one favor.

"Alright," he said. "But I don't need the expenses. I can manage."

Villiger seemed almost touchingly pleased. "Man, that's a big load off my mind, I can tell you."

"What about Hennie Marais?" Gallagher queried. "I thought he and Lorraine . . ."

"Aha. Do I detect a little rivalry there?"

"Of course not . . ."

"Hennie and Lorraine go back a long way. He's a little more keen on her than she is on him. Hennie's always assumed they'd get closer together. She has other ideas, of course."

Was that why Marais was following? Gallagher wondered. Jealousy? Would Marais jeopardize everything for something as base as jealousy? And why not? Worse things had been done in the name of passion.

Gallagher said: "How well do you know him?"

"We've never met. As you know, I keep an ultra low profile, for obvious reasons. But in my guise as servant of the state, I know an awful lot about him. He's on our files. A notorious 'agitator.' " Villiger gave a grim smile. "Every country has its euphemisms for describing those that may not always agree with the way things are run, and all such terms and descriptions are interchangeable with any country. It all depends on who's running the show at any given time. Hennie won't be going with you. He has other things to do."

Gallagher decided not to say anything about Hennie's disobedience of instructions. He saw no reason why he should rub the man's face in it. If indeed he were besotted with Lorraine Mowbray, then she would have to deal with it when they were all back in South Africa.

On the other hand . . .

"You seem deep in thought," Villiger said. "Anything wrong?"

"Nothing I can't handle."

"Here. You'd better take this." Villiger was passing him the gun. "As I said, a good piece of kit. It's so light because much of its structure is of composite materials. Tough, and very hard wearing. Virtually impervious to climatic vagaries, and pretty deadly. I know. I've used it in the field."

Gallagher was staring at the weapon as if it really was its highly venomous namesake.

"It won't bite, Gordon." Villiger sounded amused. "Legend has it that the Taipan, which doesn't just strike once but repreatedly within fractions of a second, can kill thousands of sheep with just one drop of venom. This won't do that, but it can be very devastating to an unsuspecting opposition. They can't believe why you don't run out of ammunition. It has a profound psychological effect."

"I'm not taking any gun anywhere, especially that one. Are you crazy? I'm not going to take that thing on a civil aircraft."

"I got it here."

"Bully for you. You can take it back the same way. I'll accompany Lorraine to Crete and then I'm out of it, Piet."

Villiger nodded. "Fair enough."

"Look. Piet, I'm sorry about the F-16's. I really don't think it's the right way to go about it. An international squadron, yes . . ."

"That's what it is . . ."

"You know what I mean."

They both got to their feet. Villiger placed a hand upon Gallagher's shoulder. "I do appreciate what you're doing. I know I conned you into looking after her but honestly . . . Wouldn't you have tried it on with me, if the situation were reversed?"

Gallagher smiled. "I might have done it differently."

Villiger tapped him with the envelope. "You forgot this."

"Fat chance I've got with you around. So what's our point of departure, and when?"

"Ostend, tomorrow morning. Take the connecting flight to Brussels, from there to Athens, then the connector to Chania. The helicopter will be waiting. Lorraine will be at her destination in time for dinner. You can have a quiet night on Crete and be back in Ostend the next day. A little over forty-eight hours from now, you'll be following the normal pattern of your life again."

"I have your word on that, have I?"

"Do you know one of the things I like about you, man? Your sarcasm." He grinned as he picked up the raincoat. "Let's not keep her waiting any longer."

She got out of the car as they approached, pale eyes searching each face in turn.

Villiger said: "Lorraine," and walked a short distance away.

She followed, and Gallagher watched as they talked, not really listening to the sound of their voices. His thoughts were on the BMW and the Golf. Were they still in Spa?

Villiger and Lorraine seemed to be having some kind of argument. Once, she stared at Gallagher expressionlessly before turning back to Villiger to argue with him some more. It was an intriguing sight. Villiger firm, Lorraine looking stubborn. In the end, Villiger won. It never really was a contest.

They returned together.

"That seems to be settled," Villiger said. He held out his hand. "Have a good flight."

Gallagher shook it. "You watch out for yourself."

"I always do," Villiger said. He turned to Lorraine. "I'll see you out there."

She nodded silently. He turned away and went to the Range Rover, opened the driver's door and seemed to be concealing the Taipan. Then he got in and without turning to wave, started the Rover and drove toward the border, accelerating onto the empty motorway. They stood without speaking until its sounds died away.

"You don't have to do it, you know," she said. "I know he forced you."

Gallagher looked at her. "It's really difficult trying to keep up with the way you jump from point to point. He didn't force me. I agreed."

"Conscience?"

What the hell was eating her? "Get in," he said. It was ridiculous to stand there arguing.

She did so reluctantly. He couldn't understand what had got into her. He was also annoyed with himself. He was still trying to pin down the nagging thought that had come to him earlier, but it was no nearer than before.

He started the car. "There's a road bridge further back. We can cross over to join the other carriageway."

She said nothing as he drove slowly past the roadworks truck, to turn right and up the narrow road that would lead him to the bridge. The route went through a clump of tall trees.

Just before the bridge, she said: "I've got to talk to Hennie, to give him new instructions."

That should be interesting, Gallagher thought. Marais would not be there for his call.

"Fine," he said. "When?"

"Oh I don't have to do it till this evening. He's got the number . . ." She paused, not looking at him. "He's got the number of the hotel."

"Convenient."

The pale eyes were upon him now. "What do you mean?"

"Just talking to myself. It's a habit I've picked up over the years. Must be age creeping up. It's hell being in your early thirties."

That brought one of her more prolonged silences.

"The Golf's leaving, Mr. Haslam," Prinknash said.

This was the sixth side street in which they had stopped. Haslam turned to check the rear window. Prinknash was right. The blue car, which had followed them faithfully everywhere, had apparently decided to quit.

"Perhaps he knows something we don't," Haslam said.

"Why don't we follow him for a change?"

"No. Let him go wherever he's decided to. He

won't find Gallagher any more than we shall." Haslam paused. "There has to be . . ."

"You're going to think this a non-starter, but you did say consider anything unlikely."

"Yes, yes. Go on."

Prinknash hesitated. "It doesn't sound right . . ."

"Let me be the judge. Get on with it."

"What if he went to the border?" Prinknash had spoken in a rush. Haslam was staring at him, and he began to feel foolish. "You did say . . ."

"Bloody good idea, Prinknash! You see? Those cogs do work. Get weaving. Not across the border," Haslam was saying, more to himself, "but perhaps just *inside* . . ." He paused once more. "We're probably too late by now. He's had plenty of time to get there and meet whoever he intended to . . ."

They made their way out of Spa and got back onto the main road. Soon, they were heading for the motorway near Malmédy.

"He's back," Prinknash said.

Haslam looked in the mirror. The Golf had taken up station.

"I didn't think he knew what he was on about," Haslam said with a hint of smugness.

"Why don't we just stop him?"

"Let him tag along for the time being. Best to know where he is, if he's likely to be trouble for Gallagher. We might need to lend a hand."

"To Gallagher?"

"Of course, Prinknash. Whom else? The Department has its own reasons for wanting to know what Gallagher's up to, but it doesn't mean we want him caught up in something he can't get out of."

"Why should we help him? If he wants to get

himself topped, why don't we just let him? He's always saying he's not with the Department and wants nothing to do with it. I'm not forgetting he once nearly broke my arm."

"You weren't exactly being pleasant to him, if I remember correctly. You were sent to ask him to come in, but chose to make it a summons and when he refused, you tried the strong-arm stuff. You really should have known better. In any case, that was a long time ago."

"I haven't forgotten," Prinknash said tightly. "The bastard enjoyed hitting me. He banged my knee with the sodding camera case too. I haven't forgotten," he repeated. Prinknash's eyes had become red with the memory of the pain and anger he had felt.

"Perhaps you should do something about your bedside manner," Haslam said unsympathetically. It was Haslam who had eventually persuaded Gallagher to see Fowler.

Prinknash's cheeks had become sunken, and his mouth had got smaller and tighter. It was clear he was reliving the incident. He said nothing as he put more pressure on the accelerator, taking his remembered anger out on the BMW.

The Golf, caught out by the sudden increase in speed, had fallen back, but now it was catching up.

They drove on in silence until they rejoined the motorway. Then soon after passing the Ligneuville exit, a sudden shout came from Prinknash.

"Mr. Haslam!"

"Watch the road, for God's sake! I've seen him."

The black *quattro* had appeared and was swiftly gone as it rocketed past on the opposite carriageway. Behind them, the Golf had dipped its nose in sudden braking as its driver had reacted unconsciously, clearly wanting to turn around. But the exit was now too far away.

In the Golf, Marais was not going to give up so easily. He began to reverse toward the exit. It was a stupid and dangerous thing to do. As so often happens at such times, the previously empty stretch of road was suddenly full of traffic. A big truck was bearing down, the blast of its airhorns renting the air.

Marais had no option but to abandon his attempt.

Haslam had turned around in his seat to watch the fun. The Golf was now far behind.

"It's just not going to be his day," he said as he looked ahead once more. "Slow down. Let him catch up, then take the next exit and stop."

It was another four kilometers to the Amel exit. Prinknash took it and stopped. Soon, the Golf followed off the motorway.

"Alright," Haslam said. "Block him."

Prinknash put the BMW into the classic police broadside. The Golf screeched to a halt. No other traffic was coming through. The motorway was quiet again.

Haslam got quickly out, and went over to the Golf. "Right," he began as Marais furiously wound down the window. "We've enjoyed your company long enough. Time to say goodbye."

Haslam had spoken in English, and Marais used the same language.

"What the hell do you think you're doing?" he shouted. "Get the hell out of the way!"

"My," Haslam said with infuriating calm. "We

are in a temper. Interesting accent you've got there. Bit far from home, aren't you?"

"Are you going to keep blocking my way?" Marais said tightly. "Or am I going to have to move you?"

"Dear me. I'll be terrified in a minute. No, whoever you are, we're not going to block you for much longer."

"I should damn well think so! What . . . !" Marais' eyes had grown suddenly wide.

Haslam had taken out what looked like a long and very thin knife. Before Marais knew what was happening, Haslam had bent swiftly down and punctured a front tire. Marais, at first relieved to discover he had not been the target, listened with dawning comprehension to the hissing of the expelled air. The Golf settled drunkenly on its deflated tire.

"Goodbye," Haslam said and walked quickly back to the BMW.

"Hey!" Marais yelled. *"Hey, you bastard!"*

Haslam got into the BMW, shutting the door as Marais left the Golf in a hurry and began running up.

"Move it!" Haslam told Prinknash.

The BMW squealed away just as Marais reached it. Haslam looked in the mirror in time to see Marais stamp his foot and punch at the air in impotent fury.

"That should hold him for a while," Haslam said mildly.

In the *quattro,* Gallagher had seen both the BMW and the blue Golf going in the opposite direction. Lorraine Mowbray, as luck would have it, had been occupied with looking through the CDs for one she wanted to listen to. Head down during the search, she had not seen Marais' blue car go past. Gallagher chose not to tell her about it. He still couldn't understand Marais' supposed jealousy, if jealousy it indeed was.

He didn't want to believe, despite his suspicions, that she had put Marais up to it. That would have meant going against Villiger's wishes.

Unless Villiger already knew about it.

He glanced at her. She had found the CD she wanted, and was about to play it. She paused, aware that he had looked at her.

"What?" she said, pale eyes studying him.

"Is it forbidden to look at you?"

"You never look without reason."

"They are pleasant ones."

"I don't believe you," she said.

Mainstreet came on. She closed her eyes and settled back in her seat.

"I really do like that song," she said.

Haslam and Prinknash never caught up with the *quattro*. When they eventually made it back to the Liège-Brussels motorway, Haslam told Prinknash to head for Bruges.

"Might as well," Haslam went on. "If he hasn't returned we've lost him for good . . . and if he has, he's already met whoever he'd gone to see. Either way, we've lost this one. Tomorrow, we'll take this car to Ostend and hand it in to the hire firm, then take the Jetfoil to Dover. We may as well go home. I'll have to let Mr. Fowler know."

They stopped at a service station where Haslam made his call. His conversation was brief, and contained no sensitive information; but the manner in which he delivered his message told Fowler at the other end all that was necessary.

In the London office, Fowler put the phone down slowly and tapped it once with a thoughtful finger. Then he picked up some transcripts and began to study them.

One was about a series of clashes in the African bush between South African forces and supported guerrillas, and seemingly highly successful commando-like teams that were curiously shy of publicizing their sometimes remarkable victories. No ragged bands of bush soldiers, these. The transcript indicated that they were almost wholly black, who fought with unnerving discipline. Not the normal stereotype.

Other reports had found their way to Fowler's desk, expressing similar views. Someone, somewhere, was good at training.

Fowler read through all the messages, then studied one more keenly. A Daphne class submarine had left South Africa some weeks before, but there were no further sightings of it.

Fowler tapped the paper and wondered if the commando teams, the submarine, and Gallagher, were somehow linked to FUTRON . . . and FUTRON meant Behrensen. But what was Behrensen up to?

"You're on your own, Gordon," Fowler said at the sheet of paper. "Haslam can't cover you now, even if you wanted him to."

De Vries was on the phone.

"I am satisfied it will work," he was saying. "Of course I am not a hundred percent certain. Who in this business would be stupid enough to give such an assurance?" He paused, listening, body stiffening a little. "I'm sorry if you think I'm insubordinate . . . but I'm the one in the field, and I do know what I'm doing. You'll be pleased with my result."

He listened some more, impatience plain in his attitude. He wanted to terminate the conversation. He had things to do. He continued to listen, barely managing to prevent himself from putting the phone down on the person at the other end of the line. At last, the man he had called stopped speaking.

"I'll do it!" he snarled, and slammed the phone down.

Fuck them, he thought. They were not the ones with the job. He still did not know the target.

Gallagher pulled into the courtyard of the small hotel in Bruges and switched off the engine. He remained in his seat, hands resting upon the steering wheel.

He turned to Lorraine Mowbray. "I assume you've already got your air ticket."

She shook her head. "It's in the envelope Piet gave you."

"You both had this planned all along," he said. "You worked it so that I'd be with you here today, ready to fly out to Greece tomorrow. Piet can be a devious sod when he wants to be. I know someone who'd like to meet him one day. They can compare notes."

"Piet didn't know whether you'd agree and no, it wasn't planned this way at all. This is a complete change. I'm as surprised as you are reluctant."

"I'm not reluctant. I agreed, didn't I?" She was still very touchy. What was up with her? "In forty-eight hours or so," he went on, "I'll be back here, and you'll be on your way."

"That should please you."

Gallagher was baffled. He couldn't fathom what was eating at her. Was it guilt, perhaps? Was she making plans that differed from Villiger's and which involved Marais?

The translucent eyes were looking at him with something new in them. "Gordon," she began softly, "I'm . . . I'm frightened, and I don't know why."

He reached out to put an arm about her. She did not pull away, but she did not relax either.

"Is that all?" he said. "I've lost count of the number of times I've been frightened."

"It's something more," she said. "I feel a kind of . . . oh I don't know. It's more than just being ordinarily frightened. It's a kind of dread."

"What brought that on?"

She looked as if she wanted to tell him something important, then appeared to change her mind.

"It's nothing," she said and eased herself out of the curvature of his arm.

She got out of the car, and walked toward the hotel entrance.

"Thanks for nothing, Piet," Gallagher said and after a moment's pause, climbed out of the *quattro* and began to unload it.

He had to carry her bags too.

12

"Something's happened to Hennie."

They were in Gallagher's room, having returned from a light supper an hour before. He had arranged with the hotel to leave the car in the courtyard during his coming absence, and they were planning an early night after Marais' call. The time was approaching 2100 hours.

"What makes you think that?" he now asked her.

"He should have called by now. We've been back since eight. Reception knows if I'm not in my room, I'm here with you. They'd have put the call through, wouldn't they?"

"Of course they would. Don't worry about it."

"But I've got to let him know what Piet's instructed him to do."

"Which is?"

She looked at him as if not sure she should tell, then opted for being cryptic. "He's to fly back."

"To Greece?"

She shook her head. "Africa."

He didn't ask where. It was not his business. He

decided to try a trick question. "Why not check with his hotel in Amsterdam?"

She didn't blink. If she knew Marais was nowhere near the Dutch capital, nothing in her manner betrayed her.

"We always arrange our phone calls," she said. "Safer that way. It's his turn to call."

It was a reasonable answer and Gallagher was no further along in determining whether she was aware of Marais' recent movements.

As if knowing what he was thinking, she continued: "You don't like him, do you? Why?"

"I don't know the man. Why should I like, or dislike him? I asked Piet about him . . ."

"You did, did you?" Her voice was challenging.

"I would have asked about anyone," Gallagher said patiently. "Piet wants me to look after you. I like knowing about everyone I'm likely to have contact with. I like to know, wherever possible, what's going on around me. It's my way of working. It's nothing to do with personalities. Hennie Marais could have been Joe Bloggs. I'd still have asked about him. What Piet said was enough for me. Okay?"

He remembered how subdued she had been during their meal: thoughtful, introspective, and mostly silent. Whatever was on her mind, she clearly intended to keep it to herself.

"I still think you don't like him," she insisted.

Gallagher did not have the chance to reply for at that moment, the phone buzzed.

"It's Hennie!" she said, brightening with relief.

"Better let me," Gallagher said, picking up the instrument before she could.

She was not happy about that, but accepted the situation.

"Gallagher," he said into the phone.

"Ah Mr. Gallagher," the receptionist's voice said in his ear. "Someone is here to see you."

Gallagher frowned. "Are you sure I'm the one who's wanted?"

"Yes, sir. Definitely. The gentleman has asked for you."

"Fine. I'll be down."

"Thank you, sir."

"Thank you." He replaced the phone thoughtfully and stood up. "Lock the door after me and on no account open it unless you hear my voice telling you to."

She was staring at him. "It wasn't Hennie?"

"A man wants to see me. I've no idea whom . . ."

"But why would Hennie . . ."

"We don't know it's Hennie." Gallagher studied her expression for a sign of prior knowledge. Nothing showed. "Now please do as I've asked." He went to the door. "Will you? I'm quite serious about this. Though you might not believe it, I've been very easygoing up to this moment; but if you do not do as I've asked, you'll make that trip on your own tomorrow. You can then have the pleasure of telling Piet why . . . if you make it that far."

She seemed to shiver. "That wasn't very nice."

"It was not meant to be. Piet would not have asked me to accompany you if he did not think it necessary. I know enough about him to understand that. Door locked when I've gone. Right?"

She nodded. "Yes." The eyes were staring at him, as if seeing him anew.

"Good."

He went out, paused long enough to hear her

turn the key in the lock, then continued down to Reception.

He stared at the big man waiting by the desk. Haslam.

"Ah . . . Mr. Gallagher," the receptionist began, "this is . . ."

Gallagher nodded. "I know this gentleman. Thank you."

Haslam said: "A quiet word, Gordon?"

"Do I have a choice?" Gallagher asked as they moved out of the receptionist's earshot.

"You could always tell me to piss off. But I do think you ought to hear what I've got to say."

"The courtyard," Gallagher said after a moment's pause. "We'll talk in the car. Where's the twitching bantam?"

"Prinknash? Outside, waiting in the BMW. You do remember the BMW?"

Gallagher gave a brief smile. "Enjoyed Spa, did you?"

"Wrong time of the year for me. We had company, as I'm sure you'll also remember."

Gallagher nodded again. "He of the dark blue Golf. What have you done with him?"

Haslam explained.

Gallagher gave a short laugh. "So that's what happened."

They were in the courtyard and approaching the *quattro*. Gallagher unlocked it with the remote, and they got in.

It was just past sunset, but there was still plenty of light to the day. Gallagher glanced up at his room from the driving seat. He thought he could faintly see Lorraine Mowbray's silhouette. He should have warned her about windows too, he decided.

"Talk," he said to Haslam.

Haslam studied him for some moments, before saying: "Is she here with you?"

"Yes." Gallagher saw little reason to deny it.

"And I don't suppose you're going to tell me whom you saw today out there in the Ardennes, even if I asked nicely."

"No."

"Succinct. I'll say that for you. I did wonder whether you'd come back here. I'd decided we might as well return to London, but thought of making one last check. Saw the car in here and thought as I was passing, I'd give you a little warning ... which you're quite free to ignore, or take seriously."

Gallagher took another quick look at the window of his room, and said nothing. Her silhouette was no longer there.

"I don't know what your immediate plans are," Haslam went on, "but we think you're heading into some trouble, worse than what nearly happened in Amsterdam. FUTRON, Behrensen, Quinlan, the young lady you're with, are all tied in with an arms shipment of some kind. We don't know what it is as yet. We've ... er ... done a computer intercept and some ostensibly unconnected items have appeared randomly. Taken at face value, they're just incidental bits of intelligence ... but they did have a certain relationship if one chose to look close enough. They all fell within a reasonably tight time frame, and there was a general congruence about them. I am, of course, not at liberty to tell you what."

"Of course," Gallagher said drily. He glanced up at the room for a third time. No silhouette. At least she was keeping away from the window.

"A new item has entered the pattern," Haslam

said. "A Daphne class submarine went out on an ostensibly routine patrol some time ago. It hasn't been seen since."

"What possible connection could I have with any submarine, let alone a Daphne? Sorry. This is all news to me."

"Are you quite sure, Gordon? If FUTRON and the rest have anything to do with a submarine, you'd be well advised to keep as far out of it as you can. It's bad news all the way."

"I think you've got some screwed-up information somewhere. Your official hackers have tapped into a few bits of duff intelligence and have come up with a crazy scenario."

"Duff is it? Is that what you think? Or are you just spinning me one?"

"I'm spinning nothing. I really don't know what you're on about," Gallagher said. Why the hell didn't you tell me about this, Piet? was what he was thinking.

"I can't help you if you won't let me," Haslam said. "We followed you today to lend a hand . . . in case you needed it."

"Was that the only reason?"

Haslam took a few seconds before replying. "I'll admit we were interested in identifying the person you went to see."

"The real reason."

Haslam smiled thinly in the increasing gloom. "You know how the Department works."

"To my eternal nightmare, yes."

"Adrian Fowler cares about what happens to you," Haslam said.

"Don't tell me you're keeping a straight face. I'll weep in a moment. Fowler only cares about the use he hopes to get out of me. Come off it, George. I'm not someone just off the street."

"We all get used. I should be enjoying my pension, not chasing you all over the Dutch and Belgian landscapes."

"Then do, and don't."

"If only it were so easy.

"It is. All you need is the will. Now if there's nothing else, I'm for an early night."

Again, Haslam paused. "As you're clearly not going to take my advice," he began in a resigned voice, "perhaps you'll take this. You might need it. It's one of your favorites, I think."

In the deepening gloom of the car, Gallagher could make out what "this" was. A Sig Sauer P226 automatic. The second person to offer him a gun in one day.

He shook his head. "Thanks, but no thanks."

"This might be a mistake."

"It certainly would be if I took it." Gallagher climbed out of the car as Haslam reluctantly put the gun away.

Haslam got out, leaned on the roof to face Gallagher. "Good luck," he said. "That's all I can offer you now. You might need it."

Haslam turned and went out through the still-open courtyard gate. Gallagher watched him turn the corner before securing the *quattro* and returning to his room.

Lorraine Mowbray let him in after he'd warned her he was back. She had put on one of the bedside lamps, and its soft glow made her look even more beautiful.

"Why didn't you tell me about the submarine?" he demanded bluntly as soon as he'd entered.

"Submarine? What submarine?" She seemed genuinely astonished. "I don't know anything about a submarine."

"Say it long enough, and you'll begin to believe it." Had Haslam lied? If so, to what purpose?

"I'm telling you the truth," she said. There was some desperation in her voice. "Don't you ever believe anyone?"

"It's my way of cutting down on nasty surprises."

"It's a good thing you haven't a wife," she said bitterly. "She'd have a hard time convincing you of anything."

"I had one . . . once," he said flatly. "She surprised me."

"Oh . . . oh God. I'm sorry. I didn't mean . . ."

"It was a long enough time ago for it not to matter anymore."

She stood looking at him, beautiful and to him, perhaps untrustworthy. He wasn't sure what to think. Villiger trusted her. That meant something. But Villiger had not said anything about a submarine.

Unless Haslam had indeed lied. Gallagher found himself deciding if it meant believing Villiger or the Department, he'd back Villiger. He hoped he would not live to regret it.

She said: "I've heard from Hennie."

So that's why she had no longer been at the window. "Where was he calling from?"

"He didn't say, and I didn't ask."

"What was his reason for being so late?"

"He said he'd had trouble with the car."

At least, there was some truth in it, Gallagher thought drily.

"I gave him his instructions," she was saying. "So while we're on our way to Crete, he'll be heading back to Africa. We'll be meeting up over there."

"That seems to have been settled nicely," Gallagher said neutrally. "We ought to get to bed. We've got an early start in the morning."

"I suppose I'd better stay with you tonight," she said. "You are supposed to be looking after me." Her eyes were fastened upon his.

"Alright," he said after a while.

She slept on the bed with him and later in the night, she moved close. It reminded him of Amsterdam, and Veronica Walmsley.

"Hold me," she said softly in his ear.

But nothing else came of it.

In the morning, they took the seventeen-minute train ride to Ostend, then a taxi to the airport. Soon after, they were on their way to Brussels and eventually, Crete.

Haslam had seen them take the train. The BMW made it to the Ostend station in time for him to see Gallagher and Lorraine Mowbray get into the taxi.

He had got Prinknash to follow. From the airport lounge, he now watched as the plane they had boarded took off, then went to consult an airline timetable to see which flights from Brussels connected with it. Within a two-hour span of the flight's arrival, there were too many for him to pinpoint a particular destination.

Gallagher and the young woman could be headed anywhere.

Haslam could have arranged to have them stopped at Brussels National; but that would have achieved nothing. Besides, it was not what the Department wanted. He closed the timetable, and left it on a counter.

"Good luck, Gordon," he said quietly as he went out of the building and back to the BMW where Prinknash waited. "I meant what I said. You will need it."

The *Stonefish* was following a course pattern that kept it at least a hundred miles off the western coast of Crete. It did so at an average speed of ten knots. Sitting beneath an awning on the foredeck and sipping champagne and orange, were Behrensen and Quinlan.

Behrensen gave a loud sigh of pleasure. "This is going to be a fine day, J.D. Not only will we have completed a very successful and profitable operation, *she'll* be here too. I've been waiting for this, but it's been worth it. I'm going to enjoy taking that cool bitch's clothes off."

Quinlan drank deeply. "Is that wise?" he asked, putting the glass down. "Is she worth the hassle?"

"Oh yes. She's worth it. I want a piece of that ass, and I'm going to get it. You know me, J.D. I always get what I go after, sooner or later. In her case, it's going to be sooner."

"And if she doesn't want to play?"

Behrensen gave one of his coldest smiles. "She'll play."

The flight to Athens was so trouble-free, Gallagher wondered what all the fuss had been about. There was a twenty-minute wait for the connecting domestic flight to Chania, but even that brought no alarms.

There had been no need to book a place to stay for the night in Chania. Villiger had seen to that too.

It was 1710 local time and as Gallagher looked about him, watching the tourists and holidaymakers moving about, listening to the many languages of Europe and points east mingling with each other, he decided that anyone could be tailing Lorraine Mowbray and himself. Yet again, he felt no sensory warnings. His alarm systems were still on hold.

Had he been too naive in trusting Villiger?

He glanced at Lorraine Mowbray who was sitting next to him in the departure lounge. There had been a tenseness about her throughout the flight. She had not talked about how she had hung on to him during the night nor why, and in deference to her feelings, he had chosen not to mention it. But she was nervous about something. Trouble was, he had no way of identifying the reason.

Their flight to Chania was called and after another quick look around, Gallagher followed her out. The aircraft had a full load, many of the passengers being British and American. He saw no one who looked like a possible hostile. Again, that meant nothing.

The flight took just over twenty-five minutes and was as uneventful as the one from Brussels. The subtropical heat of a Cretan May greeted them, though the sun was on its way down.

"Well," Gallagher began as they went through to Arrivals. "That was painless enough." He glanced at his watch. 1805. He looked about him. "Your party will be here soon to take you wherever you're headed, and I'll be off to my hotel . . ."

"You can still catch a plane back to Athens," she

said. "Check out the night life." She was strangely aloof.

"I'm certain I can find something on Crete if I want to."

"You don't have to wait. I can manage from here." She would not look at him.

"I am going to keep my promise to Piet. I stay with you until I'm sure you're safe."

She said nothing to that for a man had come up to them. "Miss Mowbray?" he began. "Your helicopter's waiting." He was American.

She looked at the newcomer, recognition on her face. "It's Dan Murchison, isn't it?"

Murchison smiled. "You remembered. Yes, ma'am. Here I am again."

"You didn't bring your helicopter all the way here from Portugal, did you?"

Again, Murchison gave an easy smile. "Same pilot, different chopper. I'll get your bags."

"I'll take one," Gallagher said, and did so.

"This is Gordon Gallagher," she said to Murchison. "We traveled together, but he's only coming as far as the helicopter."

Gallagher wished she hadn't made it sound like an accusation.

"Mr. Gallagher," Murchison said politely.

They went out to where the aircraft was waiting. Murchison seemed to have the run of the airport. No one challenged them. It was a five-minute walk and like the one that had taken Lorraine Mowbray to Faro, this was also an MD500.

Murchison stowed the bags while Lorraine Mowbray turned to Gallagher.

She held out her hand. "I can't pretend I'm not

disappointed you did not agree to join us . . . even though it would be temporary."

"Getting shot down is very permanent."

"He thinks you're too good for that."

"He's never seen me fly."

They were speaking quietly, on the other side of the MD500 from Murchison who had now climbed into the right-hand seat. Murchison seemed to be looking at them, waiting for her to get in.

She leaned forward as Gallagher took her hand, to kiss him on the lips.

"How touching," someone said. This was followed by a soft, humorless laugh.

The voice made Lorraine Mowbray jerk away from Gallagher to spin around with a gasp. Gallagher was surprised too, but it was a surprise tinged with a degree of chagrin, and a confirmation of the accuracy of his instincts.

I should have bloody well listened, he now thought.

"Hennie!" Lorraine Mowbray was saying in a voice high with shocked astonishment. "What are you doing here? You should be on your way to . . ." She stopped. He had come closer, and she saw something in his hand. A gun. "Hennie Marais, are you mad? What do you think . . ."

"Hennie, yes. Marais, no. Captain de Vries at your service, Miss Mowbray. Security. And I'm coming to the conclusion of a very successful operation."

"What?"

Even to Gallagher's jaundiced ears, this new shock to her and her previous surprise sounded genuine. There was something else in her voice too. Fear. She had good reason.

What now? he thought. He glanced at Murchison. Murchison was studiously going through his preflight checks. There was no way he could have missed what was going on. No help from that quarter. Marais, now de Vries, was keeping a safe distance. No chance of rushing him before he shot someone.

"Forget it, Gallagher," de Vries said. "I can almost see what you're thinking." De Vries laughed softly. "You can have a go later, if you think you can survive it. You're coming with us. We've got some talking to do, you and I."

De Vries' accent was even more pronounced than Villiger's and it grated upon Gallagher. He knew that whatever the outcome, one of them would be dead before it was all over. He had recognized the killer in de Vries. His instincts had warned him and he had not listened. He was now paying for that oversight.

"In," de Vries commanded. "Both of you."

Lorraine Mowbray was still numb with the shock of the betrayal and seemed rooted to the spot. She was undoubtedly going through all the conversations she'd had with Marais—as she had known him—through the years. The evidence against her would be overwhelming, and damning.

Then she seemed to find her voice. It was quiet, contemptuous.

"You bastard," she said. "All these years and you were just a miserable spy."

He did not like that. "Don't make your problem worse. I'm not a 'miserable' spy. I'm a very professional operative. I infiltrated you successfully, and there's still one more part of the mission to complete. I'll be doing that very soon."

"But you're on the files. You have a police record
. . ."

"And where did you get that information?"

"You told me yourself, you bloody shit."

De Vries seemed unmoved by this new insult.
"But you would have needed confirmation. You
would not have accepted only my word. Where you
got confirmation is one of the things we'll find out
from you."

Gallagher could see where this would eventually lead. He also noted with approval Villiger's rule
about keeping his identity secret even from members of the movement . . . except from Lorraine Mowbray. And de Vries had now captured her. The
unmasking of Villiger, and probably his assassination, would be the ultimate prize to de Vries. Villiger
had recognized his own vulnerability through Lorraine Mowbray, and had asked Gallagher to protect
her.

But all I did was walk her into a trap, he
thought disgustedly.

"Come on!" de Vries was saying impatiently.
"We haven't got all bloody night. Get in. And don't
try anything," he went on to Gallagher, "or believe
me, man, I'll blow you away right here. We'll be off
before any of those jokers over there can do anything
about it."

Gallagher had glanced back toward the airport
building. So near, but a lifetime away for all practical purposes. De Vries had chosen his time well. This
was no amateur.

Gallagher took Lorraine Mowbray by the arm.
"Come on," he told her gently.

"I'll sit with the lady," de Vries said sharply.

"You sit up front with Murchison, where I can keep
an eye on you."

Gallagher did as he was told. When they were
all aboard, the helicopter lifted smoothly and headed
out over the darkening Mediterranean.

It was about an hour or so later when Gallagher
found himself looking down upon what he thought
was a small ocean liner as Murchison banked left, to
come in from the stern. The ship was well lit, and the
circle of the landing pad was brightly visible.

As the helicopter descended, Gallagher saw
there were alignment bars on the superstructure to
help Murchison set up for the letdown. Murchison
was clearly on form. Two green horizontals showed,
indicating perfect alignment. Murchison landed
with barely a thump.

It was then that Gallagher saw he was aboard
the most luxurious and expensive yacht he was ever
likely to set foot upon.

As Murchison cut the power, de Vries said: "You
first, Gallagher. Out!"

"You do like giving orders, don't you?" Gallagher said coldly.

"Don't push it. Out!" de Vries repeated.

Gallagher began to climb down. The ship appeared to be barely making headway.

"You please, Miss Mowbray," de Vries went on,
ridiculously polite. It somehow gave him a greater
air of menace.

"Hennie . . ." she began, hopelessly attempting
to remind him of former times.

Gallagher turned. "Don't beg, Lorraine . . . especially not to that piece of shit."

It was deliberately done. De Vries had a short

fuse, and Gallagher wanted to see just how short. It might help in the future. Perhaps the years of being an infiltrator had taken their toll upon his nerves. Gallagher hoped so.

In the event, de Vries rose to the bait. He practically leapt out of the helicopter, planted himself before Gallagher and poked the gun close to Gallagher's face.

"You die right here."

"Nobody's going to die on my deck," a strong voice said from beyond the lights. "Put that thing away, Captain de Vries. You are Captain de Vries, I hope? You'd better be, otherwise one of my men will take you out."

"Yes," de Vries confirmed tightly. "I am de Vries." He put the gun away very reluctantly. His killer eyes glared at Gallagher.

What Gallagher actually saw were pinpricks of light in darkened sockets.

The person who had spoken came into the circle of light. Gallagher saw a big, black man.

"And you must be Gallagher." He stuck out a large hand. "I'm Behrensen." Noting Gallagher's surprise, he went on. "Hell about the name isn't it? Always catches people out. Yours too, I reckon. Irish, and all."

"My father was Irish," Gallagher said neutrally. He shook the hand. No point alienating Behrensen. At least, not yet. Not until the odds were better.

"Is that a fact. Goddam. You learn something every day. Sorry you had to be brought here like this. I wish the circumstances had been better."

Gallagher was not fooled. Behrensen had turned to the helicopter within which Lorraine Mowbray still sat. Murchison had remained at his controls and appeared to be keeping well out of the proceedings.

"How nice to see you again, Miss Mowbray," Behrensen greeted. "I've been looking forward to renewing our acquaintance."

To Gallagher, she seemed to shrink as Behrensen opened the door on her side to let her out. Behrensen held out a hand, but she ignored it and climbed down unaided. Behrensen didn't seem to mind the snub which to Gallagher was a bad sign. Behrensen did not appear to be the type of person who would take kindly to snubs, especially public ones, and Gallagher was certain he would find a way of taking his revenge later.

Another man had come into the circle.

Behrensen said: "J. D. Quinlan . . . Miss Mowbray, Mr. Gallagher. And of course, Captain de Vries, whom we've been expecting."

Quinlan looked at each in turn, glasses glinting. Gallagher felt as if he had been picked up by radar.

We'd be safer in a snakepit, he thought grimly.

He had to do something. But what? And more importantly . . . when? Timing was everything.

Never rush it, sir. Wait. Wait until the odds swing in your favor.

O'Keefe.

But would they? *I could use you now, O'Keefe.*

But O'Keefe was long dead.

Someone else had come up to the helicopter. A crewman.

"Ah Paco, take our guests' bags. Tell Ramon they've got the stateroom. He'll know which."

"Yessir Mr. Behrensen."

Paco, who was tall and big enough to warrant respect in a fight, began taking the luggage out of the aircraft.

"Dan," Behrensen went on to the pilot, "you'd better get something to eat, then take it easy. You've got an early start in the morning, to pick up our chief guest."

"If it's alright with you, Mr. Behrensen," Murchison said, "I'd like to check the ship out first."

"As you wish, Dan. I always leave chopper business to you."

Murchison nodded slightly. "Yes, sir."

As the party moved away, the landing lights went out. A faint glow remained in the cockpit of the helicopter, and Murchison was once more preoccupied with his machine.

Behrensen led the way to the main lounge where the table was set for five.

Gallagher looked about him with seeming appreciation.

Behrensen, noting, said: "She's some ship." He did not bother to conceal his pride. "She's many things to me . . . an office, a home, a pleasure boat and sometimes, a warship."

"A *warship?*"

Behrensen smiled, almost secretively. "After we've eaten, I'll show you around, if you'd like."

"Why not," Gallagher said. Behrensen's willingness was in itself an ominous sign, but every little bit helped. Gallagher fully realized he was in no position to pick and choose. It was going to be down to seizing any opportunity that eventually came his way. Provided he was still alive by then.

There was a perceptible change in the vibrations that pulsed through the *Stonefish*.

"Ah," Behrensen said. "We're working up to some speed. We've got an important rendezvous in the morning." He did not expand on that. "Please," he went on, indicating the table. "Take your seats. Miss Mowbray, you're opposite Mr. Gallagher and next to me on my left. Gentlemen." He sat down at the head of the table. "Ramon is one hell of a chef, but he excels himself with seafood."

The meal was had in silence, but there was plenty of careful scrutiny among the men. Behrensen appeared to be taking Gallagher's measure, as if calculating the chances of Gallagher being able to make trouble for him. Quinlan's attention seemed focused upon Lorraine Mowbray, but it was a clinical study that seemed more obscene than Behrensen's frequent and openly lustful gazes at her. De Vries' killer eyes seemed unable to decide whether it was her death, or Gallagher's, that they hungered after most. Gallagher for his part looked at each of the other men in turn, without seeming to. But in his mind, he was already selecting them as targets, in order of priority.

For most of the meal, Lorraine Mowbray barely diverted her attention from her plate. Once, she had looked at Gallagher. But there had been no message in the translucent eyes. It was as if they had been switched off. Gallagher hoped it was because she was aware of Behrensen's continuing scrutiny. He needed her to be in possession of all her faculties when the time came . . . whenever that might be.

At the end of the meal, Behrensen said: "I'm going to show Mr. Gallagher round the ship. I'm sure you gentlemen can entertain Miss Mowbray. But please do nothing to cause her distress." It was a warning, thinly veiled, and directed in particular at de Vries.

De Vries glanced at Lorraine Mowbray with a scowl, openly displeased by the restraint put upon

him. But he made no objection. If anyone was going
to cause her distress, Behrensen intended it to be
himself . . . at first.

But Gallagher felt relieved. At least she'd be
alright while he was away. Again, she gave him the
switched-off look as he stood up with Behrensen, and
there was no expression upon her face as they left
the lounge.

Behrensen took him on a guided tour, clearly
taking a certain degree of satisfaction in doing so.
Gallagher found it strange that Behrensen found the
need to do so. Gallagher decided it was because Behrensen had no intention of allowing either Lorraine
Mowbray or himself off the yacht alive. Neverthe-
less, Gallagher made all the right noises of admira-
tion as Behrensen showed him around.

During the course of the tour, Gallagher discovered there were 12 crew aboard, including the captain. It further confirmed his suspicions. Behrensen
was being too accommodating and was showing all
the classic patterns of behavior of someone who was
so secure, he could divulge anything he wanted to,
with the complete certainty that the listener would
not later be in a position to pass any of it on.

"I've saved the best part till last," Behrensen
was saying as they headed toward the bows on a level
that was three decks below the main lounge.

They went through a watertight door and came
to a full-width barrier that rose all the way to the
main deck. There was a door in it, to which a keypad
was attached. Behrensen swiftly tapped a series of
numbers. The door first went inward, then slid to one
side.

"My secret place," Behrensen said. "I'm the

only one with the code, which I change every day. Come on in."

Gallagher followed, and stopped to stare in amazement. Behrensen had not been joking about the yacht doubling as a warship when the need arose. He found he was looking at a miniature missile launcher system. Further along from it, closer to the bow, was what looked a multibarrel antimissile gun system.

"I've got another, not quite like it, in the stern," Behrensen said. "It's an asroc unit. Do you know what asroc means?"

"Antisubmarine missile, rocket propelled, nuclear or nonnuclear."

Behrensen nodded slowly. "Of course you would. The entire system can be operated from the bridge." He patted the missile launcher. "I've had cause to use this baby once. Devastating. They behave like exocets, but are smaller, lighter, and faster. Harder to counter too. Of course, there are no nuclear-tipped missiles aboard this ship," Behrensen added with a short laugh.

Gallagher looked about him. That entire section of the bow had been given to the yacht's armament. There was enough there to equip any self-respecting, missile-carrying fast attack craft. FACs, he knew, could be anything between 100 and 500 tonnes with a speed range of between thirty-five to forty knots. To judge by the power he could feel coursing through the *Stonefish,* Gallagher thought the yacht could top that easily. Given its potential speed and the armament that had just been displayed to him, this luxurious ship was a serious adversary indeed for any patrol boat that came nosing too close. As Behrensen had already so proudly indicated, one had paid the heaviest price.

Behrensen was again patting the missile launcher. "When going into action, the unit rises up this tube to the deck and begins tracking as soon as it arrives." Behrensen gave a cold smile. "Catches a lot of people out. One minute there's a clean foredeck, and the next . . ." He let his words die. "Came up against an OSA class," he continued. "You know what an OSA is?"

Gallagher said: "Depending on its load, 165-200 tonnes. Crew of twenty-five, max speed about thirty-two knots. Four Styx missiles, two twin 30mm remote antiaircraft mountings. Three engines, Soviet built and serving with many small navies."

"I'm impressed. You do know your stuff. Since you know so much about it, you might know the client states and guess which one's a FAC light on its inventory." Behrensen did not wait for Gallagher's comment, even if one had been intended. "It was outclassed, of course. The *Stonefish* is good for forty-six knots so as you can imagine, the bastards were sitting ducks. Blew their goddam ship right out from under them. Besides, to aim the Styx you've got to be following a straight course in a calm sea. Whereas, with my babies, you can come from any quarter, launch at any speed, in any sea state except a goddam hurricane." Behrensen grinned his pleasure at the thought.

"Why are you telling me all this?" Though Gallagher thought he already knew the answer, he was intrigued by Behrensen's possible reply.

"I figured you'd ask that question," Behrensen said. "Let's say I feel kind of sorry you've got into this. I don't like totaling a brother."

Gallagher greeted this with some skepticism. How many "brothers" he wondered, had Behrensen "totaled" in places like Africa, where his arms dealings probably flourished extremely well? Gallagher was also highly suspicious of anyone who called him brother. It usually meant your back was being measured for the right place to sink the knife into.

"You don't believe me," Behrensen said.

"Would you, in my place?"

"I can understand that," Behrensen said by way of an answer. "But I'm truly sorry you got in this far. It was not my intention."

"Your intention? What are you talking about?"

"You got a job sending you to Amsterdam. Right? A calendar."

"Yes . . ." Gallagher began thoughtfully, not liking what he was beginning to think. *"You?"*

"Me. A complicated scam was being set up. We needed you to spring the trap."

" 'We?' Who the hell's 'we?' "

Behrensen did not answer.

The words *spring the trap* burned through Gallagher's mind. But a trap for whom? Then he knew. *Villiger!*

13

"**Are you trying to tell me,**" Gallagher said, "**that** the job that came through my agency requiring a series of calendar photos for an American client was *yours?*"

Behrensen nodded. "The same. We had to cover it from all angles. Out in the bush, some pretty effective guys were causing a lot of pain. Then the hints about some people looking for aircraft and pilots began to get around. Naturally, I was approached as a possible supplier and naturally, the other side wanted to know if I had been. What they offered was an interesting proposition. Go ahead and supply the aircraft, find out who was behind the requirement and deliver both, for a quite enormous fee."

Gallagher stared at him. Behrensen talked of his treachery as if passing the time of day.

"You're going to deliver the aircraft to the other side, as well as your original clients?"

Behrensen was unrepentant. "Sure. They need something like the F-16 very badly over there too. They can't buy them on the open market, but captured . . . well that's something else again, even if they do have to pay me for the privilege."

"And you feel nothing about selling stuff like that over there?"

"Why should I?" Behrensen seemed genuinely surprised at the question. "Do you think someone else wouldn't if they could make it work?"

"So where do I come in?" Gallagher did not allow the distaste he felt to show.

"You, brother, have a very interesting history. Let's say I know people who were able to give me a brief resumé. Not nearly enough, of course, you're well covered by your guys . . . but still enough to give me the idea for the trap. Three guys are under suspicion for being behind the bush commando teams, and the aircraft purchase. They would all have access to the kind of people who could supply the money, both in national and international commerce, and in foreign governments." Behrensen gave a short laugh. "As I do. Hell, I can think of plenty in the States who would qualify. Two of the guys are innocent, or so my new clients seem to think. I have no idea who the target is, but by tomorrow, I shall. Dan Murchison will be picking him up and bringing him back here, ostensibly to take control of the goods. You see, we're also meeting the container ship that's carrying the first six aircraft tomorrow. That's where we're headed now. To the rendezvous."

Gallagher listened in mounting horror. Villiger had been neatly duped, and would fly blindly into the web that had been spun for him, unless Gallagher could come up with something that could alter the outcome.

"A submarine will be meeting up with us,"

Behrensen continued. "There are commandos aboard who will take over the container ship and sail it back, while the submarine will itself take our man—whoever he may be—and Miss Mowbray, to face their people back home. Pity about her. Nice woman." Behrensen's eyes betrayed his real thoughts about her.

"You were not expected to be in at this point," Behrensen went on. "It was hoped that once you had been placed in Amsterdam, you would be approached as a potential pilot. It was not known who would make the initial approach, but the hope was that the top man would show. De Vries' job was to take him out . . . but he blew it. Both you and our mystery man were too clever. Also, it appeared that your own guys were sniffing around. According to de Vries, they got in the way a few times, and even shot at him. He failed to do the job, and here you are. No one expected you to come out here," Behrensen repeated. "I'm real sorry about that."

"But you won't lose any sleep."

Behrensen shook his head slowly. "No. But you know how it is."

"I know," Gallagher said.

"We could get his identity out of you, I suppose. Or maybe the girl. You'd be too difficult in the time we've got. But the girl . . ." Behrensen's eyes again showed his eagerness to work on Lorraine Mowbray. "But that would be counterproductive. We want you both on deck and in good shape when the chopper returns so that our man can see you're alright. Otherwise, there's no telling what he might do. Dan Murchison would be one dead pilot for starters. I like Dan. Good pilots are hard to come by in my line of business."

Behrensen's matter-of-fact manner was more frightening than if he'd been overtly brutal which, Gallagher was quite certain, under the right circumstances he was very capable of being.

"Anything else you'd like to see?" Behrensen asked, ever the solicitous host.

"No," Gallagher said. "I've seen enough."

"My stateroom," Behrensen insisted. "You must see my stateroom."

Gallagher decided discretion was the best course to follow. "Show me," he said.

Behrensen looked at him speculatively. "You're cool. I like that. I could have used someone like you," he added, almost wistfully.

"No you couldn't."

"I guess not. You wouldn't play ball. Pity."

They left the missile section and the door hissed shut.

Gallagher allowed himself to be taken to Behrensen's stateroom and was genuinely impressed, though he found the decor questionable. But something else impressed him even more. Next to the bed, clipped to the wall within easy reach, was what he thought could be his first ray of hope: a sister weapon to the one Villiger had shown him. Behrensen took a Taipan to bed.

Gallagher looked at it only with the interest Behrensen would have expected and gave no sign of recognition. He made no comment about it either. After the missile room, anything else had paled by comparison.

That's what he hoped Behrensen would think. In reality, the fancy missiles were totally secondary to the Taipan. Gallagher began to think of ways to get into the stateroom and his hands on the weapon.

There were still twelve crewmen plus de Vries and Quinlan to deal with, but if he held Behrensen hostage . . .

A new ball game entirely, as Behrensen himself would have said.

It's all a matter of timing, sir.

O'Keefe.

Which was all well and good, but in this case the opportunity had to be created.

Gallagher thought he knew how to do it.

"What's going to happen to the crew of the container ship after it's been taken over?" Gallagher asked as they made their way back to the lounge.

"They will no longer exist."

"What a surprise."

"Don't cry over those boys. Every one of them is on a police blotter somewhere in the world, and the master's ticket is a fake. Besides, they were paid good bonuses for this job."

"That's really going to be of use to them."

"The bonuses went into bank accounts. Someone will benefit. You don't expect the commandos to leave them to talk, do you? It won't be easy, you know. The crew will fight. They've got guns, as you'd expect. Some of those commandos are going to die too." That didn't seem to worry Behrensen.

What did a few more deaths matter? Gallagher thought grimly. It was all the same to someone like Behrensen.

They returned to the lounge to find that conversation must have been rather less than scintillating. Lorraine Mowbray was studiously avoiding having to look at de Vries, but her contemptuous expression spoke more loudly than any words she could have uttered. Quinlan appeared unperturbed, and seemed mildly amused by the tension between the two. De Vries looked angry, and somehow cheated. It was clear he considered her his prisoner and as such, should be under his jurisdiction. Even he, however, knew better than to go up against Behrensen aboard his own ship.

Behrensen said to them brightly: "Having fun? No? How about something to drink? Let's have more champagne in here . . ."

"If it's alright," Gallagher said, "I'd like to go to our stateroom. I'd like Miss Mowbray to accompany me, then we might take a stroll along the deck before going down for the night. All things considered, we might as well get some sleep."

Behrensen stared at him as if checking his words out for a flaw of some kind before saying: "Sure. Miss Mowbray, you have my permission to leave us."

"I think . . ." de Vries began, about to object.

Behrensen cut into whatever he had been about to say. "Miss Mowbray has my permission to leave." The voice was cold, with more than enough warning for anyone.

De Vries would not leave it. "You're being paid to . . ."

"Captain de Vries, they're not paying me enough not to kill you if you insist on getting in my way. Don't try to contradict me again."

For one mad moment, de Vries looked as if he intended to argue the point: but some vestige of self-preservation forced its way through. He kept his mouth shut.

"Thank you," Behrensen said with heavy irony. "Miss Mowbray, if you please."

She stood up and, eyes still expressionless, went over to Gallagher. Behrensen smiled at them as they went out, but his own eyes showed something else.

As they left, Gallagher felt not only Behrensen's, but de Vries' and Quinlan's eyes upon them. Lorraine Mowbray now seemed eager to speak when they were some distance from the lounge, but he stopped her by briefly squeezing her hand. Even when they had entered the stateroom which Behrensen had previously shown him, he cautioned her against speaking with a warning look.

He went into the bathroom. There was also a shower. A quick unobtrusive check confirmed his suspicions.

"Take a look at this," he called loudly to her. "What a bathroom!"

She had been sitting somewhat tensely on one of the beds. She now got to her feet and went in response to his call. Gallagher shut the door after her, and turned on the shower.

He grabbed her suddenly and said urgently in her ear: "Don't struggle. Take off your clothes! We're going to have a shower."

"What . . . !"

He pretended to be nuzzling her ear. "For God's sake *do* it! This whole damned place is wired for pictures and sound."

"But how do you know . . ." At least, she had stopped resisting.

"I don't . . . not for certain: but I'm assuming it. A man like Behrensen would do it as a matter of routine, for all sorts of reasons, none of them good." She was sticking close to him now, allowing him to continue his pretense. "I'm certain he put us together," he went on, "just so he could listen in on our conversations. He'd expect you to say things to me that would further incriminate you, and it would all be on tape. He'd sell that to de Vries' people too. Imagine the kind of case that would make against you."

She shivered against him as the implications hit her. Still staying close to him, she began to remove her clothes, now and then kissing him for good measure. Once, she briefly stared at him wide-eyed, still trying to come to terms with the appalling enormity of the treachery committed by Marais/de Vries. It could not be easy for her, Gallagher thought, to reconcile the fact that someone she'd known all those years and who had claimed to share her beliefs, had turned out to be a Captain in the security police. Their clothes were off, and they entered the shower.

"There isn't much time to give you the whole picture," Gallagher was urgently saying to her. "If we stay in here too long, they may get suspicious and come looking. We'll have to come in here when we need to discuss anything serious: but we'll have to do so at believable intervals. We'll also have to give them something to keep them quiet. Take the lead from me, but whatever you do, don't mention any names."

He told her as quickly as he could, what Behrensen had disclosed. She seemed to get smaller as the full details of the trap were revealed and for the first time, he saw despair come into her eyes.

"We're not finished yet," he said. "I've got the makings of a plan. We won't let them get to him."

She looked at him for long moments. "You really do like him, don't you?" The water had plastered her hair into a dark golden curtain.

"I wouldn't be here otherwise."

She gave him a shaky smile and kissed him again lightly on the lips. "If we can get out of this, do you know what I'm going to do?"

"I'm all ears." He held on to her as the water coursed down their bodies.

"I'm going to let you make love to me for as long as you want, and any way you want." The words were whispered against his ear.

"I don't need that kind of bribe."

"It wasn't the offer of a bribe. It's what *I* want."

"Promises, promises," he said. He wondered if she'd feel the same way when she heard what he had in mind. "Now we'd better get out of here," he went on. "Time's up for now. Let's go for a stroll on deck."

"Can we talk there?"

"I doubt it. There are such things as rifle mikes and infrared cameras. This is to be our only place for real discussions. Now let's take that stroll." He turned off the shower and they dried themselves, dressed, then left the bathroom.

Gallagher opened the stateroom door to go out on deck. A crewman was standing there . . . with an assault rifle. He looked at Gallagher, apparently undecided about how to handle the situation. Clearly, he had not been given orders to shoot on sight. But the rifle could easily be brought into use.

"Where do you think we're likely to go?" Gallagher asked sarcastically. "For a swim?"

The deck lighting had been dimmed, so the man's features were not totally distinguishable. He seemed to be staring at them both. Beyond the deck, the darkened sea rushed past in answer to the *Stonefish*'s selected cruising speed of twenty knots. A warm breeze fanned at them.

After some moments, the silent crewman reached for a phone on the superstructure. He pulled it from its holder, and spoke into it. His accent sounded French.

"Tell Mr. Behrensen they want to go for a walk." He waited, grunted assent, then replaced the phone. "You may go for your walk."

"Thank you very much," Gallagher said as they walked past.

The crewman turned to track them with his hidden eyes, but made no move to follow. That told Gallagher they'd be covered all the way by other members of the crew. It was not going to make things easy when he decided to go after the Taipan; but he'd have to do it. The subdued deck lighting would be a welcome help.

"Let's go up to the bows," he said to Lorraine Mowbray loudly enough to be clearly heard. He didn't want Behrensen to think he would attempt to speak surreptitiously to her. "There are a couple of seats, near the railing."

The night seemed to have been made less dark when his eyes had grown accustomed. The sea was itself devoid of all other shipping within their area. It just went to show he thought, how big the Med really was, despite the amount of ships plying upon it at any given time. He wondered where the *Stonefish* was headed, and hoped there'd be a passing ship to signal in some way . . . provided Behrensen did not blow it out of the water if it got too close.

"Here we are," Gallagher said to her. "Let's sit and enjoy the night air."

They sat down, and Gallagher put an arm about her. Without his prompting, she leaned her head against his shoulder.

* * *

Behrensen was in his stateroom with both Quinlan and de Vries, watching the infrared images on the monitor.

"Looks like they're sweet on each other," Quinlan remarked neutrally. It was hard to tell whether he was having a secret laugh.

"I always thought there was something going on between them." De Vries could not disguise his own feelings.

"Sounds like a bit of sexual jealousy there to me," Behrensen said, looking at de Vries who colored slightly. "He beat you to it." The protruding eyes were challenging. "That was quite a show."

"Don't be stupid."

Quinlan stared at de Vries as if the other had suddenly taken leave of his senses.

Behrensen said: "Captain de Vries, I can see you're going to have some difficulty making it off this ship alive. Call me stupid again and I won't even talk to you. I'll just shoot you. I still say you wish you'd been there instead of Gallagher. Going to call me stupid?"

De Vries looked away, and said nothing.

Behrensen turned down the corners of his mouth, showing eloquently what he really thought of de Vries.

"Why do you think they went in there?" Quinlan asked thoughtfully.

"You saw why, J.D." Behrensen sounded amused. "They went for a shower, and some body therapy."

"But why?" Quinlan asked again. "Why just then?"

"We know from our friend de Vries here," Behrensen said with some malice, "that they've got a real thing going. We've got the evidence that they've certainly got the hots for each other. They know how much time they've got together and are making the best of it. I sure as hell would in Gallagher's place. Anyway, I'll be finding out soon enough what's got de Vries so hot between his legs. Judging by that body . . ." Behrensen stared at de Vries, who refused to meet his contemptuous gaze.

"They had a shower." Quinlan was still pursuing it.

"So? They like feeling each other in the shower. A lot of people do you know. I've had guests come aboard who turn the goddam things on just to see them work."

"Gallagher's hardly a guest."

"I know what you're thinking, J.D. Just you let me worry about that. They're going nowhere. We'll see how often they have these showers of theirs. Meanwhile, we've got the other cameras in the stateroom itself. He hasn't seen those either. Nobody ever has . . . and I've had people in there who knew what they were looking for."

"That's my point. Gallagher never even bothered to look. I find that suspicious."

"Let's see what happens, J.D. Let's see if you're right on this one."

Gallagher and Lorraine Mowbray returned to the stateroom after he felt they had been out on deck long enough. The crewman with the accent was still on station outside the door.

"Goodnight," Gallagher said to him, but the man did not acknowledge.

Inside, Gallagher switched on all the lights and

began to search. He spent a good fifteen minutes doing so while she watched him curiously.

"Well it's clean," he announced. This was not strictly true. He had discovered two of the hidden cameras, one of which was in a light fitting. "I think we can talk in here."

"I never would have suspected Hennie," she said, getting into the spirit of things. "What a bloody bastard."

"I never liked him in the first place," Gallagher said, "even as Hennie Marais. Never trusted the sod."

"He was always after me, you know. I caught him looking up my skirt once, when I was going up some stairs."

Between them, they began to lacerate de Vries.

Behrensen was smiling broadly as he watched the monitor.

"They don't seem to like you very much, Captain de Vries," he said. "Surprising what you can learn from an unguarded conversation. Looking up skirts . . ."

De Vries' face was like thunder. "That's not true! She's lying to him. She just wants him to think . . ." De Vries allowed the words to die. He seemed very angry.

Quinlan watched with keen interest, seeming to ignore the presence of both Behrensen and de Vries.

Sometime later, after talking about their fears for the morning and making some more uncharitable remarks about de Vries, Gallagher thought they had done enough for their unseen audience.

"Fancy another shower before bed?" he said to her.

She smiled, as if the prospect excited her, despite her fears for the immediate future. They undressed by the beds, and went naked to the showers where they repeated their earlier performance. He told her what he wanted her to do.

"Don't . . . give yourself away," he said fiercely in her ear as she had begun to stiffen. "There are cameras all over the place. I've found two in the bedroom. There are bound to be more."

"But you can't ask me to do that," she whispered against the roar of the shower. To someone at the monitor, it looked as if she had been nibbling at his ear, her body pressed suggestively against his. Her voice carried fear, and a good measure of disgust.

For his part, Gallagher was trying very hard not to get excited. Her wet skin felt highly charged.

"I don't want to," he said, "but it's my one chance of getting at that weapon. I'll come as quickly as I can. All you'll have to do is let him kiss you . . ."

She shivered against him, making it even more difficult to control his excitement. He forced the effect of her body out of his mind.

"That's all . . ." she said, her manner clearly indicating it was more than enough. "Don't take too long. Please."

"I promise."

"Another shower," Quinlan said.

"So?" Behrensen. "They just like it that way. Just look at them. She's eating him . . . Hey! What the hell?"

All three stared intently at the screen as the sharp report of a slap came to them.

Lorraine Mowbray was leaving the shower. "No!" came her outraged voice. "I won't do that, and I don't care about what might happen tomorrow." She walked angrily away, dripping wet.

They watched as Gallagher turned off the shower and followed. "Lorraine, for God's sake," they heard him say. "These people might well kill us tomorrow. What are you being so prudish about?"

"I'm no prude," she retorted, "but what you suggest is simply obscene. I won't do that with you. *No!*"

Behrensen grinned. "What do you know. The lady has her limits. She won't have any by the time I finish with her. She'll forget all about him." He turned off the monitor and watched as it slid back into its housing. "We'll leave them to their problems. The cameras will film their every move, and we'll see and hear it all in the morning."

Quinlan and de Vries knew it was time for them to leave.

It was about three o'clock in the morning when Gallagher left his bed to sneak over to Lorraine Mowbray. Immediately, she leapt out of her own bed, setting off the infrared camera.

"No!" she shouted, and went to bang on the stateroom door.

Gallagher, who was fully clothed, had dropped to the floor and was crawling toward the door. It opened and another crewman who had replaced the original guard, shone a torch on her. Her thin, short nightie made him pause long enough to allow Gallagher to sneak out and wait behind him.

"I want to see Mr. Behrensen," she said to the

man. "I'm not staying in here a moment longer." She shut the door, effectively blocking the camera.

"But . . ." the crewman began.

It was all he had time for. Gallagher hit him hard at the base of the neck, caught him before he fell. Lorraine Mowbray got the rifle he'd been holding before it too could clatter to the deck. Gallagher heaved the man overboard.

"What have you done!" she whispered to him.

"He was dead." Gallagher took the rifle from her.

"My God. You . . ."

"Get a move on," he interrupted. "Do you want his friends to come looking? Behrensen's stateroom is our next stop. No more whispering. Let's go."

Keeping close to the superstructure and utilizing the gloom, they made it unchallenged to Behrensen's stateroom. Then just as they'd planned, she knocked softly on the door. Gallagher waited, hidden in shadows.

After the third knock, Behrensen opened the door. "Miss Mowbray . . ." He was surprised, but her attire clearly pleased him. He smiled at her. "I'm flattered . . ."

"I didn't come here to flatter you. I came to ask for another cabin. Anything. I won't stay another moment in the same room with Gallagher. He wants . . . he wants . . ." She took a deep breath, as if swallowing her outrage. "The man outside my door said I could come."

"He should have called me, but never mind. I'll attend to him in the morning. Come in, Miss Mowbray, while I sort this out for you." He poked his head out to briefly look up and down the deck. "Come in. Please."

She entered. Behrensen shut the door, but did not lock it. Gallagher stayed where he was.

Presently, he heard: "Mr. Behrensen! But I thought . . ." the words died in a muffled jumble. There was the sound of struggle. *"Mr. Behren . . ."* More muffled sounds.

Gallagher opened the door slowly, keeping low. He peered around. Behrensen had Lorraine Mowbray on the floor, one powerful hand holding her down, the other ripping at her nightdress. Both were feet-first to the door, Behrensen on top. He was quite unaware of Gallagher. Behrensen had his work cut out. Lorraine Mowbray was proving to be no pushover; but her dress was coming apart and her increasingly bared body was exciting Behrensen. In the subdued light of the room, she fought ferociously. It was no act. She twisted this way and that, beautiful legs all over the place.

Gallagher decided it was time to move. His eyes had sought and found the Taipan. It was no longer in its normal place, but on the bed. Behrensen, not taking chances, had come to the door with it and had put it there while he attended fully to Lorraine. It was a mistake Gallagher was grateful for. It made things a lot easier. Behrensen's grunts of passion as he fought her had become animallike.

Gallagher made it to the bed in a rush, and before Behrensen knew what was happening, the Taipan had pointed its deadly muzzle at him.

"Get off her!" Gallagher commanded. "And get up!"

Behrensen, a murderous expression upon his face, rolled off and slowly released a shaken Lorraine Mowbray who also stood up, trying to put the scraps of her clothing about her.

Furious at having been tricked, Behrensen snarled: "You've just signed your death warrant, brother! You'll never get off this ship. That's a promise!"

"Guess who'll be the first to go."

Behrensen's eyes looked into Gallagher's and believed what he saw in them.

"That's right," Gallagher said. "You'll be dead long before any of your men get in here. Are you alright, Lorraine?"

"Yes . . . yes." She still sounded shaky. "I'll have to see what I can find in here to put on." She began opening up wardrobes and pulling at drawers. "I think I've got something," she said after a while. Shortly after, she came into Gallagher's line of vision.

She had put on one of Behrensen's shirts which though loose, actually looked good on her. She had also found a pair of jeans which were a slightly tight fit, but would serve for the time being.

Behrensen said: "The woman who last wore that is dead . . . as you will be, if you don't come to your senses. Gallagher's making things worse for you. I could have helped with de Vries . . ."

"Of course you could," Gallagher said sarcastically.

"I was talking to the lady."

"Oh were you?" Lorraine Mowbray spoke with loathing. "Anything Gallagher says, and anything he does, is my wish."

"Then you're both dead." Behrensen's protruding eyes blazed at them. "What do you think you're going to accomplish?"

"At the very least," Gallagher began, "your death. So your whole deal, whatever it is, will be worthless to you. After all, if you're not there you can't spend it, can you?"

Behrensen thought about that. "There are cameras . . ."

But Gallagher shook his head. "Not in here. This is the only place you haven't got them. You like watching, but don't like to be watched yourself. I knew our little pantomime would get you aroused. It worked. Your guard was down."

"You *knew*. But we heard you say you'd found nothing . . ." Behrensen stopped as he realized what he'd said.

Gallagher smiled, but not pleasantly.

"You'll never get away with it," Behrensen said; but it was all bluster. He was sufficiently a realist to know when the tables had turned. Even if Gallagher never got out of the stateroom, he knew the whole deal would be jeopardized as long as he was held at the end of the gun . . . his own goddam gun.

Behrensen knew he had to try to get away.

Gallagher had been watching Behrensen's features intently and guessed what was going on in the other's mind. Behrensen was a hard case, and Gallagher knew that first early advantage was all he was likely to get. Behrensen would strike as soon as the opportunity allowed.

Gallagher said to Lorraine: "Find me all the belts you can. Ropes, cord, anything. This is a yacht. He's bound to have such things in here."

He heard her carrying out the search and before much longer, she was saying: "I've found some tassled cord, but I don't think this was used for yachting purposes." She brought two lengths of gold-colored cord. There was a perfumed smell to them.

Gallagher said: "I think you're right. Mr. Behrensen has been indulging in a few . . . fun and games. Now check his cupboards by the bed. There's bound to be another gun. Someone like Behrensen will always have a backup. When you've got that, look by the side of the bed. You'll see the crewman's rifle. Bring that too."

"What have you done with my crewman?" Behrensen demanded.

"He went for a night swim."

"You cold bastard."

"Look who's bloody talking. Besides, he was already dead."

"I should have killed you the moment you set foot on my ship."

"Don't try that on me, Behrensen. I know all about people like you. I've had to deal with them. You didn't kill us only because you had other plans for us. You still intended to do so when you were quite ready."

Lorraine Mowbray said: "I've found an automatic."

"Can you use it?"

"Oh yes."

"Good. Hold it on this bastard while I tie him up. If he breathes the wrong way, shoot him."

"It will be a pleasure." Something in her voice warned Behrensen she meant every word.

His head jerked around at her, as if in surprise. The big service issue Beretta 92F was pointed unerringly at him.

"You wouldn't use that," he said.

"Don't try to find out, man. You'd regret it."

"I guess you would at that." Behrensen seemed to have accepted his fate.

Gallagher said: "Don't let his apparent fit of realism con you. He's at his most dangerous. He'll try to get your guard down."

"Then he's in fantasy land."

Gallagher smiled. "You shouldn't have tried to rape her, Behrensen. See where it's got you."

"You're not out of it yet, brother. Don't smile too soon."

"Don't worry about the smile. I can shoot you while it's still on. Now step back and lie on the floor on your stomach, hands behind you, legs back."

Behrensen did as he was told.

Gallagher laid the Taipan on the floor where he could get to it quickly, but well out of Behrensen's reach.

"Watch him," he said to Lorraine Mowbray.

She had taken up a two-handed stance, feet spread. "I've got him," she said grimly.

Gallagher took a length of cord, went over to Behrensen. He grabbed Behrensen's hands and began to tie them together. Behrensen suddenly rolled, bringing his feet down and pushing hard at the floor. He staggered upward, ripping the cord away from Gallagher's hands.

The Beretta roared explosively. Behrensen gasped.

"Shit!" he cried. "You fucking did it. You shot me!"

He fell to the floor, groaning. Lorraine Mowbray remained exactly where she was, the gun trained on Behrensen.

Gallagher glanced at her admiringly, went back to Behrensen.

"It was just the shoulder," she said. "I could have taken his head."

"Hear that, Behrensen? She spared you. You can handle a slight wound."

"Slight! I've got a fucking nine-millimeter round in my shoulder!"

"No you haven't. And I'm more worried about who might have heard the shot. I'll just have to work quickly. Hope for your sake the noise of the ship has drowned that shot. I don't think she'll give you a second chance. Back as you were, please."

"My shoulder . . . !"

"Is fine."

"I'll bleed to death."

"Listen to him," Gallagher said as he worked. "This is meant to be a tough man. I think you're trying it on, Behrensen, and it's not working. Good thing your arms are long." Gallagher had fed the wrists between the ankles and had secured the lot together.

Behrensen now looked like a tied chicken, back curved inward. He swore at Gallagher.

"I'll get cramp like this."

"Stop moaning. This is better than what you had planned for us. Think yourself lucky."

Behrensen's manner changed abruptly. "Right. So you've got me tied up in here. Now what? I've still got eleven men out there, plus Quinlan and de Vries. Quinlan's a killer, and as for de Vries, that boy does not love you. Then there's the submarine, and the commandos. Think you can take all that on? We'll be at the rendezvous by 0600. You're in shit street."

"Then we'll just have to wait and see what happens."

There was a ten-minute silence after that. Gallagher and Lorraine Mowbray had positioned themselves in such a way that they had both Behrensen and the door to the stateroom well within their sights, while they were in turn out of the line of fire. The only light in the room shone directly upon Behrensen, leaving them well into shadow. They sat together on the floor, backs against a wardrobe.

Behrensen said: "Look I can fix it so that you can get away in the chopper . . ."

"Shut it, Behrensen," Gallagher said.

14

O500. In his cabin, Quinlan sat bolt upright in bed.

"It was an act," he said. "The whole thing was an act. They knew about the cameras."

He turned on a light and quickly reached for the phone. He dialed a single number.

In Behrensen's stateroom, the phone buzzed. Lorraine, head on Gallagher's shoulder, started.

"And now," came Behrensen's voice from the floor, "you've got a problem. Someone must have heard that shot, after all, even if they've taken a long time to investigate."

"I don't think anyone heard the shot," Gallagher said.

"Whatever the reason, you'd better answer that phone. If you don't, someone will come looking and if you do, all hell will break loose. As I said, you've got a problem." Behrensen sounded very pleased with himself.

The phone continued to buzz.

"My men have all done their share of killing,"

Behrensen was saying, "from Duquesne the captain, to Ramon the chef who's very good at carving things other than your supper. You ought to see him go to work with the little knife of his. They won't come after you just out of loyalty to me. They have a life-style to protect and they won't like you screwing it up. These guys make salaries that any senior executive would be proud of. Do you know Ramon even runs a brand-new Ferrari? That's what you're up against."

"You talk too much," Gallagher said. "Lorraine, go to his head. If he opens his mouth within the next five minutes, put a bullet in it."

She moved over as directed, and waited. Gallagher picked up the phone.

Quinlan, clearly not expecting anyone else, began to speak immediately, and quickly.

"Mr. Behrensen I'm sorry to wake you but I've just realized it was all an act. They knew about the cameras. Gallagher is planning something. Mr. Behrensen," Quinlan went on into the silence he was receiving. "I know you don't like being woken up, but I thought you should . . ."

Gallagher slammed the phone down as if irritated by the call.

"Nice of you to keep quiet," he said to Behrensen. "That was Quinlan. He thought you should know that we know about the cameras and that we may be planning something. He apologized for waking you."

"Don't feel so good. Quinlan's sharp. You were not so clever keeping silent. He'll call again, this time expecting me to speak, if only to bawl him out for waking me again."

"That's a chance we'll have to take. Alright, Lorraine. You can come back."

In his cabin, Quinlan thought about his phone call and reached out again for the instrument. He paused. Behrensen's silence had been hostile enough. Besides, it was only an hour to the rendezvous. Nothing much could happen within that time.

Quinlan turned off his light and went back to sleep.

"It doesn't look as if Quinlan wants to risk that bawling out," Gallagher said.

Behrensen for once, had no reply.

The Daphne class submarine had been shadowing the container ship throughout the night on the surface, at a distance of ten miles. Now, as the ship began to slow down, the sub maintained its own speed of ten knots and began to gradually catch up. The commander felt pleased with the status of the mission so far. For nearly twenty-five days, he had made his surreptitious journey of 9000 miles from his home base, hiding from almost anything that floated. Sometimes he had steamed on the surface, sometimes submerged; sometimes in deep water, sometimes in shallow coastal waters. On a couple of occasions, he'd even had to hide on the surface behind rocky islands at night, while a nosey patrol boat had searched for an elusive echo. But they'd made it, after having hidden from the ships of almost every NATO navy, and some that were not.

The sub commander smiled to himself. Who would have thought the Med could be so crowded? But here he was, on the tail of the container ship, and it didn't even know he was there. Soon, it would be dawn, and he would need to submerge until it was time to put his commandos aboard the target. He smiled again. They'd be pleased to be having some action at last.

A message was relayed to him up the conning tower. Ship on the starboard bow, approaching, twenty knots at thirty miles.

Must be the yacht, he thought. Everything, wonderfully, was going to plan. Whoever had planned this mission had certainly known his job. If matters held as they were, he'd soon be heading back, with the captured ship safely in the hands of his commandos.

He turned to the Officer of the Deck. "Submerge the Boat."

Orders were passed, preparing the submarine for the dive. The commander went down the conning tower. Everyone was clear, hatches sealed.

"Dive, Dive!" came on the speakers.

The submarine began to sink quietly into the early dawn waters of the Mediterranean.

The telephone again buzzed in Behrensen's stateroom. The time was 0520.

"No rest for the wicked," Behrensen said. "What are you going to do this time?" His voice was almost gleeful, though he must have been very uncomfortable by now.

Lorraine Mowbray stared at Gallagher, who looked at the phone as it continued to buzz. He indicated that she should again position herself by Behrensen.

"Too good to last," he said to her, and picked it up.

"Mr. Behrensen," a voice said immediately, "Duquesne. We have the ship in sight. We're also picking up the sub, range . . . twenty miles. Murchison is ready and I'm about to cut speed to allow him to launch. Will you be coming up to the bridge, sir? Launch is in fifteen minutes at five knots. Mr. Behrensen . . . ?"

Gallagher coughed loudly, then said in a strangled voice which he hoped would approximate Behrensen's: "Sorry . . . yes . . . (cough) . . . I'll be . . . (cough) . . . up." He hung up. Lorraine moved back.

Behrensen said in a jeering voice: "You don't really believe Duquesne is going to fall for that, do you? This place will be wall to wall with armed men in a minute."

"It will make him pause for thought and that's all I need. Time. Lorraine, find something to gag him with, then we'll go looking for them before they come for us."

She hurried and came back with a woman's scarf. "He's got a lot of women's things in this place. If I didn't know better, I'd suspect his leanings. Perhaps he just likes to collect them."

"Right," Gallagher said, moving close to Behrensen. "Open your mouth."

"In a pig's eye!"

Gallagher hit the wounded shoulder.

"Aargh!" Behrensen gasped involuntarily.

"Quick!" Gallagher said to Lorraine. "Gag him."

She was doing it even as he spoke and soon, Behrensen could only glare his hatred and make incomprehensible sounds of anger.

"There's another scarf," she said. "Shall I use that too?"

"Yes. Cut down his noise a bit."

She hurried for the second scarf and tied that over Behrensen's mouth. It did cut the noise, but not enough to please Gallagher. Behrensen was determined to be as loud as possible.

Gallagher said: "I ought to kill you, Behrensen. Save me a lot of grief later on perhaps. Leaving you like this is certainly more than you would have done for us; but I suppose that's what separates me from the likes of you . . . I hope." Then he hit Behrensen with deliberate accuracy on the back of the neck.

Behrensen stopped making noises.

"Is he dead?" Lorraine Mowbray asked, looking quickly from Behrensen's inert form to Gallagher.

"No. Just knocked out."

"But the other man . . ."

"I had less time then and had to make sure. Now we'd better find somewhere to hide him. Hopefully, by the time he wakes up, there'll be so much going on, he won't be heard in time to make any difference."

They began to drag Behrensen toward the bed.

"The bastard's certainly heavy," Gallagher said as he hauled away. The bed was mounted upon two full-width supports that left some space in between. He lifted the floor-length quilt. "I think there's just enough room."

They managed to get Behrensen underneath, wedging him onto his side so that he could breathe more easily, then lowered the quilt. Behrensen was completely hidden.

Gallagher went to the head of the bed. "There's a big enough gap up here for air to circulate. He'll be okay for the time being."

"You're a strange man," she said. "He would

have killed us, yet you're worried about his being able to breathe."

They worked feverishly at getting rid of blood trails.

"I'm not doing him any favors. Humiliating him is already one of the worse things I could have done. He was so sure of himself. He controls a big organization. I intend to ruin his plans today and bring him down . . ."

"But how?"

"Don't ask questions like that," he told her. "I haven't got the answer yet. But when word gets around he's unreliable, he'll be finished. Now let's get out of here or we won't be left standing long enough to do anything." He stared at the carpet. There were dark patches from the water they'd used, but no blood.

"I don't think you're strange," she said. "You're mad."

He grinned at her. "Of course." He turned off the light.

They let themselves cautiously out of the state-room. Gallagher carried the Taipan with its full load of a hundred rounds and the assault rifle, a Beretta SC70/90 with a metal folding stock and carrying handle. It had a full 30-round magazine slotted in, with a second taped upside down for quick reloading. Lorraine Mowbray took the 92F automatic with her. There were still fourteen rounds to go, after the one she'd used on Behrensen. No one challenged them.

The sky had begun to show signs of lightening.

Murchison had joined Duquesne on the bridge.

"Where's the boss?" he asked.

"I spoke to him a little while back," Duquesne

replied. "Had some kind of coughing fit, but he said he'd be up. If he's late you'd better take off. Keep everything to speed. I don't want him going apeshit on me if we fuck up the schedule."

"Right."

"You just get out there, pick up the passenger, then get the hell back."

"Right," Murchison said again. "I guess I'd better get to the chopper."

Duquesne nodded, and Murchison left the bridge. As he watched the other depart, Duquesne again thought of Behrensen's cough, and frowned.

He picked up one of the phones on the bridge. "Harry, go check with the boss. He's meant to be on his way, but don't hassle him, for Chrissake. I want this thing to go well today."

"Right," the voice belonging to Harry said. "I'll go check."

Duquesne hung up.

The bridge had been designed to Behrensen's own specifications and from time to time, he would take the wheel himself. There was a captain's swivel chair, fixed to the deck, with generous padding and armrests. The wheel itself, polished wood and six spokes, fell nicely to hand. Ahead and to each side, were sloping consoles packed with dials, ergonomically designed switches, and high-tech screens that carried a multitude of information. It was a bridge that allowed the *Stonefish* to operate in all kinds of weather. The sloping sections of the consoles were finished in matt black, while the flat surfaces were of highly polished wood. The side consoles were fixed to paneling that contained chart drawers, and each had chrome handrails attached.

The central console held all the navigation and

attack systems. Behind the captain's chair was one of the yacht's two chart tables. Duquesne stood at it, studying a chart by the table's integral lighting. A skilled helmsman was at the wheel. The *Stonefish* was now at five knots.

For the day, Duquesne was dressed in full whites and upon his head was a cap that followed the US Navy's officer pattern. Its badge was of gold-plated metal, and depicted a stonefish upon a vertical oval. He wore shoulder boards with four gold rings upon them.

The same phone buzzed. He picked it up. "Duquesne." He listened briefly before saying: "Fine, Harry." He hung up and turned to the helmsman. "The boss must be on his way. He's not in his stateroom. He's taking his time so I guess he must have gone to check up on our reluctant guests. We'll have to launch the chopper whether he's here or not."

He went to the rear of the bridge to look out over the stern. The landing lights were on and Murchison was already aboard the aircraft. The day had become a steely gray that was lightening with the approach of full dawn. Over on the already distinguishable horizon, the few lights of the container ship could be seen.

Duquesne put powerful night binoculars to his eyes. There was no physical sign of the submarine. It was probably still submerged, he decided, or hiding on the other side of the distant ship. He glanced at his watch. The commando team would be getting ready to move. Another phone buzzed. He picked it up. The MD500's blades were turning.

"Ready to launch the chopper, skip," a voice said.

"Clear to launch," he said. Better to keep to

schedule instead of waiting for the boss. Behrensen was hot on exact time-keeping.

The helicopter, a sleek, ostensibly demilitarized version, had five blades and a powerful 375hp engine. Duquesne watched as Murchison wound it up and lifted cleanly off the deck. The lights were switched off as soon as the MD500 was clear. Soon, the aircraft was heading east, toward Crete. The *Stonefish* worked up to ten knots.

Quinlan came awake as soon as the helicopter had started, got quickly dressed, and phoned Behrensen. When he received no reply, he hurried out of his cabin and went to Behrensen's stateroom.

He stood by the door and stared about him. "Mr. Behrensen? Mr. Behrensen!" When silence greeted him, he switched on the lights then went straight to the nearest phone, picked it up, and dialed.

"Bridge," a voice replied.

"This is Quinlan. Where's your captain?"

"Right here, sir."

"Duquesne," the new voice said.

"Captain, this is Quinlan. Have you seen Mr. Behrensen?"

"No, sir. But I've spoken to him. He's on his way up."

"Spoken to him, you said."

"Yes, sir."

"When was that?"

"At 0520, Mr. Quinlan. It's 0539 right now.

"I see," Quinlan said thoughtfully.

"Mr. Quinlan."

"Yes, Captain?"

"I'd try the . . . er guests. I figure that's where he is."

"Yes. Yes I think I will." Quinlan hung up, looked about him once more and was about to leave, when he paused. Something was missing. He turned his head slowly, listening now, as well as searching out the anomaly. Then he saw what it was. The gun usually kept by the bed was no longer there.

It probably meant Behrensen had taken it. But why?

He was again about to leave when he glanced absently at the carpet. Fading discolorations. He went to them, and felt the slight dampness. He sniffed. Nothing. Water perhaps. Behrensen must have spilled a drink. He looked about him. There were no trails to follow.

He stood up and still thoughtful, went out.

Under the bed, Behrensen was still unconscious.

The submarine had surfaced silently after an approach at periscope depth to within less than half a mile, and had launched five inflatables carrying four men each. They had paddled noiselessly toward their quarry, as the submarine had again dived. The commander thought contemptuously that the ship's watchkeeping left a lot to be desired.

The first of the inflatables had reached the container ship which was now dead in the water. A rope ladder had been left hanging where they had been told it would be. Swiftly, the heavily armed men began to climb. The first four were on the ladder when the second inflatable arrived. Soon, the ladder became a continuing mass of silently climbing shapes.

The first group just made it on deck when there was a shout from above.

"Shit!" someone on the ladder said, not in English.

The men began to hurry as the first burst of automatic fire cut into the quiet of the dawn.

On the *Stonefish,* Gallagher and Lorraine Mowbray were crouched outside the bridge, on the exterior walkway. It had taken several cautious minutes of keeping low to make it, but they had succeeded without alerting anyone. On one occasion, the noise of the helicopter had successfully drowned out an accidental thump made by Lorraine when she had tripped against an unseen obstruction.

Now she stared at him apprehensively. This was where any real shooting would start if they did this badly. Gallagher glanced up at the twin-tower mast rising from the rear of the bridge. A ladder went up centrally, to the crows' nest which was a platform with a railing surround, positioned midway up the masts. He would have to make certain no one got up there. The vantage point gave a clear shot into the bridge.

He looked back at her and nodded. Then he was rising.

Duquesne stared disbelievingly at the gun pointing at him.

"You have two choices, Captain," Gallagher said. "One of them will leave you dead. Your helmsman too, if he doesn't stop moving."

"Can it, Bill," Duquesne said to his subordinate. "The man means business." To Gallagher he went on, as Lorraine Mowbray entered and covered the crewman with the Beretta. "Do we put our hands up?"

"No. Just continue as normal, but do nothing with them to alarm me. I might get nervous."

Duquesne actually gave a grim smile. *"You?* Nervous? Don't worry. I never argue with a man with a gun who clearly knows how to use it. And when he's got two . . . You're loaded enough to take on an army. That what you intend to do?"

"I hope it won't come to that. I have no intention of killing any of you unless I'm forced to. Quinlan and de Vries are a different matter. One is already one too many."

"One? You've killed the boss?"

"No. He's sleeping safely somewhere. One of your crew, I'm afraid. He went overboard last night. *Don't!"*

The man at the wheel had made a sudden movement when he'd heard about the crewman going over the side. The man remained still, moving only to steer the ship.

"Get down out of sight, Lorraine," Gallagher went on, "but keep him covered."

She sat on the deck, back against the chart drawers, gun pointing steadily.

"We're going to stop the takeover of the container ship," Gallagher said to Duquesne.

"There's a submarine out there too," Duquesne said. "Or doesn't your information run to that?"

"I know all about it."

"So how are you going to prevent what's happening with this pleasure ship?"

"Nice try, Captain," Gallagher said drily. "This pleasure ship has fangs when it needs them. Yes," he continued as Duquesne's eyes widened momentarily, "I know all about the missiles. We can do the whole business from here, without even going close."

"You can't!"

"Who's going to stop me?"

One of the phones buzzed. Duquesne glanced at it. "They are, for starters. Do I answer it?"

"You'd better. If you don't, they'll come looking anyway."

Duquesne picked up the phone. "Duquesne. Yes, Mr. Quinlan. I know." Pause. "I'm afraid they've already done the damage. They're up here."

Quinlan's *"What?"* was heard clearly on the bridge, before his voice continued the phone conversation more normally.

"They're well armed, Mr. Quinlan," Duquesne said with studied calm. "I'm afraid I couldn't do that. To all intents and purposes, they control the ship. If . . . *if* I do as you say, Mr. Quinlan, I'll be a dead Captain in no time at all." Duquesne stared at the phone. Quinlan had evidently hung up.

Duquesne put the instrument back and turned to Gallagher. "He's not the kind of guy to listen to reason and especially not . . . because of what's at stake. You're bucking something pretty big. There are heavy people behind Quinlan and Behrensen."

"There are heavy people behind me too," Gallagher said with a bravado he did not feel. Fowler, he thought, would have smiled to hear him invoke the weight of the Department.

"I guessed as much. You behave like a man who knows this kind of business, but it won't do you much good. Quinlan and de Vries are going to come after you, no matter what. Your people, whoever they are, are not here to help you."

"True. But you are."

"What?"

"I'm going to take a chance, Captain. I'm taking

a chance that you're not exactly like the others. I've watched you, and I have the feeling you're someone who's where he does not necessarily want to be, but who has been placed there by necessity itself."

"What are you? A do-gooder?"

"No. Just someone who's worked with enough people to know what he's looking at. A person's quality does not change with his clothes."

"Don't try appealing to my better nature. That went out of the window a long, long time ago."

"Then I'll appeal to something you haven't lost. Pragmatism. The worst case scenario is that we'll all die, no matter what. There are others. We'll make it, but you'll both die. Or we'll make it, and you'll make it. Whatever happens here, this particular line of business is finished for you. I'll do enough damage. Believe me. Then there's Murchison. He's gone to pick up a man who's coming back to a trap. By the time I've finished here, the man in the helicopter with Murchison will know something's wrong and unless Murchison wants to die, he'll be heading back to wherever he picked up his passenger.

"That passenger knows all about the shipment, because it's his. By the time he's finished digging into why Behrensen cheated him, Behrensen's stock won't be so high. He'll probably go after Behrensen himself. Do I have to go on?"

Duquesne said: "You've made a pretty good case for pragmatism. What about the young lady? She willing to die too?"

"She's been taking those kinds of risks for years and I assure you, she won't allow those people out there to take her . . . especially as Behrensen's still alive."

Duquesne became suddenly thoughtful. "I never did like him doing that," he said.

Both Gallagher and Lorraine Mowbray looked as if they were wondering what he was on about.

"Eighteen," Duquesne was saying. "That's all they were. Kids. Oh sure, they were after a good time and didn't much care how they got it. But he didn't have to do it to them." Duquesne seemed to be speaking to himself, reaching into himself for something he could still recognize. "He had his fun with them, then one morning he put them against the stern rail and had them shot."

"What?" Lorraine reacted.

"They fell into the water, and the sharks got them. He filmed it all. He's got videos down there in his stateroom of just about everyone who's come aboard this ship, doing all sorts of things. He filmed the girls in bed with him too. He's done it all before." He glanced at Lorraine who was by now looking sick. "He's got you on tape too. When you first came aboard off Portugal."

"No need to kill Behrensen," Gallagher was saying. "Those tapes will hang him in any country."

The phone buzzed again.

"Well?" Gallagher demanded. He went on quickly, using the advantage he thought he might have gained. "When this is over, take us to any of the Greek islands, and be on your way. Sell this yacht, dump it, sink it . . . do whatever you want. I promise you no one will come looking. At least, not from my side."

The phone still buzzed.

Duquesne looked at the crewman. "What about Billy?"

"If he gives me no trouble, he can go with you."

"It's as the man says, Billy," Duquesne said. "Dan Murchison's never going to land in one piece now, so he'll most likely head back to Crete with his passenger. That means this whole deal is blown. You're a good man at the wheel. As good as any I've seen and next to me, the best on this ship. You'll get another job anywhere. You've made good money since you've been with us. Might be an idea to live long enough to enjoy it."

Billy turned hard blue eyes upon Gallagher, glanced at his captain who nodded, before returning his attention to the job in hand.

"Okay," Billy said. "I got a place on one of the Keys. Plenty of people around who could use a boat skipper."

Plenty of drug barons from Latin America, Gallagher thought drily, but said nothing. This was hardly the time or place to give lectures to someone like Billy. He'd probably end his days at the wrong end of a drug enforcement officer's gun.

The phone had stopped.

Gallagher said to Duquesne: "Any weapons in here?"

Duquesne nodded. "Two."

"Get them please."

Duquesne opened a cupboard. Both weapons were Berettas. Behrensen clearly liked that particular make. Duquesne handed them over, having made no covert move to try and use them. One was a 92F automatic, like the one Lorraine Mowbray still held on Billy. The other was a twelve-gauge semiautomatic shotgun, with a 5-round magazine. It had a metal stock that folded upward.

"An M3 P," Gallagher said, passing it over to Lorraine. "Think you can handle it? It's semiauto.

One shot at somebody, and you'll frighten off all those around him. Hopefully. Better for you than a rifle in this particular situation." He turned to Duquesne. "Ammunition?"

"Plenty. Behrensen believes in leaving nothing to chance . . ." He paused, looked at Gallagher. "Well almost nothing." He took out the ammunition.

There were six pistol magazines, and another six for the shotgun.

Lorraine was dividing her attention between Billy and the M3 P. "I can handle it," she said.

"Good," Gallagher told her. "You've got plenty of ammo." He pushed the magazine box over. "And here are three mags for the pistol. I'll keep the other three." The 92F had come complete with a military-style gunbelt and holster. He strapped it on, and slipped the spare magazines into canvas pouches which hung from the belt.

Looking at him, Duquesne said: "They'll have to destroy this bridge to get at us."

"Which I doubt they'll do. It looks as if it can take punishment. Besides, this is the only ship they've got, unless they want to keep the sharks company. Right. Time we got to work. They won't hang about for much longer. Everyone else on the ship will know by now what's happened."

Duquesne still was looking at him, speculatively. "You look at home in this kind of situation. Done it often?"

"Too bloody often. But no two situations are alike. Well, Mr. Duquesne. Now's when I find out what you're made of. You wouldn't have any more weapons lying around, would you?"

"I give you my word," Duquesne said, strangely offended.

Gallagher wasn't so sure about Billy, but he had to believe Duquesne.

"Warm up the attack systems," he said, "we're going after the container ship."

Even as he spoke, a green flare curved skyward.

"The commandos have taken over," Duquesne said.

"Will they surrender?"

Duquesne gave a short harsh laugh. "Pigs won't fly, Mr. Gallagher."

"I was afraid of that."

"And their submarine? How do you propose to handle that? Sink it too?"

"Not unless it tries to sink us."

"Once you attack the ship, it will certainly attack."

Gallagher shrugged. "Then I hope Billy here really can handle a ship like this. Do you know what class of submarine it is?"

"I was not told. I don't suppose anyone thought it was necessary. I certainly didn't think so." Duquesne had flicked a series of switches, pressed a couple of buttons.

Four screens now came alive on the consoles. Each had four push-buttons at the bottom.

"Do you have a way of finding out the class of submarine? I'd like to know what we may be facing, especially if it has its own missiles. The *Stonefish* is fast enough to outrun a torpedo . . . I bloody well hope, and I know you've got an antimissile system. Even so . . ."

"This is not an antisub ship. We don't have that kind of gear. We cannot compare sound signatures."

"Then we'll go for it as we stand. Turn away from the container ship."

Duquesne gave Billy a new course. The *Stonefish* began to head away from the cargo ship putting distance between them.

The phone buzzed, seemingly with a sudden urgency.

"I'd better take it," Gallagher said. He took it off its clip. "Yes?"

"Is that you, Gallagher?" Quinlan.

"Yes."

"You're making a big mistake, guy. Turn the captain loose. Give us back our ship . . ."

"And I suppose you'll forget all about it and put us off at the nearest port."

"Listen, Gallagher . . ."

"I didn't think you would." Gallagher put the phone back. "Billy," he went on, "Lorraine's going to take her gun off you. It doesn't mean you'll get a chance to try anything. If you break your captain's word, you'll live just long enough to regret it."

"Mr. Duquesne's said it all. I'd like to enjoy my money."

"That's fine, Billy. Lorraine, they'll be trying to creep up on us. Go out onto the walkway, *but keep in cover* . . . and stay where I can see you. I want you to keep an eye on the twin-tower mast, particularly the ladder and the crow's nest. I think there's access to it from the sundeck. It's the only place from which anyone can get a decent shot into the bridge. If anyone shows his head, let the shotgun talk to him."

She nodded, and eased her way out. There was the access to the bridge itself, but he could keep an eye on that. He watched as she positioned herself. She remained within sight.

"Let's bring the anti-ship missiles up," he said to Duquesne.

Duquesne pressed a button on the console. There was a slight tremor and the foredeck began to slide open. Something gleaming came slowly up through the widening hole: the missile launcher, and the antimissile gun system.

Gallagher said: "Can they stop the engines?"

"No. All commands can be overridden up here. Besides, I've shut off access to them."

Gallagher looked at him. "Thank you. You didn't have to tell me. I appreciate it."

"I didn't like what he did to those girls."

"I see," Gallagher said.

"No you don't, but it doesn't matter."

"Thank you all the same," Gallagher repeated. "Give us thirty knots, if you please."

"Go to it, Billy."

The *Stonefish* began to come alive as the speed built. Her wake began to boil. The phone was again buzzing.

Gallagher took it.

"Gallagher!" Quinlan shouted before he could even speak. "I'm warning you!"

Gallagher hung up. "Is there another shotgun aboard?"

Duquesne shook his head. "Bridge only. Behrensen figured it was the best weapon for up here."

"For which, thank God, I'd have hated to have one pointed at us."

"At her, you mean."

Gallagher nodded.

"Fine woman."

"Yes," Gallagher said. "I'm supposed to be looking after her. I need her out there, but I don't have to like it."

"She looks as if she can handle herself."

"She can, but that's not the point."

Duquesne nodded. "Take a look at this screen. The missiles have found the target and are on lock. They're ready to go."

The screen showed a targeting box that pulsed. Across that, the word LOCKED also pulsed. As the ship moved, the screen gave a readout of the changing parameters as the missiles updated launch requirements.

"Those planes are going to the bottom of the sea. No one's going to have use of them. Launch, Mr. Duquesne."

Quinlan was working his way toward the bridge when he heard the roar of the missiles leaving. The shock made him stand up, breaking cover. No one shot at him.

"*Sweet Jesus!*" he exclaimed. "The bastard's going to sink the fucking ship!"

De Vries had run at a crouch toward him. "Those were missiles? Are you telling me the truth, man? *Missiles* on this boat?"

"Of course I'm telling you the fucking truth. What the hell do you think they were? *Didn't you hear them?*" Quinlan's eyes seemed close to madness. "Do you know what that bastard has done? He's sent your planes to the bottom of the sea and screwed up two years of careful planning. *Goddamit!* I'll kill the sonofabitch. *I'll kill him!* He's just cost us millions! *Millions!*"

"*I'll* kill him," de Vries said coldly. "I want him."

"You'll have to get to him before me. I'm not leaving him for you to . . ."

Their argument was cut short by a bellowing

series of explosions as the missiles found their target. Vivid flashes seared the sky. The *Stonefish* was curving away from the scene of destruction she had wrought and they had to brace themselves as she heeled.

"My God," Quinlan said in shock. "My God."

The submarine had been some distance from the ship when the missiles struck. Though she was submerged, the quadruple explosions rocked her and for one horrific moment, the commander thought his boat was under attack. But everyone could hear the breakup of the container ship.

He had recently received confirmation of the success of the takeover. All the ship's crew were dead, and the commandos had taken five casualties, two of whom had died. The success flare had been fired. Then this.

They could hear fast screws, but there had been no warships for miles. Where had this one come from, and why had it sunk the ship? The commander decided to go to periscope depth. All he saw was the white yacht curving off at high speed . . . and the wreckage.

Surely not, he thought. Not the *same* yacht . . .

It must have been a NATO sub, he decided. They had known of the operation and had chosen to make sure the aircraft never reached their destination. The yacht was merely getting out of the way.

The commander felt the heavy weight of defeat. After all the careful navigation, the success of the takeover . . . And all the time, the NATO sub had been waiting. Given today's technology, there were subs much quieter than his decades-old Daphne class and clearly, this one had sneaked up, and he'd never even heard it. Despite the fact that his boat had been extensively modernized and could hold its own against some older submarines, whatever was out there was more than a match. It was time for discretion to take over from valor. No one could have survived on the ship.

The commander took his boat deep, and headed home. It was not in his place to squander one of his country's precious few, but perfectly good submarines.

He was relieved when nothing sinister came his way.

15

Gallagher could scarcely believe the ease with which Behrensen's lethal little missiles had taken the ship out. Oily smoke stained the air of the new day and rose skyward. On the sea, flames of vivid colors burned with baleful intensity but of the ship itself, there was no sign. As the *Stonefish* hurled itself away from the scene at thirty knots, the plume of smoke seemed to grow thinner until it appeared to vanish.

Gallagher took a pair of Duquesne's powerful binoculars to have a better look. The smoke had not got thinner. It was simply no longer there. The ship was gone, and the flames were gone. Bits of wreckage floated dejectedly and among it all, he saw just one body.

Duquesne said: "The sub's leaving."

Gallagher put the binoculars down slowly. "What?" The word came absentmindedly.

"The sub's leaving," Duquesne repeated. He was looking at another screen. "He's going deep, moving away from us. Just out here is an area about sixty kilometers long by twenty-five, a sort of trench, where the water's nearly 5000 meters deep. 4791 meters to be more precise. That's 15,718 feet down. The deepest place in the Med. He can't go that far down, but he's running alright. Not much he can do for his men now."

"He wouldn't be trying for a shot, would he?"

Duquesne shook his head. "He's not fast enough to catch up. Something like a Soviet Alfa class could hit 40-plus knots submerged, but we know we're not dealing with one of those." He made a sound that could have been a short laugh. "Wrong country. My guess is the deal went sour on him so he's getting the hell out."

Gallagher thought about that for some moments. He glanced to where Lorraine Mowbray was crouching. She had raised her head to have a look at where the ship had been, although they were some distance from it by now.

"Keep your head down!" he told her sharply.

She ducked down again, after giving him one of her looks. Her eyes seemed to be reading something new about him.

Gallagher said to Duquesne: "Can he hear us pinging at him?"

"We're not 'pinging.' This picks up his sound waves and the computer plots it by size, speed, and course. We can't tell what kind of sub, but we do know where he is at all times, until he's well out of our kind of range. On a real antisub ship, you can hear for well over a hundred miles."

Gallagher nodded. "Yes. I know. I also think," he went on, "it's quite possible he didn't know where the missiles came from. He was submerged when *boom*. The shit hits the fan above his head. What does he do? At first, he thinks he's wandered into a nest of sub-hunters. But he hears no churning screws. He sneaks a look. All he sees is a yacht heading away. Would you, as the sub commander, imagine that the yacht you were supposed to rendezvous with had just sunk the ship your men had taken over? Would you further imagine that the yacht was armed with *missiles*. I think he believes he's run into a monster sub and he's getting out of it as fast as he can."

Duquesne was nodding slowly. "You could be right. We'll never know, I guess . . ."

The sudden blast of Lorraine Mowbray's shotgun sent them both ducking for cover. There was a sharp cry and Gallagher crawled swiftly to where she was.

"Are you alright?"

She nodded. "I think I hit him."

"I should say you did. That scream was not just for fun." He looked at the twin-tower mast. "Was he going for the ladder?"

She nodded. "You were right. I waited until he was nearly on it so I could get a good shot."

"You certainly succeeded."

"How did you know they'd try that?"

"I'd have tried it myself." He grinned at her. "But not if I knew you were up here with a shotgun. They'll have to do some thinking now."

Quinlan was in a huddle with de Vries. They'd heard the sickening thump of the body on the sundeck, preceded by the shotgun blast and the scream.

"Goddamit!" Quinlan said. "That was a shotgun. How in hell did they get hold of that?"

"It's from the bridge," a voice said from behind

them. Ramon. "There was one up there. Looks like the captain gave it to them."

"Goddam turncoat!" Quinlan snarled.

Ramon said: "Was that Paco they got, Mr. Quinlan?"

Quinlan nodded.

"I'll get them for this," Ramon vowed.

"After me," Quinlan and de Vries said together.

Ramon's dark eyes were suddenly murderous. "You do what you want, gentlemen. I'll do it my own way." He moved quickly away from them.

"Ramon!" Quinlan called imperiously.

Ramon ignored him.

"Goddam Filipino," Quinlan said.

"Are we going to wait for them to pick us off one by one?" de Vries asked.

"When this ship was designed, the bridge was built in a way to make it hard to assault. The idea was to retain control of the *Stonefish* even after it had been boarded. The nature of our business dictated it."

"A good idea, but not if it works against us eh, man? Gallagher knew what he was up to. He checked it out when Behrensen was stupid enough to give him a tour. I knew I should have killed him when I had the chance."

"And Behrensen would have killed you."

De Vries' eyes blazed. "You mean this is better?"

Quinlan said: "I wish to hell we knew where they've put Behrensen."

"What good would *that* do?"

"He may know something about the ship that we don't. Something that could give us an edge over that bastard up there."

"Well we don't have Behrensen. What we've got is a well-armed pair who know their business—at least, Gallagher does—in an apparently impregnable position. Meanwhile, the ship is getting nearer to land. There is not much time. We must *do* something!"

Quinlan looked about him. They were on the main deck, outside the forward saloon. He had sent the crew to various points from which to attack the bridge. Paco had failed, but someone else had to try for the mast ladder.

"What's keeping those guys?" he now said impatiently.

He soon got his answer. A single rifle shot echoed above the noise of the ship.

"Ours?" de Vries queried.

"What the hell do you think?"

"Not ours."

"Right."

Someone had been crawling along the sundeck and Gallagher had spotted him. He was still there, and would be there for the duration. His weapon lay unheeded by his open hand.

Duquesne said: "That was a pretty good shot. He was moving fast."

"How many now?" Gallagher asked.

"If you count the one you threw overboard, Behrensen, then Billy and I, that still leaves seven to deal with, plus Quinlan and that security man. You've got nine people, all madder than a pitful of rattlers and all after your hide. And watch out for Ramon. He'll be the sneakiest of the lot. He'll use his knife too. You won't hear it coming."

"I'll remember. How far to land?"

"Three hours, even at forty knots. Four at our present speed. You want me to take her to forty?"

"Will the engines take forty continuous for three hours?"

"We've had her doing a max burst for an hour, but never a three- or four-hour continuous, even at thirty. I feel safe at thirty, but I wouldn't give you a guarantee for forty knots all the way. Thirty is a good speed for her."

"Alright," Gallagher said. "I'll go by your judgment. What about the helicopter? Will Murchison know how to find us?"

"We've got the beacon on. He'll find us."

Gallagher nodded. "Fine. Might as well retract the missile systems."

Four hours. Would they still be alive? he wondered.

De Vries said: "I'm going."

"Where? Up the ladder?" Quinlan looked at him skeptically.

"To see if I can find another way. What about the bridge access?"

"There'll be a steel hatch over it by now. It can't be opened from below."

De Vries slapped his palm against the superstructure in exasperation. "Jesus man! We must *do* something!"

"Behrensen," Quinlan said. "We must find Behrensen. Let's go look."

"And the crew?"

"They can keep Gallagher occupied."

"So how do we do this?"

"We split up," Quinlan said. "You start at the lower deck and work upwards, and I'll begin up here and work down. We'll meet in the galley. Can you find your way around?"

De Vries nodded. "Will you start with his state-room?"

"I've already been. He sure as hell isn't in there."

In the forward lounge, Ramon was standing on the bar and working at a small hatch in the ceiling. It was an access to the foot-level lighting on the bridge walkway. His intention was to remove the light fitting and then the flat central panel of glass in the forward section of the walk-around. He was a small man and believed the space occupied by the panel would be just wide enough for him to squeeze through. He worked as silently as he could.

Gallagher looked at Lorraine. "Alright?"

She smiled up at him from her position on the walkway. "I'm fine. Stop worrying."

But he couldn't stop worrying. Nothing seemed to be happening. That, he felt, was not a good sign. The people out there were thinking. That meant they were making plans. An undisciplined rush was far easier to cope with; but after the abortive tries, they had become cautious.

He moved to the starboard side of the bridge, and looked cautiously out, beyond the sundeck. He paused. There had been movement along the main deck. He waited. Someone moved into view. Quinlan. He raised the rifle . . . then lowered it. Quinlan had ducked out of sight once more. He was certain Quinlan had not seen him.

What was Quinlan up to?

Gallagher waited, but Quinlan did not show

again. Another shotgun blast sent him scurrying back to Lorraine Mowbray's side.

"I got another one." She sounded very calm. "He was going for the ladder too. He didn't even scream." She was too calm.

"Take it easy," Gallagher said. "You're doing fine. I'd rather have you here with me, than over on their side. I can tell you," he added, mimicking her little phrase. The old thought nagged at him, but he still couldn't pin it down.

She gave him a shaky smile. "Wrong accent."

"So who said I was perfect?" He went back onto the bridge.

"Eight to go," Duquesne said. "You might make it if they keep feeding you cannon fodder."

Both de Vries and Quinlan had heard the shotgun and from different parts of the yacht, both said "Shit."

On the bar in the saloon, Ramon only stopped long enough to make certain no one had come to investigate his scrabblings. He worked at the panel with determination, the murderous look alive in his dark eyes.

De Vries and Quinlan had still not found Behrensen.

0700, Chania.

Murchison looked at the big man who had arrived at the airport by taxi and waited until he had paid the fare. He went up to the man as the taxi moved off.

"Mr. Jasper?"

Expressionless eyes surveyed him. "Yes," Villiger answered.

"I'm Dan Murchison, your pilot. I've come to take you to the ship. The helicopter's over there. Can I take your bag?"

"No, thank you. I'm fine."

"Okay, Mr. Jasper. This way, please."

Gallagher looked at Billy, who steered the *Stonefish* with unflustered ease. He seemed totally unmoved by the carnage that was going on about him. If the continuing deaths of his shipmates bothered him, he gave no indication of this.

Gallagher hoped Duquesne was right and that Billy would remain at his post and not suddenly turn on his captors.

Hardly captors, Gallagher thought.

He looked at Lorraine Mowbray. She was doing a magnificent job. Her use of the shotgun was nothing short of devastating. She had turned the ladder into a killing ground. A third man had made the attempt and had suffered the same fate as his comrades. There were now just seven people to deal with.

De Vries and Quinlan had met in the galley. Their search had been fruitless. They had heard the third shotgun blast.

"We're going to have to take out that goddam gun," Quinlan said.

"How?"

"Get behind somehow."

De Vries shook his head. "Gallagher would have thought of that. He'll be waiting."

"Dammit!" Quinlan said. "Without Behrensen, we're down to seven."

"As I've said . . . he's picking us off. And I don't

think Behrensen's on board at all. I think Gallagher threw him off."

Quinlan was skeptical of that idea. "Behrensen's a big man. Nobody throws him off anything."

"Gallagher's done something with him . . . big man or not."

Quinlan looked poisonously at de Vries.

Ramon was still working at the light panel. He had got part of it off, but was finding it difficult to remove the light unit itself. He was also trying not to give himself an electric shock. Every so often he would pause to listen, to ensure he had not been discovered. He had heard the roar of the shotgun, knowing it to be the third time.

His face hardened as he worked at the light fitting.

Gallagher heard a sudden scrabbling sound. Rifle ready, he went to investigate. A crewman was making his way up the sloping roof of the forward saloon, hurrying toward the bridge, assault rifle coming up. He was barely managing to keep his balance.

Gallagher braced himself against the bridge superstructure and raised the SC70/90. He never got the shot off.

Billy swung the wheel sharply to one side before bringing it around again. The *Stonefish* made a sudden dart to starboard, before coming around equally sharply to her original heading.

The man on the saloon roof lost his balance and was bounced off it by the unexpected swerve. He rolled, frantically grabbing at anything he thought would stop him. He need not have bothered. He bounced off the roof and over the side. He fell close to the ship and was dragged beneath it toward the screws.

Billy settled back on course as if nothing had happened.

"Six to go," Billy said.

Gallagher stared at the back of his head, at Duquesne, then at Lorraine.

She was looking at him. Her mouth formed silent words.

"I'm okay," she mimed.

Ramon had fallen off the bar, banging his elbow painfully. He rubbed at it furiously, then climbed back up. He continued to work at the light fitting.

In his stateroom, Behrensen's body had been jolted out of position by Billy's swerve. It had moved so that his feet were just sticking out from beneath the edge of the quilt. He had also begun to groan softly.

In the galley, de Vries and Quinlan had reached out involuntarily for something to grab at for support. What they had found was each other's arms. Almost as quickly, they had let go and had grabbed something else.

"What the fuck?" Quinlan exclaimed when the ship had steadied again.

"Why don't we go and see?" de Vries suggested.

Quinlan went out without speaking.

De Vries followed.

Gallagher crawled over to Lorraine. "Anything?"

She shook her head. "I think they've learned that lesson."

"Don't be too sure. They must be getting desperate by now. They'll try anything."

She smiled. "Looks as if we might make it. The helicopter must be on its way back."

"He'll know something is wrong," Gallagher said, knowing she was thinking about Villiger. "He won't come into the trap. We've done that at least. I don't know what he'll think about losing the aircraft though."

"They hadn't been paid for as yet."

"Well . . . that's something."

In the helicopter, Murchison said: "That's funny."

"What is?" Villiger was instantly alert.

"They've moved. They're not where they're supposed to be. I've just tuned to the beacon and . . ." He stopped as something hard and cold pressed into the side of his neck.

He tried to see, and didn't like what he saw.

"Christ, Mr. Jasper . . . !"

Villiger had swiftly taken the Taipan out of his bag. Its muzzle was now pressing into Murchison's flesh.

"One wrong move," Villiger said, "and you're a dead man."

"You'll be dead too, unless you can fly this thing."

"Then we both need each other alive to stay alive, don't we?"

"I . . . I suppose that's some kind of logic."

"It means you keep your head . . . for the time being. But from now on, it's on borrowed time. Now find that ship!"

Ramon had finally got the fitting off. He nearly dropped it, but managed to hang grimly on, preventing it from clattering onto the bar counter upon which he was standing. He put it cautiously down, then peered through the remaining glass panel. He could now see into the walkway. There was no one visible.

More cautiously, he began to work at easing the glass panel out of its frame. He was certain he'd be able to make it through the hole it left.

In his stateroom, Behrensen was now fully conscious. He began to have a go at wriggling as best he could from under the bed. It was going to be a long haul and he grunted fiercely with the effort. In his mind was an all-consuming hatred of Gallagher.

Gallagher had left Lorraine and was on the opposite side of the bridge, again looking out beyond the sundeck. No one was showing himself. He glanced back through the bridge at her.

"All quiet," she mouthed at him.

He nodded, gave her the thumbs up. The longer they managed to keep the crew at bay, he thought, the closer to land they got. Quinlan, de Vries, and the crew would have to try something desperate. That was when even more mistakes would be made. It should then be possible to pick off the rest of them as they came.

Ramon could scarcely believe his luck. The glass panel was coming off without a sound! The hole was definitely big enough.

Then he made his first mistake.

He tried to reach for his little knife while still holding on to the panel. At that moment, the *Stonefish* lurched gently. Under normal circumstances,

Ramon would not even have noticed it; but balanced precariously as he was, it was a major disaster. As he teetered, he had to let go of the glass panel in order to grab at the surround.

The panel dropped, making a noise that was impossible to miss. Quickly realizing all surprise was now gone, Ramon heaved himself up to get through the opening as swiftly as possible.

Both Gallagher and Lorraine had heard the breaking of glass, and both had correctly identified its source. Both rose and from either side of the bridge, ran crouching along the walkway toward it. Both saw what was happening at the same time. Both brought their weapons up.

Ramon knew he was lost. He was trapped halfway through. His head, shoulders and arms were out, but his lower body hung helplessly in the saloon lounge. Even so, he was very quick. Bracing himself on one arm and a shoulder, he threw his knife at the source of what he thought would be the greatest danger.

His aim was true, but he was still too late.

The shotgun round pulped his face even as his knife struck home and the round from the SC70/90 entered his throat, to fling him back through the hole and into the lounge below.

Gallagher heard Lorraine give a short scream as she fell, the shotgun thumping onto the walkway near her.

"Lorraine!" he shouted in fear for her as he ran up. Ramon's knife was sticking out of her, perilously close to her left breast. "Oh God," he went on. "I told you not to move from your position."

She bit at her lip, stifling the pain. "Don't . . . don't be angry with me."

"Oh, Lorraine," he said softly. "How could I be angry with you?"

Duquesne had come out to see what had happened. "Dammit," he said. "Ramon. I knew the little bastard would use his knife. Let's get her to the bridge. I've got a medicine chest, and I've handled knife wounds before."

Very carefully, to cause her as little pain as possible, they moved her to the bridge, where Duquesne went immediately to work. Gallagher went quickly back for her shotgun and his rifle.

Duquesne had opened her shirt and was cutting off her bra. The knife was an obscenity near the bared, perfectly round breasts.

"I can get this out," Duquesne said to her gently, "but we've got to get you to a doctor soon." He removed the shirt.

She bit her lip again, nodded, and said in a low voice: "Go ahead. Take it out. Only . . . only five more to go now, Gordon."

Gallagher had an arm about her shoulders, while she gripped his free hand. Her skin was smooth and warm to his touch.

"Don't you dare die on me," he said to her. "I'll never forgive you." He nodded at Duquesne to commence.

The translucent eyes looked at him. "I'll never forgive myself. We've got things to do, you and I. *Aaahh!*" Her body stiffened as Duquesne pulled the knife out, then relaxed. "That bloody hurt, I can tell you," she finished weakly. Then she passed out.

There was little blood from the wound, and that

worried Gallagher. Duquesne, working swiftly, caught his eye briefly.

Duquesne was worried too, Gallagher saw. The captain of the *Stonefish* efficiently dressed the wound, bandaged it, then with Gallagher's help, put the shirt back on and buttoned it.

Duquesne made a sling for her left arm, then they made her as comfortable as possible on the bridge. Duquesne had found a pallet in a long storage cupboard, complete with built-in pillow. She was now lying on it, safely in cover.

"It's going to hurt like hell when she comes round," Duquesne said. "She needs a doctor quick if you're not going to lose her. There's bleeding inside."

"I thought so," Gallagher said.

"Little bastard," Duquesne said, thinking of Ramon. "Well, only five of them left now, as she said. What are you going to do?"

"What about that hole out there?"

"Only the little bastard could have got through. We're alright. There's no clean shot from the saloon."

Gallagher looked at Lorraine. She was still out. "The chopper. We'll need the helicopter. That will be fast enough."

Duquesne said: "The beacon's on. Murchison's on his way."

Bloody hell, Gallagher thought. *What do I tell Piet? I was supposed to look after her.*

Gallagher said: "I think I can arrange for a doctor to be waiting. Do you have satellite communication?"

"On a ship like this? Sure we have. What do you want? Voice? Or keyboard?"

"Keyboard."

"We've got a terminal up here." Duquesne went to the left-hand console and tapped at a keypad. Doors slid open and a keyboard and screen came out. "It's all ready. Tap in your access code and send your message. When you're finished, tap DELETE, and your code will be wiped from its memory. You'll keep your security that way." He stepped back so as not to see what Gallagher sent out.

"It doesn't matter," Gallagher said. "I'll be using a code that wipes as it goes." He sent his message, then received a single AFFIRMATIVE in return. Then he shut down. "There'll be a doctor waiting."

Duquesne was looking at him with renewed respect. "Just like that?"

Gallagher nodded. But the price had been begging Fowler for help. "Talking of satellites," he said, "one might have picked up our little fireworks. We may get company."

Duquesne stared briefly out to sea, glanced at the sky. "No company yet."

"That means nothing." Gallagher picked up the shotgun, put a fresh magazine in, then hung the Taipan across his back by its sling. He'd be able to bring it to bear very quickly when he was finished with the shotgun.

Duquesne gave him a look of appraisal. "Going hunting?"

"Yes. Time this was sorted out down there. I'm leaving these weapons with you . . ." He indicated the SC70/90 and Lorraine's 92F pistol. ". . . in case anyone tries to come at you." He stooped to briefly kiss her forehead. "Keep her safe. And please, you two, don't try anything. I swear I'll kill you both if you do."

Duquesne looked into suddenly cold eyes. A wolf, he thought. A wolf on the prowl.

Duquesne said: "I don't doubt it. Billy won't doubt it, either. Will you, Billy?"

"The Captain speaks for me," Billy said emotionlessly.

"Good. And now, Mr. Duquesne, the hatch please."

Duquesne again pressed a button on one of his consoles. The hatch to the bridge access, made of composite armored material, opened silently upward. Gallagher waited; weapon poised in case someone had the bright idea of trying to come up. No one appeared.

Gallagher still waited, while Duquesne looked at him with interest. Two minutes went by. Gallagher continued to wait. Duquesne made a sign, asking if Gallagher wanted the hatch closed.

Gallagher shook his head.

Another minute. Then a face cautiously appeared. Gallagher did not move.

Quinlan and de Vries were in the forward saloon lounge staring at Ramon's body.

"The little shit won't be carving anyone up anymore," Quinlan said nastily. "That's for sure."

"You hate Filipinos?"

Quinlan glared at him. "Don't *you* give me any lectures on goddam racism." He walked out of the saloon.

De Vries stared at the body. "You're not a pretty sight." He followed Quinlan.

Gallagher was still waiting. The man had now moved most of his body into view. The moment would be soon. Gallagher was aware of Duquesne's rapt attention.

The man was coming up to the bridge. When he was halfway, Gallagher moved. The man stopped, stared in despair. He tried to use his rifle, knowing he would never make it.

The shotgun roared.

The man was virtually blown back to the deck. Gallagher moved swifly, reaching the deck almost at the same time as the body. The hatch was closing even as he began hurrying toward the stern.

Another man appeared coming toward him, but not sufficiently alert. Perhaps he thought for a brief moment, that Gallagher was another crew member. He would certainly not have expected anyone from the bridge.

Gallagher used the man's confusion to good effect. He went down on one knee as the man frantically skidded to a halt and tried to get into a good firing position, but the shotgun round was already on its way. The man was hit in the chest, seemed to try both to clutch at the wound and fling his arms outward for balance. The force of the blow sent him against the deck railing. It pitched him over the side.

"Three to go," Gallagher muttered as he got up and ran silently on.

Quinlan and de Vries were at the stern, keeping under cover.

"That sounded like it was on deck," Quinlan said. "The bastard's come down!"

"That's not such good news," de Vries said. "If he feels safe enough to come down, it means there are not many of us left."

"Meaning?"

"Meaning it may just be you . . . and me."

Another blast roared through the ship.

"Definitely just you and me," de Vries said drily. "Well, Mr. Quinlan? How does it feel to be trapped on this wonderful ship with someone like that? And I thought I was good."

"He hasn't got me yet," Quinlan snapped.

"Where there's life," de Vries said, and gave a soft laugh. "Come on, Mr. Quinlan. Let's go and see just how good he really is."

Gallagher found himself outside Behrensen's stateroom. He paused. He'd heard thumping. He waited, constantly looking about him. Only Quinlan and de Vries left now. The thumps came again. He knew what it was.

Behrensen.

Gallagher let himself in and saw immediately what had occurred. Behrensen had managed to move from under the bed and was banging his head against a wardrobe. The wardrobe's air capacity made it a good sound producer. Behrensen did not have to bang his head too hard. It had been a good try.

Gallagher remained where he was. Behrensen could not see him. The banging of the head went on. Gallagher looked about him, searching out suitable cover. He knew how to get Quinlan and de Vries.

He found a spot near the door, laid the shotgun quietly out of sight, then brought the Taipan around.

He waited.

"I can hear something," Quinlan said.

"Then you're still alive," de Vries said. He paused. "I can hear it too. A banging."

They went cautiously toward the sound, then Quinlan saw where they were.

"Mr. Behrensen's stateroom. I don't understand."

"Are we going to wait out here until Gallagher makes targets of us?" de Vries said impatiently. "Or are we going to find out what's making that sound?"

Quinlan gave him a cold stare but automatics ready, they cautiously entered the stateroom.

"*Mr. Behrensen!*" Quinlan uttered in a stunned voice. He hurried forward.

De Vries had better instincts. He hesitated.

Gallagher knew where his priority target would be.

"That will do just perfectly, gentlemen," he said softly.

Several things happened. De Vries, with the instincts of a striking snake, was already spinning toward the sound, gun tracking. There had been no pause for thought. Quinlan, more snakelike, was much, much slower. And Behrensen, recognizing Gallagher's voice, began to make loud, incomprehensible noises of both fury and most certainly, fear.

Gallagher, meanwhile, had already zeroed on target.

The Taipan seemed to chatter with glee. Gallagher was astonished by the rate of fire, and for an infinitesimal moment, it nearly went out of his control.

The bullets seemed to rip into de Vries, continuing to spin him around. He pirouetted on his toes, a grotesque dancer pointing at the ceiling with his gun hand. He fired repeatedly into the ceiling until the gun was empty. Then he simply collapsed onto the carpet.

Even before he was down, Gallagher had swung to Quinlan who took six rounds in the chest. He fell backward onto Behrensen's bed. His weapon was never fired.

Gallagher took a deep breath as the Taipan fell silent. He walked over to Behrensen, and looked down.

Behrensen had rolled over. The protruding eyes stared up at Gallagher in terror. His chest heaved with the effort of breathing.

"You're all alone now, Behrensen," Gallagher said, then he turned, and walked out of the stateroom.

As he moved along the deck, he realized there had been a change in the cadence of the engines. He glanced over the side. The ship was slowing. He hurried toward the bridge, rushed up the companionway, and banged on the hatch.

"Gallagher!" he shouted. He held the Taipan ready, just in case.

The hatch came open. Duquesne was there with the SC70/90. They stared at each other, then Duquesne lowered the rifle. Gallagher climbed through to the bridge.

"Were you thinking it?"

Duquesne shook his head. "I knew I'd be dead before I got one off. I was just making sure it was you."

"Why are we slowing down?" Gallagher hurried over to Lorraine. She looked too pale for his liking.

Her eyes fluttered open. "Gordon?"

"I'm here." He stroked her face. She didn't feel as warm as before. "Why are we slowing down?" he asked again of Duquesne without looking around.

"Chopper's coming. He'll be here in less than ten minutes. Maybe just five."

"Thank God for that."

"As you're here and alive, I guess you got them all."

"Yes."

"Goddam. Behrensen too?"

"No. He's still tied up in his stateroom."

"His *stateroom!* Then where the hell was he all this time?"

Gallagher kept fussing over Lorraine, carrying on his conversation with Duquesne with his back turned. "Under the bed."

"Under . . ." Duquesne gave a short laugh. "Well I'll be damned." He shook his head slowly. "You sure as hell gave him a run for his money."

Lorraine was looking at Gallagher. "I'm . . . I'm so sorry," she whispered. The eyes were full of pain.

"Sorry? Whatever for?"

"For making so much trouble for you."

"It was no trouble. Always at your service."

She tried to laugh, but grimaced with pain instead. "Bet . . . you . . . say that to all the . . . girls."

"No I don't. Now no more talking. We're going to get you off soon."

"Must . . . must tell you something."

"It can wait."

"No . . . it . . . it can't."

"Yes it . . ."

"Listen, will you!" Her voice came surprisingly strongly; then it was weak again as she went on: "I lied . . . to you . . ."

"Lied? About what?"

"Shh!" she said. "Don't in . . . terrupt. My parents . . . not whom I said they were. It's my father who's . . . white. You . . . you know who it . . . is."

Gallagher felt a tremor go through him. The nagging thought had crystallized. *I can tell you.* The strange familiarity of the odd little phrase . . .

Villiger's daughter.

Oh my God, he thought. What would he say to Villiger? What *could* he say?

"Don't look so stricken," she was saying to him. "It wasn't your fault that I got this and not your fault . . ." She paused, as if the unbroken string of words had tired her suddenly. "Not your fault," she went on, " . . . you didn't know . . . about my father." She smiled suddenly. "How will you . . . feel . . . when you make . . . love to me? Not . . . not afraid . . . of . . . him . . . are you?"

Villiger's daughter. But how? Villiger didn't seem old enough to have a daughter of twenty-one.

Gallagher looked around at the sudden sound of the approaching helicopter. When he'd turned to her again, her eyes were closed. Fearfully, he bent close to put an ear to her nose. It was alright. She was breathing.

He stood up as Duquesne said: "Chopper's approaching the stern. We're at five knots, and ready to recover."

In the helicopter, Murchison was preparing for the landing. He had almost grown accustomed to the muzzle of the gun that had remained in position throughout the flight, save for its having been moved back a fraction to allow him some movement.

Now, as he looked down at the *Stonefish,* he halted the descent.

"What's wrong?" Villiger demanded.

"There's a man . . . there, on the sundeck, dead. And there's no crew that I can see. Usually, at least two are by the landing pad."

"Move a little to one side, then go round the ship. Look it over."

Murchison did as he was told, talking the helicopter around, nose pointing at the *Stonefish*.

"There's another one . . ." Murchison gave a running commentary. "And another. *Three* on the sundeck. What the hell's happened here? There's one near the bridge . . ."

"Take us down," Villiger said.

"What? But there's . . ."

"Take us down! Unless you want to do it the quick way. Someone's on the bridge. Gallagher. If Gallagher's alive and those around him are dead, it usually means they tried to kill him and failed. Get us down there."

Murchison saw the person waving by the ship's bridge. How had Gallagher managed to get away and create such havoc? He was not going to argue with a gun in his face. He brought the helicopter in to land.

Taipan at the ready, Gallagher went to the stern to meet the helicopter. Lorraine had seemed no worse, but she didn't look good either. He was glad Murchison had arrived. She would soon be off to Crete, where she'd receive the proper medical attention.

The aircraft had settled and Villiger was out, with Murchison walking ahead of him. They stopped as Gallagher reached them.

"Quite a scene of carnage from the air," Villiger began. "Have you left anyone alive?"

"The captain and a crewman are on the bridge . . ."

Villiger gave a thin smile. "Not having an off day, are you?"

"And Behrensen's tied up in his stateroom . . ."

"Tied! You'll have to tell me everything, Gordon. What about my aircraft and . . ." He paused, looking at Gallagher keenly. "How's Lorraine?"

"Why didn't you trust me enough to tell?" Gallagher demanded tightly. "Why didn't you . . ."

Villiger's eyes widened, then narrowed. "Lorraine!"

"Why the hell didn't you tell me!"

"Lorraine!" Villiger said again. "Where is she, man?"

"On the bridge."

"Take me!" Villiger turned to Murchison. *"You* . . . if you take off in that machine before I say so, I'll blow you out of the air before you've gone ten feet."

"And if he misses," Gallagher said, "I won't."

"Hey," Murchison said to them placatingly, "I'm not going anywhere."

"Good," they both said together and hurried to the bridge.

Villiger entered ahead of Gallagher, and was immediately on his knees beside the pallet.

"Lorraine," he said gently, taking her hand.

Gallagher was amazed by the change in the big man. He had never thought Villiger capable of real emotion.

Her eyes were open. "Hello," she said. Even then, she didn't use his name. She smiled weakly. "We . . . stopped them. Gordon . . . will tell you . . . all about it. I'm a little . . . tired. Don't be hard

. . . on him. He didn't know . . . and it was I . . . who got myself . . . into this mess . . ."

"Took the little bastard out herself," came Duquesne's voice.

Villiger ignored him. "Don't talk anymore," Villiger went on to Lorraine. "We'll have you on that helicopter in a few minutes."

She closed her eyes again. He kissed her on both cheeks and when he stood up, there was a suspicious redness about his eyes.

Duquesne was in communication with Murchison, telling him to remove one of his helicopter's front seats to make room for a casualty evacuation. He sent Billy to help.

Gallagher walked with Villiger around the deck and gave him the complete story.

"They were after you, Piet," Gallagher said at the end. "The whole thing was a many-layered operation. You were never meant to get the aircraft. Behrensen had sold you down the river for a better price. At least, your identity's still safe, and Behrensen's finished. And as for Quinlan and de Vries . . ."

"Hennie," Villiger said grimly. "All this time . . ." He shook his head in wonder. "I owe you, man. Plenty."

Gallagher said: "You owe me nothing. I just wish I could take back what happened to Lorraine."

Villiger put a hand on his shoulder. They were by the stern, absently watching Murchison and Billy work.

"She can sometimes be . . ." He gave a small sigh. ". . . a little headstrong. You could never have stopped what happened."

"The worst of it," Gallagher said, "is that she

was right. If that little shit hadn't been so quick with his knife . . ."

"It's alright, Gordon. Don't eat yourself up, man. She's not blaming you, and I'm certainly not." Villiger took a long slow breath and let it out before continuing: "I was sixteen. Met this lovely girl. Didn't see her as colored . . . just someone I was crazy about. We . . . behaved like teenagers all over the world when an emotion is so powerful . . . Anyway, there was a child. My parents were scandalized. Made sure I never saw her. Dear God, how I've regretted this. Of course, I had no idea what happened for years, and though Lorraine's mother knew where to find me, she never tried. She married, of course.

"Then one day, in a car park, this beautiful eighteen-year-old comes up to me and says she's my daughter. Imagine the shock. As if that wasn't enough, I later find out she's an *activist*. Where I come from, that's not just bad news. It's a nightmare. She's not yet twenty-one, you know.

"This happened just after I met you in Australia. I had begun to see the rot setting in by then. As things got worse, I felt I had to do something for the land I love and for my daughter, whose land it is too. She feels so strongly about it, it's a fire in her sometimes. We've got a beautiful country, she once told me, yet we curse it. I suppose I became involved as a kind of atonement at first . . . for the things I had done, and those I hadn't. It's a damned shit world sometimes, man. We screw everything up in a kind of collective madness until we can't see our way out. So we hold on to the warped status quo because we don't know any better. The human condition is not one of continuing enlightenment with the odd hiccup of stupidity but rather the other way round, with the odd hiccup of enlightenment. But then, there are people like Lorraine . . . and like you."

"Like *me?*"

Villiger appeared to smile. "Don't sell yourself short."

Gallagher looked at him, seeing new facets all the time; seeing aspects of Lorraine. He had created something beautiful.

"Don't sell yourself short either," Gallagher told him.

"Oh . . . I've gone down a corrupt road, corrupted others . . ." Villiger paused, looked toward the helicopter. *"How much longer?"* he shouted impatiently.

"We're going as fast as we can," Murchison called back.

Villiger grunted something, then said: "I'm ready for Behrensen now. I knew something was going on . . . even suspected a hit, but never Hennie."

They went to the stateroom. In his frenzy to get free, Behrensen had moved well away from the bed. They stared at him without speaking, then Gallagher reached down to untie the gags.

"My hands and my feet," Behrensen said. "They hurt."

"Where are the videos?" Villiger asked coldly. "Don't make me ask twice. I've had a lot of practice at making people tell me things."

"Believe him," Gallagher said.

Behrensen told them. Silently, they watched part of the video of the two girls Behrensen had recently killed by the stern. They saw snippets of others, of young girls who would never be seen again. There was one of a torture session in a jungle somewhere. Quinlan was starring in that one. Then they saw the one of Lorraine taking a shower, getting dressed, walking around in what she had thought was privacy.

Villiger blew the screen apart with a burst from his Taipan. Then he began to untie Behrensen. When he had done so he stood back, gun pointing.

"On your feet!" he ordered harshly.

Behrensen did so unsteadily. He fell several times as his cramped legs took some time to sort themselves out. After a while he was able to stagger around. They took him out on deck.

"At least you're not begging," Villiger said to him as they urged him toward the stern. "Stop."

Behrensen halted, and turned around.

"This is where you had those two girls pose for your video, *isn't it?*" Villiger asked. The skin, pale beneath the tan, had tautened across his jaw.

By the helicopter, Murchison and Billy had stopped to watch.

Behrensen said nothing. He knew it would have been pointless. Villiger raised the Taipan.

A single shot rang out. Behrensen clutched at his chest and toppled backward into the wake of the ship.

Everyone turned to stare at the bridge. Standing outside, rifle in hand, was Duquesne. He remained there for long moments, before tossing the rifle over the side. Then he went back inside.

Gallagher and Villiger stared at each other. Billy and Murchison were still staring at the bridge.

Gallagher said to them, "Are you finished?"

They looked around guiltily, before continuing their work.

As they made their way back to the bridge, Villiger said: "In Australia I told you if things were different I'd invite you up Table Mountain . . ."

"And I said I'd accept."

"Let's change that. Let's say we *will* have a drink up Table Mountain together, when no one gives a damn who's sitting where, who's eating with whom, who's serving whom, who's loving whom . . ."

"Will that time ever come?"

"It had better, I can tell you. Or it's *the* nightmare."

They put Lorraine gently aboard the helicopter. Villiger insisted that Gallagher go with her. He would remain with the yacht, and Gallagher was sure Villiger's eyes were very red when the aircraft lifted off.

The helicopter was beating its way toward Crete. Gallagher was sitting behind Murchison, while Lorraine lay on the makeshift stretcher that had been fashioned by Billy and Murchison, feet toward the instrument panel. She was securely strapped in. Gallagher had an arm about her, and she was again holding on to his free hand.

He was looking at her, and she smiled slightly, saying something. He leaned closer to hear.

"Will you think of me when you play *Mainstreet?*"

"I'll get you the whole CD," he promised, "and yes, I will think of you."

She squeezed his hand. "Oh good."

He looked up to say to Murchsion: "How much longer?"

"Twenty minutes."

Gallagher turned to Lorraine. "Just twenty minutes. Hang on. Lorraine? *Lorraine?* Oh God no," he said brokenly. "It just isn't bloody fair!" There was a sudden warmth behind his eyes.

The hand no longer squeezed his.

London, three days later.

Gallagher drove up to his home in Holland Park and put the *quattro* in the carport. He had seen the white Department Rover. Haslam walked up to him.

"Fowler would like to see you . . . when you've got the time."

Gallagher looked at him balefully.

"He'd like to hear the story from you," Haslam went on. "I'm sorry about the girl, Gordon. We had a doctor waiting. She would have got the best treatment. I don't suppose you've heard. The *Stonefish* blew up rather spectacularly off one of the Greek islands. No one seems to know who was responsible. No crew members have been found. No bodies either. And we seem to have been mysteriously donated a vast selection of rather interesting videos. A lot of people will wish they never knew Behrensen. Just thought you'd like to know."

Gallagher had still not spoken.

Haslam held his arm gently. "I'm really sorry about her, lad."

Haslam left, and the Rover set off with a squeal of tires. Must be Prinknash, Gallagher thought uncharitably.

When he'd entered the maisonette, he checked his mail. The usual collection of bills for various photographic materials, agency jobs, social mail. There was one from the bank. His money had grown. There was a note from Michael Perowne telling him to the last decimal point.

He checked the answering machine. Again, the

expected collection. Nellads wanting to know if he was back, please call. A lucrative job to do with stately homes.

"Are you back yet?" Veronica Walmsley. "Guess what . . . I'm suddenly out of a job. FUTRON have mysteriously ceased to trade. Don't mind, really. I was getting ready to move on. How about lunch? Better still, dinner at my place? Daddy's offering a weekend at the pile in the country. I think he wants to talk to you, but who knows what about. Call, won't you?"

Someone else had phoned several times, but had left no message.

The door buzzer went.

"Oh shit, Haslam," Gallagher said irritably. "Tell Fowler to bloody well wait." He made no move to go.

The buzzer was insistent.

Resigned to it, Gallagher went to answer, priming himself to give Haslam a suitably unpleasant message to pass on to Fowler. He opened the door, and stared.

"I couldn't stay away," Rhiannon Jameson said.

EPILOGUE

The heat of the African day beat down upon the men. Their ambush positions had been selected days before, each man in his own individual hide. There was no communication between them. At infrequent times two men, one big and white, would move among them, checking, making certain they knew what was required of them. The black man and the white one spoke with similar accents.

Presently a low sound, growing in volume, could be heard. The two men appeared to have vanished. A dirt track meandered its way through the bush and on its surface could be seen the imprints of big-wheeled vehicles.

The sound grew into many sounds vying with each other. Then along the dirt track and in convoy, came the makers of the sounds: high-wheeled armored personnel carriers.

The hiding men waited then as if signaled, anti-armor weapons opened up on the column with devastating fury. Cries of pain, shouted orders, all were mixed within the roar of the weapons and the explosive destruction of their targets. When it was all over, the bush was strewn with broken vehicles and broken men. Oily pillars of smoke wreathed into the hot sky.

The ambushers, meanwhile, had melted away.

Born in Dominica, Julian Jay Savarin was educated in Britain and took a degree in history before serving in the Royal Air Force. Mr. Savarin lives in England and is the author of LYNX, HAMMERHEAD, WARHAWK, TROPHY, TARGET DOWN!, WOLF RUN, WINDSHEAR, NAJA, and THE QUIRAING LIST.

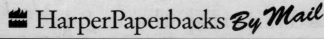

CAMPBELL ARMSTRONG

Agents of Darkness

Suspended from the LAPD, Charlie Galloway decides his
life has no meaning. But when his Filipino housekeeper is
murdered, Charlie finds a new purpose in tracking the
killer. He never expects, though, to be drawn into a
conspiracy that reaches from the Filipino jungles to the
White House.

Mazurka

For Frank Pagan of Scotland Yard, it begins with the
murder of a Russian at crowded Waverly Station, Edinburgh. From that moment
on, Pagan's life becomes an ever-darkening nightmare as he finds himself
trapped in a complex web of intrigue, treachery, and murder.

Mambo

Super-terrorist Gunther Ruhr has been captured. Scotland Yard's Frank Pagan
must escort him to a maximum security prison, but with blinding swiftness and
brutality, Ruhr escapes. Once again, Pagan must stalk Ruhr, this time into an
earth-shattering secret conspiracy.

Brainfire

American John Rayner is a man on fire with grief and anger over the death of his
powerful brother. Some
say it was suicide, but
Rayner suspects
something more
sinister. His suspicions
prove correct as he
becomes trapped in a
Soviet-made maze of
betrayal and terror.

Asterisk Destiny

Asterisk is America's
most fragile and chilling
secret. It waits some-
where in the Arizona
desert to pave the way
to world domination...or
damnation. Two men,
White House aide John
Thorne and CIA agent
Ted Hollander, race
to crack the wall of
silence surrounding
Asterisk and tell
the world of their
terrifying discovery.